Richard Whately, Elizabeth Jane Whately

Life and Correspondence of Richard Whately, D.D., late Archbishop

of Dublin

Richard Whately, Elizabeth Jane Whately

Life and Correspondence of Richard Whately, D.D., late Archbishop of Dublin

ISBN/EAN: 9783744660310

Printed in Europe, USA, Canada, Australia, Japan

Cover: Foto ©Raphael Reischuk / pixelio.de

More available books at **www.hansebooks.com**

WHATELY'S

LIFE AND CORRESPONDENCE.

VOL. II.

LONDON
PRINTED BY SPOTTISWOODE AND CO.
NEW-STREET SQUARE

LIFE AND CORRESPONDENCE

OF

RICHARD WHATELY, D.D.

LATE ARCHBISHOP OF DUBLIN.

BY

E. JANE WHATELY

AUTHOR OF 'ENGLISH SYNONYMS.'

IN TWO VOLUMES.—VOLUME II.

CONTENTS

OF

THE SECOND VOLUME.

—+—

CHAPTER VII.
1850.

CHAPTER VIII.
1851.

CHAPTER IX.
1852.

CHAPTER XIV.

1850.

CHAPTER XV.

1862.

CHAPTER XVI.

1863.

APPENDIX.

LIFE AND REMAINS

OF

ARCHBISHOP WHATELY.

———•⚬⦂⚬⦂⚬•———

CHAPTER I.

THE year 1842 opens on fresh efforts of the Archbishop
to explain mis-statements, and help his English friends to
take clearer views of Irish affairs. It is with this object
that he writes to Mr. Senior, March 10.

'Dublin : March 10, 1842.

'My dear Senior—It is a matter of great patience to
find people so readily giving credence to any falsehood,
however extravagant, relative to Ireland, even such as

are the most easy of detection. And the worst of it is, that those who don't think it worth while to ascertain facts are always quite ready to suggest measures. To feel the patient's pulse and examine his tongue is too much trouble, but they are quite prepared to prescribe.

'One most valuable stock-falsehood of the opponents of the Education Board, devised by the wickedness of a few, encouraged in circulation by many, and carelessly assented to by most of the rest (ut pessimum facinus auderent pauci, plures vellent, omnes paterentur), is that which Sir J. G. seems to have swallowed so readily, that "the plan has failed as a scheme of united education, and has succeeded only as an education for Roman Catholics." This (which is most emphatically the reverse of the truth) was most artfully devised, and has been most steadily adhered to. For there is nothing so well calculated to sow dissension among the members of the Board (if these could be persuaded either to believe it true, or to be convinced that it is generally admitted), and to set the Roman Catholics against it. M'Hale and his περί are continually striving to excite jealousy of Protestants having anything to do with the education of Roman Catholics as such and exclusively, they will then claim, with very good reason, the exclusive control of it. It is only as a bonâ fide united system that I can have anything to do with it. When, therefore (as the Duke of W. did formerly), Sir J. G. says that the scheme has "succeeded for Catholic education, and that Government are resolved to support it," I understand him to mean by "support" to abolish it in reality, retaining the name. For of course as soon as Ministers understand that it is as a Roman Catholic system they believe and design it to exist, I and the (unpaid) Protestant Commissioners shall not wait to be called on by the Roman Catholics to withdraw, but shall give it up at once. We shall not even wait, I conceive, for a grant to be made to the Church Education Society, which is earnestly petitioned for e. g. by Lord De Grey's nephew, and will be justly demanded by Protestants as soon as the national system (though it may retain the name) becomes in reality one for the education of Roman Catholics alone.

'I very much wish they could let me know at once whether it really be their wish to get rid of me as a Commissioner, that I might be saved further trouble, by having this notified to me direct, instead of measures resorted to which they must know will, indirectly, produce that result. I laid my views and intentions before them half a year ago, as you know; and up to this day I have had no answer, except that they have not yet had time to make sufficient inquiry and to deliberate.

'Yet they have had time, it seems, to make up their minds as to the truth of a representation which has been uniformly contradicted by us, and disproved over and over. In no one instance, as far as, on the most diligent examination, I have been able to ascertain, has the system failed as a united system, where a fair trial has been allowed to it, as in many cases has been allowed; and in very many instances it has succeeded even in spite of every endeavour to prevent it. Mr. and Mrs. ――――, who are bringing out a book in numbers, with plates, descriptions and stories of Ireland (δεδαιδαλμένοι ψεύδεσι ποικίλοις μῦθοι), represent the "mixed system" as having failed, on the ground of their having visited several schools in the south of Ireland in such and such places, where there were only four or five Protestant children and about a hundred Roman Catholics—these being places in which it appears by the population-returns the Protestants are not above five per cent., or less!

'If you know of any one who really wishes to know the truth, and to know how misrepresentations of it are got

up, you may refer him, among other things, to the speech
of the Bishop of Exeter in that session where the Commissioners were appointed, and my answer. The strongest
case he could put forward to prove the failure of the
system as one of united education was that of the model
schools in Dublin; for there, if anywhere, he said, it
might be expected that different denominations would be
found mixed, and yet there were very few but Roman
Catholics. I replied, that Dublin was just the place where
it was least to be expected; because (as no doubt he very
well knew) there was in almost every parish a long-
established Protestant school.

'And yet—what is really surprising, considering—there
is a proportion of Protestants in our model school nearly,
if not quite, as great as the proportion in the population of
the labouring classes! But in every place where there is
a national school without any other near it (and in many
where there is another), and where—as in many instances
the Protestant clergyman or the squire are friendly to it,
or are merely not opposed (in some, even where they are
unfriendly), the children of the mixed population attend
in proportionate numbers. And the number of such
places is daily increasing; even in a little more than a year
since Bishop Dickinson's appointment, most of the opposition in his diocese has died away, and several former
opponents have applied to the Board, or otherwise sent
in their adhesion. And it would be the same almost
throughout Ireland if ministers would but boldly declare
their intention of supporting the system; I mean the
system of united education as brought forward by Lord
Stanley.

'But if they will not do this, I wish they would speak
out boldly on the other side, and no longer "halt between
two opinions."

'The cause which operates against your continuing a Whig is one of those which have always prevented me from becoming either that, or Tory, or partisan of any kind.

'All parties, as far as I can observe, are guilty of great misrepresentation and other injustice ; and—to say nothing of any danger of contamination from " strange bed-fellows" —one is in danger of being considered more or less responsible for the unjustifiable or absurd things put forth by his party, unless he is always on the watch to put in his own protest and disown them.

'Any government, you say, is likely to be wiser than the people. According to a dissertation just put forth by me (in an additional note to the second edition of my last volume), a government is likely to be in its acts wiser than the greater part of the people of all parties, and less wise than the wisest part.

'Many thanks for your kind reception of ——. —— is nearly recovered.

                    'Yours ever,
                              'R. Whately.'

This was to be a year marked by very deep and peculiar trial to the Archbishop—trial felt by him both as a philanthropist and public-spirited man, anxious that lives he believed useful to the state should be preserved ; and as a private individual, from the remarkable warmth and steadiness of his friendships. Several whom he valued were this year withdrawn ; but two specially and preeminently dear to him, whose loss could never be in this world replaced, were removed in the course of one short month. On the 12th of June of that year Dr. Arnold's sudden decease took place, followed early in July by that of Bishop Dickinson, so long his faithful and devoted helper in all his work, and then his valued and trusted colleague and ally on the bench.

His mind was more deeply depressed by these bereavements than it had been at any previous period of his life ; and though he continued the active discharge of his duties with characteristic resolution and perseverance, it was with a saddened heart and a continual struggle for calm submission to the will of an all-wise God.

The letters that follow show in what spirit he met these losses. He announces them himself to three of his friends; and then proceeds to consult with the Bishop of Norwich, and with Mrs. Arnold, on the subject of the publication of the letters and posthumous sermons of Dr. Arnold.

'Dublin: July 15, 1842.

'My dear Hampden,—You will not wonder at my not having immediately returned your letter, considering what two stunning blows I have just received. It is a sore trial to one's faith to see such men cut off in such a career of public service.

'But God needs not our help. May He be pleased to raise up other instruments, as purely devoted to His will and to man's good! More so I cannot conceive in a mortal.

'R. WHATELY.'

To the Bishop of Norwich.

'July 19, 1842.

'My dear Lord,—It occurred to me after Mrs. W. had answered your letter, that the publication of Arnold's Posthumous Sermons, with some letters and extracts from that delightful heavenly diary (a methodising sailor might call it the log-book of a voyage to heaven) will, at any rate, no doubt, take exceedingly in a commercial point of view; but if a moderate edition, as large as a publisher would recommend at a venture, should sell off speedily and a new one be called for, there is gain indeed, but less of clear gain than if an edition more nearly adequate to the demand had been printed. Now, if a considerable number of persons who may design (as I do) to buy several copies to give away—as I shall probably forty or fifty—were to bespeak those copies, privately, of the publisher, this would have, in a great degree, the advantage of publishing by subscription, without the indelicacy which attaches to that course. I have often myself—not with any view to the pecuniary advantage of the author—taken from five up to fifty copies of some work, to give away to the clergy and others—such as various works of Hinds's and of Arnold's; the "Index to the Tracts for the Times;" and one just published (which I think would interest you), called "The Church and the Synagogue," by Rev. J. Bernard, being an abridgment of Vitringa, &c.

'Now, if I had bespoken in each case such a number of copies, and if some twenty or thirty others had done the same, there would have been perhaps 500 or 1000 copies the more printed for that purpose.

'Bishop Dickinson died the very day that had been appointed for delivering his primary Charge! I had seen the rough sketch of it, and I understand it is complete, and will be published; making, with the large extracts prepared to be appended to it, a small volume. It was on the coincidence between the Transcendentalists, now so much in vogue on the Continent, and the Tractites, and I thought it likely to be the most valuable work on a most important subject. His predecessor ate and drank for eighty-five years; and he held the diocese eighteen

months, in which time he accomplished wonders. What
a trial of one's faith!

'Ever, my dear Lord, yours most truly,

'R. Dublin.'

To ———.

'July 1842.

'My dear Friend,—You had better hear from me what
you cannot fail to hear, of the second heavy loss which I
have sustained in one short month. Bishop Dickinson
died at 12 o'clock this day. I feel hardly more than half
alive. He had been for ten years my true "yoke-fellow;"
always associated with me in every duty and plan for the
public good. How mysterious are the ways of Providence!

'But God needs not our services. If it were His will
He could send some apostle, endued with miraculous
power, who would effect more in a month than any of us
can in a life.

'It is a blessing, and in some degree a lasting one, when
men of high intellectual powers are sincere Christians; it
tends to destroy the association so apt to be formed between religion and silly superstition, or at least feeble
understanding. And of all the highly-gifted men I have
ever known, the two I have so lately been bereft of were
the very best Christians. I mean that they were not
merely eminently good men, but men who made it their
constant business to bring their religion into their daily
life and character.

'The two had some different opinions from each other;
but they were strikingly alike in making the Christian
character—the Gospel spirit embodied in the life—their
great study. "Blessed are the pure in heart, for they

shall see God," and when they meet, in his presence, they will know perfectly—and not care at all—which was the nearest the truth in his opinions here on earth.

'Pray for me, dear friend, that I may be able to bear up against the rough blasts of opposition which I have to encounter, when such props are taken from me!'

'My dear Mrs. Arnold,—You need not fear acting against my decided opinion; for in fact I have no decided opinion in this case.

'It was otherwise with the question about suppressing that Sermon. There, I never felt any doubt.

'There are strong reasons for and against every one of the three possible alternatives.

'1. The biography would certainly be the more complete by the publication of everything, great or small, that ever appeared in print. And there is no one of the occasional productions that does not contain valuable matter.

'But then there are reasons against this. For instance, some of the articles in reviews have had something of prejudice raised against them by having been served up with the sauce which the conductors of the Edinburgh think it necessary to season everything with for certain palates. The title of "Oxford malignants," and some insolent expressions in another article, that on the Episcopalian Letters, are editorial condiments of this kind; and though these may be expunged, the articles have been so long before the public with them, that perhaps some of the bitterness may, as it were, have soaked in. Then, there is the pamphlet on Roman Catholic Emancipation, which gave dissatisfaction to both parties. Now one must make up one's mind to give offence, when there is some

practical point to be carried, which requires one to speak
his mind, and this happens to be unpopular. But there is
now no practical point at issue; so that it would be gratuitously raking up the embers of a controversy which
is dying away.

'Then the letters to the Sheffield paper are wonder-
fully good, considering how very hastily they were
written; and they contain much more of valuable matter
than of what is not; but there is in them an admixture
of some crude and ill-considered views (though less than
one might have expected under the circumstances), which
one would be glad to expunge. I know the extreme
haste in which, in the midst of various other occupations,
several of them, at least, were written, being in the house
at the time. One of them, indeed, is half of it mine;
for after having written the opening of it, he asked me to
finish it for him, as he had not made up his mind what to
say. Of course it was to be expected, considering the
importance of many of the points touched on, that several
things should have been thrown out which would have
been materially altered on attentive reflection.

'2. The second alternative—to publish some of the
occasional pieces and omit some, or to omit certain passages, is, perhaps, at the first glance, what one would
most be disposed to approve. But there are objections
to that.

'It is not like selecting from MSS., for every one is
understood to write many things of which some are fit
for publication and some not; but whatever he has
printed he has, evidently, at the time, thought fit for the
public. And it is a delicate matter to make selections
out of these. Notwithstanding all the explanations one
may give as the why's, it will be apt to follow that what
is omitted is understood to be more strongly condemned

than one intends (and people know what it is that one omits; which in the case of a MS. they do not); and again, one is understood, when any omission is made, to be the more decidedly pledged to a full approbation of all that is not omitted.

'3. The objections to the third alternative—that of reprinting none of the occasional publications—are very obvious. A considerable amount of valuable matter would be withheld.

'You see, therefore, that I am quite in a wavering state of mind.

'When in that state, the opinion of Fellowes could not but have some influence. He said, that viewing the whole matter merely as a question of trade, he should suppress the whole of the miscellaneous pieces; because he thought some of them would so far raise or revive prejudices, as to do more harm than good to the sale of the work.

'Now the sale, as a matter of profit, is not the main consideration; but it is something of a sign of that which is an important consideration—wide circulation and favourable reception.

'But Fellowes may be mistaken; or, again, if he is not mistaken, there may be overbalancing considerations on the other side.

'And now I have said all that occurs to me; which, if not otherwise very satisfactory, at least must satisfy you that you cannot adopt any course which has not in my judgment strong reasons for it as well as against it.

'Ever yours affectionately, ·
'R. W.'

The following letter alludes to a matter to which reference has been made elsewhere. The Archbishop

was a good deal mortified by the opposition made to his
scheme for the establishment of a Divinity College as
supplemental to the course of the Divinity School in the
Dublin University. He was particularly pained because
many assumed the plan to be a covert attack on Trinity
College, than which nothing was farther from his mind.

Many men, however, opposed the plan, because, though
they knew the Archbishop too well to suspect him of
any motion but the ostensible one, they, nevertheless,
believed the tendency of the scheme would be, in various
ways, prejudicial to Trinity College. Some who then
took this view confessed themselves afterwards mistaken.
But amongst those who opposed the Archbishop on
conscientious conviction was the Venerable John Russell,
Archdeacon of Clogher. The Archbishop was greatly
mortified at this, the more so because Archdeacon Russell
was a near relative of Dr. Dickinson; and he feared,
therefore, that the opposition of one who had such
opportunities of close communication with those connected
with the plan would carry all the more weight. He
thought, besides, that Archdeacon Russell, being a personal friend, ought to have communicated with him
before taking any public action, and seems to have misunderstood a little the motives of delicacy which hindered
him from doing so. Be this as it may, the Archbishop
broke off his intimacy with him for some time. Immediately after Bishop Dickinson's death, the Archbishop
wrote to the Archdeacon the following letter, and he
subsequently invited him to the palace, as before, whenever he visited Dublin.

‘Dublin: July 22, 1842.

‘Dear Sir,—I have understood from Mr. Croker that it
would be satisfactory to you to receive, direct from

myself, assurance of the entire absence from my heart
of all feelings of enmity or resentment towards you, such
as my beloved friend the Bishop so earnestly deprecated.

'I beg you to receive these assurances with my most
solemn protestations of their sincerity. Any wrong, or
apparent wrong, on your part, whether with or without
your consciousness of it, I forgive, as a debt of one
hundred pence, as fully as I hope to be forgiven my debt
of ten thousand talents; and for any wrong on my part
towards you, I heartily ask your pardon. I feel a strong
hope that my departed friend did not think me a man to
cherish anger or ill-will towards any one, or to feel displeasure at all against any one for a mere difference of
opinion even on important practical points; whatever I
might, for a man's mode of expressing such difference.
To say that I think you perfectly blameless on that head,
. I am sure he could not have expected me, because that
would be to express a judgment at variance with his own,
such as I (and probably you also) have often heard from
him.

'But such words as " forgive," &c., are somewhat offen-
sive, and what I would fain avoid, as implying the existence of something wrong; while, after all, both he and
I being but fallible mortals, may have erred in our judgment, and you may have been quite blameless all through.
Still, it would not be allowable to say so without sincerely
thinking it, and yet to say the contrary may give offence;
and for this reason it is that I have all along been disposed
to decline, unless distinctly called on, to say anything at
all about the matter.

'In the mode, however, of my expressing disapprobation,
when I did receive such a call, he may have suspected
that I used harsher language than in fact I did; and if
he had seen what I said (supposing it had been in the

case of some other person, comparatively a stranger to
him) it is not unlikely he would have thought (I have
since thought so myself) that my language was more
severe than was necessary; for it was his rule, when called
on, to give his judgment in any matter, not, indeed, to
disguise his real opinion through fear of giving pain, but
to give as little pain as possible. In a similar case, I had
the advantage of being able to show to the Bishop and to
West a letter I received from a Mr. M. and my answer to
it. West has my permission to show you the letter, and
my answer as finally approved by them, from which you
will be able to judge—after making any allowance that
may seem needful for the points of difference between
the two cases—what would have been the probable result
of my having had, in your case also, the advantage of the
Bishop's counsel; but it had occurred to me spontaneously
some time before that a great part of my letter to you
would have been, on more mature reflection, erased.
For any unnecessary pain I may have caused by any part
of it (which I really believe was the case), I most sincerely
ask your pardon, and I as sincerely assure you of mine
for anything amiss in your conduct towards me. I will
only add my assurance that there is no ground whatever
for any suspicion you may have had of my having thrown
out any such imputations as you, at one time, seemed to
suppose, and from which you seemed anxious to clear
yourself.

'You assured me, for instance, that the course you took
had the approbation of your conscience, of which, I can
assure you, I had never expressed any doubt—that it
was painful to you to find yourself standing publicly
opposed to your brother-in-law and to me—that you had
no personal interest in view—that you did not yourself
draw up the memorial you signed—that you acted wholly

on your own deliberate judgment, uninfluenced by others, &c. In short, in respect of every one of the points you dwelt on in your letter to me, I must solemnly declare that I had never said anything to the contrary.

'In respect of the last-mentioned point, indeed, I certainly had heard an opposite suggestion; not, however, from any one unfriendly to you, but from those who, on the contrary, considered themselves as taking the most favourable view. By such I had heard it suggested that you had been (perhaps unconsciously) over-persuaded, over-awed, or in some way influenced by those around you, and that if you had exercised deliberately your own unbiassed judgment you would have never put your name to such a paper. This, as I have said, was suggested by those who thought themselves putting the best construction on the matter, and especially by our departed friend himself.

'But, for my own part, I repeat my assurance that I never uttered any hint of an opinion, one way or the other, on any of those points.

'With sincere good wishes to you and yours,

'Believe me, dear Sir,

'Your faithful humble servant,

'RD. DUBLIN.'

The following letter to the Bishop of Norwich is of an earlier date than the preceding; but it has been thought best to place it here, because it concerns a different subject, and one on which the views of the Archbishop were very strong. This expression of his opinion of the mode of treating the attacks on the sovereign, at that time so frequent, is too characteristic of himself to be omitted.

'Dublin: July 6, 1842.

'My dear Lord,—Allow me to lay before you, and to beg you to turn in your mind and consult others on it, what I have long been thinking and should now probably bring forward if I were in the House.

'It surely is high time that we should at length take warning by experience in respect of the attacks on the Queen; one of the papers says, " it was the more marvellous (this last attempt) on account of Francis having just been reprieved." I should rather say, if he had been hanged, there would have been a something to wonder at in a fresh attempt. I should be inclined to move for a resolution of the House preparatory to an Act, that the prerogative of pardon should be withdrawn from the sovereign in the case of attempts on her own life, except on an address from both Houses.

'It is placing the sovereign in a most indelicate predicament, because there seems something shocking in allowing the law to take its course when the individual who has the power to pardon is the one assailed; but the nation is so greatly concerned in the sovereign's life, that the public welfare ought not to be sacrificed to the feelings of delicacy of any individual. In all other cases the prerogative of pardon is very fitly vested in the sovereign; but not where there is so much of what is personal.

'I write in the midst of pressing business, therefore pray excuse haste, and believe me

'Most truly yours,

'Rd. Dublin.'

To the Bishop of Salisbury.

Countersignature of Testimonials — The Archbishop's Reasons for his peculiar Form.

'The Palace: Aug. 31, 1842.

'My dear Lord,—I am glad your Lordship has applied to me, that I may have the opportunity of explaining.

The form of countersignature *is* my usual one. I adopt it in all cases; because sometimes to add " worthy of credit " and sometimes to omit those words would be in some cases ungracious, and in some productive of inconvenience ; and again, to add those words in all cases, would perhaps be made use of as pledging me to more than I should like to stand to. I state, therefore, officially, exactly all that I mean : viz., that the signatures are, as far as I know, genuine signatures of *bonâ fide* clergymen ; and secondly, that I know nothing to the contrary of what they have stated. Then I am ready to give, privately and confidentially, answers to any bishop who may wish to inquire more particularly. In the present instance I really know nothing of the Mr. —— in question. The signers are not persons on whom I should very particularly rely in any doubtful case ; but I have no reason for believing this to be one.

> ' Ever, my dear Lord, yours very truly,
>   ' Rd. Dublin.'

Mrs. Arnold had written to consult the Archbishop on the subject of the publication of one of Dr. Arnold's posthumous sermons, to which exception had been taken by some of his friends. The following is the answer :—

' October 20, 1842.

' My dear Friend,—I am grieved you should have so much worry ; but I am happy to be able, as far as I am concerned, to cut short all perplexing deliberations. Much as I am given to hesitation, I feel none here. If Bishop Dickinson were alive, I would not lose a day's post for the sake of consulting him ; and that is saying a great deal.

' Mr. Stanley's reasons appear to me to have very little

weight. Arnold would not, he thinks, have published the
sermons himself; suppose it so (which I feel by no means
disposed to be sure of), what then?   There may be
many things not written with a view to publication, and
even which the author may be very right in never publishing himself, but which yet (for instance, his private
letters to friends on several important subjects) may be
not at all unfit to be published posthumously by others.
It is only on the supposition that he would have abstained
from publishing it on the ground of his having changed
his opinions, or of its relating to some private or local
matter not fitted for general readers, or of its having
been written under some excitement of feeling which in
his cooler moments appeared indecorous; it is only when
on such grounds we judge that the writer would have
abstained from publication, that this should be a reason
for our abstaining.

'As to its " giving pain " to several persons, I can only
say, it must be a sorry sermon that does not.   I remember one of my parishioners at Halesworth telling me that
he thought "a person should not go to church to be
made uncomfortable."   I replied that I thought so too;
but whether it should be the sermons or the man's life
that should be altered, so as to avoid the discomfort,
must depend on whether the doctrine was right or wrong.
But " what is one man's meat is another man's poison."
I dare say you have heard from me a curious and instructive anecdote about one of the " Future State "
Lectures; that on " preparation for death," two of my
friends wrote to me, pressing me most earnestly to suppress or alter it as " having given pain to many a pious
mind;" and at the same time another man, a personal
stranger, wrote to beg my permission to print it as a
separate tract for distribution!

'Mrs. W. will enter, perhaps, more fully than I shall now do, upon the merits of the sermon itself. There is no need to discuss the question whether it should be published at all or suppressed, since that is decided. The question is only as to whether it should be reserved or not, for another volume. There might be something said for this latter course, if it were on some extraordinary occasion, so as to be quite out of the course of his ordinary teaching; but to omit an Easter-day sermon, would lead people to suppose that it was, in point of matter, something of an exception from his habitual instruction. It would imply (and I have no doubt that is the real drift of the suggestion; I mean Mr. Ward's drift) that his crudest thoughts, what he occasionally gave vent to in hasty communications with his friends, were much more apparently adverse to Tractism than his more deliberate and well-considered doctrine; and that for once, by inadvertency, he let out in a Rugby-sermon some of these crudities, which he himself would on consideration have excluded from a place where they ought not to be found, as being unfit for exoteric discourses.

'If his works were now for the first time to come before the public, it might be prudent to select, for the first volume, such of his doctrines as might be the most generally acceptable, lest some readers should be scared away in the outset by too violent a shock to their prejudices; and the succeeding volumes might bring forward those opinions, one by one, which were more likely to prove a stumbling-block to some. But he has long been before the world as an author, and the volume in question is not a selection at all of the most fit for publication; but professes, as I understand, to be a continuous course, containing all his sermons that are not unfit; so that the exclusion of one from the set would be an exception, leading, I think, to such a conclusion as I have above alluded to.

'To-morrow two years Bishop Alexander died, aged, I think, eighty-five; and his successor died the July twelvemonth following, aged fifty! Mysterious and trying to our faith are some of the dispensations of Providence! Bishop Dickinson was engaged in writing, and had nearly completed a Charge setting forth the coincidence in many points between the Tractites and the German Transcendentalists, which I hinted at in the last note but one to my last volume. Dr. West will publish what is completed along with some sermons.

'Never, surely, did the world more need the warning against "false prophets in sheep's clothing;" though the fleece is so very thin it is a matter of wonder that intelligent men should so generally fail to see the wolf beneath it. So very simple a contrivance as that of using words in new senses generally the very opposite of the old, seems to answer the purpose. If Tom looks into the Corcyrean civil war in Thucydides he will see in many points, but especially in what relates to this artifice of misemploying terms, an almost exact description of much that is now going on.

'"Humble-minded" men are especially to be guarded against; the word means what used to be called arrogant and insolent; on the other hand, the worship of God only, and a deference for Him and His Word, beyond what is paid to any mortal man, is, now-a-days, "profaneness and self-conceit;" a "pure and holy man" is one who fasts twice in the week, but "neglects the weightier matters of the law, judgment, and justice, and mercy." I think the "holy men" who garbled and distorted Hampden's Bampton Lectures with the deliberate design of holding him up to the hatred and persecution of

unthinking bigots, are the genuine descendants of those
Roman emperors who dressed up the early Christians in
the skins of beasts, and then set dogs at them to worry
them to death.

> 'Ever yours affectionately,
>
> 'R. WHATELY.'

The Rev. A. P. Stanley, now Dean of Westminster, who
had commenced preparations for the biography of Dr.
Arnold, wrote to consult the Archbishop on the subject
of a memorial to him, in which many of his strongest
opponents took an active part.

To the Rev. A. P. Stanley.

'November 1.

'My dear Sir,

.   .   .   .

'Indelicacy is too mild a word to characterise the
effrontery and presumption of men who, while Dr. Arnold
was alive, repaid his kindness and friendship with the
bitterest insults, heaped on him on account of the very
circumstances which have led to the proposal of doing
honour to his memory (for if he had gone on in decent
and obscure mediocrity, they would not have reviled or
opposed him, nor would others have thought of public
honours to him); and who now come forward to take a
part in that work, when, as it appears, their scheme is to
garble his works, and to degrade his monument. They
may conceivably have been right, and he in error, all
through ; but then, let them not take their stand on the
" mountain of blessing " when their proper place is on the
" mountain of cursing." There is a passage in the
speech for the Crown which seems exactly to fit the occasion, where Demosthenes speaks of the indignant rejection
by the authorities of those who were candidates for the

office of speaking the funeral oration over the soldiers
who fell in their countries' cause, and who had been the
friends and agents of Philip. (I quote from memory not
having the book at hand).

προσήκειν τοῦτο τὸν ἐροῦντα τοτ' ἐπὶ τοῖς τετελευτη-
κόσι καὶ τὴν ἐκείνων ἀρέτην κοσμήσοντα μηδ' ὁμωρόφιον
μηδ' ὁμόσπονδον γεγενθημένον εἶναι τοῖς πρὸς ἐκείνους
παραταξαμένοις . . . . μηδὲ τῇ φωνῇ δακρύειν
ὑποκρινόμενον τὴν ἐκείνων τύχην, ἀλλὰ τῇ ψυχῇ συν-
αλγεῖν.

'Ever yours truly,

'R. D.'

It was in this year that the long Whig administration
being now succeeded by a Tory one,[1] the Archbishop felt
that decisive steps must be taken as to the Education
Board, if the national system was to continue. He accordingly wrote early that autumn to the Lord-Lieutenant,
Earl de Grey, urging the importance of a speedy decision
on the part of ministers. 'I had written,' he writes in
his note-book, 'to represent to them how important it
was not to keep people in suspense on so important a
matter; not to excite false hopes, but declare speedily,
openly, and strongly, whether they approved of and would
continue the system and the Commissioners, or not; in
which latter case I would at once retire.'

This communication had been answered satisfactorily,
and the following is the letter he wrote to the Lord-Lieutenant on the subject.

National Education System.

'Palace: Nov. 17, 1842.

'My Lord,—I have had the honour of receiving your
Excellency's communication, which I have had the oppor-

---

[1] Sir R. Peel became Prime Minister in September 1841, and remained
so until July 1846.

tunity of imparting this day to several of the Education
Commissioners. They concur with me in feelings of great
satisfaction at the announcement of a resolution so important to the welfare of this country.

' We have not felt ourselves at liberty to make to other
parties, but we conclude Government will take opportunities to make known to all who are interested in the question the course that has been resolved on. This will, I
have no doubt, go far towards allaying the distrust, anxiety,
agitation, and dissension that are to be found in the country,
and which I adverted to, as evils likely to prevail, in my
letter to your Excellency last year. I think it likely that
the decision of Government, distinctly announced and
steadily followed up in practice, may have a great effect
in obtaining the co-operation of some, and the neutrality
of others, among those who have hitherto been active
opponents; and this, without any compromise of principle
on their part, or even any change of opinion, except as to
the practicability of their designs. A man may very consistently support a system that shall appear to be the best
that is attainable, but which he had felt himself bound to
oppose, as long as there seemed a chance of substituting
what he regarded as a better; and, up to this time some
have apparently cherished in themselves and in others
hopes of bringing about a change or an extinction of the
Education System, either directly or by obtaining a separate
grant for schools on a different plan, and thus effectually
destroying the essential character of a national system.
I do not see but that those who, from entertaining such
hopes have hitherto opposed the Education Board, may
hereafter lend aid to its operations, even though believing
the system not to be the very best.

' Certainly the scruples which many have urged against
any education, not based on the religion of the Established

Church, have always been readily received, on the express
condition of non-interference with their religion. . . . .

'I am, &c.'

*Extract from a Letter to a Gentleman who had sent him a
Book treating of Church Government.*

'Dec. 17, 1842.

'It has often been a matter of wonder to me, that no
one, as far as I know, of the many writers who have
treated of Church-polity, have ever apparently had a
thought of the danger connected with such discussions.
They display great research and ingenuity, and adduce
arguments which, whether of any real weight or not, have
undoubtedly influenced many minds, to show that Episcopacy was, or was not, the form of government introduced
by the apostles, and adhered to in the earliest ages; and
each seems satisfied if he has made out this point to his
own and his friends' conviction.

'But if a man is led, or is left to conclude that it is
essential to his salvation to live under such a Church
Government as the apostles established, or at least that
he is otherwise in a perilous way, what a Pandora's box of
evils is opened, with not hope, but despair at the bottom!
There is a book—such as Bishop Wilson's, for example—
which not one in 10,000 can be expected to read, and not
one in 10,000 of those who read it are competent to
verify by consulting the ancient authorities; but to those
who can, it affords strong proofs, or at least considerable
probabilities, that such and such a form of Church-polity
is essential to Christians. Hence it is evident that all
Christians, except one in a million, have nothing to trust
to but the word of a very, very few learned men. for their
being—even likely to be—genuine members of the Church
of Christ.

'Now, if we must needs take their word for one part of what is essential, why not for all the rest, too?

'Who, in his senses, would go to analyse one-half of the medicines the doctor sends, if the other half—which he must also take—are what he cannot analyse?

'Therefore, the mass of mankind, who wish to have as little as possible of the trouble of thinking about their religion, will at once acquiesce in whatever their teachers bid them believe; and the more thoughtful few will set down the whole as a heap of priestcraft; because (they will say) our religion pretends to be a revelation, and is not;—because it is a mockery to tell the mass of mankind to prove all things, and hold fast to that which is right, and to be able to give a reason for the hope that is in them, if it is clearly beyond their power to give any reason for even hoping that they are at all members of the Church of Christ;—if this depends on their being governed on the Apostolical model, of which the apostles have left us in their writings no precise description, but which we are to collect by a comparison of what St. A. saith in such a book, with what is reported by St. B. to have been reported by St. C. as the practice in the Church of D.

'And what makes the absence of this revelation the more staggering (supposing the thing itself to have been designed to be essential) is, that it is so much easier to be put down in writing than moral precepts and exhortations, and so much more needful; and yet this is not done, and the other is. More needful, I say, because the light of reason may guide men in a great degree into moral truths—into the application of Christian motives; whereas positive regulations, as whether a church should be governed by a single overseer, or by a council, or in what other way, one could no more determine by the light of reason than whether every seventh day or every sixth should be a religious festival. And more easy also; for it would be easy in three or four pages, in one-twentieth of the space on which might be given a very slight and scanty sketch of the various modes of conduct right to be pursued on the several occasions of ordinary life that arise—to give such an outline of a form of Church-polity as would, if it had been delivered on Apostolical authority, have settled at once and for ever all the disputes on the subject that have agitated the Church for so many ages.

'Yet this has not been done.

'One of two conclusions seems to me inevitably to follow : either there is a complete failure in the professed design of giving mankind (I mean men in that ordinary degree of civilisation to which the mass of mankind may conceivably attain in a civilised country) a revelation of what they must do to be saved ; or, the design was, to leave Christian faith and Christian principles of conduct fixed, and to leave Church government, as well as various rites and ceremonies, to the discretion of each Church in each age and country.

'I can see no other alternative.'

The end of this year, so full of trial, brought him some cheering influence in the appointment of his friend Dr. Hinds, who had accepted the living of Castleknock, near Dublin. The prospect of having this valued companion of his early days again near him was the most consoling one of which his circumstances now admitted.

In the December of this year he paid a visit—to him deeply affecting—to the bereaved family of his beloved friend Dr. Arnold, in their home at Fox How in Westmoreland. In the letters written by them at this time are several notices of this visit, so highly prized by them, which give so lively a picture of his habits in social and

domestic intercourse, that we will quote one or two:
—'Have I ever described to you the Archbishop's
manner when he was here?　It was really very affecting,
and continually, without one word of profession, showed
forth his love for his friend and his mingled compassion
and affection for that friend's wife and children.　Even
what might be called the natural roughnesses of his
character seemed softened and harmonised; and it was
very striking to see him wandering about here—looking
at the flowers and talking with the gardener, with the
younger ones playing about him, just as he did at Rugby.'

'After luncheon,' writes another of the family, 'we
went up Loughrigg with the Archbishop, and a most
delightful walk we had.　As we came back we overtook
a little girl about six years old, who has daily to carry a
heavy can of milk a distance of two miles.　The poor
little thing was quite frightened at having to go so far in
the dark.　The Archbishop was shocked at her having to
carry such a load, so some of us took her can, and he
carried her himself to Fox How, whence the rest of us
walked home with her.'

In the following year (1843), we find my father receiving
and answering frequent letters of consultation on the
subject of memorials, epitaphs, and biographies of Dr.
Arnold, whose loss was still fresh in the minds and hearts
of all who had the privilege of knowing him.

The following letters are on this subject :—

'Jan. 10.

'My dear Mrs. Arnold,—I cannot resist sending you a
most characteristic note from Dr. Wilson, to whom I had
lent the "British and Foreign Review."

'I am disposed to concur with him; and, in respect of
the Anglo-Catholic, should perhaps have bestowed stronger

commendation. This may be from its being a favourable
review of my own work among others; but I believe I
am in general rather fastidious as to writers on my own
side. I think I am even more mortified by weak arguments in favour of my own views than by strong ones
against them.

'The other article is whimsically infelicitous in the
idea of compounding together Hume and Johnson to
make up an Arnold, unless he thought that, as two
negatives make an affirmative, so two red-hot Jacobites
would make a Liberal. Johnson was a most sincere and
deep-rooted Tory; and if Hume was sincere in anything,
it was in that. And they were so ecclesiastically as well
as politically; for, though neither of them thought there
was any truth in the peculiar doctrines of Romanism, the
impression conveyed by each is, that the Reformation
was not worth contending for. But a low estimate of
the claims of truth—too common as it is among men—
was carried so far by those two (though in many points
so unlike) as to be characteristic of them. They resembled
each other in their skill in dressing up a case, and in
arguing more for victory than for truth, apparently
regarding (Hume in his writings and Johnson in his
conversation) a discussion of the most important matters
as a game of chess, in which it matters not whether you
have the white men or the black, if you do but play them
skilfully and baffle your opponent.'

*To a Gentleman who had consulted him on the Epitaph
for Dr. Arnold.*

'Dublin: Feb. 14, 1843.

'My dear Sir,—A good while ago I was consulted as
to the epitaph, through Mr. Stanley, who sent me three
to judge of. I stated to him at that time pretty fully the

reasons which have long since induced me to set my face
against all laudatory epitaphs whatever—all that contain
any matter of opinion—because they are never believed;
records of facts are. Not but that many a one may
believe in the truth of that which the epitaph says; but
that is from his knowing it from other sources. It is not
the epitaph that he believes, for their exaggeration is proverbial. There is nothing in the enclosed one, for instance,
at all, beyond what we may often see said of men who
are to Arnold as copper or silver to gold. The stranger,
therefore, disbelieves, and the friend thinks too little said.

'I said that I did not like to speak truth when I had
no fair chance of being believed. I added that I had on
two occasions written epitaphs, containing nothing beyond
the truth on intimate friends of mine, with which I was
well satisfied at the time; but for the above reason I
became dissatisfied with them afterwards, and I never
after departed from the resolution I then formed; for
though I did afterwards put up a stone with a laudatory
inscription to a parishioner, a man of the lower class, I
added that it was by the rector of the parish, designating
myself as the attester of his worth; and his humble
station putting all flattery from me to him or his family
out of the question, I had no reason to doubt this praise
would be believed.

'We must make up our minds to consider that nothing
can be done that will please everybody. To see Drs.
Wooll, James, and Arnold (!) side by side, and about
equal in the eyes of those who shall judge from their
epitaphs, would not gratify me; but *de gustibus non.*
The omission of laudation (with perhaps the reason
assigned) would at least be a distinction.

'Very truly yours,

'Rd. Dublin.'

The Bishop of Norwich appears to have written to consult the Archbishop on a knotty point. His answer explains itself:—

'Palace: March 3, 1843.

'My dear Lord,—I am making inquiries about your case, and will let you know the result.

'Alas! that I cannot now resort to that counsellor whose qualities of head and heart made him so invaluable to me and to the Church!

'My own first impression is, that testimony is to be resorted to only in respect of matters of fact, such as a man's regularity of conduct, &c.; but that his orthodoxy, when it is made to turn on a passage in a written sermon, is a matter of opinion, on which one bishop has as good a right to decide as another. If any man's written or printed expressions lead you to think him unsound, that is good reason why you should refuse him a licence or ordination, but none why I should, if I happen to be of an opposite opinion, unless, indeed, the man has been convicted before an ecclesiastical court. I am supposing that there is no other objection to the man, and that you have only refused to license him on your own unlimited discretion. If this were to control the proceedings of any other bishop, the dictum of one bishop would supersede all courts, and a regular trial would be superfluous; but when there is any court in which such and such an offence may be tried, it seems to me that non-conviction is to be regarded as a decisive presumption of innocence. This is, however, as yet, only my own first impression.

'Ever, my dear Lord, yours very truly,

'RD. DUBLIN.'

Provost Hawkins had suggested to his friend that much of the perplexity in men's minds on the subject of the

now hotly-disputed 'doctrine of reserve' arose from many
really and honestly imagining that this doctrine was only
another name for that gradual and progressive teaching,
which, in the case of young or unlearned scholars, must
be essential from all who would really make their instructions intelligible.

In his answer, the Archbishop fully allows for this :—

'I have no doubt you are right in thinking that many
well-meaning, though not clear-headed men, have confounded together the necessity of teaching beginners
the first page before they come to the second with the
keeping back of Gospel truths from those able and willing
to learn them. And this may have been the case originally with the leaders (though most of them do not
seem to be wanting in clearness of head) of the Tractite
party ; but this must have been a long while ago, for it
is several years now since the " Elucidations " of Hampden
was published ; and I cannot conceive any one either
writing or reading that tissue of deliberate and artful
misrepresentations (comparing it with Hampden's own
volume) without perceiving—unless he were a downright
fool—that it consisted of the " suppressio veri " so contrived as to amount to the " suggestio falsi "—the kind
of lies which Swift justly calls the worst, " a lie guarded."
The author and the approvers of such a work (as many
as were acquainted with Hampden's) could have nothing
to learn from the " slanderer " himself!

'I am inclined to think there is another cause which
has greatly led to the double doctrine, as well as to many
other evils—the tendency which, under the garb of piety,
is most emphatically impiety, in mere men to imitate God
or His prophets and apostles in those very points in which
the imitation should be most carefully guarded against.
Hence, some " teach with authority, and not as the

scribes," because, forsooth, this is what Jesus did; hence, some profess to disdain the aid of human learning, because Paul "came with demonstration of the Spirit and of power;" some eulogise faith—viz., in their word—because faith (in God's declarations) is commanded in Scripture; and hence, since God withheld the Gospel from certain generations and nations of men, we, forsooth, are to judge who are worthy to receive, and from whom we shall "keep back all the counsel of God." It is strange, though too true, that man should be deceived by so gross a fallacy, which would make an arch-rebel and his followers imitators of a legitimate king and his loyal subjects.'

It was about this time that the 'Life of Blanco White' (who, as has been mentioned, died in 1841) was published. The Archbishop, in common with all the early friends of this unfortunate man. had greatly deprecated the publication of this memoir. which, under the circumstances, could scarcely be done fairly. They, therefore, almost all refused to contribute any letters or papers to the biography in question. The following letter from the Archbishop is on this subject :—

'April 20, 1843.

' Dear Sir—The "Life of Blanco White" I have looked into just enough to see that it is pretty much what I might have expected, considering who the editor is; for he is the very person who wrote, as I am credibly informed, a short memoir of B. White in some Unitarian periodical soon after his death, and which I happened to get a sight of a year or two after.

' In that he represents B. W. as banished by his friends, and left to pass the remainder of his days in poverty and solitude; the fact being — 1st. That he left my house

entirely at his own desire. 2nd. That he received a
pension from me, and another from another friend.
And 3rd. That I and my family, and several other
of his former friends, kept up a correspondence with
him, and visited him whenever we passed through
Liverpool.

'Now from a person who, with the knowledge of these
facts, could deliberately set himself to produce in the
mind of the public an opposite impression (as any one
may see by looking at that first memoir I have alluded
to), no great amount of delicacy or scrupulosity could be
expected. . . . . . .

'That the present publication surpasses the average (of
publications of this kind) in bringing before the public
what is most emphatically private,—in the indecent exposure of the private memoranda of an invalid in a
diseased state of mind,—this will be evident to every one
who gives but the slightest glance at the book.

'I know publications of this character are a sort of
nuisance for which there is no remedy. I am only
solicitous to clear my own character, and also that of
poor Blanco White himself, from the imputation of any
responsibility on this account.

'I myself, as I have already informed you, was applied to, to furnish letters &c. from and to the deceased;
and I declined, stating as one decisive reason that I knew
him to be in an unsound state of mind for several years;
and that I could clearly establish this, both by documents
in my possession and by the testimony of several competent persons, including two of his medical attendants,
unknown to each other; so that no memoir not adverting
to this fact (which, of course, I did not wish to proclaim)
could be correct, or could fail to convey positively erroneous impressions. I am, therefore, no party to the

publication; nor, on account of his state of mind, can I
consider Blanco White as being so, whatever he may in
that morbid state have said, written, or done.   .   .   .
And this it is right should be made known to any who
may feel an interest in the subject.

'Yours faithfully,

'Rd. Dublin.'

The Archbishop was this year again in London for the
session.   While there, Mr. Stanley consulted him on the
publication of a letter of Dr. Arnold's on Irish affairs.

To the Rev. A. P. Stanley.

'London: May 3, 1843.

'My dear Sir,—Many thanks for what you have done
for Edward, which is perfectly satisfactory.   It would be
strange indeed for me to object to a tutor for having been
in the second class.   I was elected at once against two
first-class-men; and I remember once we had eight candidates for two vacancies, and the men we elected were
the only two that were not first-class; and this, not from
any contempt of the school-examinations, for we were not
even aware of the fact till after the election.

'As general rules—subject, of course, to many exceptions: 1st. A first-class man is likely to be one who is
quicker in learning than a second-class. And 2nd. A
slow man is likely to be a better tutor than a very quick
one.

'I myself being more of a hone than of a razor, should
at this day be justly placed, at an examination, a class
below some other men in point of knowledge, whom I
should surpass in the power of imparting it.   .   .   .

'In haste, yours truly,

'Rd. Dublin.'

Again, after his return to Ireland, he writes as follows to Mrs. Arnold on the subject of her husband's biography, at that time in preparation :—

' Dublin : Aug. 16.

' My dear Friend,—If you in fact are ultimately the editor, so that you are to have unlimited power—as surely you ought to have — over every MS. before it goes to press, I think it likely that that very circumstance may check those who might otherwise endeavour to show objects through their own coloured glass.

' " A mechant chien, court lien." Let no one deter you from exercising your own judgment in this matter. The responsibility is heavy, but it must be yours after all ; since whatever others may do by your permission is virtually done by you.

' ―― and ――, I find, have discovered that Arnold was a most estimable man, and did not really differ from them at bottom !

' I dare say the same discoveries will be made of me, after I am dead, and not before. The bees will come and build their combs in the lion's carcase, but not while he lives !

' I think if this sort of patronage was to be extended to me, Mrs. W. would reject their posthumous honey—or at least I should if in her place—by saying, Why did you not find out his good qualities sooner ? I will tell you why : it is because they wanted the one circumstance which really recommends him to you—his death. Why did you not earlier declare his coincidence, at bottom, with your views ? I will tell you : it is because he was alive to contradict you. You are like the savages of the South Sea Islands, who are glad to get hold of the body of a dead enemy, that they may fashion his bones into spear-heads for future combats. " Be content," she would

say, "with having misrepresented him while living; but
expect not me to aid you in misrepresenting him when
dead. I will not help you in whitening the sepulchres of
the prophets whom you have stoned!"

'I would have you receive courteously all contributions
of letters, &c., and all various pieces of advice, with one
general answer (I have three or four "general answers"
for different classes of applicants, which my secretaries
write in each case that arrives), viz.: "that you are
obliged, and will take it into consideration." But be you
the ultimate decider on every word that goes to press.
Thank God, the decision could not be in better hands;
and at any rate yours must after all be the responsibility.'

Again, a notice in the letters from Mrs. Arnold's family
at Fox How tells of a visit there. 'You would, I am
sure,' says the writer, 'have loved the Archbishop if you
had seen his tenderness and kindness to all, and his
readiness and pleasure in teaching and amusing the whole
party. He is such a lover of Natural History, that every
ramble in the garden gives him matter on which to dwell
and impart information.' Another member of the family
adds, alluding to a later period, 'His delight in teaching
was very great. When the "Easy Lessons in Reasoning"
came out he was at Fox How, and made us all his pupils,
including my mother, whom he complimented on her
quick-witted answers, and probing our minds, I must
say, in a most searching manner.'

The following notes, occasioned by Mr. W. Palmer's
narrative of events connected with the 'Tracts for the
Times' found among the Archbishop's papers, have
already been quoted in a former volume.

'Mr. W. Palmer is quite right in recommending charity
and courtesy of language, but it should be remembered

that a most uncharitable and unjustifiable reproach to others may be conveyed by terms not applied to them, but to ourselves. For instance, a person was asked in Italy " whether Christians are tolerated in our country." The Spaniards and Italians limit that name to those of the Church of Rome ; and in like manner the " Unitarians " imply, by assuming that title, that we do not teach the Unity of the Deity. In like manner, when we are told that the Emancipation Act struck horror into all friends of " religion," this implies that those who had all along advocated the measure on religious grounds, were in reality men of no religion. This is just as strongly and clearly implied as if the abusive epithet had been directly applied to them. Again, when " Church principles " is constantly applied to designate those who hold such and such opinions (perhaps very right ones) on the subject, this is equivalent to telling all who differ from these that they do not maintain " Church principles," which they (mistakenly perhaps, but sincerely) profess to do. It is in vain to recommend charity if we do not ourselves set the example of it.'

To William Palmer, Esq. (Senior.)

'Nov. 30, 1843.

'My dear Sir,—If not too late, it would be well to suggest to your son, in a new edition of his pamphlet, to take some notice of the system of admitting students at Dublin University : answering it, if disapproved ; and if approved, defending it on some principles not applicable to Oxford.

'That the attack on Hampden was caused not really by the alleged heterodoxy of his Bampton Lectures, but by his proposing to give the same facilities to Dissenters

at Oxford as they enjoy here, most people pretty well
understood at the time; but I think the public are in-
debted to Mr. W. Palmer for the frank avowal of it.
Besides those to whom the Bampton Lectures afforded a
mere pretext, and who, by their " elucidations " of them,
endeavoured to persuade those who had never read the
work that it was quite different from what it is—besides
these, I think it likely that there were not a few who
really did see heresy in the work after he had advocated
the admission of Dissenters, and who, if he had taken an
opposite course, would have stoutly maintained, and
firmly believed, the orthodoxy of the very same work.
At least, I have often met with cases of people judging
of a book, or of a measure, by the quarter from which
it comes.   Doubtless there are several among the Whigs
who really believe the Corn-laws to be an abomination,
and have done so above these two years, but to whom
no such thought ever occurred when Lord Melbourne
declared that " it would be madness to think of meddling
with those laws."

' Trinity College, Dublin, and numerous private schools
kept by Protestant clergymen in Ireland, freely admit
Roman Catholics and Dissenters on the express condition
of non-interference with their religion ; and yet those
who approve and defend and take a part in these institutions are sometimes found deprecating the extension of
this system to the English universities, and cry out against
the National Schools for acting on it.

' Till they shall show some grounds for thus approving
and condemning the same principles in those different
cases respectively, how can they complain if their sincerity is suspected ?

'Very truly yours,
'Rd. Dublin.'

'Dec. 7, 1843.

'My dear Sir,—If Mr. W. Palmer were to say in his pamphlet just what he says in his letter to you, that would exactly meet the objection. All people might not adopt his views, but at least they would see what they are.

'I don't undertake to decide how far it was advisable to introduce at all—into a pamphlet about the Tracts—any question as to the admissibility of Dissenters to university education; but if the question be introduced, it is clearly necessary that any one who treats of it—especially a member of Dublin University—should advert to the system of that university, and should forestall the obvious question, " Why is the same thing deprecated in one place, which is acquiesced in without complaint in the other ? "

'That this question has not been asked by almost every reader of the pamphlet, I believe may be attributed to the strange ignorance that prevails. Great multitudes are totally unaware what is the fact. One of the English newspapers brings forward a bright thought, proposing as a novel and conciliatory measure that Roman Catholics should be made admissible at Trinity College, Dublin ! ! ! If any one says, " I censure those Protestant schoolmasters who consent to receive Roman Catholic boys on such and such conditions, and I lament that such is the constitution of the University of Dublin, but I am hopeless of being able to bring about such a change, and therefore I should not attempt it," people would perceive that he was at least acting on a consistent and intelligible principle, whether they agreed with him or not.

'And certainly a private individual cannot, we all

know, by his own authority change the statutes of universities. But the legislature can. It might interfere to place Dublin University on the footing of Oxford. And I presume Dr. Hampden, and also those who wrote against him, considered it as no moral impossibility that the legislature should interfere to place Oxford on the footing of Dublin, and that it might be influenced in such a matter by the publications of individuals; else they could have had no motive for writing at all on the subject.

'Believe me yours truly,

'RD. DUBLIN.'

The following letter relates to a constant subject of watchful interest—the prospects of the Education Board. It is addressed to an influential member of government.

'Sir,—The letter of which you were so good as to send me a copy seems to me the most proper that could have been written, and I heartily wish it may produce the effect desired. Nothing on my part ever has been or shall be wanting towards that object. Any altercation between the Board and any individual or body of men, I have always discouraged as far as possible, and have constantly endeavoured to guard against everything likely to lead to disputes and litigation : holding myself ready, however (and the same may be said, I believe, of all the Commissioners), to afford hearing individually, to any reasonable applications for explanation, or suggestions offered, in courtesy and in a fair spirit, by respectable persons. It is not unlikely that —— and others may have known of the application I made (by a letter to Earl de Grey) to ministers, immediately after their accession to power, urging them to prevent false alarms and false hopes, and doubts and suspicions of all kinds, among all parties, by an early, public, and distinct declaration of their designs in respect of National Education ; offering either to retain or to resign my situation, according as they felt confidence or not in the system, and in me as a conductor of it; and only entreating that they would not delay deciding, and declaring their decision one way or the other.   And if I had received within a month or two, or even within three or four months, an answer breathing the same spirit as your present letter, and followed up by corresponding measures, I have no doubt the effect would have been far beyond what the most sanguine can now anticipate. [I would not thus advert to matters that are past, were it not necessary in order to enable any one to estimate aright the present condition of men's minds.] Whether, however, they were aware or not of my application, they must have seen what actually took place. No declaration was made of the views of Government, even when (some time in Nov. 1841) the primate, in answer to an address of the clergy on the subject of education, entreated them to take no step, but to wait for the promulgation of the ministerial plans. Subsequently, most of the appointments made, and all of them in the Church (including three bishops), were of men distinguished by constant opposition to the Board, and the progress of the National System was brought to a stand for above a year ; the grants being only sufficient to support the existing schools, so that all applications for new ones were unavoidably refused.

 'It is not unlikely that the B. of ⸺ and others may have hence concluded that government would be ready and glad to receive complaints against the Commissioners, and suggestions either for the suppression of the Board, or for the establishment of a rival institution, or for such modifications as would virtually nullify its fundamental principles.

'Ultimately, ministers did signify unequivocally their determination. But, in the meantime, unhappily, many have been led so far to commit themselves anew to opposition, that I fear they will not easily be induced to draw back. And the number also of influential opponents was meantime augmenting, by the addition of all who have received preferments from the bishops opposed to the Board . . . Hopeless, and worse than useless, to all but Dr. M'Hale and his band of agitators, as reason would show such opposition to be, one too often sees men deaf to reason, when actuated by resentment for a disappointment and supposed wrong, and by a false shame at confessing error. Could they be brought to reflect calmly, they would see that the Protestant cause not only will suffer severely by their failure, but would suffer even more by their success; and the more severely in proportion as their success should be the more complete.

'Suppose, for instance, modifications were introduced into the National School system such as should meet the wishes of those Protestants who have hitherto been its opponents, the distrust which the Roman Catholic agitators have long been labouring to produce would soon arise, and become so strong and general, that there would be no resisting the demand for a distinct set of schools, to be placed under their exclusive control. Or, suppose a like object to be accomplished in another way, by acceding to the primate's proposal of making a distinct grant to the Church Education Society, the result of which would be that what is now the National Board would be unavoidably placed wholly under Roman Catholic control. Indeed, the demand for this would be so evidently just, as well as irresistible, that I for one should not wait for

it to be made, but should immediately withdraw ; as
well as most, if not all, of the Presbyterian Commissioners,
and also Mr. Blake, who has always declared he will never
have anything to do with any system of separate education.   And probably Dr. Murray would withdraw also ;
to be succeeded, most like, by some prelate of the most
opposite character.

'Now, what would be the result of this system of
separate grants of (suppose) 7000l. or 8000l. to Protestant
schools and 70,000l. or 80,000l. to Roman Catholic?
In those numerous districts of the south of Ireland, where
there are in each school not above 5 or 6 Protestant
children to perhaps 80 or 100 Roman Catholics (from
the smallness of the proportion of poor Protestants
in the population), these poor children would either
remain untaught, or, more likely, go to schools under the
unrestricted control of Roman Catholics.   And throughout Ireland the far greater part of the Roman Catholic
population would be brought up in a system, it is to be
feared, of bigoted jealousy against the Church, and aliena-
tion from their Protestant fellow-subjects.

'I need not say what would be the result of attempting
to carry out fully the principle avowed by the opponents
of the Board; which is (according to their own expression, in an address of the clergy, which I have reprinted
in a volume of tracts, p. 206), to recognise the clergy of
the Established Church as the proper and legitimate
guardians of national education; in other words, to
compel every parent to send his child to a school under
their exclusive control.

Every attempt, in short, to legislate now in the spirit
of the old system of Protestant ascendancy and penal laws,
would only tend towards the depression and ultimate
overthrow of Protestants.

'In proportion as men can be brought to reflect soberly and calmly, they will come to perceive these truths. But I fear the progress towards them will be slow. In the meantime it will be essential for ministers to follow up steadily and firmly the declarations they have made by corresponding measures.

'1. The placing of the Secretary for Ireland on the Board as one of the Commissioners, was an arrangement under the late ministry, which, besides the advantages of declaring emphatically the adoption of the institution as a part of the system of government, had also this, that it saved them effectually from troublesome and perplexing attempts to get between Government and the Board, and to excite mutual distrust . . . . . .

'2. The Board should be incorporated, and thus put at least on a level with the other Irish Board of Education, which is entrusted with the superintendence of a higher class of school. And one very great and continually increasing source of trouble, dispute, and litigation—that connected with the Vested Schools—would thus be at once and for ever done away.

'A Bill should be brought in to place National Schools on the same footing in respect of sites for schoolhouses, with railroads and other public works.

'As it is, the obstinate hostility of a few individuals enables them to defeat, throughout large districts, the operation of an important national measure, and to deprive thousands of their countrymen of an advantage which they earnestly wish for, and which the legislature has deliberately resolved they ought to have . . . .'

Lady Osborne had been writing him, in strict confidence, some particulars respecting persons who either were actually, or had been, officiating in the diocese.

The following is an extract from the letter this elicited:

'Dublin: Dec. 20, 1843.

'There is a circumstance which I think you overlook (but which you will immediately perceive on reflection) when you speak about "liking" or "not liking" such and such a person. A man in a private station will usually associate with his neighbours, because he likes companions; and with each, more or less, according as he likes them; but it is not so in a public situation; over and above my own most intimate friends, I see a great deal of a great many men (such as I should indeed be glad of as companions, if I were in a remote part of the country), but whose society, here, cannot repay me—as far as my own personal gratification is incurred—for the sacrifice of leisure and privacy. I see more or less of each of them in proportion as I am able to get something or to impart something. Any one who can furnish me useful information or counsel, or can be brought to forward in any way, under my superintendence, the great objects I aim at; and, again, any one who is able and willing to be instructed by me, these are the persons I see most of; not necessarily those who would be the most eligible companions, supposing I were in a situation to want a companion. You are not therefore to conclude—as you fairly might, of a man in a private station—that I like or dislike each, in proportion as I more or less seek his company.

'I hope the "learning" and the "architecture" of the Tractites will not lead you any further. For myself, I cannot make any such exception. Their learning and their churches both I utterly dislike. As to the latter, the Party is "edifying" in the wrong sense of the word. Their continual effort is to fix on the building of stone the veneration (as a temple) which belongs properly to the congregation—the "living stones." And their learning again tends continually to a substitution of paper-currency for gold ;—an attention to human writers which gradually absorbs and supersedes the study of Scripture.

'There was a kind of club formed at this place of clergymen who were to meet and study together certain of the Fathers; and several Non-Tractites joined it. But after a time it was found that certain members of the club were not disposed to treat the said Fathers as infallible, but to canvass freely all that was read. No open censure could be pronounced on them for this; but a rankling suspicion and jealousy was felt of them by some of the more Tractite portion; and, accordingly, by a kind of manœuvre, they managed to shake off these unruly disciples, dissolving the society, and then re-forming it with none but safe men.

'There is an account given in the Roman historians of a man who had been proscribed under one of the Triumvirates, and to save his life, disguised himself by wearing a black patch over one eye. A good while after, when the danger was passed, he took off the patch; but in vain—the sight of the eye was gone! This is a type of a great number of "sincere and conscientious men" (i.e. men who have come to be "sincere"); they have so long resolved not to see, that they are become blind.

'A union of livings cannot be made without the Diocesan taking the first step.

'I think with you that the Bible will not make a man a Protestant—i.e. a member of our Church—unless he shall have first thrown off his reverence for the priest, and reads it against prohibition. But I don't think that the Scriptures are, even to the imperfectly learned, favourable to the Church of Rome, unless they be studied in the way of scraps, picked out here and there. Each whole book of

Scripture, read as a whole, is the other way. E. g. "This is my body," seems—standing by itself—to favour the Roman Catholics; but not conjoined with "I am the true Vine," "Behold the Lamb," &c. The intelligent study of the Bible tends, not indeed to make men in Ireland join our Church (there is too much old animosity), but reform their own; for the yoke of Rome may come to be nominally borne, and yet be but a shadow.

'Yours, very truly,
'R. D.'

The following fragment of a letter to the same, probably written about this time, is sufficiently characteristic:—

'What a delightful thought, that of your residing in Dublin! And is it getting up a faction for me you are after? No, I'll have no Whatelyites! I think I could before now, if I had been so disposed, have raised myself into the leader of a party—that is, induced a certain number of asses to change their panniers. But I have no such ambition. I wish people to believe all the facts which I state on my own knowledge—because I state none which I have not ascertained to be true; and to listen to the reasons I give for my conclusions—because I never use any arguments which do not appear to me sound. And that is all the conformity I covet. Any one who tries to imitate me, is sure to be unlike me in the important circumstance of being an imitator; and no one can think as I do who does not think for himself.

'But I must not write any more where I am not required. Little do the Irish landowners know what a sword is now hanging by a hair over their heads, or how anxiously I am toiling, day after day, to keep it from falling! If the Poor Law Bill should pass in its present form, their estates will not be worth two years' purchase.

If they and the public in general were to give me credit for one-half of what I have laboured to do and been ready to suffer for their benefit, in various matters, I should have more popularity than would be safe for me.

'I would not say to one of less candour than yourself, for fear of being thought affected or fanatical, that in praying for the success of my efforts for the public good, I never omit to pray that I may meet with as much personal mortification and disrepute as may be needful to wean me from an over-regard for human approbation and popularity.'

CHAPTER II.

1844.

Triennial Visitations of the Archbishop—Conversation with his Clergy on the importance of studying the Irish Language—Letter to Miss Crabtree on Mathematical Puzzle—Letter to Dr. Hampden —Illness of his Son—Letter to Lady Osborne on 'Fasting '— Letter to Mrs. Arnold—Letter to Mr. Moore on progress of Tractarianism—Letter to Vice-chancellor of Oxford on the same subject —Spiritualism—Letter on Animal Magnetism—Death of his Sister-in-law—Letter to Mrs. Arnold on his difference from Dr. Arnold— Letter on proposed meeting of Bishops of Province of Canterbury.

THE year 1844 opens, as usual, on scenes of active and unremitting labour, ecclesiastical, political, and literary. The death of the Archbishop of Cashel had added to the sphere of Dr. Whately's labours; his province, which had only comprised Leinster, now embracing Munster also. His triennial visitations or journeys round his province were, from this change, extended to fully half the country. These provincial tours, which were never entirely omitted throughout his life till the last year of it, now brought him frequently into Irish-speaking districts; and he never failed to take this opportunity of urging on the clergy of these districts the importance of the study of the language. Such a conversation as the following would frequently take place :—

' Are any of your parishioners Irish-speaking, Mr. ——? '

' Yes, my Lord, nearly —— ' (one-half, two-thirds, or as the case might be).

'Do you or your curate understand Irish?'

'No, not a word.'

'I am very sorry to hear it,' the Archbishop would reply; 'how can you fulfil the duties you have undertaken towards parishioners with whom you cannot communicate?'

'Oh, my Lord,' the answer would be, 'all the Protestants speak English.'

'I should think so, indeed!' was the Archbishop's reply. 'How could it be otherwise? How could they be Protestants at all, unless they already knew the only language in which the Protestant clergy could address them?' And then would follow an earnest exhortation to the incumbent to endeavour to find some means of communicating with all who were resident in his parish, either by himself learning the language, or securing the services of assistants who did. And on the next tour, when the same place was visited, a change for the better was usually observed, and increased attention paid to the claims of those who could only be addressed through the medium of the Irish tongue. Thus, the Archbishop was doing continually much to promote the same objects, which were carried on in a different manner by the venerable Irish Society, and other instrumentalities. He was always of opinion that the way really to gain the attention of any people by addressing them in their mother tongue; and not, in the first instance, to urge on them the acquisition of a foreign language, whose use they cannot appreciate. When once they know how to read, and acquire a love of books, they will of themselves be eager to learn a language which can furnish them with the knowledge they desire; and in this manner, in proportion as the people are educated, a language possessing a current literature will ultimately take the place of one which has none. This

may appear a digression, but it illustrates the characteristic diligence and earnestness with which the Archbishop
applied himself to his rapidly increasing labours.

Miss Crabtree had sent, as on a former occasion, an
arithmetical or mathematical puzzle to the Archbishop.
A friend of hers had also made some objections to his
theory of ' Probabilities.'

' Dublin : Feb. 4, 1844.

' My dear Miss Crabtree,—Thanks for your enclosure,
which I have left in the hands of a friend who is curious
in such questions.

' Mr. B. must have somehow misapprehended me, or I
him; for the result he brings out in answer to that
question is not, as he seems to anticipate, different from
what I should answer, but the very same—viz. five-ninths
as the resulting probability; and this you may see (or he
may) for yourself by looking at page 76 of the " Easy
Lessons," where I give the computation of the probability
of a conclusion supposed to be supported by two independent probable arguments; for if, instead of the numbers
given (page 76), four-ninths and two-fifths, you substitute
(as in the question given in the letter) one-third and
one-third, and then proceed just as in that paragraph
(page 76) is directed, you will find the result come out
(instead of two-thirds) five-ninths.

' I fully understood Mr. B., however, to say and maintain
in that conversation, that, in the case of probable arguments, it is of no use attempting to calculate at all, because
we cannot be quite sure of the exact degree of probability
of each argument, which it is true you cannot. No more
can any one pronounce with exactitude the precise amount
of probability of any individual's life, yet so it is, that, at
the offices where life insurances are effected, life annuities
and reversions bought and sold, &c., they do reckon one

life as better or worse than another; and, forming the best guess they can from consideration of all the circumstances, they thereupon form their calculations, not conceiving that, because they cannot avoid some possible inaccuracy in the data they set out with, therefore there is no use in avoiding an additional inaccuracy in calculating from these data; and so it is that they do contrive to make their business, on the whole, profitable. So, also, there is no one who does not consider the guilt or innocence of a prisoner, for instance, or any other conclusion, to be rendered more or less probable, though not certain, by such and such arguments; and no one who does not consider, among probable arguments, some to be more probable than others, and, again, that three or four probable arguments have together more weight (other things being equal) than two or one.

'And, doubtful though we must be, after all, as to our estimate of the degree of probability of each, that is no reason why we should not estimate the joint force of them as exactly as we can. The necessity of proceeding on one rough guess is no reason why we should have two when we can avoid it.

'And the suggestion, accordingly, of such a procedure seemed to me to be needed in a logical treatise; but I knew myself to be but a very sorry mathematician. Still, a man need not die for want of medicine, though he be himself no doctor; he may consult a doctor. I applied, accordingly, for aid, and consulted (long before I saw you last summer) some competent persons; among others Sir W. Hamilton, our Professor of Astronomy, who is generally allowed to be at least one of the greatest mathematicians of the age.

'Perhaps you expect me to tell you how the trial[1] is to

---

[1] O'Connell's trial.

terminate. I not only cannot, but cannot even say which would be the greater evil, a condemnation or an acquittal! Queen and Imperial Parliament at Dublin is the only real remedy.

'Yours ever,

'R. WHATELY.'

'It seems to have been supposed by Mr. B., as it was suspected (and I own very naturally) by Sir W. Hamilton, that each of the two diseases introduced in the example (page 76) was viewed as excluding the other. To avoid this misapprehension, I have in the forthcoming edition taken an example from a totally different subject.

'But the main point which (to my apprehension) Mr. B. dwelt on again and again was, the uselessness altogether of resorting to any calculation at all in cases where we cannot be quite sure of the exact degree of probability of each separate proposition. But besides the insurance offices which proceed on calculations ready made in statistical tables for ordinary risks, there will always be found persons who make it their business to insure against all varieties and degrees of extraordinary risks, and to deal in the purchase of contingent reversions, dependent on a variety of accidents, the precise amount of each of which no one could presume to state with perfect certainty, though he may have reason for judging that his judgment will not be very wide of the mark.'

To Dr. Hampden, in acknowledgment of a Sermon received from him.

'Dublin: March 8, 1841.

'My dear Hampden,—Thank you for the sermon, which, I think, sets forth very well the different kinds of

claim of the Romish Church, and of any which puts forth
no more than can be well supported. Is there not an inad-
vertent expression in p. 10, which would seem to imply
that the literal flesh of Christ might, if it were present,
confer a spiritual benefit? He Himself having explained
that "the flesh profiteth nothing," and that "His flesh is
(means) His life," I have been accustomed strongly to set
forth that the bread and wine at the Eucharist are not
only a mere sign, but a sign of a sign.

'Your account of the "high and dry" party was news
to me. I had compared Mr. —— to the hen in the
fable who persisted in sitting on snakes' eggs, and was
greatly surprised to find young snakes come out. I am
inclined to think he will do more good than harm; but
I feel doubtful, because, in this most extraordinary age,
not merely ingenious nonsense, but dull nonsense is
tolerated.'

This year brought him some domestic anxiety in the
dangerous illness of his son at college from rheumatic
fever.

Lady Osborne wrote to him at this time on the subject
of Fasting, just then a much-agitated question in the
Church. The Archbishop—who had made it the subject
of two special sermons, afterwards incorporated in one
pamphlet—thus answers her questions, in a letter from
Cheltenham, where he had removed with his family, to
meet his invalid son from Oxford:—

                              'Cheltenham: April 16, 1844.

'My dear Lady Osborne,—I cannot, of course, develope
in a letter what I found difficult to compress into two
pretty long sermons. You must be content with a very
slight and partial sketch; but read the two "Homilies

on Fasting," and also look, by help of a concordance, at all the places in Scripture where " mortify " occurs.

'I pointed out that our Church nowhere enjoins or gives rules for either fasting or (mind this) feasting ; and that in the " Homilies " she evidently means by fasting such control of the baser parts of our nature as ought evidently to be not occasional but constant and habitual. If, with a view and as a means towards that, any one finds it expedient to adopt on certain days a more spare diet than ordinary (which she leaves to each individual's discretion), and wishes to fix on the days which his ancestors were accustomed so to distinguish, for the use of such a person, she marks in the calendar the old accustomed days. I added that fasts on certain days, though neither enjoined nor forbidden by our Church, are more apt to prove a substitute for habitual moderation and self-control than an exercise towards it ; and that in the sense of what is called in the Ascetic (Romish and Tractite) language " mortification," i. e. self-inflicted privation and pain, as something in itself—as pain—acceptable to God ; fasting, scourging, hair-shirts, flint-beds, &c., ought all to be classed together, all being alike unscriptural and alike (strange as it is) coveted by the natural man under some circumstances as making man effect atonement for himself. Witness the Fakirs, the Hindu ascetics and self-sacrificers, &c.

'I am here with three daughters, and am expecting daily Mrs. W. from Oxford with my other daughter and my son as soon as he is able to move.

'With best regards,

'Yours very truly,

'RD. DUBLIN.'

The following letter was written to Mrs. Arnold immediately after the perusal of Stanley's 'Life of Dr. Arnold:'—

'June 18, 1844.

'My dear Mrs. Arnold,—The memoir is well worthy of
the very favourable reception it has received. There is
no declamatory puffing about it; and Stanley has kept
himself out of sight with remarkable good taste. The
notice of Sismondi, Mrs. W. has, I suppose, spoken to you
about. If it had been a well-weighed and correct judgment of him that was expressed, instead of being such as
those who knew him best would dissent from, still it
would have been pity to give pain to his surviving friends,
and to prejudice them against a work from which they
might derive benefit. This, therefore, will, I suppose, be
omitted in the next edition. There is room, I think, for
a little more particular account of the appointment to
Rugby, which would be to the credit of the trustees, of
himself, and among others of myself. It might be as well
to mention, therefore, that he had withdrawn his name
from the list of candidates, at the instance of a friend who
persuaded him that it was hopeless to make head against
the powerful interest that others could command; that I,
having learned that Sir H. Halford was resolved to induce
if he could the other trustees to disregard interest altogether, urged him to come forward again, and conveyed
to Sir H. H. my full conviction that they would not find
any one so well qualified. This made him the last in the
field; and the trustees proceeding on the above plan,
found that, though stronger interest was made for others,
the award of fitness was due to A., and chose him almost
unanimously. All this is, I think, quite inoffensive, and
gives credit to those who deserve it.'

The letters which follow are on a subject of increasingly deep interest to the Archbishop—the rapid spread of Tractarian, or, as they were then called, Oxford principles. He had seen friend after friend swept off by the rising tide; and many who did not profess or even allow that they entirely agreed with the views of the 'Tracts for the Times,' nevertheless softened any protest made by them with the modifying clauses that they approved of many things in these tracts; that they saw no objection to the first, or first two, volumes; and especially that the learning, piety, and high excellences of the writers should in great measure soften the disapprobation with which their principles might be otherwise regarded.

The Archbishop dreaded anything which might even appear like a compromise with error; and in the first of the two letters before us he urges the danger of these concessions on a clergyman whom he had met and much liked shortly before at the house of a relative in England, and who had written to him expressing his intention of publishing on the subject, and pointing out that the 'Tracts for the Times' might be so understood as to be of real service in the Church :—

To the Rev. H. Moore, now Archdeacon of Stafford.

'Palace: Sept. 11, 1844.

'Permit me the liberty of suggesting to you the reflection whether you are imperatively called on (with or without the assistance of others who may agree with you) to lay before the public your views of the sense in which the Tracts ought to be understood so as to do that good service for which you think them commendable, and so as to be fully reconcilable with all that you say of the supremacy of the Scriptures—the duty of inquiring, private judgment, &c. That your interpretation is based

on good reasons I will not dispute, nor do I conceive
that it is peculiar to yourself; but you are well aware
that it is not universally adopted; that the Tracts are by
many understood in a sense quite different, and even
opposite, and reconcilable with nothing but downright
Popery, open or covert; and you also know, doubtless,
that this interpretation is far from being confined to their
opponents, but is that of a large portion of their followers.
I speak not merely of the handful who have already
joined the Church of Rome; but I dare say you are
aware that Tract 90 was elicited from Newman by the
solicitations of a great body of his followers, who insisted
on having, if they were not to join the Romish Church.
some scheme of interpretation laid before them by which
they could professedly adhere to the Articles. And they
accordingly obtained one which would have taught them,
if need were, to subscribe to the Koran. Now, if any
one were to bring into this country a cargo of cassava
root, which, if the poor Irish were to dress it like potatoes,
would kill them, I should think myself bound to teach
them how to press out the poisonous juice and retain the
wholesome meal; for it would be poor consolation, when
the mass of the people were poisoned, to reflect that there
were some hundreds of well-informed men who would be
using this meal with safety and advantage.

'An analogous duty to this is, I think, called for from
you at present. That the doctrines which you think so
salutary are actually in men's minds mixed up (no matter
through whose fault) with what you consider as deadly,
is an undeniable fact. Is it not for those who know how,
to separate the venomous juice? to point the non-con-
nexion of the principles which you approve, and which
you consider as those of the Tracts, with those conclusions,
which (however erroneously) are in fact deduced from

them, both by their opponents and a great portion of
their followers?

'You are quite right, as a general rule, not to occupy
yourself in reading second-rate books, but I would suggest
that there are exceptions. "A straw best shows how the
wind blows." Inferior men will serve as a touchstone to
show what impression is made on the multitude by such
and such teaching; they show how such a doctrine (not
ought to be, but) is actually interpreted and acted on by
the mass of mankind. With this view I recommend to
you, if you have not read them already, Mr. Percival's
and also Mr. Palmer's pamphlets (either is imperfect
without the other), giving their account of the rise and
progress of the Tractite party. They are men of no great
calibre, and yet both took a very prominent part in the
movement from the first; and they have a considerable
degree more of frankness about them than the rest of the
leaders.

'I take the liberty of sending you the transcript of an
article in my "Common-place Book" on Phenakism;[1]
begging you to understand that it is not expressed as I
should have done in a letter. I think I did not before
send you the enclosed letter on the Restoration of
Bishopricks. If the clergy and other members of the
Church are in earnest on the subject, they will importune
government with petitions, which is the only way to
carry a point, as I believe is now understood.

'Believe me to be, yours very truly,
'Rd. Dublin.'

The second letter on this subject, or at least on a
kindred one, is to the Vice-Chancellor of Oxford.

---

[1] See Miscellaneous Remains from his 'Common-place Book,' p. 213.

'October 26, 1844.

'Dear Mr. Vice-Chancellor,—I shall not, I trust, be deemed guilty of impertinent intrusion in making this application to you, and through you to the other Governors of the University, in reference to certain theological publications which for some time past have attracted so much attention, and which seem daily to be assuming a more decided tone.

' At first, principles were advocated which appeared to some persons (though not to others) to be fundamentally at variance with those of our Reformed Church, and to lead, if fairly followed out, to Romanism, or something equivalent to it. By degrees, stronger and stronger complaints against our Church, and censures of the Reformers, were put forth ; and ultimately a bitter detestation of the Reformation was avowed, the most exceptionable tenets of the Romish Church were defended, the censures that had been at first passed on that Church were retracted, the Articles were explained away in a "non-natural sense," and men were taught to look forward with hope to a penitent submission of our Church to that of Rome.

' And these publications are understood to be from the pens, not merely of members of the University of Oxford, but of resident graduate clergymen, some of them holding such situations in colleges as may be expected to give them great influence over the rising generation.

' Now, I need not remind you that I and the bishops of this province are often called on to ordain, to license, or to institute, persons educated at Oxford. And a degree at that, or at one of the other universities connected with the Established Church, is considered, I believe, by every bishop as either an indispensable requisite for ordination, or, at least, a considerable recommendation. It does not, indeed, supersede our private examinations; but it is supposed to afford a presumption that the candidate shall have received, besides mere literary instruction, a careful training in sound Protestant Church principles.

'It may be easily conceived how mortifying it must be to me to find this presumption weakened, or destroyed, or even reversed, in respect of the university at which I was myself educated, and of which I am still a member.

'And yet, can it be reasonably expected that a bishop should feel confidence as to the sound religious education of a candidate, from the circumstance of his having been trained in a university where several of the official instructors and guides of youth profess openly (besides what others of them may naturally be supposed to inculcate privately) such principles as might be looked for from the University of Salamanca or Coimbra? Are we to be satisfied with testimonials to a candidate's fitness for the sacred ministry of our Church, signed by men who have probably been avowing their disapproval of its principles, and their contempt for its Reformers?

'If the bishops should resolve that an Oxford degree should henceforth reckon for nothing, or less than nothing, and that a candidate brought up there should be called on to clear himself of the suspicion of being contaminated with such principles as he might be presumed to have imbibed in it, the university would doubtless consider itself affronted by such a mark of distrust. When, then, confidence is claimed on the one side, is it not reasonable that on the other side some sufficient ground for confidence should be afforded? I would submit, therefore, that we ought not to be deemed at all intrusive in calling on the university authorities to take such steps as in their judgment shall seem best for removing our well-founded alarm.

'I remember the case, a good many years ago, of two members of the university being expelled for a publication in favour of Atheism. The procedure was doubtless very proper, though the doctrine inculcated was not likely, either from its own intrinsic character or from any influential position of its advocates, to make progress. If, instead of obscure undergraduates, those men had been graduate clergymen and college officers having a considerable party ready to support them, and if the false doctrine they taught had come recommended by professions of piety and of zeal for the Church, their removal from the university, though it might have cost more trouble and more obloquy, would have been, in respect of the mischief they were likely to do, incomparably more important.

'It would be idle to allege that the case I have alluded to would furnish no precedent, on the ground that Atheism is a worse error than any that have recently been promulgated. This plea would manifestly be nothing to the purpose, since those men were not, I apprehend, expelled under any special statute against Atheism. The question is not as to the exact magnitude or the precise kind of each error, but as to its promulgation, and its being fundamentally "contrary to the doctrine or discipline of the Church of England."

'The bishops are solemnly pledged—and a like duty, I apprehend, lies on the university as far as its jurisdiction extends—to "banish and drive away all erroneous and strange doctrines contrary to God's Word." By which I understand not that we are literally to wage war against infidels and heretics, or to call for penal laws against those not professing to be of our communion, but to do our best to "drive out of the Church erroneous doctrines;" to protect, as far as lies in us, those members of

the Church who are placed under our care from being
corrupted through the teaching of " false prophets, who
come in sheep's clothing, while inwardly they are raven-
ing wolves," teaching false doctrine under the authority of
the Church, and as her recognised instructors. Ill should
we discharge our sacred duties if we should knowingly
and willingly suffer any such within the fold on the ground
that Atheism would be still worse.

'I do not presume to determine what particular steps
can or should be taken in the case. But I felt that I
could not clear my own conscience without distinctly
stating the alarm which is, not unreasonably, felt by myself in common with many others, and making application
to the authorities of that university wherein the causes of
that alarm first arose.

'I remain, Mr. Vice-Chancellor,
'Your faithful, humble servant,
'Rd. Dublin.'

*The letter which follows relates to a subject on which
(and its allied topics) Dr. Whately has been charged
with credulity. On such a matter it is far better to let
the subject of a biography speak for himself. He was
invariably opposed to the assumption of infallibility, and
the dictation of things to be believed, by any human
authority. It was his uniform maxim that no one can
arrive at truth, in any sense worthy of the name, who
does not discard such dictation, and examine for himself.
But though apt to be sanguine as to the results of new
discoveries in medical and similar sciences, it was by no
means his habit to be led into extravagance in support of
them.

As to the modern notion of communications with the
invisible world, or what is termed 'spiritualism,' the

reader may consult a paper in the recently published
'Extracts from his Common-place Book' (p. 381), one of
the last which he regularly dictated, and which has been
published to show what his deliberate opinion on this
point was. As an inquirer, he did not venture to reject
what seemed to him to have some, though by no means
conclusive, evidence in its support: as a religious man
he could not but maintain that, if there was any truth in
it, it was presumptuous, and, perhaps, within the actual
prohibition of Scripture.'

Letter to a Friend on the subject of Animal Magnetism.

'October, 1841.

'I have been for some time waiting for leisure to write
to you, being desirous of asking a question of you as a
man curious about philosophical investigations: viz.
whether you are thoroughly satisfied, from sufficient inquiry respecting animal magnetism, that there is nothing
at all in it, but that all the phenomena recorded are either
fabrications and exaggerations, or else may be explained
as 1st, imagination; 2nd, fraud; or 3rd, accident.

'I say from sufficient inquiry, because it has surely long
since been beyond being pooh-poohed out of court as a
thing not worth inquiring about. And I have long since
been seeking for a satisfactory solution of all that is
credibly reported (setting aside flying rumours) on the
hypothesis of fancy or chance, or collusive trick. And
this, perhaps, you can supply.

'I was a good deal staggered, several years ago, by Dr.
Daubeny telling me, soon after his tour in Germany,
that he had conversed on the subject with great numbers
of scientific men there, some of whom reported or

admitted great marvels, which others of them utterly derided and reprobated; but that he had never met with one—advocate or opponent—who did not believe that there was something in it; I mean, something that could not be explained on any of those hypotheses I have alluded to.

'And since then I have conversed on the subject with all the medical men who are in the habit of attending my family; three in Dublin and one in London. They are none of them practisers or advocates of magnetism; two of them vehement opponents; yet all admit that they have witnessed, or have had established to their full conviction, phenomena which go to prove that there must be something in it. Yet the bias of every practitioner who does not adopt it, must be against it. And so with those Germans. They are, no doubt, a very imaginative people; and this, we will suppose, is sufficient to account for all that is said by its advocates; but if any one should think that it will account for all that is admitted by opponents, he must be profoundly ignorant of human nature. These, and several like instances, have compelled me to admit that the delusion (if it be one) is one that demands investigation, and that the evidence adduced must be worth refuting.

'I am not prepared (which seems to be ——'s idea) to refuse to listen to evidence for what is unaccountable; because there are so many things which I cannot help believing (and which to the vulgar seem not at all wonderful, because they are accustomed to them), in which I am totally unable to perceive any connexion of cause and effect, and can only witness facts. E. g. take the case of mineral magnetism; it is very well to talk of a magnetic fluid (and for aught I know there may be a gravitating fluid also) which operates equally through a vacuum,

or air, or a table, but this is all mere guess. All we know
is, that some kinds, and not others, of iron ore, have a
property, which they can impart by contact to iron, which
will or will not retain that property, according to certain
laws, and may be deprived of it again, or not, according
to certain other laws; which laws have been practically
ascertained, after ages of investigation. But if a mineral
magnet were now for the first time discovered, and its
phenomena recorded, how many would at once reject the
whole as an idle tale! As for all religious considerations,
they appear to me to offer no ground of contrast or comparison of any kind with the alleged phenomena of mineral
magnetism, any more than if there were a question as to
the comparative value of steam and some other motive
power, and some one were to contrast these with Christian
motives; or should tell me, if there were a question about
the illuminating powers of gas, or some other proposed
substitute—of the light of the Gospel.

'The only point of contact between religion and these
alleged phenomena is, that there has been an attempt
made by some to explain the Scripture miracles by physical agency; and again by others, to represent these
phenomena as Satanic agency. The like takes place, and
ever will, on the announcement of every new set of facts
or fictions. Astronomy, geology, physiology (by Mr.
Lawrence), Greek-criticism—in short everything, is taken
up by the adversaries of Christianity as a weapon of
offence, and dreaded by its weak advocates. Probably
just such people as —— and ——, if they had
lived in Italy some ages back, would have exhorted all
people not to look through Galileo's telescope, or listen
to what he said; and so of the rest. But a person possessing real faith will be fully convinced that whatever
suppressed physical fact seems to militate against his

religion will be proved, by physical investigation, either to be unreal, or else reconcilable with his religion. If I were to found a church, one of my articles would be, that it is not allowable to bring forward Scripture, or any religious considerations at all, to prove or disprove any physical theory, or any but religious and moral conclusions.

' Then, as for danger, I cannot conceive how any one can apprehend more danger from doubt, inquiry, investigation, and consequent knowledge, than from adopting a conclusion at once without inquiry and in utter ignorance. When opium was first heard of (I know not when, but there must have been such a time) the accounts of its effects must have appeared excessively strange, and (which they still are, though people overlook them) quite unaccountable. Now any one who should, then, have suspected that they might be true, and that if so it must be a powerful, and, of course, a very dangerous agent, would not surely have been in more danger than one who should at once have pronounced it impossible that any drug could produce such effects. There are some few cases, it is supposed, in which that strange agent, the nitrous-oxyde gas, might produce very bad effects. Now, which would be in the less danger, one who should be inclined to believe in its effects, or one who should agree with Dr. Buckland, who stoutly maintains (or at least did) that it is perfectly inert, and that all we hear of its effects is pure fiction or fancy? My conclusion is, therefore, that animal magnetism is decidedly worthy of inquiry, and the delusion, if it be such, of exposure. And this if you can furnish you will deserve well of mankind. No one is bound (I should observe) to prove actual fraud or delusion in each individual case, only to show its possibility. And on the other hand, the clearest proof of imposition in any number of cases, if

there are others to which that solution will not apply,
proves nothing in respect of these latter.   Hume's chief
argument against miracles universally is, that there are
plenty of sham ones : he might as well have argued from
the numbers of forged bank notes that there are none
genuine.   I wish to adopt finally the conclusions that shall
imply the least credulity.   But when will people be
brought to understand that credulity and incredulity are
the same?

'You probably know the anecdote of the watchmaker
and his wig.   It is one of those which I am glad to have
by me for occasional illustrations.   He had taken great
pains with a timepiece which yet sometimes went irre-
gularly; and after watching it for many days, to try and
find out the fault, at last he could not avoid remarking
that whenever he sat before it in his nightcap it went
well, and when he wore his wig it erred.   He commenced
a series of experiments thereupon, which completely convinced him of this strange fact.   And then he carefully
examined his wig, and at length found that the steel
spring of it had by some chance come in contact with a
magnet, and thus deranged the works of the timepiece
when he sat close before it.

'Now supposing he had never been able to detect this
cause, would he have been justified in assuming that it
was impossible his wig could have anything to do with the
matter?   In truth, if he had gone on that principle, he
never would have discovered the cause; for what led
him to examine his wig was, the belief, or at least suspicion,
that the wig had something to do with it.

'How many cases of sequence will justify one in sus-
pecting or believing the connexion of cause and effect,
where such connexion is quite unaccountable, can no
more be determined exactly than (according to Horace)

how many years will entitle a poem to be called ancient; but every one must admit that there may be such a number as would establish the conclusion. An invalid who has an attack of sickness after having gone out in a carriage, would certainly be rash in supposing the excursion to be a cause of it; but suppose he took twenty drives, and was taken ill eighteen or nineteen times immediately after, and hardly ever had such an attack when he stayed at home, would not the credulity, then, be in feeling confident that this was all pure chance? Or suppose a tree is blown down in a certain grove, and he is taken ill after it, he would say it was an accidental coincidence; but if the same thing happened again and again twenty times, and he observed that every attack of a certain kind was accompanied by the blowing down of one of those trees, would he not have reason to suspect that there was some connexion, though he could not tell how, especially if he found several other invalids affected in the same manner at the same times? It might ultimately be explained, by a particular wind's disagreeing with certain constitutions; that grove being exposed to that wind. But whether that or any other explanation were devised or not, every one would be at length convinced—if not by twenty cases, at least by two hundred—that there must be some connexion between the two sets of phenomena.

'Whether sleeping in the moonlight in the East Indies brings on sickness (which is quite unaccountable), I am unable to decide. I may sometime or other meet with an East Indian (I never did yet) who disbelieves it; but the multitude of persons is so great who attest that sleeping on the one side of a wall, in the shade, or on the other side, in the moonlight, makes all the difference, and that the latter rarely or never escape, that I conceive it

would, in the present state of my knowledge. imply credulity to pronounce confidently that the thing is impossible. Yet people will reckon themselves "incredulous"
or sceptical precisely for not being sceptical, i. e. for not
doubting or inquiring, but deciding at once. . . .'

There are few other records of this year—on the whole,
an uneventful one to the Archbishop, as far as public
affairs were concerned, though marked with private
sorrow, in the death, after a long and suffering illness,
of a sister-in-law, to whom he had always been warmly
attached.

The next letter before us is to Mrs. Arnold, in answer
to one from her on some points of difference between him
and his departed friend :—

'Dublin: Nov. 17, 1844.

'My dear Mrs. Arnold,—Your letter to Mrs. W. is
what I should have expected from you, and from hardly
any one else. You seem to me to have attained the right
medium between want of due deference, and blind
deference, and blind idolatry.

'Many there are who fail to perceive that this letter is,
in truth, far less complimentary to its object than free
examination and fair trial, because rational inquiry is the
natural ally of truth, while implicit acquiescence is perfectly indifferent as to right and wrong, and may be just
as well bestowed on the most absurd priest of Brahma
as on a rational teacher.

'I once took occasion to give a warning to ——, of
which he seemed to me to stand much in need, that if
his wish were to be, as far as possible, such a man as his
father, he could not take a more effectual way to defeat
his object than by resolving to adopt all his father's

opinions and closely to copy him, since he was especially characterised by never servilely copying any one or taking any one's opinions as his standard; and he would, I have no doubt (as well as myself), have thought himself more honoured by one who should agree with him on nine points and differ as to the tenth, after having carefully examined the reasons on both sides, in all, than by one who should adopt all ten without any reason except that they were his. This latter we should have considered as being in the right only by accident.

'When we are in the act of bringing our thoughts into order on some subject, we are almost sure to entertain, for a time, some views that are incompatible with each other, and of which, therefore, some must be abandoned to make room for the others, if we would arrive at a consistent whole. It is like the compounding of some medicines, in which ingredients are introduced that are chemically incompatible, and will be sure, after a time, to decompose each other. While there is an internal action, and perhaps an effervescence going on, and before the mixture has become the compound that will remain permanent, it is something like the crude mixture of our thoughts on any subject before we have arrived at an harmonious system. A spoonful taken up here and another there, from different parts of the vessel, will exhibit different and even opposite properties.

'That it is most desirable to have the governors of any country men of true Christian wisdom, is what no Christian can doubt; but it would never do to allow that any government is, or ever can be, authorised to proclaim itself as being of that character, and therefore assume the right to dictate to the consciences of all the citizens, for two reasons—first, because any set of governors might claim this right, professing a conviction (often, no doubt,

a sincere one) that theirs is the true religion, and if any
one demanded proof of this, they would be ready (as
experience abundantly shows) to cut short all question
by an appeal to power—to the sovereignty—i. e. the
physical force—of the civil government. "There is no
arguing with the master of twenty legions." And yet
their religion might, after all, be far enough from true
Christianity. Secondly, if there even were a set of
governors who not only were perfectly in possession of
true religious principles, but also gifted, like the apostles,
with miraculous powers, as credentials from heaven that
might enable all men to know the truth of their religion,
still, the adoption of this must be left (as in the times of
those very apostles themselves) to the voluntary acquiescence of men in the conviction thus wrought, because the
whole virtue of religion must depend on its being sincere
and voluntary. Governors are, indeed, bound to offer no
impediments to what they judge to be true religion, and
to offer to their subjects every facility for learning and
practising it; but as soon as they begin to act as governors, directly enforcing the profession of a true faith, that
moment they give it a fatal stab, because they thus
change the motives from which such a profession ought
to spring.

'I remember once arguing with a man on the much-
trodden field of the National Schools, and he dwelt on the
often-repeated argument that all persons ought to read
the Scriptures, that they were inexcusable if they did
not, or if they did not have their children instructed
therein, &c. "Well," said I, "but do you think the benefit
of reading the Scriptures extends to those who do so on
compulsion or for the sake of payment, or is it confined
to those who study with hearty goodwill?" "Certainly,"
said he, "the latter; but then all men ought to read the

Scriptures voluntarily." "So I think; but I suppose there are some who will not be persuaded to do as they ought." "Why, then, they should be compelled"—i. e. compelled to read the Scriptures voluntarily!

'Now this discussion was on a question which is one part of the general question as to the employment of "power" (i. e. secular power) in religious matters.

'But I think it is no more than fair to apply the same rule of interpretation to any author whom one believes to be honest, which we apply to the sacred writers—namely, to take whatever is most clearly expressed, and which leaves no doubt as to the writer's meaning, as a guide and interpreter of whatever is obscure and doubtful, so as to admit of no sense of any passage that shall be at variance with what we are quite sure the writer taught. Now, no language can be clearer than Dr. A.'s when he says (in one of his latest works): "The highest truth, if professed by one who believes it not in his heart, is to him a lie, and he sins greatly by professing it. Let us try as much as we will to convince our neighbours, but let us beware of influencing their conduct when we fail in influencing their convictions. He who bribes or frightens his neighbour, &c." ("Life," p. 435.) Now this is so clear that I think we ought to take it as the standard by which to try anything more obscure and doubtful, concluding that anything seemingly at variance with it either is misunderstood by us, or would have been altered by him so as to be reconcilable therewith.'

The last letter of this year is one to a friend, on a proposed meeting of the Bishops of the province of Canterbury.

'Allow me to take this opportunity of asking whether the newspaper accounts are correct, of an intended meeting of the bishops (of the province of Canterbury?) to decide on questions connected with the Rubric, and what is likely to be the result?

'Some advantage I can perceive as likely to be produced by such a meeting; but I am not without apprehension of danger from it. Much benefit may result from a decision of all the bishops of the United Church, if understood to be bonâ fide unanimous, and if also coincident with the views of the generality of the clergy and laity. But what if they are not unanimous? or if it be suspected that the minority are borne down by the majority, and brought to acquiesce in something against their own judgment? In Parliament, or in any kind of legally-established convention, the decision of the majority is (if such be the law) binding on the whole. A man may, and should, submit to an act of parliament—where compliance is not clearly sinful—even though he may think it an unwise one. But it is not so with any self-convened assembly, having no legal power in a corporate capacity. The decision of such an assembly is its unanimous decision; and the individuals so met would not have even the right to bind themselves in the first instance by a unanimous vote to submit, in all subsequent proceedings, to the will of the majority—except in matters intrinsically unimportant. For a bishop who should do so, would be giving up his own judgment as to the concerns of his own diocese, which he is bound to govern according to the best of his own judgment, and endeavouring to renounce that individual responsibility of which he has no power to divest himself. And if, accordingly, some few should refuse to comply with decisions which they might deem inexpedient, would not this be making a more marked division— I may say a more organised schism—in the Church than any that has hitherto existed?

'Again, should any decision be made which seemed to savour of concession to the Tractites, even in matters intrinsically trifling, might not this excite alarm and dissatisfaction? Whether the English flag bear lions or leopards, can, in itself, make no difference in the power and welfare of the state; but if in the time of Buonaparte, we had, in seeming compliance with him, substituted leopards, all Europe would have regarded this as a step towards submission. The via media, which is now the watchword of many, and which consists in going a certain way, and no further, in the Tractite path, is regarded by many others (of whom I am one) as halting between the premises and the conclusion ; not venturing either to give up their principles or admit the consequences to which they fairly lead. And I cannot but feel apprehensions lest some such middle course as that should be adopted. If the assembled bishops would agree to petition for a Church-government, that, I am convinced, would be the only real remedy for the existing discord.'

CHAPTER III.

1845.

THE 'Lessons on Reasoning' had now been added to the other series of 'Easy Lessons,' and were received in the National Schools, as well as in others.

It was probably in the January of this year that the Archbishop wrote to Mr. Senior the following criticism on an article on the Irish Poor-Law, which had appeared in a leading Whig paper.

'Jan. 2.

'My dear Senior,—The article is less garbled than I had feared, and reads well. It seems also to have the effect of exciting great alarm among the supporters of abuses.

'It grieves me, however, that so much good sense and good writing should have the disadvantage of being understood to be a party-work, and that what there is in it good and true is said, not because true, but as suiting a party object. E. g. the Protestant religion was not more forced on the Irish nation than the Poor-law; it was not opposed by so great a variety of classes of the people ; it did not more completely fail of producing the religious harmony it aimed at than the Poor-law did of its object, &c.; the obvious reason why the one act of folly and injustice is exposed to a censure which the other escapes, every one will see to be that the one was, and the other was not, a Whig measure.

'I wish all sensible people would give up both Whigs and Conservatives, as such, and set themselves to mark out a new fort, to be built and garrisoned by a new party, having Free-trade for one of its rallying cries. Catholic Emancipation, Parliamentary Reform, and several other questions on which parties were divided at the time, are things over and past. And as for the Corn-laws, the Whigs, as such, were not opposed to the Conservatives. Lord M. said " it would be madness to touch them till a financial difficulty arose ;" and then, it was only a modification, for, though nominally a fixed duty, it was one which was to be unfixed again in the event of a dearth.

'It is time that these two armies should, as soon as possible, be disbanded, being fallen into as much disrepute as the " Rump " and " Praise-God Barebone's " parliaments. And then the " auld brass will buy us a new pan."

'The masters in training were examined a fortnight ago, as usual, publicly, at the close of their course, and, among other things, in the "Lessons on Reasoning," of which they gave a very creditable account ; and the work is spreading throughout the schools.

'I wonder if Dr. Kay-Shuttleworth knows it?'

The following letters relate in part to the proceedings

taken this year at Oxford against the Rev. Mr. Ward, author of 'The Ideal of a Christian Church,' who afterwards joined the Church of Rome.

'Dublin: Jan. 10, 1845.

'My dear Senior,—I have received communications from many and various persons, all objecting, somewhat as you do, to the new statute ; except, of course, the framers of it.   Before, however, I had received any of these, I had written to Hawkins (who had sent me a copy of it) to point out that these objections would be raised, and would probably defeat the plan.   To me it seems a great error to introduce any test of the kind.   Ward had given them a great advantage which they are throwing away ; they might have said, We will waive all questions as to what is the right sense in which a man ought to subscribe— all questions as to what is or is not conformable to the views of our church and her reformers : you do not pretend to subscribe to the Articles in any natural sense ; therefore you are manifestly, and by your own showing, guilty of a breach of faith.

'This advantage they are throwing away ; and will transfer the dread and indignation which was felt against the Tractites, to their opponents.   This, at least, was my expectation ; and every day almost brings me a letter from some Oxford man confirming my apprehensions.

'What steps should now be taken I cannot think.   I have advised Price, Merivale, Powell, Bishop, and some others who have consulted me, to meet and confer with as many non-party men as they can collect, with a view to acting together ; and to get up addresses to the bishops to join them in applying to the Queen to appoint a commission analogous to that of the reformed Poor-law, for suggesting a plan of Church government.

' Pray let Fellowes supply you with any copies of my
last two Charges for distribution, that you can think of.
' Ever yours,
' RD. DUBLIN.'

' Dublin : Feb. 10, 1845.

' My dear Senior,—I understand that high legal authorities have declared " degradation " to be illegal, though the
university may " expel," i. e. place a man in the same
situation as the majority of graduates place themselves
in, when they take their names off the books.[1]

' I pointed out immediately to Hawkins, that the
university placed itself in a false position by degrading
without expelling ; but I had not heard of the illegality.

' I should like to know what is the distinction made
by Hampden between the proposed censure against
Tract 90, &c., and that against himself. There may be a
valid one, but I have not seen it made out. My wish is
that a number of persons should apply to the Vice-
Chancellor, calling on the Hebdomadal Board to propose
the rescinding of the statute against Hampden.

' What is wanted by the persons Shiel speaks of is not
(except for the present) equality, but ascendancy and
revenge. That such is the feeling of a large portion of
the community, I have his own word.

' Education, however, is really desired by many ; and
the more education is given, the more it will be craved for.

' The Metropolitan University would no longer be the
only one in repute, or the most in repute, if my suggestion
lately given to government were carried into effect. I
am for limiting the annual number of M.A. and other

---

[1] This question was brought to an issue at Oxford in convocation, on
February 13, 1845, when two votes passed, one censuring Mr. Ward's
book, the other for his degradation.

higher degrees conferred by the new university. This would give them a value which no degrees of that class now possess, or can possess elsewhere.

'In haste, yours ever,

'R. W.'

The following tribute to his former tutor and old friend, Bishop Copleston, is too interesting to be omitted; it accompanied a copy of some publication.

'Dublin: July 7, 1845.

'My dear Lord,—I am bound to send, and you to receive, as a kind of lord of the soil, every production of my pen, as a token of acknowledgment that from you I have derived the main principles on which I have acted and speculated through life.

'Not that I have adopted anything from you, implicitly and on authority, but from conviction produced by the reasons you adduced. This, however, rather increases the obligation; since you furnished me not only with the theorems but the demonstrations; not only the fruits but the trees that bore them.

'It cannot, indeed, be proved that I should not have embraced the very same principles if I had never known you; and, in like manner, no one can prove that the battle of Waterloo would not have been fought and won, if the Duke of Wellington had been killed the day before: but still, the fact remains that the duke did actually gain that battle. And it is no less a fact that my principles actually were learnt from you.

'When it happens that we completely concur as to the application of any principle, it is so much the more agreeable; but in all cases the law remains in force, that " whatsoever a man soweth, that also shall he reap: " and the credit or the discredit of having myself to reckon among your works, must in justice appertain to you.

'Believe me to be, at the end of forty years,

'Your grateful and affectionate friend and pupil,

'Rd. Dublin.'

To Bishop Copleston.

'Dublin: Nov. 15, 1845.

'My dear Lord,—What you say about the Welsh and other provincial languages is so undeniably just and important, that the only marvel is there should be any occasion to say it at all. Those who, in this country, cultivate the Irish language, always possess at least the design of bringing in English to supersede it. They say that people are more easily brought to learn to read, and learn more easily, in the language they are well acquainted with, and that when they have acquired the art, they soon betake themselves to the language in which there are the most books. Whether they are right or not, such is their professed plan.

'There is a man at this time proposing to translate the little tract on "Evidences" into Welsh, and I have put him into communication with Tyler, to try whether the S. P. C. K. will print it. If such a version, bound up with the original, which is in very simple plain English, were circulated, perhaps it might help towards the knowledge of English. I know there are persons who use the French translation of it as an easy reading book for children who are perfecting themselves in reading French.

'By-the-bye, I lately received from Smyrna a magazine in *Romaic*, containing among other things a translation of that tract. I found I could read it with very little difficulty.

'Allow me to say a word in behalf of the persons you have censured as lukewarm in not voting for Ward's degradation. Some of them, I am sure, did not act as they did from that cause; but they felt that the degradation, not accompanied by expulsion, placed the university in a false position, and implied that a man, who, from being hostile to the Church, was disqualified for being a graduate, might still be allowed to be a member, though no officer in the army would be, for treason, reduced to the ranks, but either acquitted or dismissed.

'Ever yours most truly,

'RD. DUBLIN.'

Lady Osborne had written to propose a question to the Archbishop,—how it was that Protestantism seems more easily driven out by persecution than Romanism?

'Palace: Sept. 13.

'My dear Lady Osborne,—Though this is my audience day, I write one hurried line of remark on the very curious question you discuss.

'1. "By fair means or foul;" this furnishes part of an answer. It is almost enough to make a man cling to a false religion, to try to bribe or bully him out of it. It becomes a point of honour with him.

'2. Romanism is the religion of nature. Cast your eye again over my "Romish Errors," and see what I say on that point.

'3. In Belgium, Bohemia, Italy, Spain, &c., Protestantism was persecuted out, while Romanism stands all such attempts.

'May not this be from its being so easy a religion to retain or adopt in a state of degradation and barbarism, such as persecution produces?

'Can the poorest of the Irish peasantry (and the most ignorant) have any religion except one of external ceremonies?

'But it is a very difficult question.

'Ever yours truly,

'Rd. Dublin.'

Memorandum.

1845.

'Mrs. Whately, in going through the village of Stillorgan from time to time to look after the poor, always urges them to the practice of neatness as far as their poverty will admit, though often with no great success.

'One poor woman who is infirm and sickly, and only able to do about a month's work in the year, was found, when Mrs. Whately called the other day, to have got some neighbour to whitewash the walls of her cabin, and she had hung up a few prints which some one had given her, swept her floor, and cleaned all her little articles of furniture, mended all rents in her poor garments, and kept her person and house very neat. She was congratulated on this; but it appeared she had lost her allowance of food by it. The relieving officer, on stepping into her cabin, observed, "Oh, you seem to be very comfortable here!" and thereupon her allowance was stopped! Several of her neighbours, not at all poorer, but living in a state of swinish filth and disorder, had their allowance continued! Thus, among other many and great evils, the out-door relief system is made to operate as a direct bounty on squalid carelessness and brutish habits, and as a penalty on civilisation and efforts after cleanliness and decency.

'You may perhaps find means to communicate this specimen case to those to whom it may be usefully instructive. 'Rd. Dublin.'

'Dublin: Saturday, 1845.

'My dear Senior,—You seem to have quite mistaken the nature of my apprehensions. It is not that there is, or is supposed to be, any probability of the increase of Protestants, though some Protestant landlords might make an effort (should the measure Lord John Russell hinted at be adopted) to turn out Roman Catholic tenants and replace them by Protestants—who, as well as themselves, would be shot; but the danger I apprehended was, that it would be concluded by parity of reasoning that a further diminution of Protestants would be followed by a further reduction of revenue, and thus the tithe would be a regular bone of contention (not that either party would get much); but animosity would be increased tenfold.

'Ever yours,

'RD. WHATELY.'

'What I wished to express about O'Connell's obtaining office is this. If he is put into a political office, such as that of Secretary to Ireland, which might be held by a layman, this will be inevitably regarded as a direct reward of his agitation, and an announcement that his principles are to be acted on. The same objection would not lie against his being made "Master of the Rolls," if he would accept such an office—nor, with the same strength, against his being Attorney-General; for, though this is a political office, yet it must be held by a good lawyer, and it might be said he was put into it on account of his talents as a lawyer, and in spite of his agitation.'

In the interval between this and the next letter occurred the change of ministry by which Lord John Russell became Prime Minister, succeeding Sir Robert Peel, and Lord Clarendon Lord-Lieutenant of Ireland.

To Bishop Copleston.

'My dear Lord,—I have sent orders, though I believe it was not necessary, to Fellowes, and also to Parker, to place always at your disposal any copies of my works you may wish for. It would be hard, indeed, if a man were not free to pluck the fruit from the tree he had planted. I included, in writing to Fellowes, Bernard's "Vitringa," which is a work undertaken at my suggestion. It deserves to be much more known than it is.

'Your letter, and Dr. ——'s book, came into my hands together. I do not know him, but shall make inquiries. At a slight glance I see the importance of his argument. It strikes me, however, that he has advanced his outposts further than there was any need; and that he might have maintained, practically, the same position without insisting on so much. Suppose the three gospels were composed, in their present form, long after some of the epistles, and that John's was later than any, still, if the first three were compiled from those early documents seemingly alluded to by Luke, and John's written from his own vivid recollections, the main point is proved. If some intimate and early friend of Napoleon Buonaparte (supposing the existence of N. B.[1]) had drawn up an "éloge" just after death, and had subsequently written memoirs of his early life, it is likely we should have found him usually called "Buonaparte" in the memoirs, and constantly "Napoleon" in the other. There are many critical and other points to be elucidated by a careful study of the New Testament writings, of great importance, and generally overlooked by commentators, which I wish Hinds had leisure to write on, and which perhaps Dr. Dobbin may hereafter

---

[1] A jocose allusion to his own 'Historic Doubts.'

treat of; e.g. 1 Cor. i. 26 has often proved a stumbling-block, by suggesting the idea that the Gospel was rejected by all but the lowest and most ignorant of the populace; whereas it is plain from the context—though our translators overlooked it—that Paul is not speaking of the "called," but of the "callers." Then again in Gal. ii. 14, there is a puzzle, from its appearing that Peter had laid aside the observances of the Mosaic Law; and that too at the very time when he was reproached for having withdrawn from the Gentiles; and the rebuke of Paul seems feeble and obscure. But ζῆν ἐθνικῶς evidently is "to have life on the same terms as a Gentile, and not by virtue of his being a Jew." And the rebuke furnished all but the very words of Peter's speech immediately after, at Jerusalem (Acts xv. 11). I was looking the other day at a commentator on John xviii. 12, who says—assuming that ὁ ἄλλος μαθήτης was John—with admirable simplicity, that "the article spoils the sense;" and so it does, the sense which he had predetermined to adopt. But I should have thought the best procedure would have been to look at an author's words first, and from them to elicit his meaning. What the Evangelist does say, leaves no doubt that "the other disciple" must have been the only one, besides Peter, who had been named just before.

'What you say, and what has for a good while past been often in my mind respecting Episcopacy, often recalls to me your remark in your note on "Analogy," as to the errors we fall into by the application of the same names to offices and situations not precisely the same in different ages and countries; e.g. we often call ours a monarchical government, as if we were under a single Ruler; and, if we were under a Protector—as we probably should have been if Richard Cromwell had been at all like his father—we should probably have called our

government "republican." When a church and a diocese
were co-extensive and synonymous—which certainly seems
to have been the Apostolical model—a bishop was as different from what you and I are, as a sovereign prince
from a colonial governor. I do not say that Christian
churches had no right to make the change, on very mature
and grave deliberation. But whether they were wise in
making it, is a more doubtful question.

'RD. DUBLIN.'

To the Bishop of Norwich.

'Dublin: Dec. 28, 1845.

'My dear Bishop,—For saying that our authorised
version is not the Bible, but only a translation thereof,
and that it is not the standard of our Church, I have been
most fiercely assailed; and not the less inasmuch as what
I have said is quite undeniable.

'What you observe of Mr. ——'s speech is very just;
and perhaps if he had thought of that he would not
have said it; but I really think he is a man who would
be glad so to put the matter before the minds of his own
people as to make them remedy the evil; for though
sadly timorous, he is far from a bigot.

'What you say of Church government reminds me of
a speech of Dogberry's: "it hath been proved already
that you are stark knaves; and it will go near to be
thought so shortly." The absence and the need of a
government were unanswerably proved by me, and by
poor Bishop Dickinson, years ago; and now many people
are beginning to think it. Did I send you a copy of my
letter to the Archbishop of Canterbury about legalising
occasional forms of prayer?

'—— would be a much better bishop than any,
except one, that has been appointed since I came. But I

shall be very greatly disappointed if they appoint any but
Hinds, whom the Lord-Lieutenant has had the wisdom
to make first chaplain. Surely you know his publications? In ability (including the power of influencing
men's minds) and in learning, he would make two of
Hoare, and in moral worth four.

'Have you seen my proposal for re-establishing the see
of Kildare by uniting it with the provostship of Trinity
College? Ministers profess to be anxious that I should
continue on the Educational Board, and also that I should
attend Parliament; neither of which will, I fear, be possible, unless I am relieved of Kildare; and yet they will
not even take any notice of my proposal, though backed
by petitions to the Queen from both dioceses.

'Some, I fear, will advocate the cause in such a style as
to do more harm than good. There is a Dr. B—— who
has sent me a pamphlet on the subject, full of the old
cant against the Maynooth grant, and "driving out" false
doctrines, &c.

'I hope your daughter will not be plundered and murdered in Madeira, and that your son will not be eaten by
the Papuans; or the other by the convicts.

'By-the-bye, have you seen Mr. French Angas's travels
in New Zealand and Australia? I think it would interest
you.

'With our united kind regards to you and your party,
present and absent,

            'Believe me, very truly yours,
                        'RD. DUBLIN.'

CHAPTER IV.

1846.

Letter to Mrs. Arnold respecting the 'Model Farm'—Anecdote of
the Archbishop: tries the effect of Magnetism in curing toothache
—Opinion of Mr. Gladstone—Letter to Mrs. Arnold—Disapproves
the 'Evangelical Alliance'—Letter to Rev. R. Kyle on the subject
—Letter to Dr. Hinds on new Penal Colony in Western Australia—
Memorandum on Bill for legislating forms of Prayer—The tour to
Switzerland—Reminiscences of the visit by Mr. Arnold—Anecdotes
of the Archbishop—Translation into German of the 'Lessons on
Evidence'—Letter to Miss Crabtree on the subject—Letter to Mr.
Senior—Letter to Mr. Duncan—Lines on Australia.

THE first letter of 1846 is to Mrs. Arnold in answer to
some questions of hers with respect to the 'model farm'
attached to the Educational Institutions in connexion with
the National Board.

The next letter alludes to the objections sometimes
made by young men in choosing a profession.

'January 2, 1846.

'My dear Mrs. Arnold,—The Model Farm is a thing
which certainly ought to be visited, so as to get an idea
of the arrangement of the buildings, the agricultural implements, &c. And if a man were sufficiently bent on
becoming an agriculturist to put up with the annoyance of
attending the courses of lectures along with the farmers'
sons (a lower class than those in England) and working
along with them in the fields at all kinds of husbandry-

work—which is insisted on by Mr. Skilling, our agriculturist, as an essential part of the training—he would derive
great benefit.   But I doubt whether it would be worth
any one's while to drop in for a month or two in the middle
of a course of lectures; and Skilling has so much to do
that he would be quite unable to bestow any separate
attention on a single pupil.   So that a man would, as it
were, dip at random into the midst of a book and pick
up what he could by chance.

  'Something, no doubt, might be gained in that way:
but I should think not half so much as might be gained
in the same time by residing with a good farmer—even
half as good a one as Skilling—who had not a set of
regular pupils to attend to.   You may judge for yourself
of the difference between dropping in for three or four
weeks into the middle of a College-lecture, and spending
the same time with a private tutor.   I should not hesitate
between the two.

  'I went over yesterday to Redesdale, partly to visit some
patients whom Mr. Tennant (whom I suppose Mrs. W.
has told you of) had magnetised.   I visited and inquired
about seven; less than half of those he had operated
on in my presence.   They were all cases of acute pains,
chiefly rheumatism; and most of them had been wholly
free from pain ever since, and the rest greatly improved.
I saw also a poor woman whom I had operated on about
the same time (three weeks ago) for a dreadful toothache.   She had half the tooth drawn by a bungling
dentist who had also apparently splintered the jaw; and
had been in torture for three days, and her whole face
so inflamed that she could not bear it touched.   She
had come to our house expecting to see a gentleman
who could perhaps relieve her.   She had heard nothing
of magnetism.   I saw her waiting in the hall, evidently

in great torture; and as he did not come, I resolved
to try my hand. In seven or eight minutes she professed to be entirely free from pain; and so has remained
ever since! If all this be fancy, it is a very pleasant kind
of fancy.

'Ever yours affectionately,

'Rd. Whately.'

'P.S.—You ask whether it is a good thing that the
best measures should be brought forward by those who
propose them, not because they like them, but by those
who cannot avoid them. It is a question that does not
much affect the present ministry as compared with the
late: for the Whigs had publicly declared that it would
be madness to meddle with the corn-laws; only when they
found themselves in a financial difficulty they discovered
that cheap bread is a good thing.

'In an absolute monarchy—so far as it is really absolute—the measures adopted will always be such as the
ruler thinks best. In any free government it cannot but
be common for the subjects to force on their governors
measures not really approved.

'I think it the best thing, when a measure really good
can be carried triumphantly by men who really approve
it, that it should be so.

'Especially, anything of conciliation has a far better
effect when not extorted. Some people reproach the
Roman Catholics for not being grateful for the emancipation. I always thought them rather over-grateful to
O'Connell; but as for the Tory Ministry, to thank them
for granting what they dared not refuse would have justified the spelling of the word " great fool." You might
as well thank an ox for a beef-steak.

'But it will often happen that it will be difficult or

impossible for a certain measure to be carried, and carried in its completeness, except by those who are avowedly averse to it.   This is a paradox, but it is very true. Many men will vote and speak violently against a measure —when in opposition,—which when their party is in, they will suffer to pass.   They even think it no insincerity to oppose a measure, on the ground that they sincerely dislike it, which they are conscious at the moment they would themselves advocate if in place, as being aware that it is unavoidable.   And others, not so unscrupulous as that, will often oppose a measure which they think may be defeated; though when their own party come into power it proves necessary. Thus, the chief part of the men now in power either opposed or did not at all support the Educational Board : but when the Tories came in, and found themselves not strong enough to overthrow it, their adherents for the most part gave up their opposition in despair.   The great ground of confidence in the dispositions of the present ministry towards the Board is the conviction in most people's minds that they would have destroyed its fundamental principles if they had dared. The D. of W. when out of place spoke of its being a good thing for the Roman Catholics, but a complete failure as a united system.   I gave ministers notice that if they adopted that view, and accordingly made a separate grant for Protestant Schools, I should instantly resign. He has never said anything of the kind since.

'And so with the corn-laws. Peel is more likely to carry the abolition than the Whigs would have been ; and therefore I think it better that he should be in than they.

'What they can see in ——— I cannot think.' His

---

¹ The Archbishop is speaking of one whom he knew, up to this time, far more as a writer than a politician.

mind is full of " cul-de-sacs." He takes up a principle, and defends it plausibly, and follows it up to some absurd conclusion, and then scrambles away one can't tell how. You follow a good, well-made road, for a certain distance, and then find yourself in the midst of a thicket, or on the brink of a precipice.   And he seems quite unaware of this.'

'April 17, 1846.

' My dear Mrs. Arnold,—I am half provoked when I hear people talk of a dry study by which a young man is to obtain a comfortable and respectable subsistence.   If this is to be the general tone of " Young England;" if they think to live in Lubberland, where pigs run about ready-roasted, and the streets are paved with plum-pudding, we shall have some Young Englanders of the humbler classes telling us that driving a plough is dry work, and that they would rather employ themselves in bird-nesting.

' Why there is Senior, a man of the highest talents and most varied tastes and acquirements, who drudged at conveyancing for his livelihood ; and, I may add, had leisure hours for the study of political economy and literary criticism, which as a barrister he would have had no chance of.

' Who, except a man of fortune, has a right to say he will only follow his own tastes and inclinations ?

' In haste, yours affectionately,

' R. WHATELY.'

' Give my regards to my grafts and buds at Fox How.'

The following letter requires some explanation. The Archbishop strongly disapproved of the principles and working of the ' Evangelical Alliance,' a branch of which

had just been established in Dublin, and expressed
his desire that his clergy should not join it.   No one
who knew him could doubt that his decision proceeded
from conscientious conviction.   But in this case the col-
lision into which it brought him with the conscientious
convictions of others, was necessarily most painful both to
himself and them.   It was on this subject that he was
addressed by the Rev. R. Kyle, a curate in his diocese,
who wrote to ask him whether he considered that a disregard of the desire expressed by his Grace would be an
infringement of his vow of canonical obedience?   The
Archbishop's answer was as follows :—

                                   ' Palace: March 14, 1846.

' I have no objection to explain as clearly as I can,
the meaning I intended to convey : not undertaking,
indeed, to use such expressions as could not be cavilled
at or misrepresented by special-pleading subtlety—on the
principle of those " non-natural" interpretations which
we have lately heard of—but speaking as to a man of
honour, and candour, and common sense, as I consider
you.

' I must premise, that the question between you and
me now does not necessarily involve any consideration
at all of questions relative to the vow of obedience, and
the episcopal admonitions which a man would be bound
in conscience to obey or disobey.   For if not only you,
but I myself, thought that you were bound in conscience
to take some course which you considered essential to
peace and church unity, and which, I felt convinced,
tended to the utter destruction thereof, I could not,
consistently with duty, continue to employ your minis-
tration.   And, I cannot doubt you would, in a parallel
case, act on a similar principle.   If, for instance, you

were rector of a parish in which a certain person officiated
who could not do so but by your permission, and that
you found him imbued with some notions, suppose, of the
Tractites, which he held to be essential parts of church
principles, and of the genuine gospel, but which you
judged to be quite opposite thereto, you could not say that
it was his duty to abstain at your desire, from teaching
what he thought the only true gospel; but you would
think yourself quite unjustifiable in making yourself a
party (by continuing your permission) to what you regarded as wrong and pernicious.

'Although, however, the course I take in reference
to yourself, is independent of all considerations of the vow
of obedience to admonitions, I am ready to explain my
views thereon, in answer to your inquiry, as I did advert
to the subject in conversation with you.

'I do think then (as I have said in the pamphlet, which
of course you have seen) that the admonition now in
question, is one which the clergy of this diocese cannot,
consistently with their vow, act in opposition to, either
"openly" or secretly. The distinction which you seem,
impliedly, to make when you speak of "open opposition,"
is one which I did not make nor can recognise. Any
vow that is binding on the conscience at all, must be
binding in the dark as well as in the light. For though
man may be unable to bring home to any one a secret
violation of it, all things, you know, are open to Him
before whom vows are made.

'Were I to say that a Bishop has no right to forbid
anything "not contrary to the laws, or canons," &c.,
I should be reducing the office to that of a regulator
of mere insignificant trifles—a kind of master of the
ceremonies—an office which would not need a Bishop for
each diocese, but might be adequately discharged by one

of the humbler officers of the royal household, acting for the whole empire. And, even in these trifles, he might be obeyed or disobeyed at pleasure, wherever " the laws " had made no decision.

' In fact, the vow so solemnly made, would evidently be a mere idle mockery, if we were to understand a bishop's admonitions to be entitled to obedience only in things already determined by the church or the civil government—to be binding just in those cases, wherein one is equally bound without any admonition. This, surely, would be a " non-natural " mode of interpreting.

' And equally nugatory would it be to interpret " godly " as meaning what is, in each clergyman's opinion, conducive to a desirable religious object. For each is already bound in conscience to do, in all things left to his conduct and control, whatever he thinks likely to promote the religious and moral good of his people.

' What, then, you may say, is the limit? since some limit there must be. In the first place, the word " godly " is one limit, in the meaning in which every man of sense must perceive it was used—viz. " of, or relating to God " —pertaining to religious (as distinguished from secular) matters. Our older writers commonly use this term, and also " ghostly " (what we now more commonly call " spiritual,") to denote what has reference to religion, as distinguished from what are called " human affairs." A clergyman's voting, for instance, for a member of parliament, or the like, does not come under the cognisance of a bishop.

' But there is another most important limitation, which, even if it were not distinctly mentioned in the oath administered, would be plainly suggested to every candid and intelligent mind by the very nature of the case. As in Paul's admonition to " children to obey their parents in

all things," so here we, of course, understand the limitation
" in all lawful and honest commands." Anything contrary
to the law of the realm, or of the church—anything
immoral, or contrary to God's word—no one, of course,
can be bound to by any vow.

' And the like holds good in all other cases. Soldiers
ought to obey their officers ; and if each soldier were to
march or fight according to his private judgment, they
would be, though individually good warriors, an undisciplined rabble, easily defeated by half their number of
regular troops; but if a general should be a traitor,
and lead his troops to war against their king and country,
they would be bound to disobey him.

' If, for instance, a bishop of the diocese, in which I
held a cure, should desire his clergy to abstain from
teaching the doctrine of the atonement, or to inculcate
views which, I was convinced, were at variance with those
of our communion-service, or baptismal-service, or with
any of the formularies or articles, or if he should urge
us to incite the people to resist government, &c., I should
consider that I was under a prior obligation on the opposite side.

' But, then, in order to make good this plea, I must be
satisfied that I am under a specific obligation to that particular thing which the bishop forbids. In the supposed
case, I should be bound to inculcate those very doctrines
of the gospel and of the church, which he bid me oppose
or suppress. But as for the mere general conscientious
obligation to do everything (that is left to my discretion),
with a view to the promotion of sound religion and
morality, according to the best of my own judgment,
this would not be a valid plea in opposition to the specific admonition of the bishop, as to some particular
point. For that general obligation extends to all parts of

the ministerial duties.   And it would be as I said before, making the vow nugatory, to say that I am to obey the bishop only when he directs me to do what I felt conscientiously bound to before.

'In all things, great or small, that are left to my discretion, I am bound in conscience to act according to the best of my judgment for the good of my parish and of the Christian world ; but some step which I take with a view to that object, may appear, suppose to the bishop, objectionable; and then, if I am not absolutely and specially bound to that very step, the bishop's admonition thereon must be yielded to.   For otherwise the promise of obedience would be a mere mockery.

'For example, the bishop might prescribe to me a mode of administering the eucharist such as I could not say was "unlawful," but which (supposing I had charge of a very populous parish), would make it hardly possible for above half as many communicants to attend as otherwise would.   In such a case I should have, previously, felt it to be even my duty to administer in the way which, while I believed it perfectly lawful, I was convinced would best secure their attendance.   The bishop's prohibition I should lament ; and I should endeavour, by argument and respectful remonstrance, to induce him to withdraw it.   But if I failed in this, I should feel that there was nothing left but to submit, and to endeavour by increased labour—by trying to obtain the aid of other clergymen—and by inducing the people to attend, part on one day and part on another, to prevent or mitigate the ill effects apprehended.

'I have purposely selected a supposed case in which the episcopal admonition would have been (in my judgment) most injudicious, though not beyond the province of episcopal control.

'I myself have always done my best to avoid both of two faults which ought to be kept quite distinct, though often confounded together—the exceeding of rightful authority, and the ill use of it, by deciding amiss on points which do pertain to such authority. If the king, for instance, were to levy "ship money" or other taxes, without consent of parliament, however moderate the taxes might be, this would be going beyond the limits of the prerogative. But if he should, for instance, pardon all criminals without exception, or dissolve parliaments six times a year, this would be only a most absurd and mischievous abuse of an undoubted prerogative, and of one, too, which ought not to be removed from regal control ; for there can be no salutary power entrusted to mortal man, that shall be completely secured from the possibility of misuse.

'I have never interfered (further than by an expression of opinion, or by private advice) in matters which I regard as beyond the province of episcopal control : and in those who do, according to my view, fall within that province, I have nevertheless preferred leaving the clergy to their own discretion, except when convinced that very important religious interests were involved, and that consequently I should be myself violating my own duty if I were (as the consecration service expresses it), " so merciful as to be too remiss," either in the " banishing of erroneous doctrines," or in the " forwarding of peace and quietness, and correct-ing the unquiet, criminous, and disobedient."

'Many other such conceivable cases as the one I adduced, for example-sake, might easily be brought forward. But it can hardly be necessary to explain more fully to any sensible man, that a member of any community must, as such, part with some portion of his individual liberty, and that, too, in points where, independently of laws and injunctions emanating from competent authority, he would be allowed, and even bound, to act differently. For every man is bound in conscience to " DO THAT WHICH IS RIGHT IN HIS OWN EYES," in all points wherein he is not controlled by competent authority; now, if he were still bound to " do whatever is right in his own eyes," when the governing powers have decided otherwise, all communities must be speedily dissolved. For it is inconceivable that a multitude of uninspired men should, in all points, arrive spontaneously at precisely the same conclusions.

' All real unity, concord, harmonious co-operation, &c., must be the result of practical decisions as to what course should be pursued in reference to the common cause; and this can only be effected by leaving the decision, on several points, in the hands of some recognised authority. An army in which every soldier should march in whatever direction he judged best, would be soon dispersed.

' In the present case, I feel very strongly the dangerous tendency of the proposed alliance, for reasons of which I have set forth a part—and though only a part, yet what seem to me sufficient—in the pamphlet you have seen. And I have not heard of anything that can be considered a refutation. For I cannot accept in place of arguments mere declamation, and unsupported assertions, and texts of scripture strung together without any attempt to show their applicability to the case in hand. That concord, and Christian charity, and unity, &c., are desirable, is what all are agreed on; but what we have to do is to ascertain what course is likely to secure these advantages, or to operate the other way; else we may be losing the substance while catching at the shadow, and running the risk of creating disunion and strife (an effect, indeed, which is in some degree already produced) while unwisely seeking unity and peace. That the errors of the Tracts ought to be opposed we agree, but the point to be cautiously and clearly decided, is, how to do this so as not in fact to strengthen the party opposed, partly by sanctioning, through our example, their taking upon them to combine and form a sort of *imperium in imperio*, and partly by enabling them to point to the disorder and independence of rightful church authority which they will trace to the abandonment of what they call " church principles."

'I will only add that we may learn, in this matter, from the experience of what took place, on a small scale, in another diocese, in which, a few years before I came hither, a sort of alliance, substantially similar in objects and procedure, was introduced. The only results, I believe, were, the establishment of a new sect, which still subsists, and the separation, from the church, down to this day, of a number of families that had formerly belonged to it. As for the question however between you and me at present, you will remember that it does not (as I said at the beginning) involve necessarily any of the questions relative to the ordination vow.

'I trust you will believe me that I can never but be grieved to find myself in any case obliged to withdraw my sanction from the ministrations of a well-meaning and zealous man. But I cannot doubt that you would yourself, in a like case, feel conscientiously bound not to make yourself, by giving your permission, a party to any measures which you thought productive of the divisions and strife which you so heartily deprecate.

'Believe me to be, my dear sir,
'Yours faithfully,
'RD. DUBLIN.'

The following letter to Dr. Hinds is on a different subject, but one of lively interest to the Archbishop :—

'Dublin: May 30, 1846.

'My dear Hinds,—I am shocked at what you tell me of the design of founding a new Penal Colony in Western Australia.

'Our friend Phillips—a letter from whom I enclose to you—has often, as you know, expressed his satisfaction, in the midst of all the disadvantages the colony is exposed to, at the exemption from the curse of convicts; and once I remember his mentioning a great degree of corruption having been introduced into it by two or three emancipists who came with some cattle.

'Can nothing be done to prevent the further spread of this awful moral pestilence ?

'If I were in London I think I should make bold to wait on Earl Grey, though I have hardly the honour of acquaintance with his lordship, and plead as my apology that I know no nobleman of equal influence who is so likely to take the right side in this matter. I would lay before him the views of Governor (Royal-Resident) Phillips as well entitled to consideration. And I could explain more in half an hour's conversation than in several long letters.

'The best thing that I can now think of is, that you should ask leave to wait on his lordship, as from me; and if admitted you could say everything that I could, and say it quite as well.

'Yours, very truly,

'RD. DUBLIN.'

The following memorandum on a proposed bill for legalising forms of prayer, was probably drawn up at this time :—

'Memorandum.

' It has been urged as a reason against the proposed bill, that all the eminent lawyers who are and have been privy counsellors, are to be understood as fully concurring in Sir J. Nicholl's opinion : which must therefore be supposed to be a sound one.

' Admitting all this,—which is more than many persons would admit,—it leaves quite untouched the reason adduced for bringing in a declaratory Act. The opinions of all these lawyers can, at the utmost, only go to prove that there is no good ground for doubt.

' But the prevalence of doubt, which is undeniable and notorious, and the desirableness of having it removed, is not at all contradicted by these authorities.

' It might, however, be reasonably questioned, whether there is any sufficient reason to infer this alleged unanimity. The lawyers who are privy counsellors, may have acquiesced in a practice they found established, without having ever, even, brought before their mind a question (as to its legality) on which their opinion as lawyers was never asked. And again some of them may even have formed an opinion and yet may not have felt bound to volunteer it unasked.

' I have met with persons who have advocated the principle of allowing, in some cases, custom to supersede law ; and this doctrine may be maintained by a lawyer as well as by a layman. And moreover it should be remembered, that it is only the private opinions of lawyers that are brought forward : not any public decision. The only case (Johnson's) that was ever, as far as I know, tried, was never decided : but, after a great number of years, he consented, when worn out with legal expenses, to submit.

' There is a strong presumption, that if the law had

been clear against him, there would have been a decision accordingly.

'As for the ground on which Sir J. Nicholl's opinion is based, it appears to me not only utterly untenable, but also, even if admitted, to prove nothing to the purpose. It is that the royal prerogative is to be supposed to extend to all points from which it is not expressly excluded. Now if our ancestors had considered that any such prerogative had existed in reference to public worship they would hardly have brought in two Acts of parliament, that of Elizabeth and that of Charles II., to establish and to alter the forms of public worship, when the sovereign had power to settle all these matters without recourse to parliament.

'But admitting that there was such a prerogative, the passing of those Acts does plainly go to limit it. The sovereign (we will suppose) had full power to regulate public worship in whatever way he might think best; then he assents to an Act determining that it shall be conducted in this particular way and in no other.

'This surely is an abandonment, *pro tanto*, of all discretionary power previously lodged in the sovereign as to that matter. And this view, if it could need confirmation, would be confirmed by the clause relative to the names of the royal family, since it would be nugatory and absurd to provide for one small alteration, if there were already a power to alter the whole, or any part of the Prayer Book.

'But as I have said, if Sir J. Nicholl's opinion were fully admitted, it would leave the argument in favour of a declaratory Act to remove doubts perfectly untouched.'

In this year the Archbishop again visited the continent with his family, and spent a short time among the beautiful scenery of the Saxon Switzerland. We have a few reminiscences of this journey, from a son of Dr. Arnold, who accompanied the Archbishop and his family on this tour.

'The Archbishop,' he writes, 'travelled on the continent in 1846. I was of the party, and in my journal I find a record of a curious circumstance which occurred in Bavaria. We were travelling post from Prague to Ratisbon. On the night of the 30th July, we slept at Waldmünchen; and in order to avoid delay at the post houses the next day, notice was sent along the road that evening that our party was coming on, and would require so many horses. It seems that the approach of a bishop became generally known; for the next day, as the Archbishop's carriage passed, nearly all the people at work in the fields by the roadside, as soon as they caught sight of the three-cornered hat, left off working and went down on their knees, doubtless in the hope of receiving an episcopal bene-diction. At the little town of Rötz, as the Archbishop was standing in the street, while the horses were being changed, a wretched-looking man came up, threw himself on his knees in the mud before him, and with clasped hands and in supplicating accents began to mumble forth entreaties which our imperfect knowledge of German did not permit us to understand. The Archbishop looked at him askance, and with curious eye, as if he were some remarkable natural phenomenon, and then abruptly turned away. The peasantry in this part of Bavaria seemed to be, at that time, at any rate, a squalid, miserable, abject race, and evidently to their simple minds, a bishop was a bishop.

'At Schandau in the Saxon Switzerland, Edward and I had a good day's fishing in the little river that runs through that charming valley. Towards the evening the Archbishop joined us, and after looking on for a little while, took Edward's rod out of his hand, and after a few casts landed a fine grayling, the best fish killed that day. . . . The Archbishop relished with a hearty natural enjoyment all out-of-door sports and amusements, especially if they illustrated any novel principle, or required particular ingenuity in the use of them. Thus he delighted in making and using imitations of the Australian " wumerah " or throwing-stick, and also in throwing the " boomerang," a semicircular piece of wood which hits with great force when well thrown, and returns to the thrower's hand.

'This recalls to my recollection an incident in his former journey abroad in 1839. At Rapperschwyl, on the lake of Zurich, while the horses were being harnessed, he amused himself by teaching a number of boys at play on the border of the lake, by dumb show (for he spoke no German), to throw the spear in the Australian fashion ; and was highly delighted when he saw how eagerly they entered into the new diversion.'

'Dublin : Oct. 8, 1846.

'My dear Senior,—Yours reached me on the 6th. Your article is capital,[1] containing, like the " Homilies," " wholesome doctrine and necessary for these times." These times are indeed dreadful, and the evils you advert to have been rapidly increasing since you wrote. The exertions of the Irish, except in the way of riot (which has increased), diminish with the approach of famine. They are like the man who, having lost all on the race-course, ordered a chaise and four to drive home,

[1] See 'Ed. Rev.' vol. lxxxiv. 'On the Economical State of Ireland.'

because he could not pay for a pair. They despair of providing for themselves fully by any exertions, and, therefore, trusting that England must support them, they think it needless to exert themselves at all, and strike work for advance of wages! I wish you had added a little hit at the repealers—those whose motto is "Ireland for the Irish." O'Connell should be reminded that, on that principle, no aid should come from the United Empire. It is not fair to say I when you find a purse, and we when the hue and cry is raised to catch the thief. Perhaps you were rather hard in the opening on P. He doubtless did mean, and was understood to mean, that Ireland had the same right to good government as England. This certainly ought to be a truism, and will, I trust, ripen into one in the course of some hot summer; but a century ago it would have been denounced as a paradox, and, though admitted and cheered in theory, it has never yet been fully adopted in practice. Till the priests are paid, it cannot be said to be fully carried out. I am not easy on the subject of the Education Board. Mr. Blake, who, though absent, exercised a very important and beneficial influence, has been at the point of death, and is only just recovering. He and I together bear up against some evil influences, which I doubt neither of us singly could do.

'I have been visited by Major Jebb, Inspector-General of Prisons, seemingly a very excellent one, who tells me Government have at length resolved to adopt all my views on secondary punishments, &c. If they had done so when I first addressed Lord Grey, fourteen years ago, what incurable evils they might have avoided; but better late than never to buy the sibyl's books.

'Yours ever,

'Rd. Whately.'

The letter which follows, to his old and valued friend
Mr. Duncan, is a reply to one in which Mr. D. begged
leave to introduce a clergyman who was desirous of
officiating in the Diocese of Dublin.

'Dublin: Dec. 19, 1846.

' My dear Duncan,—I have no objection to an introduction of Mr. F., but you should tell him that there are
curates, and most deserving ones, who have been serving
in this diocese many years, for whom I have not yet been
able to find provision. So you may judge what his
chance of preferment is from me. It would be a good
thing if he could get an introduction to the Lord-Lieutenant, who has a good deal to give. My patronage is
wretchedly poor. Of the few livings in my gift a considerable portion are such that I am forced to look out for
men rich enough to afford to take them. It is a bad
plan to give a very poor living to a very poor man. He
generally falls into disrepute, either by running in debt,
or living in the style of a pauper.

' Mr. F.'s essay I began, but did not get through it, finding that his views and mine were wholly opposed, and
that he adduced no reasons for me to change mine. But
his style is respectable ; and I have understood him to be a
man of fair abilities and attainments, and good character.

' I wish I could persuade you to try a remedy for your
knee, which effected, to all appearance, a complete cure
to mine. I was suffering, the spring of last year, from so
much pain in the knee, a return of a former attack, that
I not only was quite lame, but was kept awake in the
night by pain. As no remedies presented by the greatest
physicians had ever afforded any relief, I resorted to
animal magnetism, making my servant operate. I always
found the pain abate, seeming to follow his hand. I

mended rapidly, and in a few days I was cured; and now, whenever I have a slight threatening of a return, I resort to the same, and with uniform success.

> ' There is a place in distant seas
> Full of all contrarieties;
> There, beasts have mallard's bills and legs,
> Have spurs like cocks, like hens lay eggs.
> There parrots walk upon the ground;
> And grass upon the trees is found;
> On other trees, another wonder!
> Leaves without upper sides or under.
> There pears you'll scarce with hatchet cut;
> Stones are outside the cherries put;
> Swans are not white, but black as soot.
> There neither leaf, nor root, nor fruit
> Will any Christian palate suit;
> Unless in desp'rate need you'd fill ye
> With root of fern, and stalk of lily.
> There missiles to far distance sent
> Come whizzing back from whence they went.[1]
> There quadrupeds go on two feet,
> And yet few quadrupeds so fleet.
> There birds, although they cannot fly,
> In swiftness with your greyhound vie.
> With equal wonder you may see
> The foxes fly from tree to tree;
> And what they value most, so wary,
> These foxes in their pockets carry.
> There the voracious ewe sheep crams
> Her paunch with flesh of tender lambs.
> Instead of beef and bread and broth,
> Men feast on many a roasted moth.

---

[1] The 'boomerang,' see p. 106. One of Dr. Whately's singular and favourite pastimes was the use of this curious implement, which he would throw with the utmost dexterity, at the same time holding forth on the mathematical principles which its flight illustrated.

And courting swains their fondness prove
By knocking down the girls they love.
The north winds scorch; but when the breeze is
Full from the south, why then it freezes.
The sun when you to face him turn ye,
From right to left performs his journey.
There every servant gets his place
By character of foul disgrace;
There vice is virtue, virtue vice,
And all that's vile is voted nice.
Now of what place could such strange tales
Be told with truth save New South Wales?

'By Dr. WHATELY, Archbishop of Dublin.'

CHAPTER V.

1847.

Distress in Ireland—The Archbishop's munificence—His measures for relief—Attends the Session of 1847—Letter to Mr. Senior on the distress—Bill for Out-Door Relief in Ireland—Letters to Mrs. Arnold—Injurious tendency of the Memoir of Blanco White—Takes an active part in the debates of the Session—Letter to Mr. Senior—Letter on translation of the Works of George Sand—Formation of the Statistical Society—Interest taken by the Archbishop in the Society—Letter to the Bishop of Norwich—Rumour of his appointment to the See of York.

THE year 1847 was one of peculiar trial to all who were living and working for Ireland; Dr. Whately's attention was now earnestly and painfully occupied by the distress, which was beginning to assume a more alarming form, and which called forth his energies in a new direction.

*It was the fate of Dr. Whately, of which these pages have already afforded ample evidence, to have portions of his character and opinions much misunderstood; and misunderstood partly in consequence of his own over-mastering tendency to outspokenness. He could never refrain—he held it an absolute duty not to refrain—from bringing forth his entire opinions on a given subject to its utmost extent; he would cut off, as it were purposely, all those accommodating qualifications by which persons are in general accustomed to guard unpopular avowals of opinion. In his abhorrence of everything approaching 'reserve' or 'casuistry' he would carry these tendencies

even beyond reasonable limits, and where he would himself, in practice, have admitted modifications of his doctrine,
he would have deemed it a surrender to the enemy to
allow, in theory, of the possibility of such modifications.
In nothing were these peculiarities more conspicuous than
in his contest and language on the Poor-Law question,
and in relation to charities in general. His condemnation
of the English system, such as it had been in his youth,
was absolute and uncompromising. His arguments against
them extended to the very principle of Poor Law itself,
nor would he therefore shrink from urging them. It
was not unnatural that so daring an assailant of rooted
prejudices, of the beneficent class, should be judged in
some degree by his own language, and set down as a man
of ' hard-hearted ' opinions, if not hard-hearted in conduct.
And this may be a justification for a brief allusion to a
subject which, in ordinary biographies, is best past over
in silence, as a portion of the great account between man
and his Maker, not between the citizen and the world. It
may be worth while to show how one who wrote and
thought like Dr. Whately practically interpreted his own
doctrines on ' charity.'

' Those who knew the Archbishop well,' writes one of his
most valued and trusted helpers, ' could not fail to observe
in him a strong developement of various traits of character
not often found combined in such equal proportions—
large-hearted munificence in affording relief for distress,
with careful investigation as to the merits of each case,
and sound judgment and discrimination as to the best way
of conferring the benefit ; readiness to contribute openly
and largely to public institutions for the promotion of
religious or charitable objects, with much more extensive
liberality to private cases of destitution or pressure.
These were brought before him by his chaplains sepa-

rately, or by others, as each individually happened to come to the knowledge of them ; and generally the members of his own family, and often all except the immediate dispensers of the bounty, were left in complete ignorance of the matter. When occasion required, he gave largely of his time, attention, and invaluable counsel, as well as of his money, for the alleviation or effectual remedy of distress.

"He has left little or no record of this in showy bequests and large endowments. He always advocated the wisdom as well as duty of giving as much as can be given while the donor can see it spent according to his wishes, and with the exercise of real liberality and self-denial on his part. Upon this principle he always acted ; and many churches and schools built in his dioceses by help of liberal subscriptions from his purse ; many societies either founded or largely supported by him, bear real, though silent, witness to his open-handedness in giving. For more than thirty years he continued to pay 100*l.* per annum to maintain a chair of Political Economy in the University of Dublin ; and indeed might have endowed it at less cost to himself; but, acting consistently on his fixed principle, he preferred paying the Professor out of his income. He left behind him no accumulated savings ; the larger part of the provision which he made for his family being effected by life insurances, the premiums on which were met by his private means.

In all his gifts, moreover, he was accustomed to make strict inquiry into the merits of the case ; ill considered and indiscriminate giving was a thing which he always denounced as one of the most mischievous uses that can be made of money."

It may not be out of place here, in speaking of the Archbishop's charities, to quote an extract from a friend's note-book, on his objection to the practice of giving alms in the street.

'I have heard him say,' writes his friend, 'that whatever you pay a man to do, that he will do; if you pay him to work, he will work, and if you pay him to beg, he will beg. Dr. Churchill told my wife that he had heard him say, "I have given away forty thousand pounds since I came to the see, and I thank God I never gave a penny to a beggar in the street."

'Giving to beggars, he often added, is, in fact, paying a number of wretched beings to live in idleness and filth, and to neglect and ill-treat the miserable children whose sufferings form part of their stock in trade.'

But contributions to matters of public utility did not constitute the characteristic part of Dr. Whately's beneficence. His private charities, compared with the amount of his salary and his absence of fortune, were literally princely. They were for the most part given not on system, but on the spur of the occasion, called forth by peculiar instances of want and peculiar calls for sympathy. Of beneficence like this the records are necessarily few; some who are alive, and more who are deceased, could testify to the measure and the spirit of their Archbishop's liberality. But of such he kept no nominal record. 'Many instances have come to my knowledge,' says one of those most intimate with him, 'in which large sums, from 100*l.* to 1,000*l.*, were given by him quite privately.' His agent says that in his book such entries as 'To a clergyman, 200*l.*; to a gentleman, 100*l.*; cash given away, 50*l.*;' are not uncommon. He often provided poor rectors with the means of paying a curate; and frequently, through aid timely and delicately given, enabled clergymen whom he saw overworked and under paid, to recruit their health by holiday and change of scene. Nor were the recipients of his generosity confined to his own profession and to the literary class, with the struggling members of which his sympathies were strong. But more than enough has perhaps been said on a subject only to be slightly touched. It may be added, by way of summary, that being a man of simple tastes and inexpensive life, he accumulated nothing from the income of his Archbishopric, and left to his family nothing beyond his own small fortune and his insurances. Nor did he supplement, in their favour, his own narrow means out of the public means. He has been accused, in his distribution of Church patronage, of favouring men of his own 'set,' that is, of his own intellectual following; of 'jobbing,' or personal motives, never.

The winter of 1847-8 was one of deep and painful anxiety. The Irish famine had reached its height. The failure of the potato crop through the mysterious blight, during a succession of seasons, had come upon a people wholly dependent upon this, the cheapest and simplest food, as their staff of life. Their normal condition was only just raised above starvation; and when the years of dearth came, nothing but starvation remained for them to sink to. No one who passed the years 1846, 1847, and 1848 in Ireland can ever forget that terrible life and death-struggle of a whole nation. How earnestly the Archbishop exerted himself to supply the required aid to the utmost, all who were on the spot must well remember; and how indefatigably she who was the sharer of his labours lent herself to the same service, taxing her often-failing strength to the uttermost, needs not to be recalled to the mind either of those who laboured with her, or of those who were the recipients of her benevolence. She became from that time forth more actively associated than ever in the various organisations formed to promote the

welfare, temporal and spiritual, of the distressed, the ignorant, the homeless, and the erring; and how many important works of charity sprang out of the deep misery of
those years of famine, many can now testify with earnest
gratitude to Him who thus brought good out of what
seemed at first unmixed evil.

In the session of 1847, the Archbishop was again in
London, actively endeavouring to stem the tide of public
feeling, which had taken a turn threatening much evil to
Ireland.

The English public, from a mixture of benevolence and
impatience—pity for the sufferers and hopelessness of any
real amelioration of their condition—were eager to bring
the whole Poor-law system to bear on Ireland. The state
of that country was such as to render the increased
pressure almost intolerable. There were no resources to
meet it. The increased rates, while they could not adequately alleviate distress, bore most severely on the classes
least able to endure the burden and hardest to help under
it: the smaller proprietors and householders, and the
clergy. Of the former, many who had been independent
were reduced to actual pauperism by the rates; the
latter had to struggle through an ordeal enough to sink
the stoutest spirit. Few to this day have any idea of
the suffering endured, and generally most patiently and
bravely endured, by a large number of the Irish country
clergy in those years of famine; striving in the midst of
their own deep poverty to assist the indigent, their own
income often rendered scarce more than nominal from the
nonpayment of their rent-charge, and yet expected to
pay the full amount of increased poor-rates. In very
many cases they and their families were reduced so low
as to be in want of the very necessaries of life. Their
condition in this respect having become known to the

members of the Ladies' General Relief Association, in the course of their correspondence on the subject of the distress in their respective parishes, the idea was suggested, in the early part of 1849, of forming a separate Committee for their special relief. Of this movement the Archbishop was, in fact, the originator and patron, commencing the fund by a donation of 100*l.*, on the 21st of April, 1849 ; and during the three years of the Committee's operations, he continued his unwearied attendance at its meetings, and his warm sympathy with the cases of deep distress which from time to time came under its notice. 'The united contributions of Mrs. Whately and himself to the fund,' writes the secretary of the Committee, 'exceeded 470*l.*; the total amount received and disbursed nearly reached 4,600*l.*' Dr. Whately's total contributions towards the distress of 1848–9 have been reckoned at 8,000*l.*, but such estimates must be conjectural.

The following letter to Mr. Senior is evidently suggested by the distress, though on a different point :—

'My dear S.,—What an admirable opportunity the present distress affords of paying the Irish priests ! The starving population would be more than ever grateful for being relieved of the burden. The very poorest are not allowed to enter a chapel without paying *something*, though the halfpence which are now a severe tax on those who hardly get a meal a day must afford a wretched subsistence to the priests. And yet the priests must wring from them this miserable pittance.

'But I suppose —— and —— would do their best to prevent such a measure, except in the way of taking the funds from the Protestant Establishment; a plan than which Satan himself could not devise a more effectual one for keeping up and exasperating religious animosities in this truly wretched country. Each successive government seems ambitious to outstrip its predecessor in the career of folly.'

In this year the Archbishop was again greatly occupied with the Poor-law. The government were desirous of introducing a bill for out-door relief in Ireland. This the Archbishop, in conjunction with some few others, among whom Lord Monteagle was the principal, steadily opposed. On the 26th of March, 1847, a debate took place on a motion of Lord Monteagle for a select committee to be held on this subject and other matters. His speech is an important one, and the Archbishop's name appears with those of Lords Radnor, Monteagle and Mountcashel, in the signatures to a protest against the measure of out-door relief.

The bill was nevertheless passed, the clause of out-door relief being included in the Poor Relief Extension Act, which was passed in June 1847. The numbers relieved out of the workhouse, at first very large, diminished from 800,000, in July 1848, to about 2,000 only at the end of 1850. (Ed. Rev. vol. 93, p. 246.)

'February 21, 1847.

'My dear Mrs. Arnold,—You have before now I think had a copy of this tract;[1] but you may like to give one to some of those who are talking and writing and reading about Ireland, and noticing at all the main impediments to its improvement.

'Most people have taken up some notions on the subject, which they cling to; and do not wish, or even like, to be better informed. And it must be owned, that in all

[1] Probably the one entitled 'Paddy's Recollections in the Poor-House'—a tale founded on fact.

legislation, but most especially for Ireland, the distant
prospect shows all smooth and easy, and a nearer approach
and more perfect knowledge shows more and more of
crags and swamp and tangled thickets. " It bothers one
to hear both sides."

'No doubt there are good, bad, and indifferent among
the landlords in Ireland, as among other men; and
cases have no doubt occurred of tenants being harshly
ejected. But I believe the cases are far more numerous
in which the tenants have been offered not only remission of arrears but also money in their pockets to enable
them to emigrate, if they would go quietly; and yet
they have often either attempted to maintain their position by force or have complained grievously of hardship. And I certainly do pity those who, being attached
to the house of their infancy, would endure almost any
hardship rather than leave it. And Mr. —— seems
to think that the only thing wanted is a kind landlord,
who will never exact a high rent, nor ever eject a tenant.
Now this is the very course which is, and has long been,
pursued in very many parts of Ireland ; and here is the way
it works. A small farmer rears eight or ten children, who
marry, without having any trade or manufacture to resort
to ; and so he divides his farm among them, just as the
tailor in Don Quixote divided the piece of cloth so as to
make five caps instead of one. Each of these farmers just
manages to pay his rent, and rear a family on potatoes,
and in rags; and then he divides again his farm among
them ; so that each has a patch too small to subsist on
even if rent free ; which it usually is, in fact—the rent
remaining unpaid. These cottier-tenants eke out by
occasional jobs of work, begging, and pilfering, till there
comes a hard year, and then they die of want and consequent disease.

'It never seems to occur to Mr. —— that this must be the case in one, or two, or three generations, were the land ever so fertile, and were it their own property. He attributes all to the exorbitant rent; though in general it is less than a Yorkshire or Scotch farmer would gladly give for the land if he had a good-sized farm of it; because he has five times the agricultural skill, and more than five times the capital. See how differently matters look when viewed closely and correctly!

'Again, what more reasonable, at a distance, than that the landlords should maintain all the poor, and enable themselves to do so by selling part of their land? But, first, great part of the land is mortgaged up to nine-tenths of its value; so that the rate would probably be much more, on the whole estate, than the whole amount of the rental which comes to the nominal landlord. And secondly, suppose the land not mortgaged, but that the rate amounts to more than the whole rental. This actually took place in a parish in England, and several others were approaching that state. The landlords in that case left the land rent-free to any one who would cultivate it and pay the poor-rate: but of course no one could afford to do so; and the land lay waste; the paupers being maintained by rates-in-aid on the neighbouring parishes. And I dread seeing the like very general in Ireland. Now if under these circumstances a landlord offers to sell his land, who is to buy it, even at a farthing per acre? Q. E. D.

'Ever yours affectionately,
'R. WHATELY.'

'March 9, 1847.

'My dear Mrs. Arnold,—I cannot forbear expressing the high admiration I feel for the justice of your character. It is what I have long admired in you; but the recent occurrences have forced it the more on my notice. My wife has told me, of late years, that she used to wonder at my dwelling so much on justice as the highest virtue, but that now she understands and agrees with me.   Other virtues depend in some degree on several tendencies, but the proper function of what the Phrenologists call the organ of conscientiousness, is to decide and do what is right, simply for that reason.   And the formula for calling this organ into play, is that which is furnished us by the highest authority ;—to put oneself in another's place, and consider what we should think fair then.   This formula would be of no use if we had not the organ, but the organ will often not act aright without the formula; which, yet, is very seldom thought of in practice.

'A person may sometimes be found having the material as it were, of not only a good but a great character, of a kind of heroic virtue who yet, for want of habitually applying that formula in every-day transactions, will not even escape deserved censure.   There is a kind of man, who, having fervent aspirations after pre-eminent excellence, an enthusiastic and perhaps somewhat romantic longing after distinguished virtue, frames to himself the idea of a life, which is a kind of magnificent epic poem with himself for the hero ; and deigns not to pay sufficiently sedulous attention to some humbler common duties.   He becomes, if he have a good deal of self-confidence, so full of himself, his high destinies, his own claims, his own feelings, that he somewhat overlooks what is due to the claims and the feelings of others.   What is done for him he receives very much as a matter of course ; and when anything is refused him, or any obstacle placed in his path, he is fiercely indignant, as having a great wrong done him.   And yet he will never suspect himself of being unjust, because he never designs to be so, but to assign to all their due; only he will not estimate fairly what is due to others and to himself; nor does he conceive himself capable, accordingly, of being deficient in gratitude, because he is very grateful to those who honour him, and to whom, perhaps, no gratitude is really due.

'It seems odd to say it, but so it is, that one is prone not only to feel resentment against those whom we must admit, on reflection, to have done us no wrong (a successful rival for instance, or one whose judgment was opposed to ours, and who has proved to be in the right, &c.), but also to feel gratitude to those whose judgment is flattering to us, and has benefited us. When for instance Lord Grey appointed me archbishop, I knew that he could have no partiality—no desire to benefit me, and, for that very reason, I was the more gratified by the honour of his choice, from knowing, that, whether mistaken in it or not, he could have no motive but a wish to serve the public, by fixing on the fittest man. I was careful to place before me that I was under no obligation to him, else I might have been more disposed to feel grateful to him than if he had had some private regard for me, and had preferred me partly for that reason. But it requires a vigilant and steady adherence to the principles of strict justice to view things in that light.

'Such a kind of character as I have described—the hero of his own epic—is not a common one, but it is one worth reflecting on nevertheless, because it is one of great capabilities.

                          'Ever yours most truly,
                                'Rd. Whately.'

                          'Tunbridge Wells: May 19, 1847.

'My dear Mrs. Arnold,—I am much annoyed at finding a different impression made on some persons from what

I had expected, by the Life of Blanco White. Since it appears that some not ill-disposed persons can read it without disgust and mortification, I conclude that there will be great danger from it. Some will be convinced that free inquiry must, in the end, be fatal to Christian belief, and that one by one, all doctrines will be overthrown by it : and hence, part will be led to shun and deprecate inquiry and resolve to shut their eyes and " believe all that the holy Church believes," while another part will make short work another way, and believe no religion at all.'

To N. Senior, Esq.

'Dublin: September 4, 1847.

'My dear Senior,—Yours of 14th August received. ——— a little better, but still suffers much. The rest pretty well.

'A very dry summer ; though in August, not ; all the trees and grass and springs are parched. Corn harvest very good, except beans, which had been largely sown. The potato rot prevails, though much less than last year. This partial destruction, and the much smaller quantity than usual planted, will leave the poor very ill off (unless they can afford to buy) in the winter, and as the landlords are nearly drawn dry except those of them who will never give anything, and England is tired of giving, and the people idle and demoralised, there is not likely to be much less distress than last winter. Fever is raging among high and low.

'Dr. ——— has given his adhesion to the National Schools, and has written a pamphlet which has called forth answers full of the usual trash—all that he says is triumphant, except that he fails to explain why he did not vote ten years ago.

'The Repealers are said to have gained on the elections

in Ireland; but though a few honest men have been
replaced by others less scrupulous, I do not expect that
these latter will do anything more than is requisite to
humbug their constituents. I fear the payment of the
priests will come, like other boons to Ireland, too late.
During the interval of ten or fifteen years, a poor-law will
have been going on under the control of the priests
(since they will dictate what guardians are to be chosen)
who are themselves maintained exclusively by the very
poorest class, and who consequently have a plain interest,
not only in keeping up the rates, but also in bestowing
relief chiefly on those who are not in the greatest distress,
and who consequently can spare most for them. Now
what will be the state of the country after ten or fifteen
years of this? The people of England, who are furious
at the idea of endowing the priests, have endowed them
in the most extravagant and wasteful way.

'I hear of a meeting of Political Economists of all
Europe to be held the middle of this month in Belgium,
and to be repeated annually. I should think it would
be a very good thing. Do you know anything of it?

> 'Best regards,
> 'Yours ever,
> 'Rd. Whately.'

The following letter is on a very different subject. The
Archbishop had seen advertised a translation of the works
of George Sand, published under the sanction of a clergyman, to whom, though personally unknown, he addressed
this letter:—

> 'Palace, Dublin: October, 1847.

'Rev. and Dear Sir,—I see advertised a translation
of the works of George Sand, patronised by you.

'It is not my practice to interfere in other people's affairs. But by your having dedicated a volume to me, my name has been in some degree mixed up with yours; and some persons may naturally suppose that all the publications you put forth or patronise are in some degree sanctioned by me: and it may happen that I may eventually be under the unpleasant necessity of publicly disavowing all connexion with them, or approbation of them. This being the case, I trust you will see the propriety of my adverting to the subject, first, privately.

'I cannot understand how it can be safe or allowable to bring such works before the public eye. If indeed the English were universally pure and firm in their moral principles, it might perhaps be worth while to publish some portions of works popular in France, by way of warning, as to the low tone of morality there prevalent.

'But I cannot think that we are, universally, in a state to bear such an experiment. I have even known English persons of what is called respectable character, who are little or nothing shocked at the antichristian and profligate character of that woman's writings, and who even speak of their tendency to regenerate society and place it on an entirely new footing! And it is true, a sort of regeneration would take place, if people were to act on the principles she recommends. Society would be something like that of Norfolk Island, decorated with a varnish of ranting sentimentality. It would be a kind of ragout of putrid meat, with an attempt to mitigate its fetor by a profuse seasoning of strong spices.

'Such at least is the impression produced on my mind by the little I have read of her works. I cannot boast of being well versed in them. But it is not necessary to wade all through a heap of mud in order to be satisfied of its loathsomeness. I read a good part of what was pointed out to me as the least exceptionable, and even commended by some, as exhibiting pure and high morality.

'I must say that the genius for which she is by some celebrated seems to me greatly overrated. Her tales are redeemed from flat silliness only by striking situations brought about by the most unnatural and absurd extravagances. This, however, is a question of taste, on which there is no room for disputing; but what revolted me the most was, that the characters whom she intends to be models of excellence, are such that if all the world were like them it would be a Pandemonium. They lie and cheat from morning till night.

'Now if it be proposed to translate such works omitting the foulest parts, this, I conceive, would be taking away from them their moral. The moral in fact is that "a corrupt tree bringeth forth evil fruit;"—that such and such are the practical consequences of such and such principles. If therefore there are any such omissions made for decency's sake, at least it ought to be added in a note, that the original contains the description of such conduct as naturally flows from such principles, and which is too bad for publication. Else the principles may be received by incautious youth with too much favour.

'If it be thought right to exhibit for curiosity, at some horticultural show, a plant of deadly nightshade, and to clear it of the berries, lest some of the spectators should incautiously taste them, at least the plant ought to be labelled "poisonous," lest they should imprudently give it a place in their gardens.

'But I cannot think that in any way it can be desirable that such a work should be published—especially under such auspices. A strict regard for the principles of morality and religion, and for delicacy, may be fairly expected as least from clergymen and ladies, if anywhere. "If the salt have lost its savour, wherewith shall it be seasoned?" Excuse my saying therefore, that it would be with me a sufficient reason to preclude a man from officiating in my diocese, that he had taken part in the publication of such immoral works. Over you I do not pretend to have any control; but for the reason mentioned in the beginning, it may be necessary for me to be able to say that I remonstrated against such a publication.

'Yours, &c.

'RD. DUBLIN.'

It was in this year that the Statistical Society of Dublin was first founded. The Archbishop cordially supported it, and his address at the conclusion of the first session showed the interest he took in its aims and objects. He concluded the address with an expression of hope that 'they would live to witness the good fruits of their exertions in the diffusion of sounder notions, on one of the most important, one of the most interesting, and at the present period, one of the most vitally essential subjects on which the human mind in this country could possibly be employed.'

When, three years later (in November, 1850) the Social Inquiry Society, now amalgamated with the Statistical, was founded, the Archbishop entered into it with the most lively interest, accepted the presidentship of the society, subscribed munificently to its funds, and delivered the address at its first social meeting; in which he remarked that the great advantage of such a society was, that they could deliberate on each subject according to its own merits, and through the means of the investigations which they conducted, and the observations made as to the result of them, they might so far affect public opinion as to have ultimately measures ready prepared with all that discussion which Parliament could not and would not afford to them, and thus the foundations be laid of such improvements in their social condition as they could never expect from any parliament existing in a free country, which would always be open to the disadvantage of party contests for power.'

To the Bishop of Norwich.

'Dublin: November 21, 1847.

'I cannot think what made people talk of me for York. . . . If it had been offered to me, it would have been a matter of anxious deliberation, which would probably have ended in my declining it. Unless I could have been sure of having Hinds to succeed me here (which there would have been little chance of), I believe I should have done more harm than good to the public by the change. And for myself, personally, I should have been encountering an enormous amount of trouble, beyond what anything but the hope of doing good to the public would have induced me to undertake. A new set of men all around me, a fresh set of chaplains to be selected and trained, and a new set of old abuses to be inquired into, &c. And then, if, after all, the result had been the Irish Education Board going to ruin—which, I am sorry to say it is by no means safe from—what a mortification that would have been! I don't say this with pride, for I should be far more proud of having put the system in such a state as to go on safely without me.'

CHAPTER VI.

1818.

THE letters, at the beginning of this year, need not much explanation. Constantly engaged in literary undertakings, besides his own pressing avocations, and often referred to by his friends on questions, embracing a vast range of subjects, political, religious, literary, and practically scientific, it is almost impossible to give anything like a *résumé* of the Archbishop's correspondence. At this time, he was suffering much from a sprained ankle, which he feared would produce serious consequences; but though slow, his recovery was complete.

A sermon he had preached on the often-discussed question of 'Infallibility of the Church,' was expanded into a pamphlet under the title of 'Search after Infallibility,' and widely circulated. In these letters he makes frequent allusions to it.

'Dear Lady Osborne,—I send you a paper containing the best account I have seen of the Hampden persecution. Please to return it, unless you can get the article copied into some provincial paper.

'There is something in what you say of the Roman Catholic population.

'No doubt that religion is far less favourable to civilisation than Protestantism, as may be seen best in some of the Swiss cantons, because they are on equal terms in all other respects; and yet the contrast is striking between the Roman Catholic and the Protestant cantons.

'But to try what could be done for the deterioration of Protestants, you must suppose England again conquered by the Normans or some foreign people of a different religion, who seize on all the land, and take all the Church endowments for their own Church, leaving the mass of the population—all poor—to maintain their own ministers on the voluntary system.

'And especially if this had been done three hundred years ago, when the English were far less civilised than now, what would they be at this day?'

'February 3, 1848.

'My dear Hinds,—It strikes me, on reconsideration, that there are two points which ought to be touched on in your sermon.[1]

'The vivid and beautiful picture you draw of the peace and concord of the primitive Church will throw some into despair, and lead others to advocate all the more the preceding error, as if our inferiority to the

---

[1] Preached at the consecration of Bishop Hampden.

earliest Christians were owing to our not giving ourselves up to the Church as they did to the Apostles.

'Now it is curious and important that strifes did arise among them, and false teachers set themselves up as rivals to the very Apostles, or as pretending to be commissioned by them, " to whom we gave no such commandment."

'At whatever cost, I think you must take notice of and guard against these mistakes.

'Yours ever, Rd. WHATELY.'

'Dublin: March 25, 1848.

'My dear Senior,—I suppose you will have put off your visit to Paris till the 31st of April, as it does not seem to be very safe just now.

'I should like to know what you think of —— proceeding against Mitchell and Co.[1] There are strong reasons against prosecuting, and still stronger against abstaining from it. It is a curious and instructive circumstance that in their seditious speeches and writings, they declaim against our school-books and especially the politico-economical portion of them, and endeavour thereupon to direct popular rage against me. In despotic countries, we usually find the government anxious to repress education, and the reformers to enlighten the people. Here, it is just the reverse.

'The most unfortunate circumstance of our case, is that government is in much the same fix as the revolutionary government of France. Ministers have declared, and have got the legislature to declare, that the landlords can, and shall, maintain all the people.

'The people accordingly, who are at this moment in

---

[1] The trial and conviction of John Mitchell, for seditious libel this year, was followed by the serious outbreak headed by Smith O'Brien in July, the leaders of which were tried for treason and transported.

terrible distress, are in fact urged by government to
attack all those who have any property, for not relieving
them, and to attack government itself for not making
them do so. It is vain to urge that what is demanded
is impossible; as I and many others told them a year
ago. They chose nevertheless to undertake it, and the
people call for the redemption of this pledge; unjustly,
as far as regards the landlords, who were no parties to
the promise, but justly, as regards the government
who made it. If a merchant contracts to supply me
such and such goods by such a day, it is in vain for him
to plead that ships did not arrive, or manufactures were
stopped, &c. If he cannot fulfil his contract, he must
pay the damages.'

'Cheltenham: May 13, 1848.

'My dear Hinds,—I never was in such alarm yet, about
the Repeal; I mean from the English side. People who
are not fools in other things fancy they could dismiss
from their thoughts all care about Ireland, if it were but
once completely separated from Great Britain. Not considering that the Roman Catholics would try to establish
Roman Catholic ascendency, and there would be one
civil war; then, the poor finding a failure of all the
promises of a good farm apiece as soon as the Union
was repealed, with which they have been amused, would
make war on property, and there would be another. Then
the anarchy and mutual slaughter becoming intolerable,
some would call in France, and some America, and
others recall Great Britain; and Ireland would be the
battle-field for three contending nations—ours for one!
I wish you and West would incite and help some one
else to write a tract on Repeal for the use of the British;
to show them that however indifferent about Irish misery

they may be, it is like King Zohrab's snakes, which were a part of himself. The worst of it is, the two great evils of Ireland, the non-payment of the priests and the poor laws, were and are inflicted on Ireland by the determination of the English and Scotch people against the judgment of ministers, and are consequently the fruit of the Union. The only reply is, that though the Imperial Parliament governs Ireland abominably, the Irish would make it far worse still.

'You will see in the London papers of Thursday a report of our dinner. Senior starts for Paris to-day.

'Have you seen the "Politics for the People"? I am very anxious for its success, but not confident.

'But do think of what I have said about Repeal. Till now everyone has thought only of writing for the Irish, but now there is need for English arguments. Ask Lord C. about what I have said.

'Yours ever, R. W.'

'Dublin: July 6, 1848.

'My dear Senior,—I suppose ministers have turned the corner; is it that their opponents were sensible they could not form a ministry that would stand? It is a great interruption to public business to have a change, and one that must soon be followed by another change. —— was not apparently well pleased with me (though I said very little on the subject), for not being able to express my approbation of his conduct. He had before earnestly begged me always to tell him my real sentiments; but had not, I suspect, figured to himself their proving unpalatable. I can well conceive the archbishop in Gil Blas being, " at the moment, sincere in asking his real opinion ; though when he gave it he dismissed him with all good wishes for his happiness" " et un peu plus de goût."

There is no point perhaps in which men are more apt to deceive themselves. And the way they do it is, to remain persuaded that they greatly wish to hear a friend's real opinion, only if it happen not to coincide with their own, they make out that it was given in too strong language, or given at the wrong time, or wrong manner, or wrong something; so that in short we arrive practically at Gladstone's right of private judgment—All men are to judge for themselves, provided only that their judgment concurs with that of the Church, which they are at liberty to agree with, but not to disagree with.

'Ever yours, R. W.'

The year 1848 brought an event in the Archbishop's domestic circle, which contributed more than any other to the happiness of his later life, and was a source of ever increasing comfort and blessing to him. This was the marriage of his third daughter with Charles Brent Wale, of Shelford, Cambridgeshire, which took place in September of this year. In his son-in-law he gained a valued friend, coadjutor, and companion, possessed of qualities of mind and heart of no common order, who was fully capable of appreciating his powers and entering into his pursuits and interests, and whose society and friendship were the solace of his declining years; whom he prized and valued beyond most of those still left to him upon earth, and whose life of earnest but unpretending Christian usefulness was not long to out-last that of his father-in-law. The correspondence with this valued friend and connexion was very full and frequent through life, when they were apart; but the nature of it was so strictly domestic and private, that for the most part it was considered unsuitable for publication, and only a few extracts will appear. Few other events occurred that are worthy of special record, except such as his letters give.

Extract of a Letter of the Archbishop to Mr. ——,
Edinburgh.

'Dublin: September 30, 1848.

'By-the-by, the argument of Mr. Twisleton against
the Irish landlords, which you reported to me, seems
to me to have more ingenuity than fairness. He complains, it seems, that they are not very logical reasoners
(which I believe is true enough) and that he cannot get
them to state plainly—instead of merely showing the
evils of the ministerial measures — what they would
have. " Would you do nothing and leave the people to
be starved to death ? " If this is answered in the affirmative they know that they are opening the flood-gates
to a torrent of declamatory invective against the hard-
heartedness of landlords who wish the people to be
starved ; if in the negative, then comes the question,
" What is your proposal for insuring a comfortable maintenance for every individual in the nation, industrious or
idle ? "

'Now if I were thus assailed, I should reply, I will
not set up any proposal like a Shrove-Tuesday cock,
for you to pelt at, when you are predetermined not to
adopt it, but only to seek objections to it. Make me
minister; and then it will be for me to devise measures,
and for you to criticise them. But now, you are the
batter, and I the bowler ; guard your own wicket, instead
of asking me how I should guard mine.

'Perhaps I could not succeed better than you. But
even if I be no shoemaker, I who am to wear the shoe
may be allowed to know where it pinches.

'I admit that it is not enough to show that there are
objections to your measure ; because there is no human
scheme free from objections. But if I can prove, first, that
your measure does more harm than good, and, secondly,

that you yourselves foresaw and were convinced of the
same (as I have printed and published your very words,
publicly and deliberately spoken; omitting a private letter,
which I have seen, still stronger), then I do say I have
reason to find fault with your measure, and also to complain of your defending yourselves by the *argumentum ad
invidiam*—by seeking to fix on me, or to get me to fix on
myself, the imputation of some sentiment or principle that
may be put in a very unpopular light.

'This form of the *argumentum ad invidiam* is the
battle-steed of pretenders of every kind; political, philosophical, medical, &c.: of men who profess to remedy
irremediable evils, and explain unexplainable difficulties,
and obtain unattainable goods. They represent their
opponents as delighting in those evils or difficulties, and
as indifferent to those goods. The metaphysician who
explains the origin of evil—the Owenite, or other political schemer who proposes to abolish poverty and remove
all need of charity—the political economists who rail
at Malthus, and provide for an unlimited multiplication
of mouths without meat—the miner who sinks a coal-
pit where there are no coals, because (this is a fact) " It
would be impious to suppose God would leave the people
of any district without the means of warming themselves,"—all these and other such pretenders fight with
the envenomed arrows of the *argumentum ad invidiam*.'

On the Irish Poor Law.

'Jan. 23, 1849.

'My dear Senior,—One of Beresford's Miseries of Human
Life is, " After supping on mushrooms, the lively interest
you take in a discussion of the question, whether they
were of the right sort." Similar, I suppose, will be the
interesting discussions of the Committee on Irish Poor

Laws. I entreated them to make inquiry before they took
an irretrievable step. But now, I know of no stomach-
pump. I fear the Committee will be merely a blind, to
quash all discussion in the Houses by saying, " Oh, wait
for the report of the Committee ; they know more about
the matter than the House." And then there will doubtless be some persons on the Committee, perhaps placed
there on purpose, who will take care either that there
shall be no report, or else one that amounts to nothing.
My being on it would probably only tend to mislead the
public into supposing that the interests of Ireland will be
duly looked after, and to give my apparent sanction to
resolutions—or non-resolutions—contrary to my own
judgment. But I should not mind being called up as a
witness. And I could bring up many others much more
valuable.

' I believe you were right in not suggesting any remedy,
even supposing you had one ready; for it is impossible to
get out of such a scrape without great difficulties, great
loss, and great injustice (in itself) to many. And if any
scheme involving all this be suggested, it is of course open
to many objections (you may remember that when you
were employed—*eo nomine*—to find objections to our
Poor Law Inquiry Report, you found it very easy to do so ;
and the result was that the objections to the Poor Law,
which was thereupon brought in, were overlooked); the
urging and answering of which occupies men's attention,
and draws it off from the actual evil itself that is going
on. While debating which pond to go to for water, the
fire is burning.

' I believe it is best therefore to give men time to let
their minds dwell on the magnitude of the danger till
they are ready to say, Any deliverance from such dreadful
evils, at whatever cost. They say it is best not to attempt to

rescue a drowning man till he has become senseless, and can be pulled out like a log; for just at first he clings to his deliverer, and they both drown. But what would you suggest? There would be some palliation in exempting all improvements from increase of rate for twenty or thirty years. As it is, the law operates as a prohibition.

'I doubt whether —— is right, though "peritus credendum in arte sua." In the case of a book, which a person who values it will wish to have by him to consult, a high price may not diminish the sale so far as to counterbalance the increased profit. But a book which most people wish only to read through, they will be likely, in many instances, to borrow or to buy, according to the price.

'Yours ever, R. W.'

'Dublin: March 3, 1849.

'My dear Senior,—I am uneasy at the accounts I receive of your health. Each successive attack seems to be—according to the custom of the allopathists—driven off by violent remedies, which make sad inroads on the constitution, and leave the patient more liable to a fresh attack, and less able to bear up against it. I am more and more inclined to believe that the general practice is a sort of Danegelt, which gets rid of the Danes for the present, but makes them sure to return, and to return to a country less able to bear their exactions.

'—— said, in reference to mesmerism, "If so and so could occur, it would be a miracle," and thus he thought he had disposed of the question! Pity that a man whom nature has qualified to be a philosopher, should prefer being an orator! I, for one, am not prepared to say I would reject all evidence for a miracle, merely on that ground; however great may be the preponderance of improbability against every other supposition. If the falsity of the evidence for a miracle be more miraculous (in Hume's sense of that word; i. e. more improbable) than the miracle, then, even on Hume's own principle, I ought to believe it. But again, I am not prepared to call everything miraculous which is a violation of those laws of Nature which I am acquainted with. Else, the King of Bantam would have been justified in rejecting all evidence for the existence of ice; and the cardinals for refusing to look through Galileo's telescope.

'"Oh, but that," said —— (of the torpedo) "is a case of electricity," that is, we are to believe or disbelieve, not according as we have or have not evidence; not by the results of experiments, but according as we have or have not an explanation to offer ; and what does the explanation amount to? A name! The Brobdignagians were not bound to believe in the existence of the Gulliver whom they saw before them, till they had made out that he was a "Ralplum Scalcatch!"'

On Public Executions.

(Date uncertain, but supposed to be in this year.)

'Mr. Editor,—I cannot altogether coincide with your correspondent A. on the subject of public executions; though he seems to admit what has long been forcibly impressed on my mind, the very great mischief often done by the public display of triumphant penitence which so often takes place at them. I do not design to enter into the question of the efficacy of deathbed repentance. Supposing the doctrine to be an essential part of the Christian religion, we cannot be (as your correspondent observes) justified by any fear of dangerous consequences in suppressing or denying it. But if the danger consists, as is the case in the public display which the writer of the "Times" complains of—if the evil consequences may be averted by merely avoiding the exhibition of these too striking scenes—then surely no regard for Christian duty calls on us to incur wantonly a useless danger.

'If the whole of a public execution were removed to such a distance from the crowd as to exclude them from hearing any of the "last dying speech," &c., which for the most part do such incalculable hurt, and if nothing were presented to their eyes but the distant view of the criminal launched from the fatal drop, our mode of conducting an execution would be as perfect as public execution can be. All spiritual consolation which a Christian minister might think himself authorised and bound to afford, might then be afforded in private to the only person (the condemned criminal himself) to whom it is even pretended it can be useful or safe. For no one can think that the doctrine of the efficacy of dying repentance can be edifying to anyone except the dying man.

'And if any of the consolation administered were rash and ill-grounded, at least no harm would be done by it, so long as it was private; since no one would be encouraged by it (as I fear is too often the case now) to go on in criminal courses. It is much to be apprehended that some of that rashness I have alluded to in cherishing this ill-founded confidence in the dying is to be found where one would least expect it. I would not take upon me to say that no divines, even of the Church of England, have ever been so ignorant or unthinking as to resort to those topics your correspondent alludes to—the case of the penitent thief, and that of the labourers called at the eleventh hour; though a very humble portion of learning and intelligence would suffice to show that these are far indeed from being parallel to the cases with which they are compared.

'The labourers in the vineyard had been standing idle till the eleventh hour because no man had hired them ; they are not represented as being at all in fault, as having been invited before and refused to come. Whatever, therefore, we may judge of the case of a hardened sinner repenting at the approach of death, it is plain it can have no sort of connexion with this parable. And no less foreign to the purpose is the case of the thief on the cross. He acknowledged as his Saviour and Lord, about to enter on a kingdom, One whom he saw perishing by an ignominious death amid the exulting taunts of his enemies and the despairing lamentations of his disciples. Such a strength of faith as this not many of us perhaps possess ; but it is what no one in the present day can possibly display.

'I have proposed what seems to me a great improvement in our public executions. But, surely, it would be much better if all executions were private. That familiarity which breeds contempt is most effectually generated in the unthinking and profligate mobs which assemble for the enjoyment of what they call "Hang Fair," and who are chiefly anxious to see a spirited and becoming submission to death, in those who (in common with many of the spectators) have long been accustomed to regard hanging as their natural death. I invite your readers to a fuller discussion of this important subject from those of more leisure and more knowledge than I profess ; and am, &c., &c.

'CLERICUS.'

'Now, I must say it is a strong presumption against your view—what Baron Pennefather would call a *prima facie* evidence—that ninety-nine in a hundred, both of Roman Catholics and Protestants, decide the other way.

'I myself agree with them; and I attribute the Reformation mainly to the increased diffusion of scripture reading.

'For the Romish Church, though insulated texts may be adduced in its favour, perhaps nearly as many as against it, is peculiarly endangered by the continuous perusal of any entire book of the New Testament—much more of several—on account of their all omitting what are the most prominent parts of the Romish religion. For instance, the foundation of all is the supremacy and infallibility of their church; yet throughout the Acts and Epistles no allusion is made to any such supreme and infallible tribunal, present or future. You have probably seen my "Search after Infallibility," published about a year ago, in which this omission is pointed out. It was answered by a Dr. O'Connell, one of their most popular preachers; who laboured to draw off the reader (very nicely) from the examination of Scripture to the Fathers, &c. There was a reply to him by an anonymous writer, which seemed to me to demolish him. At any rate, neither he nor anyone else has taken the field since.

'Again, if a stranger were to visit Europe, he would not fail to describe most of the inhabitants as worshippers of a certain goddess, whose image, decked in tawdry petticoats he would see them everywhere venerating. Indeed, I have heard of some colony where the aborigines distinguish the settlers into "worshippers of Christ," and "worshippers of Mary." Now, in the Gospels we find

her pointedly excluded from taking part in her son's
ministry; and in the Acts and Epistles she is never
named or alluded to at all. Again, the sacrifice of the
Mass is the main part of their worship; and in the
epistle to the Hebrews, the imperfection of the Jewish
sacrifices is contrasted with that of Christ " once for all,"
and no sacrificing priest (sacerdotal or hierarchical) is
appointed by the Apostles; while in the Church of Rome
everything is made to depend on that.

'Ever yours truly,
'RD. DUBLIN.'

'Dublin: Feast of St. Pancake, 1849.

'My dear Hinds,—I write this to you instead of to ——
because you will perhaps modify or amplify what I say.

'There is a certain morbid state of mind which I
suppose few thoughtful persons have ever been wholly
exempt from throughout the whole of life, except those
who with a sanguine temperament have "Hope large and
Cautiousness small." I mean a tendency to unreasonable
doubts and suspicions, especially on any point whereon
we are the most anxious to feel fully assured. This,
like any tendency when it goes beyond a certain point,
may become monomania. But in a minor degree most
people have been, at some time or other, thus haunted.
In some, it takes the turn of fancying oneself about to be
ruined; in some, of all men being hostile and conspiring
against one; in some, of ill usage from those dearest to
us. There was one of my clergy who was rational except on one point; he fancied his wife (whom he doted
on) was unfaithful, and was trying to poison him. One
patient I remember hearing of, whose own reason and
that of his friends never could satisfy him that his person
was clean; and having a great horror of dirt, he was all

day washing and scrubbing his unfortunate carcase, till
he at length caught his death of cold.   And some again
are haunted with groundless fear for the safety of a beloved child, whom they will hardly bear out of their
sight; or doctor themselves to death for imaginary
diseases, &c.

'Others again are haunted with a philosophical scepti-
cism, which I regard as only another form of the same
disease.   They are always labouring to convince themselves that sleep and waking are two different states, and
that the whole of life is not a dream; that there is an
external world; that there is such a thing as personal
identity (Des Cartes, with his "Cogito, ergo sum," was
evidently haunted in this way): and, not least, to satisfy
themselves of the truth of their religion, so as to preclude
all possibility for ever of any doubt creeping in.   Now,
how is this state of mind to be combated?   Direct arguments to prove the desired conclusion do not succeed in
such a case.   At least, they are not alone sufficient practically to exclude doubt.   And the worst of it is, that
when a man's understanding assures him, more or less
certainly, that he ought to be fully convinced, and yet his
feelings suggest doubts, he is apt to be haunted with a
fresh doubt, whether this be not a sinful want of faith.

'When I have found myself in this state, the first thing
I do is to convince myself that there is such a state.
Next, I place myself in a jury-box, and resolve to give a
verdict according to the evidence, not leaving out of
account the authority of competent persons who have
pronounced such and such evidence good; just as a juryman does, whether there be a great or a small preponderance of probability.   And then, just as a juryman does
not try the cause over again, but sentence is pronounced
according to the verdict, I resolve to set about acting

according to the decision I have come to, and withdraw
my attention for the present from the question already
tried; always keeping in mind that faith, in the sense in
which it is a virtue, does not consist in the strength of the
conviction, but in readiness to act on the conviction; in
being " willing to do the will of God," and hoping to be
rewarded by " knowing of the doctrine whether it be of
God."

'And I have commonly found that some points of
evidence come out incidentally when the mind is occupied with collateral inquiries. E.g., while I was discussing
the corruptions that have been introduced into Christianity, it struck me most forcibly that these would surely
have been the original religion if it had been of man's
devising, &c.

'You must have often observed that the side sight of
the eye is the strongest. You get a brighter view of a
comet, or some other of the heavenly bodies, when you
are looking not outright at it, but at some other star near
it. And so it often is with evidence. Discuss some
other point allied to the one on which you have been
unable to satisfy yourself, and it will often happen that,
just as when you are hunting for something you have
lost, you find other things which you had lost long before.
Some argument will strike you with its full force which
had failed to make a due impression when you were
occupied in trying the very question it relates to; when
a certain anxiety to be convinced produced a sort of
resistance to evidence. Observe : I have said, " Withdraw
your attention for the present from the question " that
puzzles you; for it would be not only unfair, but would
tend to keep up an uneasy suspicion in your mind to
resolve never from henceforth to debate such and such a
question, but put off the discussion to some definite or

indefinite time, and turn your mind to some different
subject.

'I dare say you have often, like my other pupils, received that advice, which I always acted on myself, for
your studies. When a man has got thoroughly puzzled
at some passage in an author, or at a mathematical
problem, I have known him sit over it for hours, till
he was half distracted, without being any the forwarder;
and when he comes to look at it again a day or two
after, having been occupied in the interim with other
things, he finds it quite easy. And it is the same when
you are trying to recollect some name. I always told my
pupils, " When, after a reasonable time, you cannot make
out a difficulty, pass on to something else, and return to
the point next day;" and many a weary hour have I
saved them. I have known a gamekeeper act on an
analogous plan. When the dogs failed to find a winged
bird in a thicket, he called them off and hunted them
elsewhere for half an hour; on coming back, they found
the bird at once. He assured me that if he had kept
them at that thicket all day, they would never have found
the bird. The phenomenon is curious, and I do not profess to explain it. But of the fact and the practical
inference I cannot doubt.

'And now I have sent you the medicine, which, if
you approve of it, you may administer.

'Ever yours,

'RD. WHATELY.'

In this session the question of out-door relief for
paupers was again brought forward, and a debate took
place on the second reading of the ' Rate-in-Aid ' Bill.
The Archbishop in a short speech opposed the Bill, but
without effect.

'My dear Hinds,—What you say about the Scotch Church is very reasonable; but may they not object, that, by getting an Act passed to unite them to the English Church, they would be placing themselves under the control of Parliament? And this some would dislike, not wholly without reason; and I know you prefer the apostolical plan of several independent churches, in full intercommunion.

'Perhaps the object would be equally attained by their simply laying aside all the non-existing differences between the two; for, as you observe, if they hold them non-essential, they cannot object; if essential, they cannot blame objectors. And it is an awkward thing for a man to be using the English offices on sufferance, just so long as his congregation happen to prefer it. I shall suggest this to Bishop Terrot.

'What can be done for Ireland, is a question more easily asked than answered; but this is certain, and is being established before the Commissioners, that in those places where out-door relief has been resisted, the distress has been far less; so that I should be for cutting off that, and retrieving, so far, the false step made in 1847. A rate in aid I would cheerfully vote for, as you suggest, limiting it to one year and one 6d.; but who is to limit it? Can any parliament or any ministry bind their successors not to do the very thing they are themselves doing? The 6d. is called for on the ground of necessity. If that necessity continues and increases, as the very relief afforded encourages it to do, why should not this necessity be a plea next January for a 1s. or 2s. rate, and, a little later, for 10s. or 12s.? If it be in our power to say to pauperism, "Hitherto shalt thou go and no further," why not say so at the outset? If it be not in our power, it is idle to pretend to it. I would have cheerfully paid ship-money—and so, no doubt, would Hampden—if there could have been any security that the alleged necessity of the King would never recur; but it was claimed, as Clarendon observes, "by a sort of logic which left no man anything that he could call his own."

'Universally I have a distrust of measures which are called "temporary" or "final." They hardly ever prove so; for those words are used precisely because there is an evident danger that another step will be called for on the very same ground as the first. Surely the burden of proof is on those who declare that so-and-so shall be final, or shall be temporary. Where is their security? They promised that eighty workhouses should be sufficient for all Ireland; they built one hundred and twenty, and there were not sufficient. They promised that mendicancy should be suppressed; it was never even diminished. They promised that there should be no out-door relief, but the workhouse test always enforced; they failed to fulfil this. They promised that this out-door relief bill should make each district maintain its own poor, and within two years they find this impossible; and now they promise that the bottomless pit of a rate-in-aid shall swallow up no more than a given quantity. May we not fairly call on those who have hitherto broken every promise to find securities?

' Yours ever,
' R. WHATELY.'

To the Bishop of Norwich on the Jew Bill.

' June 24, 1849.

'. . . I took a different view of the question (as you will have seen) from many others on both sides. I may perhaps have even damaged the immediate cause of Baron Rothschild by advocating a principle (to the great dismay of one at least of the supporters of the bill) which would leave Parliament as open to a Mahometan or a Pagan as to a Jew, and by waiving altogether the question whether a Jew is a fit person to sit in Parliament; but I must maintain my own principle, which is, that a law, giving to Christians generally as such, or to Christians of any particular Church, a monopoly of any civil rights, is to make Christ's kingdom, so far, a kingdom of this world, and is a violation of the rule of "rendering to Cæsar the things that are Cæsar's." I cannot doubt that the apostles were suspected of designing that, whenever their party should become strong enough, their followers should, by law, enforced by secular power, compel all men to profess Christianity, or at least exclude others from office; and I cannot doubt that they always intended to be understood —and were understood—as denying any such design. If this denial were insincere, they must have been base deceivers. If it were sincere, one who studies to conform to their principle cannot deserve to be reproached with indifference to Christianity.

'And no answer has ever been, or can be given, to this argument, that, if removing Jewish disabilities implied indifference to Christianity, then manifestly the opening of Parliament to Dissenters must imply (what I will never acknowledge in myself) indifference to our Church.

'Some, indeed, of the opponents of the bill expressed their disapprobation of the admission of a Dissenter; and they would have been—though in my opinion quite wrong—at least consistent if they had proposed to add to the words, "on the true faith of a Christian," the words, "of the Established Church." But, as the matter now stands, we are in a palpable false position, unless we are prepared to say that it is of no consequence at all what a man's religion may be, provided he will but profess Christianity!

'Those who cast imputations of infidelity or of indifference on all who supported the bill, should remember that there once was a Person so circumstanced as to have it in His power completely to exclude from all offices everyone who did not embrace the Gospel; nay, and to oblige all men, without need of resorting to actual violence, to profess Christianity; and who yet chose to forego this exercise of power, and to leave all men to their own free choice to embrace or reject the religion.

'Was not He a traitor to the good cause? So thought the Jews themselves; for, when He rejected temporal dominion, and resisted their attempts "to make Him King," they put Him to death as a false pretender for disappointing their expectations; and it does seem to me that it is in their steps we are treading if we exclude by law from civil rights all who will not profess Christianity.

'I do believe, however, that (besides those who opposed the bill merely as members of Opposition) there were several well-disposed men who either could not or would not consider clearly the question really before us, and ran away with the general vague notion that it was a question whether it is or is not a matter of indifference whether a man is a Christian or not.

'As for the argument (?) that the present is an unsuitable time for passing such a measure, because Providence has blessed our arms with success in India, and because we are exempt from the civil discord which rages on the continent, I cannot but feel the greatest wonder that anyone should suppose it possible such a reason could convince anyone. Those who are advocates for the removal of the disability must either believe that such a course does imply contempt for Christianity, which of course they must reject and contemn, or else must be persons who think that the law as it stands is adverse to the religion which they venerate, and is a reproach instead of an honour to it.

'Now the former class will never surely be made pious men and good Christians by our victories in India. The victories gained by Frederick of Prussia and by Bonaparte had no such effect (nor was there any reason they should) on them or their followers. If our Indian victories depended on our exclusion of the Jews from office, they may say, how came the Americans to defeat the Mexicans? In the United States, Jews are not excluded. Then, as for the other class, if I am convinced that the attempt to monopolise civil rights for Christians is to make Christ's a kingdom of this world, how should Lord Gough's victories change my opinion? My gratitude to Divine providence can never lead me to run counter to what I believe to be the Divine will. Nor can it alter my view of what that will is, unless there be a special revelation for the purpose.

'If I were to urge (as I might equally well do) that the potato-rot is a judgment on us for the Jewish disabilities, it would be sufficient to reply—as in the other case also—what proof can you offer of this? The Egyptians could not have been expected to conclude that it was the God of Israel who sent plagues on them for the deliverance of His people, but for the circumstance that " in the land of Goshen there was no hail." Such wanton, and I must say presumptuous, interpretations of current events are not merely idle and useless, but in many ways mischievous.

'Ever yours,

'R. Whately.'

'My dear Senior,—Yours received, and highly satisfactory. You will perhaps have seen that we have lost the good Bishop of Norwich.[1] As a public loss, I think more of him than perhaps many others who knew and esteemed him.

'A bishop, who in Galileo's time supported astronomy, would have saved many from infidelity. There is always a danger in such times that men should form an association between the Church, or religion generally, and opposition to all reform and all advance.

'Cholera is making frightful ravages both here and in London, much more than is publicly proclaimed. Poor Dr. Taylor was carried off yesterday.

'There is a good deal of blight in the tops of the potatoes, but as yet very few of the roots have suffered; and, though there have been heavy showers, the harvest, on the whole, is reckoned pretty good. But a good deal of land is out of cultivation, and the idlers are eating up the country. In fact, the Poor Law is producing just the effects we anticipated, making the famine permanent. There is no other cause that I know of why the country should be worse off now than it was ten years ago.

'The Queen's visit is reported to have been mainly due to Lord Clarendon, and to have been rather deprecated by ministers especially. Sir G. Grey is said to have dreaded her visiting the schools. Nothing could have gone off better. She spoke to me, both at the time and two days after, of her great gratification at seeing the schools; and a new building for training masters, and a new agricultural training school are to be named respec-

---

[1] Bishop Stanley; succeeded by Archbishop Whately's friend, Dr. Hinds.

tively after her and the prince, as a memorial of their satisfaction.

'Will it not be necessary for the Whigs and Tories to combine against their common enemies—the Radicals? Each is too weak separately.

'Will Austria ever dare, now, to employ Hungarian soldiers? and will she not be prostrate at the feet of Russia?'

'Nov. 2, 1849.

'My dear Mrs. Arnold,—I shall direct Parker to send you a copy of the French translation of the "Lessons on Worship." I have advised him to procure the "Edinburgh Review," for the sake of the first article.[1]

'I do not wonder that there should be persons who consider that a teacher of history has only to examine the pupils in some books they had been reading, and see whether they remember the date of each king's accession, and the locality of each battle. But, if the lecturer is to direct attention to the various influences on nations of various modifications of true and false religions, and to develop any of the workings of Divine Providence in human affairs, then I do think any who regards the soundness of his religious views as a matter of no consequence, must have forgotten Hume and Gibbon. F. Newman, however, we are told, is a very pious man. And so he is, in a certain way of his own. As far as I can judge, from what I have read of him (for I have not gone through his book), his piety seems to consist mainly of a sort of self-adoration. His system seems to be that of "every man his own apostle." But he possesses two qualities which, to a large proportion of persons in the present day, are high recommendations—inordinate self-

---

[1] 'Reason and Faith: their Claims and Conflicts.'

confidence and mystical obscurity. To me, I must confess, cautious modesty and perspicuity are greatly preferable. But there are many who give their admiration, as
they would give their money to a highwayman, on loud
and vehement demands. And I have heard the maxim
laid down by somebody, earnestly maintained, that "a
clear idea is a little idea." I am accordingly set down
as a third-rate or fourth-rate kind of person by many,
because I condescend to write intelligibly. But I am old-
fashioned enough to admire Bacon, whose remarks are
taken in and assented to by persons of ordinary capacity,
and seem nothing very profound; but when a man comes
to reflect and observe, and his faculties enlarge, he then
sees more in them than he did at first; and more still, as
he advances further; his admiration of Bacon's profundity
increasing, as he himself grows intellectually. Bacon's
wisdom is like the seven-league boots, which would fit
the giant or the dwarf, except only that the dwarf cannot
take the same stride in them.

'It is curious to observe how the brothers Newman,
starting east and west, have gone so far that they have
nearly met. Both have come to the conclusion that there
is nothing of what is commonly called evidence for Christianity; the one resting his belief (if he has any) of that,
and of the silliest monkish legends alike, on the Church;
and the other on the infallible oracle within him.

'The disparagement of evidence among persons who are
professed believers is characteristic of the present age.
I have pointed out some of the many curious coincidences
as to this in the parallels between Hume and the "British
Critic," and the "Edinburgh Review" and Coleridge.

'Such a notion as that of Coleridge is, I conceive, doing
incalculable mischief, on account of the large admixture
of truth in it; for error and poison are seldom swallowed

undiluted. It is true that internal evidence is a great
and an indispensable part of the foundation of faith ; and
hence he makes it the whole (as I have observed in the
last edition of the "Evidences"), and makes each man's own
feelings the sole test of what he is to believe. And there
are some very good people who, though they do not themselves feel all evidence for Christianity (as F. Newman
says) " crumble away under them," yet regard it as a
great triumph of their religion that it should so recommend itself to the inward feelings of those who hold that
no reason can be given for their hope, that they yet do
believe it. But if my tenants were to deny that I had
any legal claim to my rents, and call my title-deeds mere
waste paper, but to offer to hand me the money as a free
gift, because they thought me a worthy man, I should
decline the compliment ; because next year they might
think I only deserved half the sum, and the year after,
perhaps, none at all. And so with Christianity. If a
man believed the truth of it merely because he likes it, in
the first place, another, who does not like it, may, by the
same rule, reject it ; and secondly, everyone who does
call himself a Christian will receive just such portions of
.the religion as please him, and reject the rest. He will
consider this Apostle as mistaken in one point, and that,
in another, and Jesus Christ Himself as faulty in so and
so ; and in short he may believe much less of the Gospel
than a Mahometan does ; and yet forsooth his so-called
belief in Christianity is a great triumph to it ! though he
is not taking the Gospel for his guide, but making himself
the guide and ruler of the Gospel. It is like the worship
in the cave of Domdaniel of an idol made by the worshippers. But still he is called a Christian ; just as the
Mayors of the Palace called themselves subjects of the
rois fainéants. When will men get free from the thraldom
of words !

'I have been as tedious as a king. But I am writing about matters connected with what seems to have been marked out as my own especial province—to combat the prevailing tendencies of the age. I was in reality the first writer of the "Tracts for the Times;" for my "Romish Errors" might well have been so entitled; and it came out before the storm burst which I had seen gathering. And I have also observed, and fought against, the tendency in the present day to discard all moral reasoning, and to encourage the practice of making one's opinions on all moral and religious questions a matter of taste. A person who was conversing with one of my daughters said once: "Oh, you had that from your father; I remember it in some of his works." "Perhaps so; but I have given you my reasons for it; and if it is true, and the proof of it sufficient, it has a claim to reception on its own account." "Oh, your father is an eminent man in his own way; but I prefer different views."

'All this I consider as characteristic of the age. Men did indeed formerly reason on little and ill; but they professed and attempted to reason; they sought, if they did not always find, some rational ground for their conclusions; and though no doubt often biassed by their feelings, they did not, as now, avow and glory in this. The evidences of Christianity again were contemned; but it was by avowed unbelievers; not, as now, by persons professing a veneration for Christianity, and even a belief in it. In short, it is an age not particularly perhaps of disobedience to logic, but of open rebellion against it. So I have unfurled my standard, and mustered a respectable minority.

'Ever yours affectionately,

'R. W.

'P.S. I need hardly say that I have inflicted all this

upon you with a view to have your opinion of my ideas. You are not accustomed perhaps to have so much deference paid to your judgment as I should consider you entitled to. But Mrs. W. and myself, though we feel bound not to be led implicitly by anyone, should feel that we were neglecting one of the talents committed to us if we did not avail ourselves of our intimacy with you by listening attentively and with deference to your opinions.'

To Bishop Hinds.

'Nov. 7, 1849.

'.   .   .   There is on its way to you, through E., a MS. which I shall beg you afterwards (at your leisure) to forward, as directed, to Mr. Rogers, the reviewer.

'He is a very modest and candid man. I suggested as an improvement on his illustrations of faith and reason, that the anchor of faith, however strong, must be cast in the right place and on good holding-ground, which reason supplies. He admitted this as an improvement. See Hebrews vi. 19.

'I also remarked that the will and determination to adopt the major premiss is the work of faith; the minor (so and so is well established) belongs to reason.

'In this also he concurs.

'Yours ever,

'R. W.'

'Dec. 10, 1849.

'My dear Hinds,—I should like to hear how your consecration and bishop's sermon came off; and also some particulars of that correspondence with your opponents, of which something has appeared in the papers.

'Your refusal to sign any declaration dictated by a self-constituted authority was very well expressed. I am

not sure, however, that I should not have administered, in
very calm language, something of a more decided rebuke
of the absurdity as well as impertinence of the application. I think I should have said that, to impute to
me views which to myself appear at variance with those
of the Church, is what everyone is bound in Christian
charity and in gentlemanly courtesy to abstain from, and
is an imputation which it would be both lowering oneself
and also vain to reply to, since a man who plays the
hypocrite for thirty years would be likely to do so still.
But as for views at variance with what somebody else conceives to be those of the Church, it is a thing which though
one may regret, one cannot avoid. If I could express
myself so that no person could possibly differ as to my
meaning, I should do more than, notoriously, has been
done, either in our Church's formularies or in Scripture.
But to attempt not only to accomplish this, but to make
my meaning acceptable to all persons, including those who
take different and even opposite views of the doctrine both
of the Church and of Scripture in many points, this would
be a palpable absurdity. And I think I should have
concluded by asking them to reflect how they would feel
and act if five or six different parties were to call on
them to sign a list of Articles drawn up in conformity
with the views of each respectively.'

CHAPTER VII.

1850.

Family anxieties of the Archbishop—Illness of his son—Accompanies his family on their journey to Nice, but leaves them at Paris—Letter to Mr. Senior—Letter to Lady Osborne on Epicureanism—Letters to Mrs. Hill on literary matters—Letters to Bishop Hinds on the Baptismal Question—Letter to Mr. Senior on his Review of 'Lewis on Authority in Matters of Opinion'—Spends part of the summer with his family at Cromer—Miss Anna Gurney—His friendship for Mrs. Hill—Letter to Mrs. Arnold—Letter to Mrs. Hill—Letter to a Friend—Letter to Bishop Hinds on his Address to his Clergy.

THE year 1850 opened with much trial to the subject of this memoir, not only from sickness in his family, but from other causes known and shared only by them.

The precarious health of his son obliged him to leave a curacy in England to which he had been recently ordained, and try a winter in a warmer climate. Accompanied by a sister, he started for Nice in December, 1849 ; the Archbishop accompanied his children as far as Paris, but his journey was a hurried one, and early in 1850 he was again at his post.

'Feb. 1, 1850.

' My dear Senior,—It strikes me that there is much wanted an article on National Education. It might be a review of the "Minutes of Council," our Irish Reports, and a whole host of pamphlets, including the appendix to my last Charge. I find that —— is traversing England, and disseminating, and gaining credence for, his misstatements. And there is much excitement and discussion prevailing relative to the English schools also. In Ireland the Roman Catholic agitators are assailing the Board almost fiercely as the ultra-protestants. And there is also a great opposition in the colonies to the introduction, which Lord Grey is disposed to attempt, of our system.

'Such an article would, I think, not only be interesting but needful, to meet the inquiry why none such appears. If you do not write it, cannot you set some one else to work?

'We have heard only incidentally of our children's arrival at Nice, their letters to us having apparently been lost. How they are, we are still in most painful uncertainty.

'Ever yours truly,
'RD. DUBLIN.'

To Lady Osborne on the Opinions of the Epicureans.
(She had written to ask him on the subject.)

'Dublin: Feb. 28, 1850.

'I have never read, nor do I know of, any work written by an Epicurean, except Lucretius. And as for all that has been written about them, and about the other philosophical sects, you may easily find people who have read three or four times as much as I have.

'But as most of the ancient philosophers were Tractites, having a "double-doctrine," it would be rash to decide what they really thought.

'Perhaps I might say with Hobbes, "If I had read as

much as some men, I should be as ignorant as they."
Certain it is, that I have met with persons who know by
heart much more of Plato and Cicero than I do, who
have not found out, first, that they really believed nothing
of what they taught of future rewards and punishments;
secondly, that the immortality of the soul which they held
was practically equivalent to annihilation.   In like manner
Pope and others, who had all the heathen mythology at
their fingers' ends, were so ignorant of it after all as to
imagine that the Pagans worshipped the same creator
with us, only under the name of Jove.

'I have not yet read much of ——'s sermons.
But I have been reading a paper of his in the "Irish
Ecclesiastical Gazette" on the 23rd Article, which he,
I think, expounds rightly, though he might have com-
pressed all he had to say into half the space.   But he
attributes to Burnet (on the 23rd Article) and to me,
a doctrine which I do not think either of us can be
fairly considered as maintaining: viz. that the Article
excludes from the English Church all who hold the
necessity of episcopal ordination, and who do not admit
that one ordination is just as good as another.   I myself
have no doubt that among our reformers there were
differences of opinion on this point, and that they intended
to exclude neither.'

The following letter is to a much valued correspondent,
with whom he had recently become intimate :—

To Mrs. Hill of Cork.

'March 26, 1850.

'Dear Mrs. Hill,—I do not quite recollect whether you
have any of my works.   I will send you either the whole,
or as many as may be deficient.   You may return them

on the 30th of February. The cost to me of such a gift to any one not likely to be a purchaser, is next to nothing ; and, accordingly, Dr. West is allowed to give them away to such persons at his discretion, as from himself. But I do not ordinarily give copies as " from the author," for fear of giving offence to those omitted. The line that I draw is, to give to those who have in some way assisted. And your pretty book of selections brings you within the category of having done something.

'You do not mention the Proverb copies at the end of " Sullivan's Spelling Book." If any periodical you are writing for would take them they are at your service, as he has no copyright in them.

' The apophthegms I was speaking of would, I should think, all go into two or three octavo pages. Perhaps if you were to add to them some others from different authors, you might make a collection which would be acceptable to some periodical. Several of Bacon's " antitheta " (selections from which I have printed at the end of the Rhetoric) would be jewels in such a collection, if so translated (which is not easy) as to lose none of their force.

' Macaulay's writings would furnish several. If you should undertake any such collection for the amusement of your leisure, or for any other purpose, you will find that some passages will require to be a little altered in expression to make them intelligible apart from the context, e.g. (in S. V. on the Shepherds at Bethlehem) " When the illumination from heaven, the rays of revelation, failed to she 1 full light on the Gospel-dispensation, they brought to the dial-plate the lamp of human philosophy." I have published nothing, and hardly written anything, on language, except what is to be found in the Logic (including the Easy Lessons on Reasoning) ;

but, in fact, Logic, as treated by me, relates altogether to language; as I am a zealous Nominalist, and reject all the stuff that so many talk about " Ideas." I dare say you have heard the story of a lady who had had very little education, but was anxious to improve herself, and borrowed instructive books of a learned gentleman, who, despising female intellect, lent her Locke's Essay, as a joke; and when she returned it asked her what she thought of it; she replied, " that there seemed to her many very good things in it, but there was one word she did not clearly understand, the word idĕa (as she pronounced it, which by the way, is just as we do pronounce it—" not idéa "—in the original Greek); he told her it was the feminine of "idiot." My remark on the story was that I quite agreed with the lady; and, moreover, that I verily think neither the learned gentleman nor Locke himself understood in what sense he used the word, any more than she, only that she had the sagacity to perceive that she did not.'

To the Same.

'Dublin: March 29, 1850.

' The " bush " is supposed by all commentators to have been the commonest bush in the Arabian Desert, the dwarf palm. It is now naturalised in some parts of Spain. Whether this is the origin of its branches being an emblem of victory, or whether it was merely that it is a fine-looking branch of a common shrub, is a doubtful matter.

'The Polynesians use a plantain leaf as a flag of truce. But the idea of the phœnix is very ingenious, and worth considering. Now for another question: Can you connect a bay horse with a bay tree? 1. As in Ireland, the substitute for a palm-branch is a sprig of yew; and in

England, a sprig of willow with its catkins ; so in Italy, the substitute for a palm-branch was the "laurus"— the bay-tree. 2. Now the Greek for a palm-branch is "baïon" (which is in the Greek Testament, where "they cut down branches from the trees," &c.). And 3. The Latin for baïon is "spadix;" which is also 4th, used for a bay-horse (Virgil's *Georgics*), from the colour of the young shoot.

'As for the cases, I have often remarked that the genitive, denoting the source from which anything arises, is used when our attention is directed primarily to our own feelings ; and the accusative, denoting the object acted on, when our attention is called to the effect produced on another. When you strike your hand gently on the table you say, " I feel the table ;" when strongly, you say, " I feel pain in my hand from the table." Now sight is the faintest sensation, and the most vivid perception. The Greeks therefore spoke of sight as acting on the thing perceived, and all the other senses as giving a sensation from the object. So also φιλῶ, to love, governs an accusative case ; we seem to be acting on the object ; but ἐρᾶν or ἐρᾶσθαι, to " be in love," " to suffer love," governs a genitive.

'Mr. Sullivan, in his next edition, is to insert another proverb—

> Silver gilt will often pass
> Either for gold, or else for brass.

With the comment that some men who, at the first glance, give the idea of something very superior indeed, rather beyond what they really are, ultimately are either underrated or overrated. Your remarks on Apophthegms occurred to me in my sermon to-day, in which—as often —I had summed up the substance in one sentence : We

must " watch " as if all depended on our own vigilance,
and we must " pray " as if nothing depended on it.

'Very truly yours,

'Rd. Dublin.'

To Bishop Hinds on the Baptismal Question.

'Dublin: April 1, 1850.

. . . .

' If by " baptism for the remission of sins " it be meant
that all Adam's descendants are doomed to punishment
in the next world for his sin, unless they are made members 'of the Christian Church, then surely that practice
(of infant baptism) is right; and also the baptism by
midwives.

' But as you know (in the Essay on imputed righteousness), I do not see any grounds in Scripture for supposing
that anyone is liable to punishment after death for any
sins but his own. And, therefore, is not baptising the
infant savage, like presenting him with the title-deeds of
a valuable estate, with a full knowledge that, whether he
die young or grow up, he will never be able to read them
or claim the property?

' Again, it is generally admitted by both parties that
the baptism of an adult is accompanied with the grace of
regeneration if the sacrament be rightly received, and
not otherwise; not if there be a want of repentance and
faith. But though no benefit accrues to the unworthy
recipient, may he not (to his own condemnation) have
been really regenerate in the sense of being enrolled in a
society gifted with certain spiritual privileges, though he
does not think of availing himself of them? Just as a
man may be truly made a freeman of some city, or
graduate of a university, though he may never use his
rights. As we shall certainly both of us have to write

on the subject before long, I throw out what occurs to me, with great desire that you should do the same. I was thinking of making a reference to that essay and those sermons, as saving me a great part of the discussion. I fear Parker is impenetrable, and will rather be killed *secundum artem* than try any novelty. I have talked to him several times.

' Yours ever,
' RD. WHATELY.'

' Dublin : April 16, 1850.

' My dear Senior.—I have received the " Edinburgh," and read your Article.[1] I can't help doing so when I know of one, though the superior vigour of your style is apt to make your colleagues seem flat. So also with the authors reviewed, though they may be what would read well when not thus contrasted. E. g. your extracts remind me of glass beads set in gold.

' As for what you say of the impaired authority of the supporters of what it would be unpopular to oppose, I need not say I concur in it, having in several places made the same remark. And this (which is all that is needed for your purpose) may be extended to other cases. E. g. I know of several who are believers in mesmerism, " but secretly, for fear of the Jews." And as I know not how many more such there may be, this impairs the authority of the professed disbelievers.

' But when you speak of theological literature as " protected," do not even the examples you give disprove it? Many men may, indeed, be deterred from writing against the prevailing religion by dread of odium; but if any one hopes to escape odium in writing for it,

---

[1] Upon ' Lewis, On Authority in Matters of Opinion.'

he is likely to be disappointed. If he defend the peculiar tenets of his own Church, he will have half of its members against him, besides all those of other Churches. And if he write in defence of Christianity generally, he will be more assailed by Christians than by infidels. Look at the parallel columns (to which I might have added many more) at the end of the Logic. Even at this time there is a strong body of Roman Catholics (besides Protestants) pressing the Education Board to suppress the "Lessons on the Truth of Christianity," which the Commissioners put forth several years ago. And Warburton was assailed more by Christian than by Antichristian opponents. He was like Samson, whom the Israelites bound hand and foot and delivered into the hand of the Philistines, "And he snapped the cords as a thread of tow is broken when it toucheth the fire."

'There is also this additional penalty against writers on the side of religion, that they are denounced (as you have remarked of Hampden and me) as traitors to their own cause. The defender of the doctrines of his Church is stigmatised as heterodox. The defender of Christianity as impiously raising doubts and "unsettling" people's minds. Πάσχειν δὲ κακῶς ἐχθρὸν ὑπ' ἐχθρῶν οὐδὲν ἀεικές, but to be assailed by one's own brethren is more trying. Now he who supports his own views on geology or politics is, indeed, liable to be opposed, but not by those on his own side.

'I think you might have added, therefore, that those who do brave obloquy by advocating unpopular views, ought to have a corresponding weight attached to their authority on all points. And I think this is in a considerable degree the actual result.

'Yours ever,

'R. W.'

'My dear Hinds,—I know you have little time either for business or for relaxation. I at least mean, however, that the enclosed should come under the latter head. Should you find it, after reading the first three or four stanzas, to be of that description which men and gods can't endure, you need go no further; but if you like it, it will be rather an amusement than a toil to you to suggest any improvements that may occur to you. If you should think well of the verses, what would you think of their being printed at the end of the " Evidences," having been suggested by the perusal of the last two Lessons?

' Bishop Wilson, in talking of the Regeneration controversy, remarked that it is extravagant to refer to the Creed—" one baptism for the remission of sins " as decisive of the whole—though he afterwards seemed to admit that, to a member of a Church which baptises infants, it is pretty nearly decisive. I suggested, and he concurred with me, that, in most questions pertaining to the Gospel dispensation, the first thing to be done is to look at the Law, considering that from that the first preachers of the Gospel would naturally take their notions, wherever they were not specially directed otherwise.

' 1. When a sojourner Gentile wished to partake of the Passover, &c., " let all his males be circumcised ; " and then his family became adopted Jews. Hence, surely a man and his children would all be baptised (unless the contrary were enjoined) on his embracing Christianity, and would thus be adopted as members of the people of God under the new dispensation.

2. ' When any Jew or proselyte, whether circumcised as an infant or as an adult, failed to take advantage of

his privileges as one of God's people, he would be exhorted not to become an Israelite—but to walk worthy of his calling—to return to the Lord, &c. ; and so also the early Christians would call on the careless members of the Church not to become regenerate saints, &c., but to awaken, to seek for a renewal, &c.

' And the parallel might be carried, I think, fairly through many more points.

' But the advocates of baptismal regeneration labour under this difficulty, that they represent regeneration as two different things — to an adult and to an infant. The adult, they say, is regenerated only if he is a right recipient—if he have that deep repentance and full faith which are required, and which are followed by the immediate actual enjoyment of the sanctifying influence of the Holy Spirit on his heart and conduct.

' To the infant, incapable of being a moral agent at all, most would only make " regeneration " an offer and promise of all this hereafter—a right of admission to the treasury of divine grace, supposing him hereafter to apply properly.

' Now, supposing all this correct, it is plain that regeneration is two different things—to the infant and the adult.

' It is as if I defined " inheriting an estate " to mean, in the case of an adult, a man's actually entering on the enjoyment of the property, taking possession of it, and spending or otherwise disposing of the revenue [so also, becoming a freeman of a corporate city, &c.]; and as if I decided that if he neglect thus to use and enjoy the property, he is not to be said to have inherited it. Now, an infant cannot, in this sense, " inherit an estate," but, if at all, in some different sense.

'But if I define inheriting an estate to consist in a person having a legal title to it bestowed on him, and his becoming a freeman his name being entered on the roll, &c., then there is but one sense in which this is predicated of an adult and of an infant; and he who, either through negligence if an adult, or through incapacity if an infant, fails to avail himself at once of the advantage acquired, may be admonished to seek, not to acquire, a new possession, but to make use of what is already his.

'Now which of these views is the right, or is either of them?

'Yours ever,

'RD. WHATELY.

'P.S.—Will people be found to pay 3l. per acre for land in this settlement?'

Part of the summer of 1850 was spent at Cromer with his family, where he formed an acquaintance with one whose rare powers of mind rendered her peculiarly capable of entering into his—the late Miss Anna Gurney of North Repps. None who have enjoyed the privilege of her society will readily forget it; and the Archbishop's intercourse with her, brief as it was, was much enjoyed by him, and was kept up by occasional correspondence.

Another acquaintance, renewed this year, ripened into a friendship which contributed much to the interest and pleasure of his later years—namely, with the late Mrs. Hill of Cork, whose high qualities of mind and heart were such as to recommend her peculiarly to the Archbishop. With no one, perhaps, at this period of his life, did he carry on a more intimate and unreserved correspondence.

She was able to assist in many of his literary labours, and wrote many papers from his suggestions; and their intercourse by letter was only broken by the illness which ended in her death.

'October 6, 1850.

'My dear Mrs. Arnold,—" What in the world can have possessed the Archbishop that he sends us a parcel of haws?" Now, guess! Do you give it up? They are some of the fruit of the red-flowering hawthorn which dear —— budded with her own fair hands. They are sent, however, not merely to show how well it has flowered, but in case you and she have a mind to try the experiment of sowing them, and trying what will come. I have been trying several such experiments, and should follow them up if I had leisure; for the subject of Varieties, both of plants and animals, is particularly interesting to me. Among other things, it is connected with the question whether all mankind are of one species. The two extreme opinions are, 1st, that of those who teach that negroes, Europeans, Tartars, Red Indians, &c., are distinct species; and 2nd, that of Lamarck and the " Vestiges of Creation," who hold that men are descended from apes, and those again from cockles and worms; and between these there are very many shades of opinion.

'I have sown the seeds of the white black-currant and the white variety of the woody nightshade, and all of them —as many as have flowered—have come true. On the other hand, I have sown berries of the Florence-court yew (which the botanical books speak of as a distinct species), and all that have come up as yet have been common yews.

'One thing that has, till lately, been an obstacle to experiments of this kind, is, that with many trees the seedling must be a good many years old before it flowers, so as to show what it is; but this is now got over. If the young seedling is grafted on a bearing branch of a tree of the same species, it will flower and fruit speedily; so that there are now many new apples, plums, &c., to be had at the nursery gardens, which were raised from the seed only a very few years ago. I have some hawthorns thus grafted with seedlings from the red-flowered, which I hope will flower next spring.

'Haws usually lie in the ground a whole year before they come up; but they (and the same with the hips of roses), if mashed up in water with some meal, or anything else that will ferment, and so left for several weeks, will be so softened that they will, many of them, come up the first spring.

'One day, while waiting for the train at Windermere, on my way from Foxhow hither, I was attracted by a very fine wild rose-bush of the deep-red kind, close to the station; and I pulled up a sucker and brought it home, and (though this was in June!) it was so good as to grow, and I have now two plants of it.

'Did they tell you of our excursion to see the charcoal-works? It was very interesting. I had known two years before how well plants will grow in peat-charcoal, having tried it; but I was astonished at the neat contrivance for charring, and they sell it at 35s. per ton! I have bought a ton, to try it in my few fields. If the thing succeeds as it has promised, it holds out a prospect (barring Poor-laws) of regenerating Ireland, and, by-the-by, a good deal of your part of England too.'

The following is to Mrs. Hill, who was at this time engaged in a work undertaken at his suggestion.

'It may seem strange that I should think of drawing you off, in any degree, from the work you are about. But there is a work wanted (not, by-the-by, altogether unconnected with it) which I have not time for, nor any of the (few) clergy and others who would be qualified for it, and towards which I could furnish hints.

'The public, especially in England, are in a great fright, and great anger; and I dread their terror and rage taking a wrong direction. If the people of London, &c., should take to pelting priests and burning chapels (as in 1780), or if any indecent demonstrations of alarm or resentment should occur, this will cause a strong reaction towards Romanism. And this is to be apprehended the more, because the Tractites, and some of their favourers in high station, are seeking (in order to clear themselves) to hound on the mob, and aggravate their rage against the Pope, for sending officers to take charge of the recruits whom they have been enlisting for him.

'Almost any publication on the subject, of any merit, besides many of none, would be likely just now to have a sale. And it would be an important public service to turn the alarm and indignation towards the right quarter

'I would send you some hints, if you think it worth while, from which you could judge whether you could work them up in a popular style. Sometimes I have thought of the form of an Address to the Protestants of the Empire, sometimes of the form of a dialogue. But every writer will do well to follow his own taste as to that.

'A great work is a thing I have never undertaken. Any one, on examining the formidable array of my volumes, would find that all the most considerable have grown out of sermons, lectures, &c., which I was called on to deliver, and which I then published with some

additions; and any work purporting to be a "refutation
of so and so," or an "answer to such a one," would be
quite at variance with the general character of my works.
I am an armourer rather than a warrior. I have manu-
factured powder and ball, and leave you and others to
make them up into cartridges and fire at the enemy.'

Extract from a Letter to a Friend.

'You are quite right in disregarding misrepresentations.
It has always been, as you well know, my practice. I
mean what are properly called misrepresentations, arising
from malicious design or inexcusable carelessness. If any
one chooses to impute to me, in report, something I never
said, in some work which perhaps he has never opened, I
leave the error to correct itself.

'But misapprehensions, such as a man might innocently
fall into through deficiency of learning or of logical acuteness. I feel bound to guard against as well as I can, and
to correct, if they do arise, whenever I am able. This is
what I feel bound to, both in justice to my own character
and to the public.

'Now, allow me to suggest that on this principle I
should feel myself called on, were I in your place, to produce a work on the evidences of our religion. Of course,
I do not mean that every Christian minister is bound to
publish such a treatise, but that circumstanced as you are,
it may fairly be demanded from you.

'A man may conceivably believe some conclusion as
firmly as his neighbours do, though on quite different
grounds. He may think, and may have laboured to prove,
that the reasons on which they believe are futile; and he
may have reasons of his own which he thinks better. But
then he is bound, if the matter be one of importance,
publicly to state those reasons; having endeavoured to

remove their belief from what he regards as an unsound foundation, he ought to place it in some other. Then (and then only) he will have cleared himself (whether his reasons are thought satisfactory or not) from the suspicion of insincerity and inconsistency. But if he neglect to take this course, he cannot complain of misrepresentation, since he will in fact have been misrepresenting himself.'

'Dec. 21, 1850.

'My dear Hinds,—Your admirable Address[1] seems not published for sale as a pamphlet. I think it should be ; at any rate, I shall be glad of five or six dozen copies to distribute.

'West will have sent you a copy of my letter to the Archbishop of Canterbury. The primate thought it excellent, and when he and I agree, we must be right. I was the more induced to write it by a letter from Lord ——, in which he speaks of Ireland having always had an unbroken succession of Roman Catholic bishops (which is a strange ignorance of history), and of the necessity of " the Church of England disconnecting itself at this crisis from the Irish Church."

'While Ireland was an independent kingdom, the substitution there of a Roman Catholic establishment for a Protestant might not have endangered that in England. But if this is done (and Lord ——'s expression prepares the way for it) in a part of the United Kingdom, the next step called for may be that Liverpool or all Lancashire shall change its establishment, on account of the numbers of Roman Catholics there, and so on.

'What we, the Irish Protestants, have to do is, not to try to aggravate the rage in England, but to implore that

[1] Reply to an Address from the Clergy of Norwich Diocese on what was called the Papal Aggression.

we may be kept in the same boat; that is our only chance. I can't say I much like the tone of Lord ——'s letter, in the early part. Neither resentment nor fear should ever be avowed, except in action. If we apprehend an attack on a fortress, instead of wringing our hands and screaming with terror, we should strengthen the fortifications. If an enemy appears before it, let us not scold him; but if weak, let him alone; if formidable, cannonade him.'

CHAPTER VIII.

1851.

The Papal Aggression—Publishes the 'Cautions for the Times'—
Correspondence with the Archbishop of Canterbury on the Papal
Aggression—Letter to Mrs. Hill—Letter to Miss Crabtree—Letter
to Dr. Hinds on the Marriage Laws—Letter to Lady Osborne—
Letter to Mr. Senior on the late French Revolution—Letter to
Lady Osborne on Good and Evil Angels—Letter to Mr. Senior on
the Ecclesiastical Titles Bill — His Suggestions for a Universal
Coinage—Father Ignatius—His Interview with the Archbishop—
Letter to Mrs. Arnold on the State of Ireland—Letter to Mrs.
Arnold on her Proposal to answer the 'Creeds of Christen-
dom'—Attends the Session—Harassed by Family Anxieties—
Letter to Mrs. Hill on the Spread of Mormonism—Letter to the
Archbishop of Canterbury on the Gorham Controversy—Letter to
his Son-in-Law.

THE year 1851 was memorable for the excitement caused
by the subject to which the last letter of 1850 refers,
namely, the 'Papal Aggression.' The Archbishop was
anxious to point out to all concerned, that the real danger
lay, not in the irritating bravados of the Church of Rome,
but in the quiet and secret labours of her emissaries to
win the confidence of individuals, and to undermine simple
faith in the Scriptures. To open the eyes of the public to
this less noticed and latent evil, was the object with which
the 'Cautions for the Times' were commenced; they
were most of them not actually written by the Archbishop,
but composed under his directions, with his revisal and
minute superintendence.

The Bishop of Oxford had sent him a copy of the protest made by the clergy of his diocese against the 'Aggression.' The Archbishop's answer to this letter was as follows :—

Archbishop of Dublin's Answer to Letter (and Protest) of Bishop of Oxford on the Papal Aggression.

'Dublin: Feb. 1, 1851.

'My dear Lord,—I have to acknowledge your favour of January 30, accompanied by a copy of the protest of your clergy against the proceedings of the Pope.

'It would be superfluous for me to express my concurrence in the denial of the claims and censure of the peculiar doctrines of the Church of Rome, a subject on which I have written and published so much within the last thirty years.

'And as for the present particular occasion, the Addresses to the Archbishop of Canterbury and to the Queen, from the Irish prelates (which were drawn up chiefly by the Archbishop of Armagh and myself, and signed by all the bishops), sufficiently express our views on the most important points.

'Your Lordship will observe that in those documents we earnestly deprecate the introduction of any legislative measures for the protection of the Church in England, exclusively of Ireland, as a violation of the Act of Union, and fraught with danger to both countries.

'That an adherence to this principle will prevent any penal enactments at all is my conviction, for no administration is likely to propose any that shall extend to Ireland.

'A zealous and far-sighted Romanist would, I conceive, rejoice at any enactments against the Church of Rome for England exclusively. They would afford a pretext

for raising the cry of "persecution," without the least
risk of their being enforced, like firing at a mob with
blank cartridge, which enrages without repelling; and
they would give plausibility to his Church's claims in
this country, without practically weakening its cause in
England.

'In most of the speeches, pamphlets, addresses, &c.
that I have seen on the subject, there is a confused blending together of three quite distinct subjects:—(1.) The
claim of the Romish Church to universal supremacy.
(2.) The peculiar doctrines and practices of that Church;
and—(3.) The appointment of bishops denominated from
districts in England, in place of Vicars-Apostolical.

'The third alone is the novelty. The others are just
what they have long been, and yet they are often confusedly mixed up with what is said of the third. And all
three are, in themselves, quite independent of each other.
For—(1.) The Church of Rome might conceivably have
reformed (and many at the time cherished this hope), at
the Council of Trent, a multitude of abuses, and yet
might still have retained its claim to be the Universal
Church. (2.) It is possible to retain most of the peculiar
doctrines and practices of the Church of Rome, without
acknowledging any supremacy of that Church, as was in
fact done by Henry VIII., and is done by the Greek
Church. (3.) To appoint bishops over particular dioceses
is what is in fact done by the Scotch Protestant Episcopal
Church, which repudiates both the claims and the doctrines of Rome.

'Some would admit that, supposing the Romish Church
to be pure, and its claims to supremacy well founded, the
step taken by the Pope would have been unobjectionable;
and consequently is in itself unobjectionable. Others
seem to think it would at any rate have been an infringe-

ment of the royal prerogative. And some again seem—
I cannot understand how—to hold both these opinions
together—that the procedure would have been legal, and
politically right, but for its connexion with theological
error.

'In reference to the protest of your Lordship's clergy
permit me, with all respect, to suggest a doubt as to one
passage of it, where it is declared to be their conviction
that the doctrines and practices of the Church of Rome
would be condemned by the judgment (could that be
obtained) of the "Universal Church."

'The experiment indeed is not one that any one can
expect to see tried; but each man will be likely to form
his own—not unreasonable—conjectures, as to the result
of such a trial, if it were made. And I apprehend, the
conclusion most would come to on this point would be
such that the Romanists would be but too happy to join
issue thereon.

'Strictly speaking, the Universal Church (on earth) must
comprise all Christians, and the majority of these have no
original and natural right—none except by express compact—to dictate to the minority. The decision of Christian
men, like the verdict of a jury, must be that which they
all agree in. By law, the decision of the House of Commons is that of the majority of members present; of the
House of Lords, of the majority of those present in person or by proxy. But where there is no law laid down
on the subject, the decision of fifty-one men in a hundred
against forty-nine, ought not to be called the decision of
the hundred.

'Now it may be said, "If all Christians disapprove of
the Romish doctrine and practice, how comes that Church
to exist?" or if it be assumed—which is an entirely
groundless assumption—that the majority are to represent

the whole, and to be accounted the Universal Church, it may surely be said, "The Roman Catholics actually are a majority; and moreover, those of the Greek Church would vote in favour of the far greater part of the doctrines and practices of Rome. There would therefore be an overwhelming majority in favour of Romish doctrines and worship.

'It is melancholy to reflect—but so the actual state of the case is—that if we go to decide questions by collecting votes (i. e. by an appeal to human authority) the Protestants must be outvoted.'

The following letter was sent to his friend and literary assistant and employée Mrs. Hill, with a copy of the 'Lessons on Morals;' another of that series of 'Easy Lessons,' which he considered as belonging to the most important and difficult class of his works.

It was his rule to give copies of his work to all those who had in any way helped him, either in copying, making indexes, offering suggestions, or in any other way; and no one was ever more ready to acknowledge such obligations.

'Dublin: Feb. 4, 1851.

'My dear Mrs. Hill,—I am obliged to send you this in conformity with my rule of presenting a copy to every one who may have, more or less, contributed. And in this I have adopted a suggestion of yours.

'This little, very little book, has been in hand constantly for between two and three months; during which I never passed a day (for that I find an essential rule) without doing something to it. It is true I have been of late unusually busy; else I might have got through it in six weeks. But then, on the other hand, full three-fourths was already written, in the form of sermons, and I had only to arrange and retouch. I mention this to show how absurd it would be for me to undertake a large original work, requiring many books to be consulted, and the whole to be composed from the beginning.

'That little tract the "Lessons on Religious Worship," though merely a compilation, cost me six months of incessant work.

'Original works must be left to those who can command unbroken leisure; if at least they would produce anything really valuable.

'Believe me to be,
'Yours very truly,
'RD. DUBLIN.'

To Miss Crabtree.

'Feb. 13, 1851.

'It is painful and disheartening to observe how much, in times of excitement, most men fall below themselves. They gather together in meetings, and are then like half-kindled firebrands, which heaped together soon kindle each other into a blaze. Then they pour forth speeches and resolutions according to the dictates of feeling and not of reason; and ever after, all their ingenuity is employed in defending and justifying what they have just said and done, in order to avoid what a man generally regards with more shame and dread than anything else; confessing himself to be wiser to-day than he was yesterday. Hence if you judge a man from what he appears in such cases, you will perhaps greatly underrate him.

'But the worst of it is, this kind of paroxysm often affords advantage to enemies greatly inferior on the whole in general ability, and in goodness of cause; e. g. a Roman Catholic of very moderate common-sense might reply to what you lately saw urged, the "ingratitude" of the Roman Catholics for the removal of restrictions (which they repay by persisting in claims which they never abandoned, and which are an essential of their creed), " Why, if you conceded no more than could be done consistently with the public safety, you did nothing but bare justice, and have no claim to thanks ; but if you conceded something inconsistent with the public welfare, you are fools for your pains, and must of course expect that fresh attempts will be made to take advantage of your folly." '

To the Same, with some Copies of No. I. of the 'Cautions for the Times.'

'Feb. 22, 1851.

. . . . 'I dare say several good men who have been petitioning for legislative protection without saying what, and leaving it to government to adopt such measures as they in their wisdom may see fit, would be shocked at the enactment of penal laws ; and do not perceive that if none such be enacted, it is no thanks to them.

' One of these days I shall publish a curious document to show how trusting to legislative protection paralyzes exertion. In this diocese, the whole time the penal laws were in force, though the Protestant population must have greatly increased, in the general increase not a church was added, except one or two in the City, by Act of Parliament. They trusted to the penal laws. The Roman Catholic priests were active and successful in spite of those laws. Then, when these were abolished, the Protestant Church began to bestir itself. In ten years seven new churches were opened ; in the next ten years eleven ; in the next fourteen ; in the next eighteen ; and so on, up to this day ; and still there is a demand for many additional ones ! When will people learn from experience ?'

'Dublin: Feb. 20, 1851.

'My dear Hinds,—When it is that a desirable measure is advanced, and when retarded, and when neither, by bringing it forward in Parliament, must be judged of by intelligent persons on the spot.

'In either of the two former cases, the right course is obvious. In the third case, how much trouble and, perhaps, obloquy it is worth while to encounter for the sake of protesting against a wrong, and asserting a right principle, and clearing one's conscience, must be determined by the nature of the case. I have more than once come forward to advocate some important principle, or to protest against some bad measure, with a full knowledge that I could not succeed, except in clearing myself.

'The opposition to Lord St. German's bill, which is, it seems, so overpoweringly strong, is founded chiefly, as far as I can judge, on misapprehension. And whether this misapprehension be or be not incurable; and, again, whether it is more likely to be remedied by bringing forward the bill, or by abstaining, I cannot undertake to decide.

'The misapprehension I mean is, that almost all the advocates of the restriction, and a large proportion of those who are for removing it, seem prepared to join issue on the question " whether a marriage between a brother and sister-in-law is or is not a suitable, desirable, proper thing."

'If you will ask the ninety-nine of every hundred women, who, as you say, are opposed to the bill, what are their sentiments thereon, I think you will find ninety of them taking for granted that that is the question ; and that those who approve of such marriages ought to vote for the bill, and those who disapprove thereon ought to vote against it.

'Now this is, according to my view, not the question, and it is a point on which I decline giving any opinion.

'This, however, I am ready to declare ; that if any one should consult me as to the desirableness of a marriage where there was a very great disparity of age, or of rank, or where there was a taint of hereditary disease on either side, I should pronounce against such a marriage. But Heaven forbid we should have laws to prescribe the relative ages of parties who are to marry, or to require so many quarterings on each side like German nobles— or to have the parties examined by a jury of surgeons, like horses for sale !

'My principle is that the presumption is against all restrictions. Some we must have. But the burden of proof lies on those who advocate either the imposition or the continuance of any restriction. We are not bound to show that everyone who is left to judge and act for himself will decide and act first in the way that the majority of his neighbours would think best ; but the others are bound to show some great and palpable evil that would in such and such a case result from leaving men free. I am no friend to late hours, or to carelessness about fire, or lavish feasting and dress ; but I do not vote for the old curfew law, or for laws prescribing how many dishes of meat a man may have on his table, &c.

'Then, as for the Mosaic law, there again I decline giving any opinion, because I cannot bring myself to be-lieve men serious in bringing forward arguments about that till I find them themselves conforming to that law. That consistent procedure would alone entitle them to a hearing. And that is what they therefore may fairly be challenged to. This would be περιτέμνειν τὸ πρᾶγμα.

'But if they say this is part of the moral law of
Moses, how can we in any case judge of that but by the
light of reason? And when the very question is about a
point of morality, to resort to the Levitical law is a most
palpable begging of the question. "Such and such a
thing is immoral because it is forbidden in the moral law,
and that it is so is proved because it is immoral!" If
then the Levitical law (and the same may be said of the
canons of foreign churches and councils) be not binding
on us, it is better to waive all questions about it; unless,
perhaps, to make these two remarks :

'(1st) That anything distinctly enjoined in that law
ought not to be pronounced in itself, universally and
necessarily, criminal ; and the marriage, under certain
circumstances, of a brother and sister-in-law was enjoined
in that law.

' (2ndly) That the Levitical law is no guide for our legislation, even in cases where all admit that morality is concerned; e. g. no one doubts that gluttony and drunken-
ness, and disobedience to parents, are moral offences, yet
no legislature has (in conformity with the Mosaic code)
affixed the penalty of death to them.

' Waiving then the irrelevant questions of what marriages are suitable and desirable, and of the Mosaic law
and foreign canons, let people be brought to the discussion
of the true question ; which is, whether a sufficient public
benefit from the restriction can be proved, to justify the
abridgment of a man's liberty? Whether the evil of
leaving all men to judge for themselves in this point be
greater than that of meddlesome legislative interference
with domestic concerns.

' It savours of puerility and of barbarism to be for
always keeping men in the leading-strings of legislative
injunction and prohibition. "There ought to be a law to

make men do this, and to prevent their doing that!" is just what occurs to an intelligent and well-disposed child of twelve years old.

'We have been told in discussion on this subject, that "men must learn to control their inclinations." There is one inclination which it would be well for members of parliament to control—the inclination to over-governing, the lust of legislation, and of imposing or keeping up restrictions.

'If the opponents of the bill can be brought to confine themselves to the real question—to the making out a sufficient case to justify an abridgment of liberty—I think many of them will themselves perceive that their cause has very little to rest on.

'"There would arise a scandal," they say, "at a sister-in-law residing in a widower's house, if they were allowed to marry; but none at all as long as a marriage is quite out of the question : viz. unnatural by Act of Parliament!"

'I can't believe that in either condition of the law any scandal would arise among people of any sense of decorum, and as for those who are dead not only to virtue but to shame, they would be out of the reach of the law. But whatever little danger there is of scandal, is greater now. If some gossiping neighbours suggested that Mr. A. was likely to marry Miss B., because she was taking charge of her deceased sister's children, the rumour would soon wear away when it was found they did not marry when they might. But if the marriage is illegal, then an attachment might be suspected, such as might tend to illicit intercourse. And the sister-in-law would feel it much more a matter of delicacy and doubt to reside with the widower. But I don't think any decent people would incur suspicion in either case. It is plain, however, that the more shocking and atrocious is any act, the less likely

are tolerably respectable persons to incur the suspicion of
it. Now, undoubtedly, to have illicit intercourse with a
sister-in-law would be doubly atrocious, when the parties
are left at liberty to marry if they will. And it is, therefore, less likely to be suspected if the law were altered,
than as it stands.

' As for legislating with a view to guard any possible
jealousy between husband and wife, we should surely
have enough to do if we were to attempt that !

' A man, or a woman either, had better be at once
prohibited from any second marriage ; or, perhaps, from
marrying any one he had ever seen before his first wife's
death ! For it might be argued " he may become
acquainted after his marriage with some lady who he
thinks would have suited him better than his actual wife ;
and if this be suspected, jealousy may arise !" Now in the
case of sisters, it is worth observing, that a man is in most
cases acquainted with the whole family, and singles out
of all the sisters the one he prefers. So that this is
precisely the case in which jealousy is the least likely to
occur.

' There appears to me, therefore, a total failure in all
the few attempts that have been made to support this
restriction on the true grounds. But the advocates of the
bill have often—to their loss—been seduced into arguing
a different question, on which, though they may be very
right, they are not so triumphantly and clearly in the right.

' They should reiterate that the question is not " whether
a man should or should not contract such a marriage,"
but " whether each should be left to act in the way that
he thinks best, or whether the minority should be
oppressed by the majority, and compelled to conform without any sufficient cause, to the opinion of another, in their
own private concerns !"

'That minority, though it be such, is considerable and respectable.   Lord Campbell, indeed, says in one of his books, in a note, that it is pleaded in behalf of these marriages that they are common ; and the same may be said of bribery and cheating.

'I cannot say I ever heard such a plea urged ; though I cannot prove that it never was.   What I have heard urged, and I think fairly, is that such marriages are common among worthy, respectable, well-conducted people.

'Certainly experience proved for a century and more before the Act of 1835, that the evils to society now apprehended are chimerical, for there was till then no real prohibition of such marriages.

'They were nominally illegal ; but at the expense of a little trouble the law was evaded ; and, I believe, was never enforced.   At any rate, it is quite certain that at that time, and long before, such a marriage was not looked upon as a thing quite impossible and out of the question, as much as between brother and sister.   It was well known that those marriages might and did not seldom take place, and yet no such evil results to society as men are now dreaming of, ensued.   Those dreams are refuted by experience as well as by reason.'

To Lady Osborne.

'Dublin : March 4, 1851.

'One would really wonder at the number of people, not wanting in intelligence or knowledge, who have yielded to the seductions of Tractism or Romanism, were it not that one may see the habit in so many others also of laying aside common-sense in matters pertaining to religion, and thinking it a duty to do so.

'What is found in revelation is what we could never

have learnt or conjectured by reason; else there would have been no need of any revelation. And this most true and evident proposition they confound with another, i. e. that we ought not to use reason in deciding what it is that revelation does teach. This is compared by Locke to a man's refusing to use his eyes, because he has been supplied with a telescope.

'And may it not be that some also have accustomed themselves to tamper with truth, and impair their devoted reverence for it till they have gradually lost the power of distinguishing it at all, and God has "sent them a strong delusion."

'Is it not possible that some may have been trained in the notion that it is allowable and right to join a party with many of whose principles you do not concur, and much of whose conduct you disapprove, on account of the increased efficiency they may give you—the powerful aid in carrying out some objects that you do approve? And when you have once allowed yourself to do this, it is not easy to stop. You will proceed to (1) wish, (2) hope, (3) believe, that those you are acting with are right throughout; and then you obtain the consolation of a thorough-going conscientious conviction, having fashioned your own conscience to suit your convenience and inclination. It is thus that Dean Swift instructs the cook to have dinner ready exactly at the appointed hour by putting the clock back.'

'March 18, 1851.

'My dear Senior,—I wonder to hear you talk of going to France. I hope it is a sign you consider the insurrectionary Jacquerie as nearly put down.

'The revolution did not surprise me. I only wondered some such stroke, on one side or the other, did not occur sooner. I do not know enough of the state of things to form any judgment as to the right and wrong; but my impression was pretty much what you describe Lord Lansdowne's.

' "Kings," says Burke, "will be tyrants from policy when subjects are rebels from principle."

'The description of the Corcyrean sedition in Thucydides is so exact a description of what is now realised, that I wish you would look over it to refresh your memory. You will observe, I think, only one difference, that, while in Greece there were only two parties, in France there are more; and, when this is the case, the strongest party may have a majority opposed to it, which is a temptation to use the more violent means for keeping its power.' . . .

To Lady Osborne, in Answer to a Letter asking various Questions about good and evil Angels, and also on the Romish Practice of Invocation of Saints.

'Dublin: March 23, 1851.

'It was urged that the invocation of saints—which I understood you to have reprobated, not on the ground of its being unscriptural, but of its intrinsic absurdity—implies nothing more incredible than a certain doctrine generally held by Protestants, which you, thereupon, give up. Now, when thus driven from your moorings, there is no saying whither you, or at least some others, may be drifted; for I would undertake to produce (as several Roman Catholics have done) arguments that should appear at least plausible, and would be to many convincing, to show that such and such things which we censure in the Romish system are not at all more at variance with what we should expect and reasonably conjecture, and not more hard to be reconciled with our notions of the Divine nature than the doctrines of the Incarnation, the

Atonement, &c.; and when my opponent had either given up these, or admitted that the Romish doctrines might be true, I would proceed to some other point, and so lead him on step by step, to become Socinian, Rationalist, Deist, Atheist, or else Roman Catholic; and this kind of process is continually going on. A large portion of those who listen to an ingenious Roman Catholic disputant, from whom they fancied themselves quite safe, are by this course converted to Romanism; while probably a still larger proportion become infidels.

'Now, I go to work in a far different way. If anyone suggests to me that perhaps those many millions of pious Christians, who have departed during eighteen centuries, are made ministering spirits by the Most High, along with millions more of angels created long before; and that the Virgin has all these placed under her control as Queen of Heaven, and that she gives them directions, and receives from them reports of all that passes in the Christian world, and intercedes for her worshippers with her Son—I reply, not by setting forth any antecedent improbability or alleged impossibility in all this; I do not urge that it is beyond the reach of omnipotence, or that it is what I cannot reconcile with my own notions of the Deity; nor do I pretend that the Gospel which I do receive is a scheme which I could have conjectured, or that it contains nothing strange and startling; but I ask for Scripture proof. "What you tell me," I say, "is not, indeed, what I could not believe if revealed to me; but it certainly needs a revelation, and I will not believe it without. Show me, therefore, the passages in which the apostles are recorded as practising and enjoining the invocation of the Virgin," &c.

'I lately heard from France of a priest who met the ordinary objections against transubstantiation by saying

that we know nothing at all of substance, all that our
senses inform us of being the attributes, which yet we
never believe to be the very substance, for we do not
consider snow to be whiteness and coldness, &c., but a substance which has those properties; and why may not the
Almighty, if He sees fit, cause one substance to assume
the attributes of another? And I was asked what I
should reply to this. I answered, that, if Christ and His
apostles had expressly declared this, I should believe that,
in some sense or other, quite unintelligible to me, the
substance of bread was changed; but that since it is plain
the disciples did not so understand Him, either at the
time or afterwards, but spoke of the sacramental bread
expressly as bread, I cannot doubt that He was understood, and meant to be understood, as using just the same
kind of figure by which He had (just before) called Himself a door, and a shepherd, and a vine.

'In short, I always cast anchor on the Scriptures,
which is common ground to both parties. I never pretend
to say that the Romish doctrines are to be rejected on
such and such philosophical grounds, but simply because
they are such as we should be sure to have found plainly
revealed if true; and instead of finding this, we find plain
proof that they must have been quite unknown to the
apostles and their hearers. The very authority, therefore,
which they (the Roman Catholics) acknowledge is brought
against them; and this I regard as the most decisive, and
also the most safe (indeed, the only safe) mode of procedure.'

' Dublin: March 27, 1851.

' My dear Senior,—Ministers, you will see, have (in the
Commons) carried their bill[1] by a large majority; not,
however, of real well-wishers, but of persons, I conceive,

---

[1] The Ecclesiastical Titles Bill.

who hope to gather the pear as soon as ripe. No doubt
Lord John's most absurd letter to the Bishop of Durham
was the immediate cause of most of the disturbance and
perplexity. But I think the remoter cause was the
haughty and insolent tone of the papal Bull. All who
vindicate the measure itself speak of its intrinsic reasonableness, but say not a word in vindication of the arrogant
assumption of the language. True it is, a Roman Catholic must think that the Pope has a right to supreme
dominion over all Christians. And it is no less true that
a Protestant thinks that that Church has grossly deformed
and corrupted Christianity. But the Roman Catholics
don't like to be openly and bitterly reproached as cor-
rupters of religion. And they should therefore consider
that Protestants do not like to be spoken of as rebellious
heretics. I suppose, however, that if anyone tells them,
as Decius does Cato—

A style like this becomes a conqueror !

They will answer as Cato does—

A style like this becomes a *Roman* !

Still they ought not to wonder that if they choose to spit
in a man's face, he should knock them down.

‘Some intelligent persons, however, strongly suspect
that the Bull was purposely made as insulting as possible
for the very purpose of provoking a quasi-persecution ;
with a full confidence that they would be safe from anything like penal laws being really enforced, and with a
hope that a plausible cry of persecution being raised,
would produce (as I think not unlikely) a reaction in
their favour. I have been exerting myself to quiet men's
minds so far as to prevent anything of violence being
resorted to ; and also to prevent what the “Times” is

labouring to bring about—a separate legislation for England and for Ireland; than which nothing could more favour the cause of Repeal.

'That article in the "Edinburgh" which I alluded to is written by a Mr. ——, who holds an office in the castle, and who has published some things before.

'There is a most amusing blunder in it, for which he is getting well derided. He writes a great deal about the eminent services of the Roman Catholic priests without any (intentional) allusion to the Protestant clergy, who certainly did exert themselves, even beyond their means, during the famine; but among these priests he gives a conspicuous place to a Mr. Moriarty, who happens to be not only a Protestant, but one who has a very large congregation of converts.'[1]

In the midst of these higher and grave interests, the Archbishop was always ready to turn his mind to any scheme of practical utility, in whatever department. And at this time he drew up and sent to the managers of the first Great Exhibition, the following "Suggestions for a Universal Coinage," a plan which had occurred to his mind many years before.

Suggestions for a Universal Coinage.

'The most selfish man should, on national grounds,

---

[1] "The language of Archbishop Whately, especially in a charge about this time, at once condemning the views of the framers of the Ecclesiastical Titles' Act for England, and condemning the government for not extending it to Ireland, was signalised by Lord Monteagle amongst others as an instance of eccentricity and inconsistency. Whether his doctrine on this subject was practical or not, it was based on a principle which had taken very deep root in his mind; that all exceptional legislation for Ireland was to be deprecated, however plausible the arguments for it, as tending directly towards Repeal."

prize any advantage to himself not the less from its being an equal advantage to his neighbour. And so the most narrow-minded patriot ought to seek a benefit to his country not the less from its being an equal benefit to other countries. But long rivalry and hostility have bred such associations that men often regard with indifference or aversion what may benefit their own country if it give no superiority over other nations, but benefits them equally. If the Exhibition of 1851 shall tend to do away such feelings it will have done great service. The advantage of a uniform currency for all the world need not be dwelt on. The trouble, and often fraud, occasioned by having to change all one's coins in going from one State to another, and the continual fluctuations in the rate of exchange—for instance, between the franc and the sovereign—are evils which no one is unaware of. The Spanish dollar has in many countries approached somewhat to a common currency, being received freely in many places unconnected with Spain; on account of its known purity of metal.

'The additional requisites for a current coin that should be nearly universal, would be: 1st. That it should have no indication of Nationality, so as to awaken national jealousies by appearing on the face of it, to be anywhere a foreign coin. 2ndly. That it should be as far as possible conveniently measured by the known coins or weights of many countries. 3rdly. That it should have some inscriptions intelligible to as many different people as possible.

'Now Troy weight is in very general use throughout the world. And, accordingly, an ounce Troy of silver duly stamped, would be in most places nothing strange; moreover, it is not very remote from many of the coins or moneys of account of many states. It approaches near to the English crown, to the Spanish dollar, to the Portu-guese mil-re, to six francs French, and to definite numbers of several other coins.   It should be inscribed, not with the name and arms of any state or sovereign, but with its designation as an ounce ; together with the time of its being struck.   It should be of a somewhat purer silver than the existing standards ; suppose 34 parts of silver to 2 of copper.

‘ And both sides might be covered with inscriptions in various languages, denoting the equivalent in the exist-ing moneys of the respective nations—something in this way :—

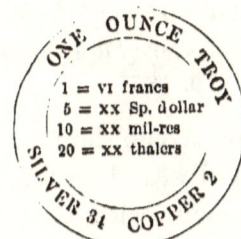
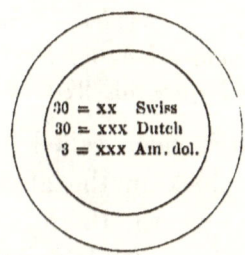

Of course the most elaborate care should be taken in the execution of the die, and if the State which first issued such a coinage should declare it to be a legal tender (without superseding however the non-current coin) and should denounce penalties against impairing or forging such coinage, it is likely that other nations would, one by one, follow the example, to the unspeakable benefit of all the parties concerned.   Of course it would be easy to issue at the same time half-ounces or quarter-ounces, one-tenths and one-hundredths.

‘ If some public-spirited individual concerned in metal-works would try his skill in producing and exhibiting a specimen of such a coin (which might be inferior metal) for exhibition in 1851, he would at any rate gain deserved repute for himself, and might be the means of bringing about a great benefit to all the world.'

It was at this time that the Hon. and Rev. G. Spencer, who had become a monk in the Roman Catholic church under the name of " Father Ignatius," was making a kind of progress through the United Kingdom, with the view of exhorting all Christians, of whatever communion, to engage in earnest prayer for unity. He visited Dublin in April 1851, and held a long conversation with the Archbishop, notes of which were taken down by one of his chaplains.

Notes of an Interview between the Archbishop of Dublin and the Honourable and Rev. George Spencer (Father Ignatius) at the Palace, on Wednesday, April 9, 1851.

'Mr. Spencer called upon the Archbishop at about three o'clock in the afternoon, and was shown into the parlour, where there were present with his Grace his domestic chaplain, Dr. West, two of his examining chaplains, Mr. Mason and Mr. Dixon, and his agent, Mr. Carroll. Mr. Spencer was dressed in the costume of his order, which consists of a loose gown of coarse dark cloth, secured round his waist by a leather belt, and meeting close round his throat; over this was a short cloak of the same material and colour. On the left shoulder of each was a badge apparently of tin, painted black, of the form of a heart surmounted by a shamrock. On the heart was printed in white letters, " Jesu Christi Passio," and on the shamrock was a cross. He had a brass crucifix, probably a reliquary, hanging by a small iron chain from his belt ; and he wore a peculiarly-shaped hat, with a very broad brim turned up at the sides, and a round crown. In stature he is rather below the middle size, his countenance is more of the Celtic than of the

Saxon character, and his features resemble on a small
scale those of the celebrated O'Connell. His voice is
feeble and undecided, and his accent slightly nasal. In
manners he is mild and courteous.

' After the usual salutations had been interchanged, the
Archbishop remarked to Mr. Spencer that he had called
upon a day of the week when he would be always sure
of finding him at home and attended by his chaplains,
" for," said his Grace, " these gentlemen are all, my chaplains, though they are not, all my chaplains."

' " I see," said Mr. Spencer, taking his seat, " that you
have not forgotten your Logic."

' " Talking of Logic," said the Archbishop, " you know,
I suppose, that my work on Logic has been prohibited
by the Pope?"

' Mr. Spencer professed ignorance of the circumstance.

' " It has then," said the Archbishop, " and I have been
variously congratulated and condoled with by my friends
on the occasion. There is nothing in the circumstance,
however, to cause me any surprise, except that the Pope
should have considered the work of sufficient importance
to be formally prohibited, as I never either intended or
professed to exclude from it controverted points. You
know, I suppose, that Dr. Cullen has also condemned the
book, and has stated that my object in writing it was to
corrupt the minds of the Catholic youth?"

' Mr. Spencer was not aware of the fact.

' The Archbishop then informed him that Dr. Cullen had
brought forward the charge in a letter addressed to his
(Dr. Cullen's) clergy in December last. " The work, however," pursued his Grace, " was written originally for the
use of my pupils in Oxford, and was published for the
sake of any who, with my name on the title-page, might
desire to read it. In books which I write for the use of

schools where education is given to children of different
religious persuasions, I follow of course a different plan.
In these I abstain from all points of controversy; but in
my other works, the only rules I lay down for myself in
reference to such points are not to misrepresent the
opinions or statements of those who differ from me, and
not to speak uncharitably of them. And I wish that
Mr. Cahill, of whom you were just speaking," said his
Grace, turning to Mr. Dixon, " would observe the same
rules. You have heard, I suppose," continued the Archbishop, addressing his visitor, " that Mr. Cahill has been
publishing sermons and letters containing the grossest
misrepresentations of the actions and intentions of the
government and of individuals, and calculated to inflame
and exasperate in the highest degree the minds of the
ignorant people into whose hands these publications will
fall ?"

' Mr. Spencer deprecated imputing to Mr. Cahill the
intention of producing the effects which his Grace had
anticipated from his pamphlets.

' To this the Archbishop replied, that of course we should
be very cautious in imputing a bad motive to any person,
where a reasonable doubt could exist as to his intention,
but that this was not the case in the present instance; for
the avowed object of Mr. Cahill was to excite the indignation of the Irish people against the English government, and he sought to effect this object by making
statements respecting individuals which he must have
known to be false. Thus he accused Mr. Drummond of
having not only spoken disrespectfully of the Virgin
Mary, but having also applied to her epithets applicable
only to the most abandoned of the female sex. " Now,"
said the Archbishop, " though I am very far from desiring
to defend Mr. Drummond, though I think his speech a

most unfortunate one, and though I heartily wished he had been at the bottom of the Red Sea when he made it, yet, as they say even a certain black gentleman should receive his due, it must be admitted that Mr. Drummond was not guilty of the charges brought against him by Mr. Cahill."

'Mr. Spencer said that he had read Mr. Drummond's letter, in which that gentleman had, as he conceived, exculpated himself by stating that he had not meant to speak disrespectfully of the Blessed Virgin, and that he, Mr. Spencer, felt that credit should be given to Mr. Drummond's statement.

'The Archbishop replied, that it did not require a knowlege of the letter to prove that Mr. Cahill's charges were unfounded. No newspaper had reported Mr. Drummond to have used disrespectful language of the Virgin Mary, much less to have applied to her the epithets referred to by Mr. Cahill, although they all condemned or lamented his speech, and described the dissatisfaction excited by several passages of it which they reported, and which were certainly bad enough.

' Mr. Spencer replied, that for his part he must confess, that when he first read Mr. Drummond's speech, he thought he had spoken disrespectfully of the Blessed Virgin.

' " How ? " said the Archbishop, " the only allusion he made to the Virgin Mary was, to speak in a tone of contempt of some relics ascribed to her, and, as he believed, without sufficient evidence. Would you think I spoke disrespectfully of you, if I spoke contemptuously of some letter which I believed and pronounced to be a forgery and falsely ascribed to you ; or would you accuse me of speaking disrespectfully of our Lord, if I said that I did not believe the holy coat of Trèves to have been His,

and that even if it had, I did not think it should be made
an object of adoration?"

'Mr. Spencer did not seem disposed to continue his
defence or apology for Mr. Cahill, he preferred passing
on to the object of his visit, which was to make some
remarks on a letter he had received from Dr. West,
relative to the subjects discussed at a former interview
which he had with the Archbishop, and in which he
sought to press upon his Grace's attention the importance,
at the present crisis, of all serious persons making a combined effort for the promotion of Christian unity.   He
said that he fully concurred with the opening remarks in
this letter on the importance of making truth the first
object in all our pursuits, and that he also admitted the
justice of the observation made by the Archbishop and
repeated by Dr. West, that different persons entertain
very different notions of Christian unity; some, for instance, holding that it implies submission to a central
government and a visible head of the church, while
others believe that it is of a purely spiritual character.
He felt, therefore, the force of the objection, that while
persons hold such contradictory opinions as to the nature
of unity, it is impossible for them to be united in their
pursuit of it; but it occurred to him that his original proposal might be so modified as to evade this objection.
He thought that all might unite in praying that God
would promote among mankind, by such means as seemed
best to His infinite wisdom, unity in the truth as it appeared to Him.

' To this the Archbishop replied that such a petition was
equivalent in point of fact to the second clause in Our
Lord's Prayer, " Thy kingdom come ;" that, moreover, as
Mr. Spencer must know very well, we are in the habit of
offering up a petition in one of the prayers of our daily

service, that " all who profess and call themselves Christians may be led into the way of truth, and hold the faith in unity of spirit, in the bond of peace, and in righteousness of life," and that we thus show that we are not insensible of the importance of that unity in the truth which Mr. Spencer was now advocating, nor negligent in praying for its promotion among mankind.

' Mr. Spencer admitted that all this was true. He remembered, moreover, that on one occasion when he waited on the Bishop of London, his Lordship had called his attention to a prayer for unity in the service appointed for the day of the Queen's accession, which embodied almost all the Scripture phrases relative to the subject. Still he desired that greater prominence should be given to the topic at the present time, both in our prayers and exhortations. He believed it to be one of paramount and vital importance. " When a great people," said Mr. Spencer, " like the English and Irish are disunited on a subject in which they take such an interest as that of religion, they cannot be united in the pursuit of any political or social object."

' The Archbishop replied that he fully concurred with all Mr. Spencer said as to the desirableness and importance of unity in the truth, and the evils of disunion. That the only point now at issue between them appeared to be the best mode of attaining to this unity. Mr. Spencer seemed to think it should be sought directly ; he (the Archbishop), on the contrary, thought it should be sought through truth. " For," said the Archbishop, " it is obvious that if any number of persons, individually, hold the truth in its integrity, they will all agree and be united in their views of it. The best mode, therefore, of promoting unity in the truth is to promote the dissemination of truth. Truth is one ; all who hold the truth will be

at one. And so, if we desire to promote among children
at school that unity and harmony which result from
mutual forbearance, &c., the most effectual way of gaining
our object will be to press upon every child individually
the duty of exercising those feelings of charity, toleration,
and forbearance. This is in fact the only practical way
of seeking to attain the end we have in view. If we seek
to attain it directly by pressing upon the children the
importance of being united, the evils resulting from disunion, &c., the most turbulent in the school, the most
intolerant, and the least forbearing will heartily assent to
the justice of our observations, and will immediately proceed to inculcate and enforce a unity which shall consist
in subjection to themselves; and thus our attempts to
promote unity will end in increasing dissension. No;
the right way is to press upon each individual child the
duties of forbearance, toleration, and charity; and this is,
in fact," continued the Archbishop, " the course adopted
in the schools in connexion with the National Board.
There are nearly five thousand of these schools through
Ireland, giving instruction to nearly half a million of
children; and in every one of them is hung up a card,
containing what are called general rules, the object of
which is to inculcate upon the children the duties which
I have so often referred to of forbearance, &c. The best
way then," said the Archbishop, "and in fact, as I have
shown, the only way, to promote unity in the truth
among men is to impress upon them the duty and the
necessity of their individually seeking after truth, and
embracing it when found, and of being tolerant, forbearing, and charitable towards all who differ from them in
opinion."

' The Archbishop then dwelt upon the importance of
cultivating a love of truth for its own sake, and of form-

ing such a habit of mind as shall lead its professor to embrace any opinion, however contrary to his prejudices, which he may be honestly convinced is true, and to reject any, no matter how congenial to his tastes or sentiments, or how strongly supported by authority, if it were proved to him to be false. And the Archbishop professed himself always ready to act by this rule.

' Mr. Spencer seemed startled. He inquired whether his Grace held all his opinions thus loosely ; whether for instance, he regarded as a doubtful and unsettled point the inspiration of the sacred Scriptures.

' The Archbishop replied that Mr. Spencer appeared to misunderstand him. He did not mean to say that his opinions on such points as he had examined and made up his mind on were wavering or undecided. He meant that having embraced the opinions which he held because he believed them to be true, he was ready to renounce them if they were shown to be false. While he held them, he was of course convinced of their truth. He would explain his meaning by an illustration. Mr. Spencer was probably acquainted with the different methods in which type was set up for printing. It was sometimes cast in stereotype plates, sometimes arranged in moveable forms. The latter was just as steady and solid as the former, and possessed this additional advantage, that if any word or passage was found to be incorrect, it could be altered and corrected : this was impossible in stereotype plates. In these if an error was detected, there was no means of remedying it. "Now," said the Archbishop, "I hold my opinion in moveable forms and not in stereotype."

' He said he would give an example. About five or six years ago he had preached an ordination sermon on the subject of the prevailing tendency in the human mind to desire an infallible guide in religious matters. In this sermon he had dwelt upon the fact that when St. Paul was taking leave of the elders of Ephesus at Miletus, under the impression that he should never see them again, and warned them of the dangers which threatened them and their flocks, he yet never once alluded to the existence of any infallible guide, of any visible head of the Church on earth, St. Peter or St. Peter's successor at Rome, Antioch, or elsewhere, to whom they should have recourse in their difficulties, and by adherence and obedience to whom they should keep themselves and their people from error. From this the Archbishop had concluded that St. Paul did not know of the existence of any such guide. He could not on any other supposition account for the Apostle's silence on such a subject at such a time. And he felt the more strongly convinced that this view of the matter was correct from the circumstance that, although Dr. O'Connell of Waterford had undertaken to reply to this sermon, yet he left this point, the prominent one in the discourse, unnoticed. "Still," said the Archbishop, " if you, Mr. Spencer, or any member of your church, can give any satisfactory account of the Apostle's conduct on this memorable occasion consistent with the views of the Church of Rome as to the existence of an infallible and visible head of the Church on earth, I am open to conviction; I am ready to change my opinion on the subject, when it is shown to be erroneous."

'Mr. Spencer, however, was evidently unable to furnish any such explanation. He appeared restless and uneasy from the moment the Archbishop introduced the subject of infallibility. He rose from his seat, and his good manners alone prevented his leaving the room before his Grace had finished speaking. As soon as he concluded, however, he briefly remarked that Dr. West had kindly forwarded him a copy of the sermon to which his Grace had been alluding, and without making any comment upon it, said that having now disposed of the business in reference to which he had taken the liberty of waiting upon the Archbishop, he would beg leave to withdraw.'

The following letter to Mrs. Arnold throws more light on the then state of Ireland, and especially of the suffering clergy. The little book alluded to in it, 'Paddy's Leisure Hours in the Poor-house,' is a tale illustrative of the effects of the Irish famine and Poor-law, written by a friend, and published under his patronage, which at the time excited much interest, from the truthful and vivid manner in which the facts of the case were brought forward.

'Dublin: April 15, 1851.

'My dear Mrs. Arnold,—The second part of No. 5 of the "Cautions" I do not send you, as it does more good to have it ordered at a shop; so I only notify to you, and beg you to make known its being out. But I have ordered for you the new edition of "Paddy's Meditations," with an addition which I think excellent. I trust you will promote the sale of this also, if you can, as any profit from it will go to the starving clergy of Ireland. Our funds for their relief are nearly exhausted; but their distress is far from being at an end. Several have to pay, out of a small income, eight or ten or twelve shillings in the pound for poor-rate, and withal they have not the satisfaction of seeing the poor relieved. The workhouses are crowded with paupers doing nothing, while the fields are lying untilled, from the capital which would have employed labourers having been abused in keeping men idle. The paupers are like Pharaoh's lean kine, who ate up the fat ones, and yet were still as lean as ever.

'Miss ——, the friend of Jane's friend, Mrs. ——, is much pleased with numbers three and five, but does not like two and four—I suspect from the very circumstance that makes those the greatest favourites with most, the familiar illustrations. There are persons of minds so constituted that I am convinced many of our Lord's parables would seem to them (if seen for the first time, and without knowledge of the author) extremely indecorous. They cannot distinguish between comparing together two things or persons, and comparing the cases or transactions relating to those things; and thence would suppose it affirmed that Christians are actually like fishes, or fig-trees, or sheep.

'And again, if any fallacy or folly which has been connected with religion is ridiculed, they cannot distinguish this from ridicule of the religion itself; as if they were to deem it an injury to a tree to clear away the lichen and moss, and other parasites that had overgrown it.

'And again, there are some whose organ of veneration seems to be concentrated on words instead of things. Such a person is not scandalised at F. Newman's saying, with most decorous gravity, that our Lord was a faulty character; but when a piece of modern history is narrated in the style of our authorised version of Scripture, for the purpose of showing how open it would be to the kind of cavils with which sacred history has been assailed, this is regarded as horrible profanation! I could not but compare this whimsical inconsistency (as it seems to me) to the conduct of the people of Hawaii (Owhyhee), who murdered Captain Cook, and cut his body to pieces, but—regarding him, as it seems they did, as a being of superior order—carried about with them pieces of his bones as a kind of amulets, which they regarded with superstitious veneration. You may show this to K. (I beg pardon,

Mrs. Forster), as I know she does not mind my speaking my mind freely.'

The 'Creeds of Christendom,' by Mr. Greg, had just appeared; and many were naturally anxious to see this attack on Christianity answered by an able hand. Mrs. Arnold wrote to the Archbishop, mentioning the earnest wish expressed by Mr. Graves, a clergyman in her neighbourhood, that he (the Archbishop) should undertake this task himself. The following is his answer:—

'April 26, 1851.

'My dear Mrs. Arnold,—After reading the enclosed, please to forward it.

'I am honoured by Mr. Graves's belief that I am capable of answering Mr. Greg, but I trust he is mistaken in thinking that no one else could, for it does not answer to have many irons in the fire. Men sometimes make the same mistake as to their powers and their time, that many do as to their income. I have known a man who thought, and truly, that he could afford to keep hounds, and that his income would admit of a fine conservatory; and that he might sit in Parliament; and that he could keep a house in town, and give fine parties; but, like many others, he attempted all, and was ruined. In like manner, some are tempted to engage in this and that and the other work, from feeling conscious that they could accomplish any one; and so they leave them all unfinished, or so ill-done that they had better have been left alone.

'I, in particular, have less work in me than many others, and my only chance of doing anything well is—though I cannot exclude interruptions, yet—to be very careful not to attempt too much. It may seem strange to many that those little volumes of lectures—most of them ready written, as sermons—took me, in merely preparing for the press, about four months' incessant work; I mean that I never let a single day pass without doing something to them. And the little tract on religious worship, which was almost entirely a compilation, took me, in like manner, six months!

'I am now engaged with the "Cautions;"[1] that is, in merely giving suggestions from time to time, and revising. If anything in Mr. Greg's book should seem to call for notice in the "Cautions," we will see about it. But if, in addition to all my unavoidable official business, I were to turn aside from the "Cautions," and enter on some new field, the result would be that I should fail in all. It is vain for me to set up for an "admirable Crichton."'

The Archbishop was now in parliament, but not attending very regularly.[2] He was residing near London, and much harassed by family anxiety and sickness.

---

[1] The compilation entitled 'Cautions for the Times.'

[2] He spoke, however, this year rather more frequently than usual; on the bill for removing the disqualification of the Jews, on transportation, and on the projects for the revival of convocation—as to which he always abode by the opinion, that a regular government for the Church was desirable, but a clerical convocation most objectionable. Speaking of the assumption that the party calling for its assembly was the most numerous, he told, after his manner, the following story:—'He was informed once that a violent opposition existed in a particular parish to a proposed alteration of a road, at which he was very much surprised, because the alteration was conducive to public convenience. In order to ascertain the real opinion of the inhabitants of the district, he sent to each house a black bean and a white bean, with directions that those who were opposed to the alterations should return a black bean, and vice versâ. The return was twenty-nine black and three hundred white beans. Yet the twenty-nine black beans called themselves "the parish;" and it was hardly necessary to say that they made twice as much noise as the three hundred white beans.'

The following is to Mrs. Hill, who had asked him as to the truth of some report she had heard of a remark he had made on desultory tendencies of mind :—

'Nov. 23, 1851.

' My dear Mrs. Hill,—Very likely I did say what you report, though I have no recollection of it.

' Certainly I should not recommend mathematics as the remedy. Though one might naturally expect that the fault of mere mathematicians would be an over-rigid demand for demonstration in all subjects, I have found the fact to be the reverse. They generally, when they come to any other subject, throw off all regard to order and accuracy, like the feasting of the Roman Catholics before and after Lent. With them, mathematics is " Attention ! " and everything else " Stand at ease ! "

' The defect of mathematics as an exclusive or too predominant study is, that it has no connexion with human affairs, and affords no exercise of judgment, having no degrees of probability.

' On the comparison between that, and what is called moral reasoning, you will see some remarks in the dissertations appended to the "Logic ;" and, in the "Rhetoric," you will see remarks on the importance of imagination in the study of history, which are, as far as I know, not to be found elsewhere.

' Do you know anything of the Mormonites ? They are an increasing sect in some parts of England, especially about Leamington, where a servant of ours picked up some of their tracts and became a half convert. The ground is ready ploughed for their seed by such writers as are noticed in " Cautions," xi. and xii., and by those who act on their principles.

' I want some one to write a little tract to open the eyes

of the poor people in England, in a style and of a shape
and size suitable to them; but I myself, and all those I
have been accustomed to employ, have their hands more
than full for a good while to come. I wish you would
try your hand. I can get you the materials—viz. the
Mormonite tracts, and the true history of the rise of the
sect; for it has been well described, and the matter well
investigated for the upper classes, but not so as to reach
the lower. The poison is retailed in the streets in
halfp'orths, and the antidote is to be had only in large
casks. Do pray try.[1]

' Yours truly,
' RD. DUBLIN.'

*To the Archbishop of Canterbury in reference to the Bishop
of Exeter's Proceedings in the Gorham Controversy.*

'Dublin: Nov. 30, 1851.

' My dear Lord,—In ordinary circumstances, I should
deem it impertinent to come forward unmasked to give an
opinion on the proceedings of one of my brethren; but
the censure which some clergymen of another diocese
have presumed to pronounce on your Grace, in a tone of
no small arrogance, makes it, I think, not only allowable,
but a duty for me to return my thanks for the firm,
temperate, and dignified protest which your Grace has
put forth in reply.

' The brevity and the forbearance of what you have
said is the more to be commended, because no one could
have called it unreasonable if your Grace had strongly
rebuked them for having studied the Articles so little, or
to so little purpose.

---

[1] This trial was afterwards made by Mrs. Whately, in a little tract on
Mormonism, which had considerable circulation.

'My views on the subject are expressed in pp. 151–2 of the little tract I take the liberty of transmitting, in case your Grace should not have been acquainted with the publication.

'These little tracts are drawn up in a popular form, with a view to extensive circulation among the people, by one of my chaplains, with my assistance and supervision; and their very low price has even already enabled some who think with me on the subjects in question to disseminate them pretty widely, though not near to the extent that the present crisis requires.

'I might have added to the passage just referred to, that the Rubric prefixed to the Ordination Service is utterly misrepresented by those who pretend to find in it what they have vainly sought for in the Articles. Our reformers are evidently vindicating their own practice, not laying down a rule that is to bind all men; and they vindicate themselves from any suspicion of introducing any novelty by an appeal to the precedent, which, they assert, may be established from Scripture and ancient writers. They do not pretend that Scripture alone would be sufficient for this; and, therefore, if they are understood to be laying down a dogma as to one of the essentials of salvation, they must be regarded as grossly contradicting their own article on the sufficiency of Scripture.

'But if any Church should determine (which it would undoubtedly be competent to do) to re-establish such an order as the Deaconesses (or "widows"), and should state, as a justification, that "it appears from Scripture and ancient writers that such female ministers were appointed in the apostolic age and long after," would anyone in his senses consider this as amounting to a denial of the character of a

Christian Church to any community that had not deaconesses?

'Yet such an interpretation is exactly such as some persons put on our Rubric!'

To his Son-in-Law, Charles Wale.

'Dec. 20, 1851.

'My dear Charles,—I am greatly alarmed at the tendency I see in some good and (generally) sensible persons towards a reaction, in favour of anyone who will but join in denouncing Tractism.

'The revolutions, past and present, of France, are instructive (to those who have ears to hear) on the subject of reactions. A long and galling tyranny had so embittered every mind against kings and nobles, that they were ready to throw themselves unsuspectingly into the arms of any who did but deny and oppose them. By-and-by, the excesses of terrorists, socialists, red republicans, &c., became so shocking that the people were ready—and appear now to be so—to trust anyone who will but assume despotic power, and preserve order at any cost.

'Much the same is our case now in religious and ecclesiastical matters. Many, even of those who have had opportunities of availing themselves of the experience and good judgment of candid and intelligent men, seem resolved to throw away all these advantages, and to trust implicitly to those who are but of the opposite party to the Tractites. Anything said by them—even by those who have proved themselves careless of truth—is at once believed, without seeking for evidence or listening to it. Anything said against any of these, however well authenticated, is at once set down as a falsehood or as the result of prejudice; for this last word is most in the mouth of those who are in reality under the influence of the thing—

a " prejudice " being, in reality, a judgment formed without evidence.

' And thus I see people throwing themselves into the arms of a party, and even conscious of doing so, but satisfying themselves that at least this party is not so bad as the opposite, and that at least they do not avow deception; but " many sell stinking fish who do not cry it," though it is reasonable to conclude that it is sold by those who do cry it.'

CHAPTER IX.

1852.

IN the early part of 1852 he paid a short visit to England, but the rest of the year, with the exception of his regular visitation tours, &c., was spent at Redesdale, where his daughter and her family were again their guests. During a great part of the seven following years, much of their time was spent under the Archbishop's roof, and this was to him an increasing source of comfort and pleasure. In his son-in-law's society he had the kind of intercourse he most enjoyed and valued; that of a discerning, right-judging, and intelligent companion entering into all his pursuits, and fully sympathising in the high moral tone of his mind; while his grandchildren, as they grew up around him, were sources of continued pleasure and interest. Naturally fond of children, his delight in these little ones was a prominent feature in his declining life; his tenderness and affection for them, and interest in their sports, were such as could hardly have been looked for in one so habitually absorbed in matters of the highest moment.

To the children of his son he showed no less constant affection and kindness; the eldest was for a considerable time an inmate of his family, and treated as an adopted child; and when at a later period, these children were all permanently established under his roof, his interest in all their pleasures and concern for their enjoyment and comfort was manifest.

To Charles Wale.

'Dublin: Feb. 15, 1852.

'I need not say how fully I concur in what you say about party. It cannot be too often and earnestly urged; for I find many men, and more women, not wanting in intelligence, and what is more, who have seen and bitterly experienced the evils of party, who are led by that very circumstance to throw themselves into the arms of a party, merely because it is the opposite of that which is the immediate object of their dread; just as if experience of military science should induce some simple people to invite an army to rescue them. "For my part," says a poor woman in the Tales of the Genii, "I think all women are rebels, for they all plunder us alike."

'It is wonderful and shocking to perceive how those who are calling on men to throw off popish thraldom will submit, and try to force others to submit, to popes of their own; and how the disregard of truth, the narrow and uncharitable bigotry, and the bitter persecuting spirit which they loudly censure in Roman Catholics, they will at the same time approve in their own party.'

The following letter to Lady Osborne explains itself. Much interest was excited at this time by the newly-published disclosures as to the working of the 'Sister-hoods' at Plymouth and Devonport.

'April 10, 1852.

'My dear Lady Osborne,—Have you read Mr. Spurrell's pamphlets, and Miss Campbell's, on Miss Sellon's establishment, and her answer? They are very curious and important documents. You may be very sure I am fully aware that the High Church party are quite as ready to persecute when they get the upper hand, as the Low Church. Both are men. And both parties are equally aware how utterly I am averse to every party. And it is quite true, as you observe, that the one will do everything in the name of the church-formularies, as the other does in that of the Bible. In truth, however, neither party makes either of these the real standard, but their interpretation; which may chance to be very different from yours or mine. The one is ready—even avowedly—to understand our formularies " in a non-natural sense;" and the other set down everyone, however well-read in Scripture, as "not knowing the Gospel," who does not adopt their views. And it may be added, that as they adopt virtually the Romish notion of an infallible interpreter of Scripture to whom everyone must submit his own private judgment, on pain of being set down as heterodox (only substituting their party for the Pope of Rome), so they are equally ready with the Romanists to resort to Tradition when there is no Scripture to their purpose. For they appeal to (an alleged) tradition of the apostles having transferred the commands relative to the Sabbath from the seventh day of the week to the first—a transfer of which certainly Scripture gives no hint, but rather contradicts it. Still they have this advantage over the opposite party; that they really do encourage everyone to study Scripture, bitterly as they revile him if he does not adopt their interpretation of it; and a man is thus enabled to have a chance, at least, of detecting any errors in the system he may have been taught. The opposite party—as is set forth in one of the " Cautions "—do certainly lead men to neglect, and ultimately avoid the study of Scripture.'

'May 29, 1852.

'My dear Hinds,—I have been devouring your Report.[1] It is an admirable one, and though too good to be at once fully carried out, I cannot but hope it will produce an effect, in some points, even independently of any legislation.

'You seem to have had a great hankering after Senior's proposal for a Government nomination of Heads, though you shrank from decidedly recommending it. I think you might have hit on a compromise by recommending something like the Oriel mode. Every fellow is at liberty to name whom he pleases, and the Lord Chancellor to choose from among them. I believe, indeed, that in practice they have always contrived to agree, so as to leave the Chancellor no choice. But the elections have been, I know, very different from what they would otherwise have been. Provost Eveleigh was elected, by a small minority, against an unfit man whose supporters knew that the decision would be likely to go against them.

---

[1] That of the Commissioners to inquire into the State of the University of Oxford.

That election at Lincoln would not, under such a rule, have taken place.

'I rather wonder you so readily acquiesce in the fraud (for it is no other) of the degrees of M.A., B.D., &c.   It is the more a fraud and the more a disgrace to the University, since at the London University M.A. does imply a severe examination.

'The same censure applies to Dublin University, and I am thinking how we can mend the evil.   Perhaps it might be allowed to each professor to give, on reception of a small fee, a certificate to anyone of having attended his lectures, and passed (on paper) a satisfactory examination in them; and then, three such certificates (in such and such specified courses) might be accepted as equivalent to an examination for degree; and if a man had only one of these certificates, or had them from some other course, this would still be a benefit to him as far as it went.

'What do you think?

'If you have time to look at that little tale I mentioned ("Early Experiences"—Grant & Griffiths, Paternoster Row), I should like your opinion on a short discussion in it of daily services in church; at which discussion some are scandalised.

'The services were no doubt designed by our reformers, who, indeed (most unfortunately), have no special service for Sundays.   But, then, in the days when so few could read, domestic worship and private reading of Scripture could not have been so general as they might be now.

'If there were daily service in church, in those cases only where the minister's other duties would be equally well performed, it would be so far well (I mean as far as regards the minister).   But there is surely a great danger that the mere mechanical performance of a duty (by the clergyman), which requires neither learning nor ability, nor sound judgment, nor assiduous care, nor anxious responsibility, should seduce those who are, in mind, indolent, to substitute this for labours which call for all those qualifications; that the mere turning of the handle of a barrel-organ should be found easier though more monotonous work, than qualifying oneself for the part of a good musician.'

To Miss Crabtree.

'Dublin: June 15, 1852.

'I wish you would try your hand at a little parable for young folks; I and my assistants are too busy with other things. You have often observed, I dare say, the cabbage-caterpillar (and perhaps others) that had been pierced by the ichneumon-fly. It goes on quite sound and thriving throughout its larva-life, feeding till the time comes at which it should become a pupa, and then a butterfly (psyche, the soul, as the Greeks called it); and then the ichneumon grubs come out, and leave an empty skin, having fed merely on the enclosed embryo-butterfly. How many of our fellow-creatures seem to be in an analogous condition!

'You might throw this into a little dialogue between a parent and child.[1]   'Ever yours, truly,

'RD. WHATELY.'

In this year the Cork Exhibition was opened. A course of lectures was delivered in the pavilion of the Exhibition building, and the Archbishop was requested to deliver the inaugural lecture of the series, on Tuesday, June 29, 1852. The subject of the lecture was 'Popular Education,' and in it he took pains to confute the favourite common-

---

[1] A dialogue on this subject, though not by the lady addressed, did afterwards appear in the 'Leisure Hour.'

places about the danger of 'a little learning,' and to point out the fallacy of the assertion—at that time put forth strongly by the Roman Catholics—that all departments of secular education should be under the direct control of religious teachers.

Mrs. Hill had made some objections to the tone of some of the late 'Cautions for the Times.' The letter suggested the following answer :—

'August 29, 1852.

'My dear Mrs. Hill,—You may easily conjecture how earnestly we have been appealed to by those who are not exactly Tractites, but of somewhat High Church principle. "True, the Tractites have some of them gone much too far ; but they have done on the whole great good, by protesting against irregularity and insubordination, and fanaticism and schism. Let your censures be confined to those who are causing disorders in our Church such as must end in its overthrow, and thus remove the strongest barrier against popery as well as against infidelity. Men who, after obtaining orders in our Church, seek every opportunity of hurling defiance at its authorities and ordinances ; who are ready to exchange pulpits with self-ordained tinkers and cobblers for the purpose of opposing or converting papists, but who end in making converts to the Darbyites and the Plymouth Brethren and Irvingites ; who show their Christian charity and meekness by assuming to their party the title of ' evangelical,' calling every one a ' Socinian,' who does not adopt exactly their opinions ; who presume to take on them the character of inspired prophets, calling everything they put forth a suggestion of the Holy Spirit, and without in words claiming infallibility, denouncing all who do not agree with them as 'not knowing the Gospel ;' men who declare that 'God's people ought not to feel any uneasiness on account

of their sins, since it is God that suffers his people to
commit grievous sins in order to humble them, and who
all the time regards them with no diminished favour!'—
these and avowed infidels are the persons on whom your
censures should be poured, but spare the maintainers of
Church principle!"

'Thus it is that you will always find the rats crying out
for mercy to the rats, and destruction to the mice; while
the mice say kill the rats, but spare the mice. If we
were to listen to such suggestions from both sides (and
this would be more fair than to listen to one, and to be
deaf on the other ear), we should spare all faults of all
persons. But if we listen to the voice of truth and justice, we shall spare none. And I think you will perceive,
on reflection, how much strength is added to our censure
of High Church faults, by our censuring the opposite also.
It is then seen that it is the love of truth and not party-
spirit that influences us. And we shall be proved to be
opposing error, not because maintained by such and such
persons, but because it is error. You will also, I think,
readily understand that it is not from thinking lightly of
your judgment, and that of others who deprecate our procedure, that we are incited by your disapprobation to act
the more decidedly and earnestly in the very way you
deprecate. On the contrary, the more widespread and
deeply rooted any views are which we cannot adopt, and
the more they prevail among sensible and well-disposed
people, the more we must exert ourselves against them.
The greatest compliment to an invader's power is to
submit to him at once; the next greatest is to raise as
powerful an army as possible to resist him strenuously.

'Very truly yours,
'Rd. Dublin.'

Mrs. Hill was at this time planning an article on American slavery, apropos of 'Uncle Tom's Cabin.'

'Sept. 14, 1852.

'My dear Mrs. Hill,—It is of little use to write on such a subject convincingly to all except the holders of slaves, and those connected with the system. And these will escape if you leave them (as the author of "Uncle Tom" has) a loop-hole.

'Indeed, it is very easy to gain the approbation of those who are already of your opinion, and so very difficult to change anyone's opinion, that one is sometimes tempted to doubt whether it is of any use at all to write, except for fame or profit.

'I received a letter the other day from an old friend, a man not at all below the average, relative to the "Cautions;" great part of which he highly approves, but utterly dissents from what is said of Apostolical Succession. And so doubtless it is with ninety-nine in a hundred of the readers; each approving of what coincides with his own previous conviction, and rejecting what does not. If I could think that forty of the four thousand readers of the "Cautions" had been led by them to change any opinion, this I should account a rare success. You yourself are above the average both in intelligence and candour; yet I don't know that there is a single point on which I have altered your views. Where, then, I have sometimes said to myself, is the good of writing at all?

'I believe it really does produce an effect in time, whether for good or for evil.

'Anything falling in the way of a mind that is—on that point, fallow — not pre-occupied with any decision, or wavering—may instil, or keep out, much that is either useful or noxious, as the case may be. And this I conceive is nearly the whole real effect of writing, as far as concerns propagation of doctrines.

　　　　　　　　　　　'Yours very truly,
　　　　　　　　　　　　　　'Rd. Dublin.'

Mrs. Hill replied by mentioning several distinct instances in which the Archbishop's arguments had led her to change her mind. His answer follows :—

　　　　　　　　　　　　　'Dublin : Sept. 18, 1852.

'My dear Mrs. Hill,—To you I need not say what I have said in the Charge, that I value not a man's professing truth which is not truth to him. And my intimacy with Dr. Arnold is alone a sufficient proof of my practical toleration. But what I wish you to keep in mind is that the vehemence of my opposition to anyone's views is no mark of my thinking lightly of him, but the reverse.

'I had no idea I had altered your views on so many points. But you are no rule for the generality.

'As a general rule, the water from the engine should be poured on the places adjoining the conflagration, but which are not yet on fire.

'It is a very curious fact that you advert to, of our unequal sympathy with physical and mental suffering. As for the inflicter, he may sometimes not perceive the pain he is giving ; but often he does, and delights in it. But the bystanders, perhaps, do not so fully enter into the sufferer's feelings. It is remarkable, again, that to insult and triumph over bodily weakness is always reprobated as the basest cowardice ; but not so if it be natural weakness of understanding.

'Query : Is there not something besides sympathy in the case of physical suffering, that kind of nervous shudder which makes some people faint away at the description of wounds? And may not this partly account for your phenomenon?'

Mrs. Hill was inclined to shrink from the task her correspondent had proposed to her. She urged the Archbishop rather to undertake the work himself.

'Sept. 27, 1852.

'My dear Mrs. Hill,—Every sermon costs me as much time and labour to write as to furnish the matter and subsequent corrections for six or seven. And I have more business to occupy my time and thoughts than you probably suppose. When you see me lounging about the garden and pruning a rose-bush, you probably suppose that I am thinking of nothing else; when, perhaps, I am in fact deliberating on some weighty matters on which I have to decide. And all the time I can spare from duties which I have no right to neglect, is absorbed by the "Cautions." You, I dare say, would advise me to drop the "Cautions," and turn my mind to other matters. But though this advice might be right in itself, I should be very wrong in following it against my own deliberate judgment. I have undertaken a difficult and painful task, which appears to me of great importance; and having put my hand to the plough, I must not look back. Since inspiration has ceased, I do not see what fuller assurance anyone can have, that God wills him to do so and so, than his own judgment resulting from deliberate and prayerful reflection. His decision may not be infallibly right. If he could be sure of that, he would be inspired. But it must be right for him to follow the best guide Providence has vouchsafed him. God made the moon as well as the sun; and when He does not see fit to grant us the sunlight, He means us to guide our steps as well as we can by moonlight.

'I dare say you will not write the article as well as it conceivably might be done; but the question is between that and nothing. If by the subject being such as a "powerful and practised hand ought to deal with," you mean merely that it deserves that, I agree with you; but not if you mean that a slight and imperfect notice would be worse than none at all.

'But you have, in the letter I enclose to you, nearly all the materials needed for a very useful article. It only needs hammering out. I send you also an American paper, lent to me, from which I would suggest your extracting the whole of the attack on Mrs. Stowe, as a proof that they are very angry and much alarmed, and have no answer except vituperation. For they cannot and do not attempt to deny that all she relates may take place every day. You might also notice the narrative of a man's cropping his slave's ears off, in which it is implied that no amount of flogging would have been censured. Indeed, how could it? unless every slave had to be brought before a magistrate, who should allot the due amount of punishment, and see it inflicted.

'I hope this will find you at home and recovered.

'Very truly yours,
'Rd. Dublin.'

The following letter to Mr. Senior, on the subject of the conversions from Romanism, which were at this time attracting a large share of public notice in Ireland, shows that the Archbishop was no uninterested spectator of the struggle.

As much misapprehension has existed as to the part he took with respect to Protestant missions in Ireland, it may be needful to add a few words of explanation here.

It has often been alleged, and much too hastily assented to, that the Archbishop was opposed to controversy, especially upon the subject of the distinctive doctrines of Romanism. One who was intimately acquainted with him for many years writes: 'I am not greatly surprised that such an impression should have prevailed to a considerable extent. I can recall the time when I was myself influenced by it. I should think it was partly caused by the limited sale of his "Origin of Romish Errors," compared with the great popularity of most of his other works, the decided manner in which he openly expressed his disapproval of certain "controversial discussions," which had taken place; and the frequency with which he was in the habit of quoting the proverb: "No sensible person thinks of catching birds by throwing stones at them." But that it was not controversy *per se* to which he objected, but only the manner and spirit in which it was often conducted, there is overwhelming evidence to prove. In fact, I cannot help saying that I look upon Archbishop Whately as one of the most decided, extensive, and varied controversialists of the present century. The work already referred to, " The Origin of Romish Errors," was published before he became Archbishop of Dublin. I have often heard him express his regret that he had been persuaded, against his own judgment at the time, to adopt that title, as it gave an inadequate idea of the design of the book, in which he traces not only Romish errors, but unsound religious doctrines and practices generally, whether heathen or so-called Christian, to the corrupt tendencies of our fallen nature. In 1847 he preached as a sermon, and subsequently published in an enlarged form, his most able and conclusive essay,

"The Search after Infallibility." In 1852–3 he published "Cautions for the Times," as a check to the Romeward tendency of the higher and intellectual classes; and about the same time he furnished to the "Catholic Layman," in a series of articles, the admirable tract for the unlearned, "The Touchstone, with Answers," containing a complete reply to the Roman Catholic publication of that name. At the same time he was extremely unwilling to have his name mixed up with the proceedings of any societies of an avowedly proselytising character, lest he should thereby seem to sanction some matters of detail of which he did not quite approve. But that he did not object to the general principle and objects of such societies is proved by the fact that he licensed for divine worship the Mission Church in Townsend Street; and so lately as in the year 1856 he gave, through my hands, 50l. to each of the two principal organisations for direct missions to the Roman Catholics of Ireland—" The Irish Society," and the "Society for Irish Church Missions." The evidence, however, which seems most conclusive in this matter, is that which rests upon the fact that he was one of the original founders of the "Society for Protecting the Rights of Conscience in Ireland" in 1850; and continued to take an active part in all its proceedings until his death; that society having been formed for the express purpose of meeting and neutralising the bitter and wide-spread persecution excited in Ireland by the success of the operations of the two reformation societies above mentioned. I can bear testimony as well as yourself to the warm interest which he manifested in the progress of the religious movement, at the same time that he exercised his characteristic caution as to the manner in which the temporal aid administered by the "Conscience Protection Society" was to be applied; viz. that it should be simply for

the protection of those who, from an honest conviction
of the falsity of Romanism, had openly separated from
its communion, and not as an inducement or temptation
to any to profess what they did not conscientiously
believe.'[1]

It was also with his full knowledge and sanction that
his son-in-law, for whose judgment he had the highest
value, was, whenever resident in Ireland, an active and
efficient co-operator in the work of Protestant missions.
The influence Mr. Wale exerted in the mission dormitories
and training-schools for boys and young men is remembered and felt to this day. The Archbishop was ever
ready to allow grants of his works to be made to their
libraries; and these volumes have been studied by the
Scripture readers and youths training for teachers with
an eagerness and diligence hardly to be equalled in many
schools of a higher class.

And how precious and tender a memory of two others
of the family, now also ' bidden up higher,' is interwoven
with the Ragged Schools and the ' Bird's Nest' for destitute little ones, all who remember them well know, for
they ' being dead yet speak.'

It may not perhaps be out of place to allude here to a
circumstance which occurred between four and five years
later, and which has been represented in such a way as
to give rise to much misapprehension. In a parish in the

---

[1] "The accusation that ' Dr. Whately was habitually opposed to controversy,' if ever made, was a singular charge against one of the most active and
hardy controversialists of his time. But this much is true, that he had a great
dislike to see the weapons of controversy, particularly in favour of causes in
which he felt an interest, wielded by the hands of the ignorant and self-
confident, to the serious damage of their own party, if not of truth. And
no doubt, in his outspoken way, he had often made free with the perform-
ances of these mischievous auxiliaries in such a manner as to render him
subject to misrepresentation."

immediate environs of Dublin a branch of the Irish Church
Mission Work was carried on for some time. Serious
charges against the agents employed there, and against
the society itself, were formally brought under the Archbishop's notice in the latter part of the year 1857 ; and it
has been alleged, that in consequence of what occurred
upon that occasion, the Archbishop desired the agency of
the society to be removed from the parish. This is by
no means a correct statement of the facts. A lengthened
investigation of the charges took place in the Archbishop's
presence. Several witnesses were examined on both
sides ; but none of the charges against the Irish Church
Missions were proved so as to draw from the Archbishop
a verdict or decision. At the conclusion of the proceedings, however, the Archbishop said that the fact of the
incumbent of the parish (who was also present) being dissatisfied with the state of things, was sufficiently decisive
as to the necessity for discontinuance of the operations of
the Mission in the district, in conformity with the fundamental rules of the society. The agency was accordingly
withdrawn at once, without, however, affecting in any
way its working in other parts of Dublin.

'Nov. 4, 1852.

'My dear Senior,—I know a great deal of Mr. Greg,
but I did not know those were his articles. I thought
the one on France had been yours. It is very good. I
know his article on Socialism, which is very good ; and I
know the general outline of his " Creeds of Christendom."
He writes well (as is the case with many men) on any
subject where he is not run away with by enthusiastic
feelings, and then very absurdly. The peculiarity of him
is, that his is anti-religious enthusiasm.
'He takes as representatives of the creed of Christendom

two or three individuals, whom almost all, even of their
admirers, consider as very crotchety, whimsical, and
singular in their views—views which are not adopted by
as many individuals in the world as there are millions of
Christians; and no one else is to have any voice at all,
and no one is a competent judge, moreover, of the question
who has been brought up a Christian; it must be decided
by those alone who have rejected Christianity, or never
heard of it. And so, by choosing his jury and his witnesses as suits him best, he obtains whatever verdict he
pleases!

'It is somewhat remarkable that I am never noticed
(so far as I know) by any antichristian writers, either as
affording any specimen of what the religion is, or as a
defender of it.

> 'Yours ever,
> 'R. WHATELY.'

The following memorandum, on a pamphlet published
about this time by a Roman Catholic gentleman of high
station and influence, ascribing the conversions which
were taking place to bribery, may find a place here, as it
treats of a subject already mentioned.

Memorandum.

'I agree with Mr. de Vere on most points,[1] as I have
always thought so; but two points I except against
strongly: First, He has read Bishop Hinds with attention,
and quotes from him whenever it suits his purpose; but
he does not at all meet what he says of the peculiar
difficulty of dealing with Roman Catholics from their

---

[1] This agreement refers to another subject canvassed in the pamphlet.

owning allegiance to a spiritual head who is also an independent temporal sovereign ; so that the tendency which
every religious body has to encroach occasionally on the
civil power cannot be so readily and effectually checked
as when the body or person to whom they owe spiritual
allegiance is, like John Wesley, or Johanna Southcote, or
Mr. Irving, a subject of the state, or even of some other
state.   The Pope is, in all questions of the kind that may
arise, judge in his own cause ; and this has always, in all
states, Roman Catholic or Protestant, occasioned peculiar
difficulties.

'I acknowledge it is not easy to meet what Bishop
Hinds says on this point.   Perhaps the only course for
Mr. de Vere to take was, boldly to deny that the Roman
Catholic hierarchy ever did interfere, or claim any right
to interfere, in civil concerns.

'But who can be expected to believe this, in the face
of such a multitude of indisputable and notorious facts ?
He might as well have said that everyone knows no rivers
ever overflow their banks !

'Secondly, He speaks of apparent conversions, effected
by direct or indirect bribery, as being the general if not
universal rule.   As far as my knowledge goes, and I
have made a most rigorous scrutiny, nothing of the kind
has ever occurred.   I do not, however, undertake to prove
a negative.   There may have been such cases that have
not come to my knowledge ; but what he gives us to
understand—that such is the general character of the
conversions that have taken place—I know to be utterly
the reverse of truth.

'And as a large portion of the Protestant clergy are
not favourably disposed towards me, I am—at least on
that side—an unbiassed witness. . . .   But though the
first deviser of a calumnious falsehood deserves the most

blame, I must protest against those who lend their aid to the circulation of calumnies without inquiring and ascertaining the truth.

'Most of his points are very soundly reasoned; but his arguments will have less weight than they merit, partly from his having put forward two statements so easily disproved; partly, and much more, from his being suspected of a bias, and therefore regarded with distrust by those who are little competent to judge of reasoning by its own sole merits.

'For this reason, the letters from the "Witness," and the pamphlet on "Papal Aggressions, how they should be met" (which advocate the very same practical conclusions as his), will have more effect.

'One thing, however, towards his object he might do more effectually than any Protestant—to procure from the Roman hierarchy a formal condemnation of all persecution, a censure of all who have written in praise of Queen Mary and the Inquisition, and of all those bitter persecutors in Ireland of the Protestant converts.

'This would go far towards softening the animosity of a great number in England.

'I am not for repaying intolerance in kind; but many are, and ever will be.

'P.S.—I trust no coercive legislative measures will be adopted against Roman Catholics; but if I were a zealous Roman Catholic, there is nothing I should anticipate with so much joy. As for any danger of penal laws being enforced in England in the nineteenth century, that is out of the question. It is only like firing blank cartridges, which just allows people to complain that "they have been fired upon," without doing them the smallest damage.

'And nothing would be more likely to create a reaction.

The breaking of chapel windows, and even the violent speeches made lately at public meetings, have done great service to the cause of Romanism.

'It has nothing to fear in England at this day, except from calm discussion, enlightenment of the people, and study of the Scriptures.'

At this time the Archbishop received a visit from Mr. Senior, during which much interesting conversation passed, which was recorded by Mr. Senior in a journal he was in the habit of keeping whenever he was staying from home. Some extracts from the pages of this journal may find a fitting place here.

Extract from Mr. Senior's Journal.

'Oct. 8, 1852.

'We posted to Redesdale, Archbishop Whately's country place, about five miles from Dublin, nearly opposite to Kingstown Harbour. Nature meant the road to be an open terrace, between the sea and the mountains. Man has made it a dirty lane, twisting between high walls. Almost all the country near Dublin is cut into squares, each with its wall without and its fringe of trees within, merely ugly in summer, but damp and unwholesome in winter.

'We talked after dinner about Puseyism. I asked if it was prevalent in Ireland?

'"Not so prevalent," answered the Archbishop, "as in England; but it exists. I was told that we should escape it—that, as we have the real thing, we should not adopt the copy—but I was sure that it would come. Ireland catches every disease after it has passed over England.

Cholera came to us after you had had it, so did the potato
rot, so did Puseyism."

' "I am inclined." I said, " to think that it is diminishing
in England."

' "Diminishing," said the Archbishop, " in its old head-
quarters, Oxford, but increasing in the country parishes.
The tidal wave, after it has begun to ebb in the ocean,
still rises in the bays and creeks. Those who were taught
Puseyism fifteen years ago, are now teaching it in their
villages."

' "I heard the lessons read," said —— " by a young
Puseyite, and they were mumbled over, so as to be
scarcely intelligible."

' "I heard, or rather did not hear them read in the
same way in Margaret Street chapel," said ——.

' "What is the explanation of this?" I said. "The
Puseyites cannot wish to show disrespect to Scripture?"

' "I do not pretend," said the Archbishop, " to be
master of all the details of Puseyism; but its general
theory is, religion by proxy. The priest is not only to
pray, but to believe for the laity. To them the raw Bible
is dangerous. They ought not to receive it until he has
cooked it. The lessons ought not to be read at all, or
they ought to be read in Latin; or, if they must be read
in English, they should be hurried over, so as to let them
give as little knowledge and do as little harm as possible."

' We conversed on the appointment of bishops by the
ministry. The Archbishop said, that to choose them
without reference to their opinions on the education
question, was to send arms and ammunition to the Cape,
and to be utterly indifferent whether they fell into the
hands of the Queen's troops or of the Caffres. He had
observed this to a leading statesman, who answered that

this impartiality would give him a much wider choice. " I ventured," said the Archbishop, " to doubt this."

' " Of course," I said, " if you mean, that, by ignoring the existence of the opposition between the friends and the enemies of mixed education, you will be able to select your bishop from among a larger number of clergymen, that is obviously true. I even believe that, if you were to select exclusively from among its enemies, you would find more clergymen to choose from than if you selected exclusively from among its friends ; but if your object be to choose from the fittest men, I do not think that con- sidering hostility to mixed education no disqualification will enlarge your field of choice in the least. If I had to point out the half-dozen best men in all other respects— the men who, if there were no Education Board, would be the fittest for promotion— I should have to take them all from among the friends of mixed education." I do not think, however, that I convinced him.

' " I suppose," I said, " that you adhere to your old opinion as to the abolition of the Lord Lieutenancy ? "

' " I feel it," he said, " more strongly every day. No friend to the Union, no friend to good government, can wish to retain that office. Those who hear that the Lord Lieutenant is kept at work all day, and perhaps half the night, infer that he must have much to do. I have served the office for months at a time. The Lords Justices, in the absence of the Lord Lieutenant, perform all his duties, except those connected with patronage and representation. They are not employed for three hours in a week. The Lord Lieutenant's days and nights are wasted on intrigue and party squabbles, on the management of the press and the management of 'fêtes;' on deciding what ruined gambler is to have this stipendiary magistracy, and what repealer is to be conciliated by asking his wife and daughters to a concert—in short, on things, nine-tenths of which cannot be so well treated as by being left alone. The abolition of this phantom of independence is the first step towards the consolidation of the two countries. I must add, that, attached as I am to regal government, yet, if we changed our sovereign every time that we changed our ministry, I had rather take refuge in some more stable form of constitution, though of an inferior kind."

'" Would you retain," I said, " the Irish Office ? "

'" Certainly not," answered the Archbishop, " I would no more have an Irish Office than a Welsh Office. The bane of Ireland is the abuse of its patronage; what Lord Rosse says of the stipendiary magistrates is true of every other Irish appointment. Fitness is the only claim that is disregarded ; this would be bad enough anywhere, but it is peculiarly mischievous in a highly centralized country, where the bureaucratic influence is felt in every fibre. Now the concentration of the Irish patronage in the hands of one or two persons resident in Ireland is favourable to this abuse. The English public is accustomed to consider Irish appointments as things done in Ireland by Irishmen, and for Irishmen, with which it has no concern. It thinks it probable that, like everything else that is Irish, they are very bad, but does not hold that the English government is responsible for them. A Prime Minister or a Home Secretary would not bear the disgrace of the jobs which are expected from a Lord Lieutenant or from a Secretary for Ireland. He would both be subject to a less pressure, and would be better able to resist it.

'" In a country in which the aristocratic element is strong," continued the Archbishop, " we must submit to see men promoted in consequence of their birth and connexions; in a country subject to parliamentary govern-

ment we must expect to see functionaries selected rather
to serve the party than to serve the public. It is only a
government like that of Louis Napoleon that can give its
patronage only to merit. But in Ireland a third element
interferes to disturb all our appointments, that is to say,
the religious element. It has been the principle of some
viceroys to favour the Roman Catholics ; that of others
to favour the Protestants, and I have heard of departments in which the vacancies were filled from each sect
alternately, and Papists and Protestants were disposed like
the squares on a chessboard . . . We probably could not
escape this abuse altogether if the appointments were
made in England, but I think that there would be less
of it."

'" Do you find," I asked, " any marked difference between your Roman Catholic and Protestant inspectors ?"

'" Not," he answered, " a marked difference ; the Protestants I think are rather the best. I am told that in the
higher departments of the public service the difference is
marked, and that the Protestants are by far the best
public servants, and I should expect it to be so. In the
lower and middle classes the education received by the
children of both sects is nearly the same ; but in the
higher classes the Protestants have until now been
educated, not well perhaps, but much better than the
Roman Catholics. Let us hope that the Queen's Colleges
will remove this distinction, and place both classes on an
equality, elevating each, but raising most that which is
now the lower."

'" Under any training," I said, " Catholicism must be
unfavourable to mental development. A man who has
been accustomed to abstain from exercising his reason on
the most important subjects to which it can be applied,
can scarcely feel the earnest anxiety for truth, the deter-

mination to get to the bottom of every question that he considers, which is the principal stimulus to improvement in the higher branches of knowledge. This does not apply to higher laymen in France or Italy, for they do not believe in the peculiarities of Catholicism, but it must always injure the minds of the English and Irish Catholics who do."

'The Archbishop is president of the "Society for protecting the Rights of Conscience." For some time a considerable conversion to Protestantism has been going on in Ireland. The converts are to be numbered by thousands—not by hundreds.

'I asked to what these conversions were to be attributed? What were the causes which had suddenly opened men's minds to arguments which had been addressed to them for years without success.

'"The causes," said the Archbishop, "must be numerous; it is not probable that I am acquainted with them all, or that I assign to those which occur to me their relative importance . . but I will tell you all that I know or conjecture, and I will also tell you what opinions are current. Many persons think that it is owing to the general diffusion of Bibles, Testaments, and Prayer-books, by the societies instituted for those purposes. But those societies have been at work for many years, and the conversions on the present scale are recent. Others believe, or profess to believe, that the conversions are purchased. This is the explanation given by the Roman Catholics. An old woman went to one of my clergy and said : ' I am come to surrender to your reverence, and I want the leg of mutton and the blanket.' 'What leg of mutton and blanket?' said the clergyman; 'I have scarcely enough of either for myself and my family, and certainly none to give. Who could have put such nonsense into your head?'

'Why, sir,' she said, 'Father Sullivan told us that the converts got each a leg of mutton and a blanket, and as I am famished, and starving with cold, I thought that God would forgive me for getting them.'

'" But our society has for months been challenging those who spread this calumny to prove it. We circulate queries, asking for evidence, that rewards or inducements have been held out, directly or indirectly, to persons to profess themselves converts. Not only has no case been substantiated, no case has been even brought forward. Instead of being bribed, the converts, until they are numerous enough in any district to protect one another, are oppressed by all the persecution that can be inflicted in a lawless country by an unscrupulous priesthood, hounding on a ferocious peasantry. Another explanation is, that it is owing to the conduct of the priests during the O'Brien rebellion. The priests, it is said, lost their popularity by exciting the people and then deserting them. The fact is true, but it is not enough to account for conversions in many parts of Ireland which were not agitated by that movement.

'" Another theory is, that it is mainly owing to the different conduct of the Protestant and the Roman Catholic clergy during the famine. The Protestant clergy literally shared their bread, or rather their meal, with their parishioners, without the least sectarian distinction—they devoted all their time, all their energy, all their health, and all that the Poor Law left them of their small revenues, to those who were starving round them. Their wives and daughters passed their days in soup-kitchens and meal rations.

'" The Roman Catholic clergy were not sparing of their persons—they lived, and a great many of them died, among the sick; but the habit of that clergy is never to give ; there is a division of labour between them and the laity—they take faith, and the laity good works, at least, as far as almsgiving is a good work. A great part of them, indeed, during the famine, had nothing to give ; they starved with their flocks, when their flocks ceased to pay dues. But others had means of their own, and many of those who took part in the distribution of the Government money or of the English subscriptions, helped themselves out of the funds which passed through their hands to what they considered to be the amount due to them from the people. But no part of their revenues, however obtained, found its way to the poor. Their incomes were spent during the famine as they were spent before it, and as they are now spent—on themselves, or hoarded till they could be employed in large subscriptions to chapels or convents. And this was not the worst. In many cases they refused to those who could not or who would not pay for them, the sacraments of their church. In ordinary times this may be excusable ; a clergy unendowed and unsalaried must be supported by voluntary contributions or by dues. In so poor a country as Ireland voluntary contribution cannot be relied on. The priest might often starve if he did not exact his dues, and as he has no legal rights, his only mode of exacting them is to make their payment the condition on which his ministrations are performed. But during the famine payment was obviously impossible. When, under such circumstances, the sacraments which the priest affirmed to be necessary passports to heaven were refused, the people could not avoid inferring either that the priest let men sink unto eternal torment, to avoid a little trouble to himself, or that absolution or extreme unction could not be essential to salvation.

' " I believe that this explanation is not without its

truth, and that the influence of the Roman Catholic clergy has been weakened by the contrast of their conduct to that of ours. But I am inclined to attach more importance to the acquisition by the Protestant clergy of the Irish language. Until within a few years Protestant doctrines had never been preached in Irish. The rude inhabitants of the remote districts in Munster and Connaught believed that English was the language of heretics, and Irish that of saints. The devil, they said, cannot speak Irish.

'"About ten years ago, on my first visitation, after the province of Cashel had been put under my care, I asked all the clergy what proportion of their parishioners spoke nothing but Irish. In many cases the proportion was very large. 'And do you speak Irish?' I asked. 'No, my lord.' 'I am very sorry to hear it,' I replied. 'Oh,' the clergyman always said, 'all the Protestants speak English.' 'That is just what I should have expected,' I replied; 'under the circumstances of the case it would be strange indeed if any who speak only Irish were Protestants.' This sort of dialogue became much rarer on my second triennial visitation, and at my last there was scarcely any occasion for it. There are now very few of my clergy who cannot make themselves understood by all their parishioners, and I am told that the effect of this vernacular preaching is very great.

' " The great instrument of conversion, however, is the diffusion of Scriptural education. Archbishop Murray and I agreed in desiring large portions of the Bible to be read in our National Schools; but we agreed in this because we disagreed as to its probable results.

' " He believed that they would be favourable to Romanism. I believed that they would be favourable to Protestantism; and I feel confident that I was right.

For twenty years large extracts from the New Testament
have been read in the majority of the National Schools,
far more diligently than that book is read in ordinary
Protestant places of education.

'" The Irish, too, are more anxious to obtain knowledge
than the English. When on the Queen's visit she asked
for a holiday in the National Schools, the children submitted to that compliment being paid to her, but they
considered themselves as making a sacrifice. The consequence is, that the majority of the Irish people, between
the ages of twenty and thirty, are better acquainted with
the New Testament than the majority of the English are.

'" Though the priest may still, perhaps, denounce the
Bible collectively, as a book dangerous to the laity, he
cannot safely object to the Scripture extracts, which are
read to children with the sanction of the prelates of his
own Church. . . . But those extracts contain so much that
is inconsistent with the whole spirit of Romanism, that it
is difficult to suppose that a person well acquainted with
them can be a thorough-going Roman Catholic. The
principle on which that Church is constructed, the duty
of unenquiring, unreasoning submission to its authority,
renders any doubt fatal. A man who is commanded not
to think for himself, if he finds that he cannot avoid
doing so, is unavoidably led to question the reasonableness
of the command. And when he finds that the Church,
which claims a right to think for him, has preached doctrines, some of which are inconsistent and others are
opposed to what he has read in the Gospels, his trust in
its infallibility, the foundations on which its whole system
of faith is built, is at an end.

'" Such I believe to be the process by which the minds
of a large portion of the Roman Catholics have been
prepared, and are now being prepared, for the reception

of Protestant doctrines. The education supplied by the National Board is gradually undermining the vast fabric of the Irish Roman Catholic Church.

' " Two things only are necessary on the part of the Government. One is, that it adhere resolutely, not only in its measures but in its appointments, in the selection of bishops as well as in making parliamentary grants, to the system of mixed education. The other is, that it afford to the converts the legal protection to which every subject of the Queen is entitled, but which all her subjects do not obtain in Ireland. Some of the persecutions to which they are exposed are beyond the reach of the law. It cannot force the Roman Catholics to associate with them, or to employ them, or to deal with them. . . . It cannot protect them from moral excommunication. To mitigate, and if possible to remedy, those sufferings is the business of our Society; and I hope that, as soon as the public is aware of its necessity, we shall obtain funds enough to enable us to perform it. But good legislation and good administration, good laws, good magistrates, and a good police, are all that is wanting to protect the converts from open insults, injuries to their properties, assaults, and assassination. This protection the State can give to them, and this protection they do not now obtain.

' " I quite agree with Lord Rosse, that an improvement in penal justice is the improvement most wanted in Ireland."

' My brother and I walked with the Archbishop to Blackrock. We talked of the Education Board.

' " A year ago," said my brother, " the country gentlemen of the north, who used to be its fierce opponents, were gradually coming round. They would prefer, indeed, a grant for Protestant schools, but, as that seemed impossible, they were beginning to support mixed educa-

tion. The change of ministry, by reviving their hopes of
a separate grant, has stopped them. They are waiting to
see how the Government will act."

'"In England," I said, "we believe that Lord Derby
will not venture to propose such a grant. He cannot
propose a grant for purposes exclusively Protestant without proposing one for purposes exclusively Catholic, and
the Maynooth debate must have convinced him that such
a grant as the latter he cannot carry."

'"What I fear," said the Archbishop, "is a measure
which, though not avowedly sectarian, may be so practically. I fear that a grant may be offered to any patron
who will provide such secular education as the Government shall approve, leaving him to furnish such religious
education as he may himself approve. If this be done
the schools in the Roman Catholic districts will be so
many Maynooths, so many hotbeds of bigotry and religious animosity. Nor will the Protestant schools be
much better. The great object of the teachers in each
will be controversial theology, and secular instruction, and
even moral instruction, will be neglected. I believe, as I
said the other day, that mixed education is gradually en-
lightening the mass of the people, and that, if we give it
up, we give up the only hope of weaning the Irish from
the abuses of Popery. But I cannot venture openly to
profess this opinion. I cannot openly support the Education Board as an instrument of conversion. I have to fight
its battle with one hand, and that my best, tied behind me.

'"One of the difficulties," he continued, "in working
the mixed system arises from the difference in character
of the parties who have to work it. Much is necessarily
left to their honour. If the patron or the master choose
to violate the rules of the Board, he may often do so
without detection. Our inspectors are too few to exercise

more than a partial superintendence, and too ill paid to be always trustworthy. Now I must say that the Protestants more strongly feel, or at least observe more faithfully, the obligation of honour and of promises than the Roman Catholics. The more zealous Protestants keep aloof from the system of mixed education, because it ties their hands. They cannot, without a breach of faith, teach in our schools their own peculiar doctrines; or, rather, they can teach them only at particular times and to particular classes; they naturally wish to make them a part of the ordinary instruction; they support, therefore, only schools of their own, where their hands are free.

'" The zealous Roman Catholics are less scrupulous; their hands are free everywhere. With all its defects, however—and many of those defects would be remedied by a grant not so grossly inadequate as that which it now receives—we must adhere to the system of mixed education.

'" The control which it gives to us is not perfect, but it is very great. It secures the diffusion of an amount of secular and religious instruction such as Ireland never enjoyed before its institution, and certainly would not enjoy if it were to be overthrown; and it prevents the diffusion of an amount of superstition, bigotry, intolerance, and religious animosity, I really believe more extensive and more furious than any that we have yet encountered."

'" Would you support," I asked, " Maynooth?"

'" I am not sure," answered the Archbishop, " that its original institution was wise. Mr. Pitt thought that the young priests were taught disaffection and anti-Anglicism at Douai, and he created for their education the most disaffected and the most anti-English establishment in Europe; but, having got it, we must keep it. While the grant was annual, it might have been discontinued; now that it is permanent, to withdraw or even to diminish it would be spoliation. It would be a gross abuse of the preponderance in Parliament of the British members. We have no more right to deprive the Irish Roman Catholics, against their will, of the provision which we have made for the education of their clergy, than they would have, if they were numerically superior, to pass an Act for the sale of the colleges and the estates of Oxford and Cambridge, and the application of the produce in reduction of the national debt.

'"I hear," he said, turning to my brother, "that you reason somewhat in the same way respecting the Ecclesiastical Titles Act; that, admitting it to have been a very unwise measure, yet, now that it has passed, you would act on it. I agree with you, that to advance in order to retreat, to pass an Act and then to be afraid to enforce it, is very mischievous. But in this case we have to choose between two mischiefs; and I am convinced that to attempt to enforce the Act would be the greater mischief."

'"And yet," I said, "you concurred in wishing the Act to be extended to Ireland."

'"What I concurred in," said the Archbishop, "was not in wishing that such an Act should be passed for the British Islands, for I utterly disapprove of it, but in wishing that it should not be passed for England alone. I believed the Act, if general, to be a great evil, but a still greater evil if confined to England. It was saying to the English Roman Catholics, You are weak and loyal, therefore we trample on you; to the Irish, You are strong and rebellious, therefore we leave you alone."

'"To return," I said, "to Maynooth; what is your impression as to the education there?"

' "I believe," said the Archbishop, "that it is very poor; that little is studied except controversial theology, and that very imperfectly. Hercules Dickinson, a son of the poor Bishop of Meath, had a long discussion the other day with a Roman Catholic priest. The priest maintained that if the authority of the Church was not infallible we had no certain guide; that the text of the Scriptures might be falsified; and that we could not rely on our Old Testament, as we do not possess it in the original Greek." '

'Nov. 7, 1852.

' My dear Hinds,—Your client, I suppose, never knew, and you had forgotten, that the Lords Justices have nothing to do with any appointments. We are left without the three great things that belong to the Lord-Lieutenant: pomp, pay, patronage; but we are charged with all the really important functions of government pertaining to his office; and this occupies us, on an average, about one hour per week.

' I have sent the letter to Lord Eglinton,[1] in London (though I don't suppose it will be attended to), because he occupies just the place which the applicant supposed to be mine.

. . . .

' I see the difficulty which you advert to in extending the proposed Glossary to the Old Testament.

' I will wait till your publication is out, and then reconsider the matter to more advantage. And now I want to consult you on a question on which some far from

[1] Lord Eglinton had become Lord-Lieutenant under the administration of Lord Derby, which lasted through this year. During the absence of a Lord-Lieutenant the Archbishop of Dublin acted as one of the ' Lords Justices.'

contemptible men are divided, and which is of no small practical importance in these days of conversions, viz. :

'If a man, feeling bound to quit the Church of Rome, is convinced that he ought, if possible, to join some religious community, on what principle ought he to make his choice?

'1. It is admitted that establishment by law does not of itself constitute any claim on the conscience; but

'2. Some hold that he is allowed, and consequently bound, to join whichever may seem in his judgment the best—the most adapted on the whole to promote the objects for which a Church exists.

'3. Others say that he is bound to adopt (if he can with a safe conscience) the prevailing religion; to join the Church to which most of his neighbours belong, provided he is not convinced that it is un-scriptural; even though he should think some other preferable. E. g. Suppose (to take a case actually put) there are two brothers, who have been both convinced that they ought to quit the Romish Church; A. happening to be fixed in Scotland, and B. in England. A. thinks episcopacy and a liturgy far preferable to the kirk system, though neither is imperatively enjoined or prohibited in Scripture; and B. thinks exactly the opposite on these points; yet A. is bound to join the kirk, and B. the Church of England.

'4. I presume (though this is only matter of inference) that the decision would be the same if instead of Scotland we were to put the province of Ulster, or at least some counties of it, in which Presbyterians greatly predominate. And I don't see why the principle should not apply equally to some town or district in England or Wales, in which it might happen (as I believe there are such) that the Methodists e. g. or the Independents might be the majority.

' 5. For in applying the principle, the question arises, " Who is my neighbour ?" The majority which a man is to follow is evidently not the majority in the empire, else the man living in Scotland (in the case put) would look not to Scotland, but to Great Britain and Ireland.

' 6. The argument on the one side is, that since a man is authorised and bound to exercise his own best judgment as to the absolutely un-scriptural character of a Church, and to decide as well as he can what errors are sufficiently important to require separation, he is equally authorised and bound to decide as well as he can what is more and what less agreeable to Scripture and conducive to edification. If he is to judge what is good and true, and embrace that, and reject what is radically bad and false, absolutely, it should seem that he must be also bound to decide comparatively as well as absolutely. If he is to judge what is good, he is to judge what is better. If he is not allowed to adhere to what he thinks bad, instead of what appears to him good, neither ought he to embrace the worse in preference to what he thinks the better.

' And it is urged that in entering the religious community which he judges to be the best, he is not creating any schism; as a man is who wantonly or on slight grounds quits the Church he is actually a member of, merely from liking another better. It is admitted that he should separate from his Church only when he is convinced that it is fundamentally wrong. But, by supposition, he has already separated from the Church of Rome on that very ground. A single man may choose one woman for his wife in preference to another, on grounds which would be far from justifying a divorce.

' 7. On the opposite side it is argued that to have several distinct religious communities in any one locality tends to disunion among Christians, rivalry, and eventually hostility; that everyone should seek to avoid and counteract such evils by acting in such a way that if all men did the same discord would be avoided; and that on that ground he is to conform to the prevailing religion as long as he finds it not fundamentally wrong, even though there may be some other system which he thinks to be abstractedly better.

'This is the best summary I can give of the pros and cons on this, which is likely to become with many an important practical question.

'Yours ever,

'RD. WHATELY.

'P.S. When you have read No. 21, I will tell you my reason for asking your opinion of it.

'Monday Evening, Nov. 8, 1852.

'P.S. Through forgetfulness I directed my letter of to-day to Norwich, so I suppose you will get that and this together.

'Fitzgerald was authorised by me to put in any additional observation; and he has shown me what he added.

'It seems to me to have no bearing on the general question, unless he supposes me to be speaking of a man's right of seceding or not from the Church of which he is actually a member. But in the case before us this has been, by supposition, already done, and done on good and sufficient grounds. The question is what religious community a man shall join who is at this moment a member of none.

'The parallel, in reference to the case of civil communities, seems to me to be this: there are now hundreds of French exiles, of whom many probably are hopeless of any deliverance of France from the tyranny which has outlawed them; if any of these can be naturalised either as British subjects, or as citizens of an American State, or of Prussia, &c., are they, or are they not, free to choose, each for himself, what State he shall become a citizen of?'

'Nov. 14, 1852.

'My dear Miss C.,— . . . . Not only are partisans accustomed to have the budget before for their neighbour's faults, and that behind for their own, but moreover several who do not belong to any party are for passing by all the faults (whose existence they do not wholly deny) of those who join with them in opposing what they regard as the worst extremes. Now to that plan I and my coadjutors object;[1] though certainly it would save us no small portion of censure. We remember that it was not to Jews but to a Samaritan that Jesus set forth the superior claims of the Temple at Jerusalem; and it was not to Samaritans but to Jews that He dwelt on narrow bigotry and national prejudice against Samaritans. It was to the Sadducees that He adduced an argument in favour of the Resurrection; it was to the Pharisees that He addressed His censure of traditions, which had overloaded and overgrown the law.

'It is true, as you observe, that there are not very many members of our Church who distinctly declare that every one is to take up the Bible and make out a religion for himself from that, unaided; nor again, are there many who distinctly set up the Church and its formularies as superseding Scripture.

'But when people dwell every day, and all day long, on the " rights of labour," and the " claims to liberty,"

---

[1] In the ' Cautions for the Times.'

and the " duties of the capitalist" and of governments, and
say little about any other rights and duties, it is usually
found that people are gradually brought to be Chartists,
and to doubt whether all rich men and all kings are not
an incubus on society. And so also when (without distinctly denying, any more than the others, any true political doctrine) any one dwells exclusively on good order
and submission, &c. he will be likely to train men to a
slavish or oligarchical spirit. And so it is in religious
matters as well as in political.

' I did indeed know a man, well educated and intelligent, and believed to be sincerely religious, who used to
maintain that it would be much better if all books on any
religious subject were burnt, all over the world, except
the Bible. And I assure you he was not without something plausible to urge. He was a physician ; and I
might have met him by a suggestion that inasmuch as
teeth are undeniably liable to decay and to give pain, we
should cut short all possible toothache at once, by making
every one have all the teeth in his head drawn ; and a
similar rule might be applied to other members, till one
had reduced the human body to a torso.

' Of course all sermons and other oral instructions he
would have equally prohibited, since it would be absurd
to allow people to hear what they should be debarred
from reading.

' Just such a case as this, however, is not, I believe, very
common, though perhaps less uncommon than some may
think ; for if there had been but one person in all England
of this opinion, the chances would have been enormous
against my meeting with that one.

' But what we have had in view is, as we have said,
those who undesignedly and imperceptibly lead others,
and perhaps themselves, into an undue neglect and

depreciation of something which they do not (or at least did not originally) mean to discard.

'Very truly yours,
'Rd. Whately.'

The following is an extract from a letter to a young writer of some promise, in whom he was interested :—

'[The Archbishop agrees with Mr. Senior, that "logic does not need a lengthened defence;" but thinks it would be "going too far to say that it needs none."] The Bishop of London e.g. speaks with great contempt of "what Oxford men call science;" and I should think you would find few Cambridge men of his standing—or ten years junior—who do not hold the same tone.

'There is a good deal of it in Macaulay; and in Scotland, though the juniors and some of the seniors value logic, you will find a strong majority of men, of forty-five years old and upwards, against it. See "The North British Review." Perhaps the best way would be to make a short defence, with the air of one who is on the triumphant side, and who is allowed to speak with some scorn of objections that are nearly obsolete.

'You may write to Mr. Senior, saying what I have here said, and so save my writing it to him.'

'Dublin: Nov. 24, 1852.

'My dear Senior,—We are now alone, the Wales and also Pope having departed.

'I have been occupied (the little scraps of time I can find) for about two months in drawing up "Easy Lessons on the British Constitution," as a sequel to the money matters.

'It is to appear first in a periodical called the "True

Briton," and is to be a surprise on my ladies, who have
not been told of it. It is excessively hard writing, though
I trust it will prove easy reading.

'Miss Edgeworth speaks somewhere of persons who
" divide all mankind into knaves and fools, and when they
meet with a sensible, honest man, don't know what to
make of him." Thackeray answers that description. He
draws the base and the bad with a vigorous pencil; but
he seems utterly incapable of even imagining a worthy
person who is not a simpleton. I remarked long since
that he considered mankind as consisting of only two
classes—the knaves and fools.

'Yours ever,

'RD. WHATELY.'

'Tuesday Morning, Dec. 7, 1852.

My dear Senior,—We want to know what is thought
of the Budget. I should like to know also whether you
have done anything with the letter from Italy. I understand, on pretty good authority, that a great sensation is
excited in Italy by the efforts made on behalf of the
Madiai, and that the English documents relating to them
are eagerly though secretly circulated. I have been very
hard worked, with a confirmation. Besides the general
one, every other year, for the whole of the dioceses, I
have one on the intermediate year (which is this) for
Dublin city and suburbs. Now, here is a problem for
you in statistical computation. I confirmed 1,150 : these
were, with a few exceptions, from thirteen years old to
eighteen ; now how, from this, to make a rough guess at
the Protestant population ? The above number excludes,
you will observe : 1. Nearly all adults ; 2. All children ;
3. Protestant Dissenters (who, though much fewer than
those of our Church, form several large congregations) ;

4. All those who were confirmed last year (of whom there are many between the ages specified); 5. All those whom the clergymen judged not quite prepared (and keep back for confirmation next year); 6. All those who are careless about religious duties, though nominal Protestants.

'When all these are computed together, the Protestant population will appear to be much beyond the mere handful some suppose it. But I remember that a good many years ago you had taken up the notion that nearly all the Protestant population of the south of Ireland was congregated in Dublin. The reverse is nearer the mark; for, in most parts of Wicklow, the Protestant population is larger in proportion than in Dublin. And the same is the case, not generally in Kildare, but in some districts of it. Since the famine, the Protestant proportion has in most parts greatly increased, not so much by conversions (though of these there are several thousands) as by the greater emigration of Roman Catholics. They go chiefly to the United States. And it is remarkable that (as is stated, and complained of by Roman Catholic writers) the greater part of them quit their Church soon after their arrival, and so do the children of many of the rest. There even seems reason to believe that the whole number of Roman Catholics in the Union does not equal the number of Roman Catholic emigrants from Ireland in the last twelve years. I can supply you with the computations if needful.

'You may decorate part of your journal with some portions of this letter.'

Notes on an Article which had recently appeared in a Paper.

'It seems rather strange that a "Hater of tyranny" should be so fiercely enraged at that letter from Italy, considering that the writer is evidently an advocate for complete and universal toleration. No one surely can doubt that he is for leaving religion between each man's own conscience and God; and that he would have every one allowed to hold and teach — without violence, or insult, or sedition—his own belief, whether it be in the opinion of the magistrates a right or an erroneous belief.

'But perhaps "Hater" limits his hatred to tyranny exercised against those who agree with himself, and adopts the principle laid down in the "Essays on the Church" (as quoted in the letter), that the magistrate does well in punishing those who teach a false religion and is not a persecutor.

'This principle—as is remarked in the letter—would be readily acceded to by all the persecutors in the world, since each professes to regard his own as the true religion.

'As for the denial that the Madiai did violate the laws of Tuscany, the "Hater," when he becomes a little cooler, will perhaps perceive that this is nothing to the purpose; for the letter-writer asserts nothing on this point except that the Grand-Duke would of course maintain that the law had been violated. And that he must do so is evident, since the Madiai were tried and pronounced (however wrongfully) to be guilty.

'The plea is indeed a worthless one, if the law itself is (as the letter evidently assumes) a cruel and unjust one; for, in that case, they ought (if they did violate such a law) to be immediately pardoned and the law repealed. But a persecuting ruler would, instead of repealing, enact such a law, if there were none already existing.

'For the rest, amidst much vehement vituperation, there is not even an attempt to refute any one argument in that letter. And this may be considered as a strong presumption that no refutation can be found.'

'Dec. 12, 1852.

'My dear Hinds,—I find some are much startled at hearing it said, as indeed I had said in my last charge also, that a translation is of the nature of a commentary—is a kind of explanation of the sense of the sacred writers —and·that punctuation also is another human help to the sense of Scripture.

'We guarded[1] against its being inferred that we are bound to take the word of any translator or editor, any more than of any catechist or preacher. We may derive assistance from the variorum notes in Maret's Bible, and in Bloomfield, without at all pinning our faith on them; but folks are startled at the novelty of the language, though there is no really new sense attached to the word.

'They will have it that nothing can be called a commentary which does not profess to give a full and complete explanation of all that the Bible contains. Now, a man is as truly a commentator who expresses his judgments as to the meaning, e. g. of the one word μετανοεῖτε, as one who undertakes to explain the whole meaning of all that the evangelists and apostles wrote, though he is not a commentator to the same extent; but I should like your opinion on this.

'Exception is taken also against a passage in which it is said that the gift of the Spirit is not more a gift of Christ than the ordinances of a Church. It was not meant that both are equally important and valuable, but only that He has ratified whatever is " bound on earth ; " but perhaps the expression was not well guarded.

'The Education Board is—between ourselves—on its last legs. A majority of the Commissioners are for excluding books unanimously sanctioned by the Board

---

[1] He is speaking of the ' Cautions for the Times.'

for general instructions from the District Model Schools,
of which the Board itself is patron, thus proclaiming that
we are either insincere in recommending those books, or
else overruled by those who ought to have no voice in the
matter.   If they follow up this course—which is greatly
to be feared—I must withdraw, and make public my
reasons; and if I am followed—as is to be expected by
all those who are really friendly to the original principles
of the system—I don't see how the Board can continue,
nor can I guess what Government—whether this or
another—can do next.   But the choice will not be
between the systems being continued or not, but between
its being put out by an extinguisher, or dying away in
fetid smoke, like a candle blown out.

> ' Ever yours affectionately,
> ' RD. WHATELY.'

> ' Wednesday, Dec. 22, 1852.

'My dear Senior,—They say here that a dissolution
would unseat a great many of the Irish Radicals.   The
late election was such a triumph of priestly influence as
is not likely to recur.   The riots at Stockport and the
Ecclesiastical Titles Bill (commonly called " Lord John's
leaping-bar," to afford exercise in jumping over it)
caused an excitement, which has since died away a
good deal.

'I suppose a good many English members also would
lose their seats, so perhaps the fear of a dissolution may
do instead of an actual dissolution.   " If you will let us
stay in, we will let you stay in."

'I suppose I am to see an eleventh Lord-Lieutenant.
How I do wish they would abolish it, and let Lord
Chancellors be as fixed as Judges.   'Yours ever,

> ' RD. WHATELY.'

'Dublin : Dec. 29, 1852.

'My dear Senior,—I wish you would send to Bishop Hinds that extract of a letter from Italy, or a copy of it, telling him you had it from me ; and that if any provincial paper would be glad of something to fill their columns up during this lull of debates, they may insert it. Is a dissolution now looked for? If there is one, I shall be out of Parliament. They call the Ministry Lord ——'s Christmas mince pie.

'I wish they had retained ——. When the former refused to be Chancellor without a place in the Cabinet, they should have offered the same to his successor, both to mark that it was no personal slight, and also to put the office on the footing on which it ought to stand. The fewer removeable offices the better.

'Yours ever,

'RD. WHATELY.'

CHAPTER X.

1853.

In the year 1853 we find his earliest letter to Mr
Senior on the again-revived subject of Transportation.

The 'Lessons on the British Constitution' were now
appearing in a periodical, which, though short-lived,
received much able support during its brief span of
existence. They were afterwards published as the former
series had been.

'Jan. 4, 1853.

'My dear Senior,—I am glad to hear of the proposed
abolition of transportation, though I suppose I shall die
soon after, as the system was born with me, and I was
sent into the world for the express purpose of opposing it.
Here it is currently reported that the Ministers are bent
on abolishing the Lord Lieutenancy, and appointing a

vice Chancellor.   The thing might have been easily done at the time it was attempted, if Lord John had not, as his custom is, publicly announced his design (just as he did with Hampden's bishopric) long enough beforehand to give opponents time to muster their forces against him. There are many people who think it would be a great evil to cut off the expenditure of so much money on the poor tradesmen of Dublin.   I have been accustomed to proceed by a *reductio ad absurdum*, for the benefit of those not versed in political economy.   If this be a real benefit to some hundreds of labourers, with no counter-vailing loss or evil of any kind as a set off against it, then why not do more good of the same kind, by giving each mayor of every town in Ireland 20,000*l.* per annum, on condition of his spending it, and 2000*l.* per annum to each clergyman in like manner?   It is a benefit which ought to be multiplied a thousand-fold.

'Do you know of any better popular argument?   I hope, in reforming Parliament, they will profit by that excellent article in the last "Edinburgh," and also do away with the vacating of seats by taking office.

'Yours ever,

'RD. WHATELY.'

'Jan. 12, 1853.

'My dear Senior,—I have read your article, as usual, with delight and instruction; but I am the less able to judge, from not having been able to get through any of Thackeray's novels except "Vanity Fair."   "Pendennis" I got weary of, and laid it aside; "Vanity Fair" I got weary of, too, but went through it.   His characters are either so disgustingly odious, or else so mawkishly silly— some of the characters are so unnaturally "inconsistent," viz. they are too good to be such fools as he represents them—that I cannot take an interest in them.

'If you were to serve up a dinner with top dish a roasted fox, stuffed with tobacco and basted with train oil, and at bottom an old ram goat, dressed with the hair on, and seasoned with assafœtida, the side dishes being plain boiled rice, this would give an idea of what his fictions are to my taste. You will see that I agree with your censures, as I do also with your commendations, only that I should make the former stronger, and the latter fainter.

'What you formerly said about the "amusing" being preferable to the "interesting," I fully agree with; but the amusement afforded by Thackeray is so mixed with disgust, that, as I heard an intelligent person say the other day, "I should never think of reading a page of his a second time." Now, Shakspeare and W. Scott, and Miss Austen and Mitford, &c., I can look at again and again with amusement.'

It was in this year that the events occurred which led to the Archbishop's final withdrawal from the National Education Board. Much misapprehension has existed with respect to the reasons which occasioned this withdrawal; the letters which follow will best point out the motives which actuated him; but a few words of explanation may not be out of place here.

When the rules of the Education Board were first drawn up, the Archbishop had been far from expecting that extracts from Scripture would have been permitted in the regular lesson books, but they, as well as the 'Easy Lessons on Christian Evidences' drawn up by the Archbishop in 1837, received the distinct and full sanction of Dr. Murray, then Roman Catholic Archbishop of Dublin.

It is important to dwell on this point, because it has been alleged that Dr. Murray did not give his formal sanction, but only abstained from prohibiting it, and that this negative approval was taken as a deliberate and official sanction. This statement is sufficiently answered by recalling the rules of the Board with respect to books brought before them.

No book could be placed on their list without the unanimous sanction of all the members of the Board. If there was a dissentient voice the book was not placed on the list at all, therefore such a thing as a negative sanction was utterly impossible. The very rules of the society put it out of the question; and thus the fact of these books being placed on the list, and used in the schools, was a sufficient guarantee for their having had the sanction of every individual member.

Dr. Murray, to whose high character all who knew him, however differing from him in views, bore full testimony, never shrank from avowing his approbation of the works in question; and this is proved by a letter referred to by Dr. Sullivan, in page 382 of the Report of the Committee of the House of Lords on Irish Education in 1854. This letter, dated October 21, 1838, was addressed by Dr. Murray to all his brother prelates in Ireland, with one exception. In it he expresses the strongest approbation of the Scripture extracts, and adds, 'They are so constructed that they may be used in common by all the pupils. The notes, therefore, that are appended to them do not advocate the discriminating doctrines of any particular class of Christians. It would be unfair in us to expect that a book to be used at the time of joint instruction should unfold any peculiar views of religion. The sacred text which it contains supplies much of sacred history, and much of moral precept, with which it is highly important that all should be acquainted; while the notes which are added are such as can give no just cause of offence to any other denomination of Christians.'[1]

Such are Dr. Murray's views of the extracts, and the request made (with one exception) by his brother prelates that he would continue to act as commissioner (in reply to his proposal of resigning) did in fact commit them all to the same view. But when, at the death of Dr. Murray, a new primate was appointed, a change took place in the course pursued by the members of the Church of Rome as regarded the National Board. The lessons on Evidences and the Scripture Extracts were voted prohibited books, and the Roman Catholic children and teachers forbidden, one and all, to use them.

The Board on this resolved to meet specially to discuss what steps to take. The Archbishop intimated to them that he would take no part in the discussion, and even avoided attending the meetings till their decision had been made.

The resolution to which the majority of the members came, was to take the obnoxious books off the list. The Archbishop considered this as virtually a breach of faith with the public. In the first instance, the Board might have decided as they thought best, as to receiving or rejecting any given work, and in such decisions he would

---

[1] Archbishop Murray ever bore a generous and candid testimony to Archbishop Whately's merit. In the same letter in which he speaks of the Scripture extracts, he thus alludes to him : 'No matter how he may differ from me in his religious belief, I am sure nothing that was not kind and liberal could come from that eminent individual.' This testimony was the more striking, because all knew that Archbishop Whately was no neutral or lukewarm Protestant, nor one inclined to make light of the difference between his views and those of the Church of Rome. It was as an honest and fair-minded opponent that Dr. Murray esteemed him. It may here be observed, that although through their life they were on terms of cordial good understanding and friendliness, their intercourse together was entirely official, and this by mutual agreement, each seeing that the course pursued was the most expedient under the circumstances.

have acquiesced, even though differing in judgment from them as to details; but having deliberately sanctioned these works, and used them for years, and many having been induced to place their schools under the Board on the strength of these very books, he felt they had no right to withdraw the sanction they had given. On this ground, and as a question of justice and straightforward dealing, he considered it his duty to withdraw his connection with the Board.

That this was a step not taken without much pain and mortification, no one who knew him could doubt; but his personal feeling to the Board was so far from unfriendly, that he continued to pay the salary of a regular catechist, a clergyman of the Church of England, who attended the model schools in Dublin weekly, to give religious instruction to the members of the Established Church, both pupils and teachers in training. And up to a few weeks before his last illness, he came himself from time to time, to see that the instruction was regularly and steadily given. He also continued to give Bibles and Prayer-books to the pupils and teachers in training, as he had done during his connection with the Board.

His views with regard to the system can best be given in his own words, at page 166 of the Report already alluded to. He adds, ' I approve of the system as much as ever, and am as ready to carry it on, but I feel that I should be deserting it in the most disingenuous and the most mischievous way possible, were I to pretend to be carrying it on when in reality subverting it.'[1]

---

[1] It may be well to notice here, that the story which has recently been brought forward, of the Archbishop's having manifested his displeasure against the Resident Commissioner, the Right Hon. Alex. Macdonnell, by deliberately omitting his name and title in addressing his letters, and directing to —— Macdonnell, Esq., is entirely unfounded. The truth is, that the concentrative habit of mind which distinguished him led to con-

Both the Lord Justice of Appeal (The Right Hon. F. Blackburne) and Baron Greene, who retired from the Board with the Archbishop, entertained and expressed the same view. The former, in his evidence before the Lords' Committee in 1856, says, 'I consider the expunging of the books from the list as a breach of faith,' and he gives this as the reason for his resigning.

The Government subsequently caused the Board to draw up and insert among their fundamental rules the following one : ' The Commissioners will not withdraw or essentially alter any book that has been or shall be here-after unanimously published or sanctioned by them with-out a previous communication with the Lord-Lieutenant.'

It may be well here to insert the letters of the Arch-bishop to the Lord-Lieutenant relative to his retirement from the National Board, although they were not printed till the following year.   They are taken from a printed ' Return ' of the House of Lords, April 11, 1854.

From the Archbishop of Dublin to the Lord-Lieutenant.

'July 5, 1853.

' My dear Lord,—I have heard from Baron Greene that (as your Excellency is doubtless aware) he means to move next Friday that the Board should make and announce a formal decision on the points at issue.

' There seems good reason for his objection to leaving matters in their present state ; an anomalous state, which is unsatisfactory to all parties, since each must be dis-satisfied that their own views are not fully and generally carried out.

tinual forgetfulness of etiquette and petty forms; and the instance of careless-ness alluded to might have taken place, and often did, with his most intimate friends. No one who really knew him could for a moment suppose him capable of such a mean piece of spite.

'I have to acknowledge also your Excellency's communication (which I should have replied to immediately but for the pressure of business), in which you suggest to me to reconsider the determinations I had formed. I thought I had sufficiently explained how fully, and with what anxious care I have, for many months, considered and reconsidered the subject. But perhaps I may have failed to express myself with sufficient clearness, or it may be that I have confused together in my memory what I have said to your Excellency and to the late Lord-Lieutenant.

'I may add, that I have also fully and frequently discussed the subject with my most confidential advisers, to one of whom, the Bishop of Norwich, I took the liberty of referring Lord Aberdeen, as a person thoroughly acquainted with Ireland, and with the national system, and with my sentiments, and who could give any needful explanations orally much better than I could by letter.

'Having the advantage of possessing intimate friends of eminent good sense and worth, I felt bound to consult them, and listen with deference to what they might say. I will not say, however, that I was prepared, in case of finding their views different from my own, to alter my course, unless they offered me stronger reasons than any I have ever heard. But I found them all fully agreed with me in thinking that no course is open to me, consistently with honour, but the one I have resolved on, and that a departure from it would be no less unwise than unjustifiable.

'As for any personal motives, such as regard for my own ease or my own credit, no one can think me capable of being influenced, in the present case, by any such considerations, who knows but the half of the toil I have endured, and the obloquy and vexatious opposition I have encountered in the cause for above twenty-one years. And in any minor question I have always been ready to sacrifice my own views of expediency to the judgment of the other Commissioners. But I regard the present as a question, not merely of expediency, but of principle also. I consider it as not only one of vital importance to the public, but also as one on which good faith is at stake. And, doubtless, your Excellency would be as far from wishing as from expecting that I should take any course at variance with my conscientious conviction of duty.

'What leads some persons to take a different view from mine seems to be their confounding together two totally different questions; that concerning the original adoption of some rule or some book, and concerning its removal afterwards. And yet no one would say that freedom to make, or refuse to make, a compact, implies freedom to break it; that because a State is allowed to ratify, or not, a certain treaty, therefore it is allowed to violate a treaty, or to modify its conditions at pleasure; that because a man might lawfully have remained single, therefore he may obtain a divorce whenever he thinks fit!

'Whenever any rule or any book was proposed, if any one Commissioner objected to the whole or to a portion of it, I always at once acquiesced in its withdrawal. And in fact several parts of some of the books now in use were originally thus altered to meet the objection of a single Commissioner. If, accordingly, when some of the books now so much discussed were first proposed any Commissioner had said, "Although Archbishop Murray and all the other Commissioners have carefully examined this book, and pronounced it sound in doctrine, and suitable for united education, yet I think otherwise," he would have been yielded to without even any remonstrance.

'But when some books or some rules have been deliberately sanctioned by the unanimous voice of the Commissioners, and have been for many years appealed to in vindication of the system, and as a ground on which cooperation was invited and obtained, if, afterwards, this decision is reversed, and this sanction withdrawn, such a gross breach of faith could not fail to deprive for ever the Commissioners, and all other public men who may be parties to it, of all public confidence, and of all just claim to it. It would be vain to say, "We think this or that a matter of very small consequence." The answer would be: 1. It is plain you did not reckon it so when you brought it forward before the public as a strong recommendation of the system. 2. Who is to be the judge of the comparative importance of a certain innovation? You? The very party introducing it? Why, every first encroachment is either in itself small, or is so represented by its authors. And 3. Why should we expect that the first step will also be the last? When once you have departed from an implied pledge to the public, what security is there that you will not introduce fresh and fresh violations of it? Is it to be expected that you will go on following all the changes and conforming to all the variations of a Church which boasts of being unchangeable and united, but whose highest dignitaries pronounce that heterodox now which was in the judgment of others equally high quite orthodox some years ago?

'When, however, I speak of the ruinous effect on public confidence which I am convinced would result from the proposed innovations, I wish it to be distinctly understood that, even if I thought quite otherwise on that point, and saw a present worldly expediency in them, I should still feel not at liberty, morally, to be a party to them, I should feel this to be an abandonment of principle. But, as it is,

I am convinced that nothing would be gained—very much the reverse—by my continuing a Commissioner under such an abandonment of the system hitherto pursued. I approve the system as much as ever, and am as ready as ever to carry it on; but I feel I should be deserting it in the most disingenuous and most mischievous way possible were I to pretend to be carrying it on when in reality subverting it. I should make the proceedings of the Board even more open to suspicion (if possible) than they would be without. For if a man is liable, as he must be, to incur distrust and contempt for making unwarrantable concessions, under a mistaken belief that he is acting rightly, how much more when it is known that his conviction is the very reverse! All the influence I have possessed has been based on the general belief (partaken of by many, even of those most opposed to me in practice) of my firm and conscientious adherence to what I deliberately judge to be my duty. If I were to come forward acting against that judgment, and which moreover is known to be my judgment, for the late proceedings are no secret, I should forfeit all public confidence, and my support of any measure would be thenceforward utterly worthless.

'I have endeavoured, at the risk of being tedious, to lay before your Excellency as plainly as possible the grounds of my convictions. And whether there shall appear to you sufficient grounds or not, at least you will perceive that with these convictions I cannot possibly swerve from the course I have resolved on.

'Believe me, &c.,

'RD. DUBLIN.'

' Palace: July 21, 1853.

' My dear Lord,—When I received the favour of your Excellency's last communication, in which you inform

me, in a perfectly courteous and friendly manner, that
you do not take the same view of matters with myself, I
was at first disposed to consider this as a sufficient and
final answer; for it is manifest that two persons cannot
satisfactorily act together in carrying on any system whose
views on some fundamental points connected with the
system are radically different. Your Excellency is, by
office, the head of the national school system, the Commissioners being merely your agents; and no one of them
can properly retain that office whose views are opposed
to those of the head of the department. I had accordingly
declared, in appealing to your Excellency against the late
decision of the Board, that if that decision was ratified by
Government, either expressly or tacitly, I should consider
myself as dismissed, and this ratification seemed to be
implied in the words used by your Excellency.

'But then, as there was reference made to a Cabinet
Council that was shortly to be held on the subject, I
thought this might mean that the decision of that council
might possibly alter your Excellency's view, and I accordingly resolved to wait a few days longer before finally
announcing my withdrawal.

'I have received no communication since, and I find
that a Cabinet Council did meet last Saturday, in which,
considering the debate that was to come on on the
ensuing Monday, I cannot doubt there was a full discussion
of the Irish education question.

'Any further delay now would add to all the evils of
the false position in which I find myself placed. I am
naturally considered responsible for all the acts of a Board
of which I am a member; and that Board has passed a
measure which I have protested against as an unjustifiable
breach of faith with the public; and, moreover, there are
many hundred schools, of which the patrons will, if they

follow my example or advice, refuse compliance with the order which the Board will, I presume, proceed to issue, and will appeal to Government, and then to Parliament, for redress.

'If it be contended that the Commissioners were intrusted with a "power" to remove any books from their list, I shall not contend about a word, provided it be admitted (which I must ever maintain) that to do so is an abuse of their power, and one which it is plain was never contemplated by either the advocates or the opponents of the system.

'The "full control over the books to be used," was always understood to mean that no book not sanctioned by the Commissioners should be used. But if there had ever been an idea of their prohibiting books which had been unanimously so sanctioned, the appeal to the books, as an inducement to join the system, would have been a mere fraud, and all the debates respecting them nugatory.

'I shall not, under these circumstances, trouble your Excellency or Lord Aberdeen with any further discussion on the matters in question; but on Tuesday next, if I receive no communication from Government to the contrary, shall send notice to the Education Board that I am no longer a Commissioner.

'I remain, &c.,

'Rd. Dublin.'

'July 24, 1853.

'My dear Lord,—I collect from your Excellency's letter to Baron Greene that you have been misinformed as to some important points. I have not seen him, and perhaps he may have explained those points. But I will take the liberty at the risk of saying what is superfluous, of correcting the misstatements, as they are of much importance, which appear to have been made.

' 1. You seem to have been given to understand that the eighth rule has hitherto been so acted on as to allow the objection of one child to exclude a book from the rest; and that Baron Greene's amendment goes to introduce a new practice.

' This is contrary to the fact. If your Excellency will obtain from the secretary the correspondence of the Board a good many years ago with a Mr. Tattenham, you will see that the interpretation then (and always) given of the rule coincides with Baron G.'s view. Never has it been so acted on as to exclude a book in consequence of the objection of some children. Baron G.'s object was to prevent a threatened change;—a practical interpretation of the rule contrary, not only to reason, and to the known design of the framers, but also to their constant practice.

' 2. I fully concur in the general proposition, and so I doubt not would Baron G., that " the Commissioners are not wrong in prohibiting the use, at the time of combined instruction, of a religious book which Roman Catholics believe to be inconsistent with the doctrines of their Church."

' This is a point on which all are agreed, and always have been. But your Excellency seems to have been given to understand that Baron G., or I, or some one else, have endeavoured to introduce such a book.

' But I wonder that any one should have ventured to throw out a calumny against us, which is so easily refuted. No book ever was, or could be, placed on the list of those sanctioned by the Board that had not obtained the approbation of all the Commissioners, Protestant and Roman Catholic. And, as far as the particular book in question is concerned,—the " Lessons on the Truth of Christianity,"

— so careful was Dr. Murray that he sent it to Rome to be submitted to the late Pope, who had it read to him in Italian, and pronounced it unobjectionable. [By the way, it has been translated into Italian since, by a priest at Florence, with the approbation of his diocesan.] That, therefore, as well as all the other books of the Board, is not " inconsistent with the doctrines of the Church of Rome," such as they were at least some years ago. If their fundamental doctrines have undergone such a change since, that that which was orthodox sixteen or twenty years ago is heterodox now, it cannot be expected that the Commissioners or the Government should follow all these changes.

' 3. When your Excellency says that " no Commissioner ought to act as if the decision of the Board had been confirmed by Government," you seem to understand that a decision of the Board does not come into action at all till it has been so confirmed; in short, that it is like a bill which has passed both Houses, and is waiting for the Royal Assent to become law. But the reverse is the fact. A decision of the Board takes effect at once, if Government does not interfere. Silence amounts to a ratification ; and therefore, if Baron G. defers his withdrawal while Government is deliberating, the decision will be acted on, and the evil (as he regards it) will be going on in the meantime ; and we shall be considered as responsible for the acts of a Board of which we are members.

' Now, this, I think, he will consider as the proposal of a truce on one side, and not on both ; it is as if an invading army should propose an armistice while negotiations are pending, on the condition that we should lay down our arms, and they should proceed in their career.

' If the proposal were that the late decision of the Board should be rescinded for the present, and that then his withdrawal should be deferred, though I do not say he would accede to this, at least it would have some appearance of fairness. But that he should recall his decision, and the Commissioners not recall theirs, does seem to me, I must say, anything but reasonable.

'On this, however, and on any other matter of opinion, I cannot pronounce how far Baron Greene may concur with me. But as regards matters of fact, I have no doubt he will be ready to confirm all the statements I have made.

'I remain, &c.,

'Rd. Dublin.

'P.S. It may be worth while to correct one other misapprehension that has gone abroad. Baron Greene did not propose his explanation of Rule 8 as a substitute for that rule, but as (what I have here called it) an explanation of the sense in which it has always hitherto been acted on.

'It was in his absence, and without his knowledge, or Mr. Blackburne's, that it was, through some blunder, entered on the minutes as a new rule.'

'Palace: July 26, 1853.

'May it please your Excellency,—Pursuant to the communication made a short time ago, I have now to announce to Government, through your Excellency, and to the Commissioners, that I am no longer a member of the Education Board.

'When I found myself under the painful necessity of appealing to your Excellency against the recent proceedings of the Board, which I regard as a departure from the existing system, such as we were not justified in making, I added, that if I obtained no redress from Government I should consider myself dismissed.

'I have purposely avoided using the word "resignation," lest I should be understood to have altered my
views of the National system, and to withdraw from it as
no longer approving it. The reverse is the fact. I am
as much attached to the system as ever, and as ready as
ever to carry it on ; and it is precisely because I do retain
these views that I am driven to the present step. Feeling
that the system, which has flourished for above twenty-
one years, is virtually abandoned, and consequently that
the office I have hitherto held is in reality suppressed, it
would not be fair for me to deceive Parliament and the
public by pretending to go on carrying out the system,
which, in truth, is fundamentally changed.

'If I were to wait for the final determination of
Government on the matters in debate, the decision of the
Board in the meanwhile taking effect, I should be placed
altogether in a false position. By withholding my decision
to withdraw while the Commissioners do not withhold
theirs, but carry it out in practice, I should be held
responsible, and justly, for proceedings which I not only
believe, but am known to believe, to be unjustifiable.

'When I spoke of the Commissioners having exceeded
their "powers," and of their having no "right" to prohibit books that have received the unanimous sanction of
the Board, of course I was speaking of fair and equitable
rights. As for legal rights, or obligations enforced by
legal penalties, these were not in my mind. I am considering what a man of honour would hold himself bound
to do, or debarred from doing, in the faithful discharge of
a public trust solemnly confided to him. I am well aware
that a man may sometimes find himself so circumstanced
as to have the "power," with legal impunity, to break
faith with his neighbour, — to disappoint reasonable
expectations which he knows to exist, and has himself

contributed to raise,—to " keep the word of promise to the ear, and break it to the hope."

' But to any one judging fairly it must be evident that " the full control over the books to be used " given to the Commissioners was always understood to mean, that no books were to be used without their unanimous sanction, and that any book thus sanctioned was to be supplied to any school in connection with the Board, and might be used therein if the patron approved it.

' That a book so sanctioned should be liable to be afterwards prohibited is what never was at all contemplated by any of the Ministries which have supported the system, or by any Parliament that has voted grants to it, or by any Member of Parliament favourable or hostile to the schools.

' This is plainly proved by all the debates, and they have been very numerous, that have ever taken place on the subject.

' In the debate lately, on a motion of Lord Clancarty's, and in every debate on the motion for a grant for the schools, and on many other occasions, reference has been made (both by advocates and opponents) to the list of the books sanctioned by the Board. Never did any opponent come forward to say, " This is all a delusion ; we are wasting time in discussing the merits of these books, since some of them may probably be struck off the list next week, and some more the week after. The list of books is merely a bait to allure the over-trustful into placing schools under the Board, and as soon as the deception has succeeded, the books which had chiefly aided in it will be prohibited."

' And if any one had brought forward such a surmise, it cannot be doubted that it would have been repelled with indignation and disgust.

'This being the case, it is plain that to depart from the system in this point, and to introduce an innovation never contemplated by any one when the grants were moved for and voted, would be to divert the public money from the purposes for which it was granted; and it is also a gross injustice towards the many hundred patrons of schools who were invited and induced to place them under the Board on the strength of an implied promise, fully understood by all parties, and acted on for twenty-one years, but which it is now proposed to violate.

'When on various occasions attempts were made by some parties among Protestants to introduce for their purposes such a "modification of the system" as would have amounted to a subversion of it, I always strenuously opposed any such unwarrantable changes. I never would nor never will consent to break faith either with Roman Catholics or with Protestants.

'And that the recent proceedings of the Board (even if not followed up, as I cannot doubt they will be, by further steps in the same direction) do amount to a breach of faith with the public, and involve a misapplication of the public money, is a conclusion which appears perfectly evident, both to myself and to all those confidential advisers, including some of the ablest and most upright characters in existence, with whom I have discussed the subject.

'I will take the liberty of suggesting, in conclusion, not as a Commissioner, but as a patron of a National School, that measures should be taken to secure at least the schools (amounting to several hundreds) which are actually using the books proposed to be discarded, from being deprived of the advantage they have hitherto enjoyed.

'The patrons of these schools, if thus grievously

wronged, will be likely to bring forward their complaints
in a manner which may lead to such contests as are much
to be deprecated.

'I have the honour, &c.,

'RD. DUBLIN.'

In the midst of these turmoils, he found time to write
to his old friend Bishop Hinds, on hearing of a domestic
bereavement.

'Dublin: Feb. 1, 1853.

'My dear Hinds,—After what you had said in a former
letter, I could not feel surprised or even sorry to hear of
your good mother's departure. As for the sufferings
previously undergone, it is hard to check the imagination
so as to keep within the bounds of reason; but I always
endeavour to recollect in such cases that what is past and
over, for ever, is no legitimate source of grief. The only
thing which reason cannot get over in such a case—the
suffering of the good—is only one portion of the one great
difficulty, the existence of evil; and when the suffering is
such as to exhibit an edifying example of patient faith,
one perceives, which is not always the case, one good
brought out of evil.

'Far more afflicting to all parties, except the patient
herself—and sometimes to her or him also—is the piteous
spectacle of decaying intellect, gradually reaching the
point of complete dotage, and presenting for perhaps
years an object of unmixed pain to those around.

'I congratulate you and your sisters on having been
spared everything of this kind. Pray God my family
may be spared it too!'

'Feb. 4, 1853.

'My dear Senior,—It is curious to find Lord John, of
all people, saying that a Commission would bind Govern-

ment to carry out its recommendations, he being the Minister who appointed a Poor Law Enquiry Commission for Ireland; and, on being dissatisfied with its report, employed you to criticise, and then brought in a bill quite at variance with both our judgment and yours.

'There is much to be said, both for and against the ventilating of any plans, in every case; but the character of each plan makes a great difference.

'When there is some one distinct and complete measure contemplated, not admitting of modifications, then it is best to say nothing about it till the last moment. Thus, the appointment of Hampden to a bishopric, and the abolition of the Lord Lieutenancy, should have been privately resolved on, and (without giving time to organise opposition) brought forward as things to be done at once.

'Now, in both these cases he did just the reverse, and was defeated accordingly in one and harassed in the other; but when there are very many details, there are strong reasons the other way.

'True it is that the Reform Bill did owe to suddenness and secresy its immediate success; but did it not to the same cause owe its ultimate failure? For a failure it must be called, since in twenty years it requires a thorough re-reform.

'Perhaps it would be best that the Commissioners should be instructed to collect evidences as to the facts of the actual working of the present law, and to make no recommendations except where quite decided and unanimous, else to state the pros and cons for each suggestion; and then Government could not surely be at all committed.

'Yours ever,
'R. WHATELY.'

It was about this time that he wrote the following letter of lively 'chat' to an old and valued Oxford friend, who had been the companion of many earlier and happier days.

To Philip Bury Duncan, Esq.

'Dublin: Feb. 17, 1853.

'My dear Duncan,—I was glad to receive a few lines from an old friend, just forty-two years from the time of my first making acquaintance with him in a coach between Bath and Oxford.

" Here you may see with vast surprise
How spiders are devoured by flies."

I suppose you reprint those verses with the latest additions. I suppose you have seen them with the additional couplets about the bower birds. By-the-bye, did you ever see the epigram which I sent to be inserted? I do not know whether it was in the visitors' book of the Bavarian Valhalla?[1]

'From Fitzgerald you have his respectful regards to his patron, and from me a recommendation to read, if you have not, his "Historic Certainties." Have you seen his edition of extracts from Aristotle? There is an English description prefixed, which deserves letters of gold. What you propose for Oxford may be effected there, and there only, when my suggestion, which I suppose you have seen in the evidence, of a preliminary examination, is adopted. For the οἱ πολλοί take a degree, with that amount of proficiency which may be fairly expected of a lad of seventeen or eighteen, on entrance; and this they would bring to the university, if we would insist on it. Thus they would begin their academical education where they now end it, and then all that you propose might easily be superadded.

'P.S. Did you ever hear of the Cambridge tutor who

<hr>

[1] See the 'Miscellaneous Remains,' where this is inserted.

rebuked a man who had quizzed him for continually introducing the expletive, " I say "—

> " I say, they say, you say, I say, I say."

'This rebuke is an English verse. Can you put it into a Latin or a Greek verse?'

Again we find him urging Mrs. Hill to continue her anti-slavery labours.

'Feb. 12, 1853.

'My dear Mrs. Hill,—You must get on now with your slavery article, or it will be thrown out to make room for some of the trashy theology and metaphysics which Mr. Fraser is dosed with. Some of his contributors are eccentric geniuses—all but the genius, and they approach (to use their own language) " to the verge of unintelligibility." There is one who writes about " sevensomeness," in an article on the Sabbath, which he calls Sabaoth! But there is in the last number a capital article on France.

'Your article should be chiefly occupied—1. In doubts about the plan of redeeming slaves and sending them to Siberia, which I suspect is a plan for getting rid (like the crypteia of the Spartans) of the most dangerous to the slave system. 2. On the contrast between a poor hard-worked labourer in Europe, and a slave. The sense of wrong is a great aggravation of any suffering to one who has the feeling of a man. It is unpleasant in going through a wood to have boughs bang against one's face, and drops from the trees wet one; but who feels this as he would a man's spitting in his face, and slapping him at pleasure? True, many a slave has lost the feelings of a man; so much the worse!

> " Wretch whom no sense of wrong can rouse to vengeance!
> Sordid, unfeeling, reprobate, degraded,
> Spiritless outcast!"[1]

---

[1] See Canning's ' Knife Grinder,'

3. Suggest the greater profitableness of free labour, when fairly- tried.   4. Bishop Hinds's suggestion should be noticed, and the pros and cons briefly stated.   5. Something about Abbeokuta and Sierra Leone, and the effects now being made to introduce agricultural industry into Africa.   Better for all parties that cotton and sugar should be grown there (which succeed perfectly) and thence imported, than to carry away the negroes to cultivate them 1,000 miles off.

‘I could write the article myself; and I could also do this, and I could do that, and I could do the other ; but that therefore I could do all the things that I am pressed to do, is a fallacy ; and if I were to wait till my advisers were all agreed which task should have the preference, I should do nothing at all.

‘I must inquire about that Jewish version of the Old Testament.   I should like to know what they make of those points touched on in the “Tractatus Tres;”[1] and, by-the-bye, I should like to know what you think of the theories of those Tractatus.   The Latin is far from elegant, but not very hard to make out.

‘Those lines on Webster you might insert in your article, if they have not been published.   I think you will give as “general satisfaction” as my would-be hangman—i. e. to all except the hanged.’

In April this year the Archbishop was staying with his daughter and son-in-law in Cambridgeshire.   The letter he writes from thence to Mrs. Arnold gives a slight but characteristic touch of that delight in his grandchildren which was one of the solaces of his declining years.

---

[1] A little tract published in Latin on the Continent, by the Archbishop.

'My dear Mrs. Arnold,—In case your folks should be as dilatory as usual, I send you a " Caution," which you can dispose of if you have another copy.

'You should inquire for the new edition of Mr. Cookesley's letter to me, and my answer.[1] It is in the press, and is much enlarged.

'I am enacting the part of a camel, and sundry other beasts of burden, to carry my grand-daughter on my back.

'I trust you have come in for your share of this fine growing weather.'

He writes as follows to Miss Gurney, of North Repps. with whom his daughter was at that time staying, on the Jewish Emancipation Bill of this year.

'London: May 7, 1853.

'My dear Miss Gurney,—Many thanks for the seeds, which I have sent to Dublin; and much more, for your kindness to my Jane. How much rather would I have been of your party, puzzling out etymologies, than amidst all the turmoil of London!

'My speech was very meagrely reported, as mine usually are; but, though my views differ much from those of most of the supporters of the bill, they do not differ at all from those I published (in a speech on the same subject) about twenty years ago, and again in my Charge of the year 1851. So that if you wish to see them fully set forth, you may look at those.

'The supporters of the bill were, many of them, as lukewarm as its opponents were zealous, or we should have had a much better minority. But I plainly told

---

[1] On Miss Sellon and the 'Sisterhood,' at Plymouth.

Lord A—— that, I hoped they would next time bring in a better bill, taking the bull by the horns at once, and sweeping off all religious disabilities. One might then say, consistently, that this is not from indifference to Christianity, but from a persuasion that all attempts to monopolise by law civil privileges for Christians, or for Christians of any particular communion, are contrary to the spirit of the Gospel, and tend to make Christ's a kingdom of this world. As it is, we are in a most absurdly false position, in many ways: 1. A Jew is admitted to the elective franchise. 2. Since to let a Jew take his seat when elected, would, it seems, unchristianise the legislature; to admit a Roman Catholic must, by the same rule, unprotestantise the legislature; and to admit a Dissenter, must unchurch it; and so on. 3. Since to remove the existing declaration would, it seems, proclaim indifference to Christianity, the retaining of it proclaims indifference to all but the name; since there are men (and much more numerous than the Jews) who are ready to call themselves Christians, and who themselves avow what they mean by it, as denying all revelation except the impressions on each man's own mind, and rejecting the chief part of the Gospel-history and Gospel-doctrines. Such are the followers of F. Newman and Greg. 4. We are proclaiming that the English people are so desirous of electing Jews, and the House of Commons (four different parliaments!) of allowing them to sit, that it is necessary for the House of Lords to throw out this bill, in order to show that we are a Christian nation!

'And yet, after all, this honour to Christianity (!) is bestowed only by a side wind, and accidentally; for, the declaration was never designed as a religious test, but as a declaration of loyalty; but it so happened that the wording of it proved an obstacle to Jews taking their seats.

'Well, therefore, did Lord —— say that logical conclusions and reasoning must be laid aside by the opponents! If they would be consistent, they should let no
person have a vote for a member, or be eligible without
declaring himself a Christian. As the law now stands, it
is a mass of absurdity.' [1]

'My dear Senior,—I have received from —— an
acknowledgment of my last (of which I sent you a
copy), saying that he does not agree with me; and that
no doubt the Cabinet will decide on the matter as soon
as they have leisure. My belief is that they mean not
to find leisure till after the close of the Session. But
this I shall not acquiesce in. My character will be in
more and more danger every day that I am a member of
a Board which has departed from the system. And after
the lapse of a few days I shall inform them that if by
such a day—say the end of this month, at latest—I find
the late resolution still standing on the minute-book, I
shall consider myself dismissed.

'They wish, I conceive, to avoid any battle either with
the Irish brigade or with the opposite by throwing the
matter over, and saying (if pressed) that there has been
a small difference of opinion among some of the Commissioners, and that it may end in the unfortunate resignation of one or more; but that they mean to supply their
places, and go on with the system, &c.

---

[1] 'The debate to which allusion is here made took place on April 29. On
this occasion the Archbishop spoke out, on the general subject of tests, with
even more than his usual fearlessness. He was dissatisfied with the present
bill, not merely on account of what he conceived to be an erroneous title, in that
it purported to be a bill for the relief of the Jews, instead of for the relief
of electors; but because it did not do away altogether with all declarations
required from members of Parliament. 'He did not approve of this patch-
work legislation—this passing of laws, first for the relief of Separatists, then
of Quakers, then of Jews.'"

'But this must not be.

'I have appealed against the Commissioners, and if the appeal is rejected, I shall regard myself as dismissed, and the system as abolished and replaced by a new one.'

The Archbishop was now returned to Dublin; and we find him writing to his old friend, Dr. Daubeny, of Oxford, on one of the subjects which formed a pleasing relaxation to his mind from more pressing cares. His love of natural history and botany never failed; and the College Botanical Gardens in Dublin bear witness to his many and varied experiments, and the interest he took in collecting plants from all parts. His correspondents in various quarters of the globe, knowing his tastes, frequently sent him seeds or cuttings, which he always took to the College Gardens that they might have the benefit of the careful superintendence of Mr. Baine, to whose admirable management and scientific knowledge he always bore ready testimony; and many of his pleasantest hours were spent in watching the effects of these experiments.

'Palace, Dublin: June 11, 1853.

'Dear Dr. Daubeny.—Many thanks for your book, of which I have read as yet only the passage relating to myself.

'There is a case of what may be called acclimatisation, which seems very curious. The red-flowering ribes when first brought over was remarked as flowering freely but never fruiting; after some years it began to bear here and there a berry, and every year more and more, and now is every year loaded with fruit. The *ribes aureum* and the prickly species have also begun, after several years, to bear a few berries.

' All the plants of the Garrya in our country bear only catkins, though it is said to be a monœcious plant.

' There are some differences between England and Ireland, which it seems hard to explain from differences of climate. The Buddlea flowers freely in England, but the flowers are almost always abortive. When I lived in Suffolk I had one which once produced a perfect seed-vessel, and my neighbours came to see it as a great curiosity. In Ireland they are loaded with seed-vessels every year. How is this to be accounted for ?

' When I lived in Suffolk I had a laburnum tree, one of whose branches, about as thick as a finger, swelled out towards the extremity nearly to the thickness of one's wrist, and from this bulging part pushed out a dozen or more luxuriant shoots. I cut off the branch and sent it to a horticultural society in London, who considered it a great curiosity. In Ireland nearly half the laburnums we see put forth such branches.

' Yours truly,

' RD. DUBLIN.

' June 12.

' P.S.—It was in the Sandwich Islands that taro was cultivated, not in New Zealand, where they had only the sweet potato.

' The inspissated juice of the cassava is called cassaripe, not cassarine. I doubt whether the poisonous juice is ever used by the Indians to poison their arrows, though they do use for that purpose some vegetable poisons. It is a curious circumstance worth noticing that there is a variety of the cassava, not a distinct species, which is not at all poisonous ; it is eaten boiled or roasted, like a potato.

' I believe you will find that the tripe de roche is not a seaweed but a lichen.'

Again he writes to Miss Crabtree :—

'Dublin : August 23, 1853.

'I send you the last published of the "Hopeful" Tracts,[1] which have been found very useful here. The great difficulty in Irish questions is, that they usually seem at the first glance so *easy*, that a man of intelligence who has spent two or three months in Ireland, or, like ——, two or three weeks, is apt to fancy that he understands the country, and sees how it should be governed ; but if he has patience and inquires further, with *great* diligence and great candour, he begins to find that he understands far less than he fancied he did, and, on still further inquiry, he finds that further yet is needful, like Simonides in the well-known story, who asked first for a day to answer a question, and then two days, and then four. If Mr. —— ever should come to know half a quarter as much of Ireland as I do, he would burn his pamphlet.

'Because Ireland is poor and half-civilised and full of ignorance and error, it is generally thought that a very little knowledge and study are sufficient to govern it ! I am reminded of the young medical student who thought he had learnt enough of medicine to cure a very little child !'

To Mr. Senior.

'September 20, 1853.

'Those who regard man as a very consistent being, and accordingly look on any instance to the contrary as a kind of prodigy, may well wonder at a Roman Catholic sanctioning a Work on Evidences. And if they look about them a little, they may find other matters for

---

[1] A series of Tracts, published in Dublin, under the Archbishop's sanction.

marvel; e.g. that the study of evidence should be discouraged by a professed successor of the apostle Peter, who charged us to be "ready to give a reason of the hope that is in us;" and that *Logical* Studies should be tolerated, and encouraged by Roman Catholics, and among fallacies that of the "*Circle*" enumerated by them; when they bid you take the truth of your religion on trust, on the word of their Church, without seeking any further proof; and if you ask *why* you are to trust that Church, refer you to certain passages of scripture; and when you urge that those passages do not seem to bear any such meaning, tell you that you must interpret scripture according to the teaching of the Church; and so round again. A man may go round the world fancying he is travelling in a straight line; but it is strange he should not be giddy in running round a circle of ten paces diameter.

'But when you talk of wonders, what more strange than to find men of mature age, and who were supposed to possess common sense and common honesty, and to have some regard for their character, talking about the fitness or unfitness of such and such a book for Roman Catholics, as if that had anything to do with the present question? The book was (whether wisely or unwisely) deliberately sanctioned for fifteen years by the highest Roman Catholic authorities; and to say that now they have changed their minds, and may fairly prohibit that book, and that whole course of study to those who do not object to it, and many of whom were invited and induced by the bait of such books to place schools under the Board—this is like saying that if a man thinks he has made an imprudent marriage, he is entitled to a divorce. Indeed, if man's conduct generally were of a piece with such a profligate system of morals, the whole framework of society would be broken up.

'In the case of an action for breach of promise of marriage, if it be proved that a man has, though without signing any regular bond, given a woman to understand that he designs to marry her, only half as plainly as men were assured of their right to use the books of the Board, every judge and jury gives heavy damages against him; nor is he ever allowed to plead that he was not originally bound to enter into the engagement, and that therefore he may break it at pleasure.

'P.S. I am continually receiving fresh and fresh proofs that Ministers will find themselves in a sad scrape if they persist in supporting the Commissioners whose proceedings, in proportion as truth comes to light, are daily exciting fresh disgust, indignation, and alarm, both in Ireland and England. For, their plan and that of their advocates is to circulate gross falsehoods and misrepresentations (one of them you saw in the "Times" a good while back), which are credited for a short time, but when detected double the disgust felt, not only for their conduct, but also for their mode of defending it. Many of these falsehoods cannot indeed be traced exactly to the Commissioners themselves; but as some can, the public will not give them credit for being scrupulous about the rest: e.g. they have published the answer to my letter of resignation, in which is a gross misstatement, which no one will suspect *him* of having invented, and which in fact can be proved to have come from them; viz. that the rule by which they make the objection of one child, exclude a book from the whole school, was on one occasion only interpreted in a different way; the fact being that it was always, for thirteen years, so interpreted.

'And again, that rule, though ambiguously worded, did not appear to them quite sufficiently to bear them out in their procedure ; and so, in their Report just published, they have forged a different rule, putting in the words, " separate—religious—instruction," which are not in the original rule ! Now this is what Fouché would call " worse than a crime, a blunder." Their tricks, according to the proverb, are " sewed with white thread," for such a clumsy artifice is sure to be detected and exposed.'

The letter which follows, to Mrs. Hill, unlocks a recess of his inner life, and shows the reality of the struggles he was called on to undergo ; not only against outward difficulties, but inward hindrances.

'Sept. 29, 1853.

'My dear Mrs. Hill,   I sent you, yesterday, a copy of the vol. of " Cautions." The principal good that we expected to do (and that was our object) was among those who would only partially approve. For what people most readily and most cordially approve, is the echo of their own sentiments : and they admire one who, perhaps, expresses these better than they could. But then, this leaves them much where they were, only, perhaps, better pleased with themselves. If there could be a book (on moral or religious subjects) which every one thought very convincing, this would be a sign that it had convinced nobody. But when a good many people read what they approve in part, about five per cent. may, perhaps, be brought in time to reconsider their opinions and practice in reference to the parts they did *not* like ; and in time some of them may come to alter their views a little. But this, one is not likely to hear much of. The " cheers " come from those who were already convinced.

'There are thoughts that I have long been accustomed habitually to bring before my mind, and to suggest to myself, continually, that it is better to have a chance of doing even a very little good, which, perhaps, may not even take place in my lifetime, and which I am not very likely to hear of if it does ; and to incur ever so much censure from various parties, than to obtain the applause of millions, by flattering their inclinations. We were— and are—convinced that we might have gained a much larger amount of popularity, and have escaped nearly one half of the disapprobation we have encountered, if we had pursued a different course. But even if this course had been in itself a better than the one we did take, it would not have been right for *us*, if at variance with our convictions.

' All this, most would admit in words, but in practice there are many temptations to depart from the rule, and these temptations are different to different persons. Perhaps you have heard that, according to the Hindoo law, infidelity in a wife is severely denounced, except only in case of her being offered the present of an Elephant. That is considered a douceur too magnificent for any woman to be expected to refuse. Now in Europe, though an actual elephant is not the very thing that offers the strongest temptation, there is, in most people's conscience, something analogous to it ; and different things are elephants to different characters.

'To myself, the "scandalon" most to be guarded against —the right hand and right eye, that offended, and was to be cut off—was one, which few people who have not known me as a child, would, I believe, conjecture. It was not avarice or ambition. If I could have had an Archbishopric for asking it of a minister, I would not have asked, though the alternative had been to break stones on the road ; nor would such a sacrifice have cost me much of a struggle. But my danger was from the dread of censure. Few would conjecture this, from seeing how I

have braved it all my life, and how I have perpetually
been in hot water, when, in truth, I had a natural aversion
to it. But so it was. Approbation I had, indeed, a natural
liking for; but so immensely short of my *dislike* of its
opposite, that I would not have purchased (by my own
choice) a pound of honey at the cost of chewing one
drachm of aloes.

'So I set myself resolutely to *act* as if I cared nothing
for either the sweet or the bitter, and in time I got
hardened. And this will always be the case, more or
less, through God's help, if we will but persevere, and
persevere from a right motive. One gets hardened, as the
Canadians do to walking in snow-shoes [raquets]: at first
a man is almost crippled with the 'mal raquet,' the pain
and swelling of the feet, but the prescription is, to go on
walking in them, as if you felt nothing at all, and in a
few days you feel nothing.

'There was a very dear and valued and worthy friend
of mine, who was excessively sensitive, though I believe
not more so than, originally, I was, and who exerted his
eloquence and ingenuity in descanting on the propriety of
not being wholly indifferent to the opinions formed of one
—the impossibility of eradicating the regard for approbation—and the folly of attempting it, or pretending to it,
&c. I used to reply, that, though this was all very true,
I considered my care and pains better bestowed in keeping
under this feeling than in vindicating it. I treat it, I
said, like the grass on a lawn, which you wish to keep
in good order; you neither attempt, nor wish to destroy
the grass; but you mow it down from time to time, as
close as you possibly can, well trusting that there will be
quite enough left, and that it will be sure to grow
again.

'This seems to be all about myself, but there is some

general use in warning all people to be on the look-out, each for his own Elephant.'

Mrs. Hill, in her answer to this letter, objected that a total want of deference or concern for the opinion of wise and trustworthy friends, is an extreme to which many are liable, and would be an equally trustful one with the opposite. The Archbishop's answer is as follows:—

'October 6, 1853.

'My dear Mrs. Hill,—I rather suspect that you are confounding together two things in themselves quite different, though in practice very difficult to be distinguished:—love of approbation, and deference for the judgment of the (supposed) wise and good, &c. The latter may be felt towards those whom we never can meet with;—who perhaps were dead ages before we were born, and survive only in their writings. It may be misplaced or excessive; but it is quite different from the desire of their applause or sympathy or dread of their displeasure or contempt. A man's desire to find himself in agreement with Aristotle, or Bacon, or Locke, or Paley, &c. whether reasonable or unreasonable, can have nothing to do with their approbation of him. But when you are glad to concur with some living friends whom you think highly of, and dread to differ from them, it is very difficult to decide how far this feeling is, the presumption formed by your judgment in favour of the correctness of their views (see " Rhetoric—Presumption "), and how far it is the desire of their approbation and sympathy, and dread of the reverse.

'It is of this latter exclusively that I was speaking: you, I think, in the instances you adduce or allude to, were thinking of the other. A man who is—like one of those you mention—excessive in his dread of excessive deference, will be very apt to fall into the opposite extreme, of courting paradox and striving after originality.

'But I was thinking entirely of a different matter, the excessive care concerning what is said or thought of myself.

'Elizabeth Smith (whose vol. of "Remains" I have unhappily lost; she was an admirable person) says that if she were to hold up a finger on purpose to gain the applause of the whole world, she would be unjustifiable. If, said she, I obtain the approbation of the wise and good, by doing what is right, simply because it is right, I am gratified; but I must never make this gratification, either wholly or partly, my object.

'Yet she had, and avowed, much deference for the judgment of others, and was reluctant to differ from those who she thought likely to know better than herself. It was not this deference but the desire of personal approbation, that she felt bound so severely to check.

'One difficulty in acting on this principle is, that it often is even a duty to seek the good opinion of others, not as an ultimate object and for its own sake, but for the sake of influencing them for their own benefit and that of others, "Let your light *so* shine . . . . Glorify your Father in Heaven."

'But we are to watch and analyse the motives of even actions which we are sure are in themselves right.

'And this is a kind of vigilance which human nature is always struggling to escape. One class of men are satisfied as long as they do what is justifiable, i.e. what may be done from a good motive and what when so done would be right; and which therefore may be satisfactorily defended. Another class—the ascetic—are for cutting off everything that may be a snare. They have heard of the "deceitfulness of riches," and so they vow poverty, which is less trouble than watching your motives in gaining and spending money. And so of the rest. But if you would cut off all temptations, you must cut off your head at once.

'Yours truly,

'RD. DUBLIN.'

The persecutions inflicted in the poor-houses on many converts to Protestantism, forced from poverty to betake themselves to this only place of shelter, had been brought before the Archbishop's attention specially at this time. At a somewhat later period his son-in-law, Mr. Wale, made very minute inquiries into this subject, visited several places where these abuses were carried on, and obtained much important information. But such sufferings were easier to ascertain than to remedy.

It was on this subject that the following letter was written to Mr. Senior :—

'October 24, 1853.

'My dear Senior,—I send you a paper (which pray acknowledge) which has an account of poor-house persecution. I had always foreseen and foretold, that besides other evils of the Poor Law in Ireland, there would be that of incessant squabbles, on a fresh battle-field between Protestants and Roman Catholics. But, of late, this has increased tenfold; because many of the Protestants are converts; and the object of the Roman Catholic priests in each locality, is to keep all converts from being employed, so as to force them into the workhouse; and then, when they are there, to have them persecuted without hope of redress. For, most of the officers in the generality of the workhouses, and a vast majority of the inmates, being Roman Catholics, it is hardly ever that the most notorious outrages can be *legally* established by testimony. I doubt whether even in Tuscany greater cruelties are practised than in several of our workhouses. For, what I send you now, is I believe only one case out of very many. As for the man who was only imprisoned for a day, and forced to be bound over to keep the peace, for handing a paper to another, it is true, this was far short, in point of severity, of the Tuscan proceedings. But I wonder you should overlook, as you seem to do, the important circumstance that the one was wholly illegal; and that when once men in office are allowed to set at nought law, no one can tell what may come next. The other was according to law, though a most absurd and cruel law; but still, when law is adhered to, a man can know what he may and may not do. The insolent and overbearing proceedings of Roman Catholics, and the disgust and dread felt by Protestants, increase daily. The sanction afforded by Government means to allow Roman Catholic "ascendency" to the same extent as Protestant "ascendency" formerly prevailed. 'Yours ever,

'R. W.

'P.S. If you receive a printed petition, remember that I never saw it till printed.'

To the Same.

'November 25, 1853.

'I am glad you think the Ministry [1] a strong one; not only because (as I told Lord A.) I think they stand between us and anarchy (for I cannot think of any others that could hold their places for one *session*); but because they will have the less need to truckle to the Irish Brigade, commonly called the "Brass Band." But I fear they will think the establishment of the separate-grant

---

[1] That of Lord Aberdeen.

system will really conciliate permanently *both* parties. I must own they have good reason for thinking so; for the ultra-Protestants and ultra-Roman Catholics both press for it; and they together form a considerable majority. But when this has been done, the Protestants finding that about four-fifths of the grant goes to Roman Catholic priests (who will think it too small a proportion; and the others, too large), will look back to their own arguments against the Maynooth grant, and will see that all the objections to that lie with double force against the other, and will assail ministers with redoubled fury for complying with their own desire.

' The Roman Catholics, on the other hand, will complain bitterly of Government giving aid to proselytising schools; for though their own will be in many instances the same, still, since there are many more Roman Catholics than Protestants, there will be a greater number of Roman Catholic children compelled to receive Protestant instruction, than the reverse. There are schools, now, of this description; but the complaints are met at once by the patron's urging that he may do what he will with his own; he maintains the school wholly at his own expense and will insist on teaching in it whatever he thinks fit.

' But the case will be different when it is supported by public money.

'I am convinced therefore that Government, by adopting this course (as I expect they will) instead of satisfying both parties, will double the discontent of both.'

Mrs. Arnold had asked the Archbishop's opinion of a recently published work which had excited much attention.

' Dublin: November 25, 1853.

' My dear Mrs. A.,—I can give you no opinion as yet of Professor Maurice's book. I am now reading it by proxy (which is what I often do), having put it into the hands of an intelligent critic. What I *have* read of his, gives me the impression of being much clearer and more satisfactory in each separate passage, than as a whole. It reminds me (as the works of several other writers do) of a Chinese painting, in which each single object is drawn with great accuracy, but the whole landscape, for want of perspective, is what no one can make head or tail of. Thus I have sometimes read a treatise in which I have understood, and assented to, almost every sentence; and when I have come to the end, and ask myself what is the author's *general drift*, it has generally appeared that he never had any.

'But I lately saw in some periodical an extract from his work, and one from No. 29 of the "Cautions" (one of the finest compositions by-the-bye, in our language), about a "luminous haze" which the writer thought must have had especial reference to Mr. Maurice; though in fact Fitzgerald had not, I believe, any one particular writer in his mind.

'I forget whether I told you that Governor Grey has sent me some copies of a translation into Maori of the "Lessons on Money-matters," which he says has proved highly acceptable to the natives. He is about to publish a translation of the "Lessons on Religious Worship." I have sent him some more books, and among others ——'s "Lessons on Paul's Epistles." So perhaps *they* may appear in Maori.

'I sent him, along with the books, a present of some hips and haws and holly-berries! The weeds of one country are precious in another.'

To Dr. Daubeny.

'Dublin: December 1, 1853.

'Dear Professor,—I thank you for the pamphlet, with the general views of which I am disposed to agree; though I am hardly a fair judge, not having read the "Quarterly." You might I believe have brought in this University as a witness; for there are men among its Fellows who, I believe, are allowed to stand very high in physical science, particularly (but not solely) Professor Lloyd.

'But I wonder you should allude to Homœopathy as a thing to be pooh-pooh-ed out of court, as not deserving even to be attended to. Be it truth or error, good or evil, it has made, and is making, far too great a progress to be thought lightly of. For, as our old friend Aristotle says, καὶ γὰρ τὰ ἀγαθα καὶ τὰ κακά, ἄξια οἰόμεθα σπουδῆς εἶναι.

'You cannot possibly think it more indefensible, than I do the peculiar tenets and pretensions of the Church of Rome; which yet I should never think of treating as if they could never gain any considerable influence, or be worth contending against.

'Paradoxical, certainly, is a great deal of the homœopathic doctrine; but this, which is a strong presumption *against* anything in the outset, becomes a presumption the other way when there is a great and steady, and long-lasting advance. For, as our friend Aristotle again remarks, what men believe must be either probable, or else true; and therefore the great improbability of anything which gains and retains great and increasing belief, is, to a certain extent, a presumption that something so strange must have strong evidence in its favour, or else no one would have listened to it.

'Now, in this case, when I first came here, there was

not, as far as I knew, a single homœopathic practitioner in all Ireland ; at present there are four or five in Dublin alone, in very considerable practice ; besides several in other cities.   I believe there are now more in London alone than there were twelve or fourteen years ago in the whole British Empire.   And from what I saw on the Continent, I am inclined to think that it is there spreading still more.   And when I inquire into the causes of this, I am referred to the statistics of several Foreign Hospitals, and to the returns of Homœopathic and Allopathic practice in Ireland during some frightful visitations of fever, of dysentery, and of cholera : all which returns, if falsified, would, one might expect, have been reported and exposed long since.

'Now such being the evidence adduced, and such the results produced by that evidence, I cannot think that it is to be overthrown by a slight and contemptuous touch. You cannot disperse the Turkish and Russian armies and send them quietly home, like a swarm of bees ; "pulveris exigui jactu."

' Yours very truly,

' RD. DUBLIN.'

' December 14, 1853.

'My dear S.—I am reading the third volume (which is quite independent) of Miss Bremer's (the novelist) "Homes in the New World," which I think would amuse you.   Negro life, free and enslaved, in United States and in Cuba, compared, is one of the most interesting points.

'By-the-bye, Mr. Thackeray was saying, at a party where I met him, that the cases of ill usage are only here and there one out of many thousands ; and that Mrs. Stowe's picture is as if one should represent the English as humpbacked, or a club-foot nation.   Wonderful people are the Americans! In all other regions it is thought at least as likely as not that a man entrusted with absolute power will abuse it. We jealously guard against this danger, and so do the Americans. But of the many hundred thousands of their people, taken indiscriminately, who are nearly all so humane and just, why do they not choose *one* to be their absolute monarch? I think the only excuse for Mr. T. would have been the supposition that he was so *very* favourable in his judgments of human character as to reckon men much better than they are. But in his works he gives just the opposite picture. ALL his clever characters, and a majority of his weak ones, are utterly selfish and base; and none but a few simpletons have any moral good about them. I cannot, therefore, but conclude that he knew better about slavery.

'I send you a corrected copy of the verses. If you will get some one to correct yours by it, that will be an acceptable present to some one.

'Just after I wrote last, I saw an account of one of the Scripture readers having been (for no other offence) assaulted, three ribs broken, a tooth knocked out, &c., and the assailant being brought before a magistrate was sentenced to pay a fine of no less than five shillings! If the Government go on thus, what shall we come to?

'Yours ever,

'R. W.'

'Dublin: December 3, 1853.

'My dear Mrs. A.—I send two copies of a Prospectus of a journal[1] which is to be conducted by some men in whom I have great confidence; among others, Professor Fitzgerald. I hope .it will be such as to do

---

[1] The 'Irish Church Journal,' which was carried on for some years under the Archbishop's sanction.

away the prejudice existing against the Irish branch of
the Church, which I believe is in great measure owing
to the very bad tone of the existing Periodicals.

'I forget whether I sent you before copies of my
circular relative to the Tractite Memorial.

'The "John Bull" has been bellowing at me for inter-
fering with the "right of private judgment." Bishops, it
seems, are to allow full right of private judgment to everyone but themselves; and though solemnly appointed, and
sworn, to check disorderly proceedings as far as they can,
they are to leave everyone to do whatever seemeth right
in his own eyes, and yet to remain (nominally) acting
under their superintendence and control.

'When a new Church was formed (in everything but
name) some years ago, under the title of an Evangelical
Alliance, with articles of faith to be subscribed, and
congregations for prayer and preaching, and synods for
passing decrees, &c. (I am only calling things by their right
names) I was censured, as you are aware, by some well-
meaning persons, for not allowing my clergy to join this
self-constituted body. And my censurers did not, I believe, perceive that they were in fact objecting to all
government, and advocating complete anarchy.

'Now, to me, anarchy does not appear a good thing;
but if I did disapprove of all Church-government, I should
be bound not to hold office in the Church.

'As for the right of private judgment, if any man is
fully convinced that Episcopacy, for instance, is wrong, or
that the Quakers or the Roman Catholics are in the right,
he ought to leave our Church; but not to insist on retaining his position in it, and yet set its rulers and government at nought, like the memorialists.'

A petition for the regulation and inspection of nunneries

brought forward by Lord Shaftesbury in May this year, led to debates in which the Archbishop took a prominent part, and expressed his hearty concurrence in the effort.

A few words of explanation may be useful here, to remove misapprehension. He did, in common with most enlightened Protestants, strongly disapprove of the conventual system, and believe it to be totally unsanctioned by the spirit of the New Testament. And no doubt his feelings on this subject influenced him in advocating the measure in question. But he maintained the broader principle that every public institution, whether school, hospital, asylum, or other establishment, ought to be open to public inspection, and that in no other way can the abuse of power be guarded against and the subjects of a free country protected from tyranny. Those, he alleged, who were conscious of no abuses being permitted in their establishments would surely be willing and ready to allow of an inspection which could only redound to their credit; and if any shrank from such an inspection, this was in itself a presumption that the conductors of such institutions felt that their work could not bear the light of day. He held that, in the case of any public institution being completely secluded from all outward observation, it is manifestly impossible to guard against the danger of persons being detained against their will or otherwise constrained: that if the advocates of convents assure us that no such abuses take place, they should remember that we cannot be expected to take their bare word for it, and that the only proof they can give of being wholly free from this reproach is to be ready to invite inspection.

A Roman Catholic gentleman who was on friendly terms with the Archbishop requested his perusal of a letter from a female relation of his who had taken the veil, and who wrote to her friends in terms expressive of the most perfect and exalted happiness as a nun. The Archbishop, on reading the letter, asked whether, if this lady was indeed enjoying a life so blessed, she would not rejoice that others should see and know it, and have an opportunity of personal observation of the happiness of convent life?

If the system, he thought, be indeed so perfect, let all men see and judge of it; but as long as these establishments are kept cautiously veiled from the public eye, those who conduct them have no right to complain if suspicions are entertained that what is concealed is something which open examination would hold up to blame.

It was with this view that the Archbishop lent himself, heart and hand, to the efforts made to procure a general inspection, not of convents only, but of all public institutions.[1]

[1] The debate to which allusion is here made took place in the House of Lords on May 9.

CHAPTER XI.

1854.

Letters to Mr. Senior on Thackeray's Works, &c.—Publishes the
'Remains' of Bishop Copleston—Letter to Mrs. Arnold—Letter to
Mrs. Hill—Letter to Rev. C. Wale—Letters to Mrs. Hill—Letters
to Mr. Senior on his 'Sorrento' Journal—Letter to Mrs. Hill—
Letter to Mr. Senior on his Review of 'Uncle Tom's Cabin'—
Extract from a letter on 'Slavery.'

OF the year 1854 we have few events to record directly
connected with the Archbishop's public or private life.
His correspondence will show the subjects principally
occupying his mind. He entered with unflagging earnestness and lively interest into all that was going on in
literature or politics, and continued to write new works
and revise new editions of former ones, and find time for
extensive correspondence, without relaxing in his incessant attention to the special work of his diocese.

The first letter before us in this year contains a criticism
on his friend Mr. Senior's Review of Thackeray's Works,
now published in a volume under the title of 'Essays on
Fiction.'

'January 13, 1854.

'My dear Senior,—I think some censure should have
been passed on Thackeray's sneer (cited at p. 209) against
piety and charity. He might have been asked whether
he knew many instances (or any) of a person utterly destitute of all principle, and thoroughly selfish, being "the
fast friend" of the destitute poor. Such will, on *some*

grand occasion, make a handsome donation, and join when
solicited in a bazaar; but a life *habitually* devoted to
such works is not consistent with such a character; at
least, I never knew an instance. And he implies that it
is quite common and natural. The truth seems to be
that he has about as good a notion of moral qualities as
the heraldic painter had of a lion, who when he saw a
real one was convinced it was a trick put upon him; he
had been painting lions, he said, all his life, and he knew
that was not one.

'I suppose Ministers will escape having much attention
called to the Education Board, by the Turks; as one may
be freed from the pain of a sore finger by the amputation
of a hand. And perhaps again the Reform Bill will
suffice to smother the Turkish question.'

'January 24, 1854.

'My dear Senior.—I send you by to-day's post the MS.
of the Lessons,[1] which I will beg you to acknowledge.
Pray make any remarks on a separate paper, that the
MS. may be fit to go to the press.

'I hope you will not have been expecting, as some have,
a much more extensive and more profound work than I
designed; either (1) a Constitutional History of England
from the time of Alfred, (2) a Treatise on Government
generally, or (3) a Treatise on Jurisprudence, or (4) a
Scheme of Parliamentary Reform, or (5) a Digest of the
Laws, or all of these combined, any one of which would
make a very large volume, even though too brief for popular use, and too meagre to be satisfactory. The common
error is to oblige anyone who wants a mutton chop to buy
and kill a sheep.

'I wish merely to give children, and those who in know-

[1] On the British Constitution.

ledge and intelligence are not above thirteen or fourteen, a general notion of what our government actually *is*; not of what it *was*, or *may* be, or *might* have been, or ought to be. And any notice of anything else is introduced very rarely and very briefly, and incidentally, when it could hardly be avoided. If you can detect any error in the execution of this design, or suggest any improvement in the execution, your hints will be of course very acceptable.'

He was now engaged on a volume of remains of his lamented friend Bishop Copleston. To this he alludes in the following letter :—

'Dublin : January 28, 1854.

'My dear Mrs. Arnold,—An old bachelor in my father's neighbourhood used to tell with great exultation a story of a pair of canary-birds he had long kept in a cage, and which never sang. One morning he was surprised to hear the cock in full song; and on looking into the cage, the poor hen was seen lying dead. I hope the case of —— is not analogous, and that her versifying powers are not limited, like the canary's song, to a state of celibacy.

'If you mean to read my publication, you must read the Memoir of Bishop Copleston already published (and which does really contain interesting matter, especially two letters to me, each worth the price of the whole volume), since, though I *could* perhaps have done it better, I cannot now *ignore* the book and write as if it did not exist, but must make references to it, which is a disadvantage, but unavoidable.

'I find it harder work than writing an original book. But competent judges think what has been done very interesting.'

Mrs. Hill was at this time preparing an Index to one of the Archbishop's Works.

'February 10, 1854.

'My dear Mrs. Hill,—I do not think there is anyone I employ who *saves* me so much trouble. Fitzgerald, who is now transcribing for me from Bishop Copleston's Commonplace Book, bears witness to the value of your excellent Index.

'This reminds me that in the new edition of the volume of Sermons, which is now in the press, I mean to have an Index; a thing which adds 10 per cent. to the value of any instructive work. If you like to undertake it, write to Parker to send you as much as is printed, and each sheet as it comes from the press. It is a kind of work you do right well, and it will not take you long, for six or seven words, on an average, for each sermon, will be quite enough.

'Is it not strange that my Sermons when called Essays —though avowedly they were written as Sermons—sell five times better than Sermons so called?

'In all the accounts one reads of myrrh, frankincense, and other "medicinal gums," one always finds different qualities mentioned; the *best* being what exudes spontaneously, and not by tapping, or boiling down, &c. And so it is with apophthegms. If a man taps himself to draw them out, he will be the more likely to sacrifice "truth to antithesis." What is said of human approbation, as compared with intrinsic rectitude—that it is a very good thing when it happens to come incidentally, but must never be made an object—may be said of forcible or elegant expressions, &c as compared with truth. The desire of truth must reign supreme; and everything else be welcomed only if coming in her train.

'You may do what you will with my lobsters.[1]   I wish you could boil and eat all the two-legged ones.

'You will find out, if you reach my age, and probably much before, that people of different parties are much more *alike* than at first one is inclined to suspect.

'Certain persons who agree with you on several important points (whereon others are not only greatly in error but also argue most unfairly), you will be inclined to judge of from yourself; and you will be mortified and surprised to find them ready to practise equal unfairness when they have occasion.   You have seen some samples of that in what is said by some persons (agreeing with you on the whole) in reference to my views of the Sabbath. And you will meet with much more of the same kind.

'Every now and then a case occurs which affords (Bacon's) *experimentum crucis*, whether the truth a man actually holds and for which there is good evidence, is held by him *on* evidence, and *as* truth, or as part of the creed of a party.'

To Charles Wale.

'February 18, 1854.

'My dear Charles.—It is the tendency of the Calvinistic school to represent man in his natural state as totally without moral sense, or as even having a preference for evil for its own sake; not considering that (as is remarked in one of the " Cautions") this destroys not only virtue but vice.   When —— was a little girl, she rebuked a great tame gull we had, who was bolting a large fish, saying, "Don't fill your mouth too full!"   She had been taught that for a little girl this was bad manners.

---

[1] An addition he had made to an article on ' Food,' written at his suggestion, and nearly the same as the one in his ' Commonplace Book.'

'It is curious to see Paley, who was far from Calvinistic, taking the same view!

'One might ask one of these moral teachers, "Do you think it right to obey the Divine will?" I don't mean merely *prudent*, for it might be prudent to deliver your purse to a robber, holding a pistol at your head; but do you think that God has a just claim to your obedience? For, if you do, then to say that it is "morally right" to obey Him, and yet that all our notions of morality are derived from our notions of His will, is just to say that what He has commanded is—what He has commanded!'

To Mrs. Hill.

'T. Wells: April 18, 1854.

'Certainly one may reckon among the obstacles to the attainment of truth, presumptuous speculations on what is beyond our reach. Instead of ploughing a fertile soil, a man breaks his tools in attempting to dig in a granite rock. One may read much of such speculations in the schoolmen and some who came after them, about the celestial hierarchy and such matters, when there was an utter want of practical elucidations of the New Testament history.

'In a sermon of mine which I think you never saw or heard, on the sacrifice of Isaac, I have remarked on those who profess to explain the atonement of Jesus Christ, and who at the same time pretend to pre-eminence in *faith*; now, if Abraham had *known beforehand* the issue of the whole transaction, there would have been no trial of his faith or his obedience. One who on a dark night at sea fancies he sees land before him while gazing on a fog bank, should at least not pretend to have as much faith in the pilot as one who believes on the pilot's word that the land is near, and does not pretend to see it. For "Faith is the evidence of things *not* seen."

'Fitz[1] wants me to follow up the "Lessons on the British Constitution" by "Lessons on Morals;" I am afraid the task is impossible, at least to me.'

The Archbishop was anxious to employ Mrs. Hill in writing more articles for Reviews; but her shrinking diffidence and distrust of her own powers, made her often draw back from the undertakings he suggested to her. On this subject he writes :—

'May 21, 1854.

'My dear Mrs. Hill,—My friend John Hughes went out one day a-trolling for pike, and caught one of 23 lbs. He carved and painted a model of it, which he hung up in his study as a trophy; and from that time he never would go a-fishing any more, that he might have it to say "*The last time* I went out I caught a pike of three-and-twenty pounds."

'Now, perhaps, something like this is your case. You wish to be able to say, "The last article I wrote for a Review was eminently successful." If your article had been rejected or thought meanly of, I should have urged that you ought not to be vexed or disheartened by the failure of a first attempt, &c. But as it is, I am quite at a loss. For if complete success does not satisfy you, one can't say what you *would* have.

'What I said about being charged with legalism was not thrown out at random. There are not a few such narrow-minded bigots, that anyone who does not treat and treat exclusively on the same topics with them, and in the very same order, and in the very same words, they set down as not knowing the Gospel.

[1] A playful name for Dr. Fitzgerald.

'But there are a good many partisans who are like the ancient Stoics. Those taught that all faults are equal; since a man whose head is one inch under water is as infallibly drowned as if it were ten fathoms.'

'June 9, 1854.

'My dear Mrs. Hill,—It is worth your while to look at (I would not sentence you to read it through) Coleridge's Dissertation prefixed to the "Encyclopedia Metropolitana." If you have not access to it, I can show it you when you come. I had thought to cut it out and burn it when I had the volumes bound, but I resolved to keep it as a curious specimen of what trash a very clever man *can* write.

'Those "fragmentary writers," as Bishop Copleston observes, men whose wealth may be said to consist in gold-dust—who deal in striking insulated passages of wisdom, or wit, and in mysterious hints of what wonderful systems they *could* construct, if they had leisure—are, as he observes, greatly overrated. Some are led to form expectations from them destined not to be realised till February 30, and others give them credit for being at least unrivalled in their own department. Now, if you should prove to the world that such writers can be rivalled by selections from one of a far different stamp—that the shreds and parings of some complete treatises can furnish almost as much gold-dust as those can produce whose gold is only dust—you will have accomplished much.

'The great Montrose, on one occasion, had to engage with a very superior force; and he put nearly all his soldiers into the wings, having nothing in his centre but a great deal of brushwood, with a score or two of men popping their heads out of bushes, which kept the enemy in check, who took these for the main army. Is not this something like the procedure of these " fragmentary writers? "'

Mr. Senior had sent the Archbishop a portion of a journal he had written during his stay at Sorrento. He was in the habit of recording conversations he had held with various distinguished persons ; and in this portion were notes of several which had taken place between him and M. de Tocqueville, on the respective merits of the ministers of the Roman Catholic and Protestant Churches. On these conversations the Archbishop makes the following remarks :—

'July, 24, 1854.

' My dear Senior,—It is but very lately that I have had leisure to look at a small portion of your Sorrento journal. I am greatly surprised at the record of some of your conversations with Tocqueville. He seems to have greatly mystified you ; for though he probably believed a good deal more than was true, he could hardly have believed all that he said. And you seem according to the most obvious interpretation of your words to have assented to much, and also added much, contrary not only to facts, but to your own knowledge of facts.

' I suppose you did not really mean—though most would so understand you — that all Protestant ministers are worldly and interested men, and that Roman Catholic priests are all disinterested and heavenly minded ; or that Roman Catholics do not consider what they call ' heresy' as ' destructive,' but regard it with tender compassion ; or that hatred for erroneous or supposed erroneous and mischievous tenets, which is so apt to degenerate into *personal* animosity, does so degenerate among all Protestants and no Roman Catholics? You are acquainted

with several Protestant clergymen, though not with a
twentieth as many as I am, but enough, I should think,
to know as well as I do that there are good, bad, and
indifferent among them, as in other professions. But as
for what relates to the respective Churches, as such, the
impression anyone would derive from the most obvious
sense of the language used is just the reverse of the truth.
There is a little penny tract by Napoleon Roussel, widely
circulated in France, and which no one ever did or can
answer—though the Roman Catholics would of course be
very glad if they could—called "La Religion de l'Argent,"
exposing the established and sanctioned system of *traffic*
which is peculiar to the Romish and Greek Churches, a
traffic in the sale of Masses, Relics, Indulgences—in short,
νομίζοντες πορισμὸν εἶναι τὴν εὐσέβειαν.

'Then as for tender compassion felt by Roman Catholics
towards heretics, it is shown here by pelting, beating, and
sometimes murdering them, refusing to employ them, refusing to sell to them any article, &c. In some of the workhouses, the persecution has been so fierce that all Protestants who would not give up their faith have gone out
in a body, to take their chance of begging or starving
outside rather than endure it any longer. And no legal
redress can be obtained; because those who are eye-
witnesses of the most violent outrages either *will* not or
dare not give evidence.

'Perhaps you may think all this appertains to the Irish
as *such*. I, however, know something of the treatment
which Protestants receive in Italy and in France.

'Now, Protestants, it must be admitted, are often violent and bitter, often avaricious or ambitious, &c., and
Roman Catholics often the reverse. But the difference is
this: on the one side you have gardens often sadly over-
run with weeds; there are nettles in the cabbage plot

and groundsel among the celery beds, and so on.   On the
other hand, you have a garden *laid out* in noxious plants;
there are beds of nettles and parterres of thistles.   A
Roman Catholic who does *not* seek to extirpate heretics
by force, if fair means fail, is transgressing the regular
deliberate decrees of his Church (look at the first article
in the July number of the "Irish Church Journal," which
is very well and fairly written).

' I wonder you should have apparently acquiesced in the
very shallow defence by Tocqueville of the celibacy of
the clergy as qualifying them for the *Confessional.* Could
he have been ignorant, or could you, that in the Greek
Church, where there is confession also, the clergy must
be married men? or would he have supposed that a
priest's *niece* would be less likely to be made a confidant
than a wife? or would either of you doubt that if the
experiment were tried, and priests allowed to marry, all
decent women would choose a married confessor?

' As for the real cause of the greater interest in religion
among the Protestant laity, you may see it clearly set
forth in the "Cautions," No. 18, p. 341.   The Roman
Catholic priest is to the people what the lawyer is to his
client, and the physician to the patient; the Protestant
minister is to his people what the lawyer and physician
are to the legal and medical pupil.'

Mr. Senior in his answer suggested some explanation
of the remarks he had made, which he had never intended as conceding so much to Romanism as they had
appeared to the Archbishop to do.

'Dublin: August 4, 1854.

' My dear Senior,—I do think some such explanation
as you allude to might as well be inserted in your

journal. If you had recorded *nothing* at all of your own remarks, the whole would have appeared merely as " a mirror" showing what was said by another. But, as things stand now, the impression conveyed is something considerably different from what I conceive to be your real meaning. I believe that sometimes a *partial* knowledge of some country misleads more than utter ignorance. "Per incertam lunam, sub luce maligna," may, in some respects, be worse than pitch-darkness. I have no doubt that a large proportion of the educated Roman Catholics on the Continent have no hostility to Protestants. But there are enough of them who have, or pretend to have, such hostility, to make them leaders of the vulgar, who are, many of them, fierce zealots. Probably, the Roman magistrates at Philippi had no hostility of their own to Christianity, but they were willing to earn popularity by scourging Paul and Silas.

'I have lately been raising contributions for some poor French Protestants, to enable them to build a church at Agen; and no means were left untried by the authorities, leading or rather led by the populace, to prevent them.

'The "Cautions" is out of print, and there will be a few words added to that note in the new edition. But there is one remark which will not be inserted there; when you speak of some differences of interpretation being designed, but not *all*, this seems an arbitrary distinction. If, according to your own illustration, you infer a designed difference of construction of a deed from its actual occurrence, this must hold good equally whether the differences of construction be few or many, trifling or important. The whole resolves itself into the difficulty of the permission of evil.

'I see Lord Monteagle has given notice of motion of a series of resolutions amounting to the request which the

Education Committee would have made if they had agreed to make one conformable to the evidence. But I suppose it is too late in the session to bring forward his motion.'

The following extract from a letter written about this time is characteristic :—

'What you and I think about asking for a Bishoprick is not I believe in accordance with the opinions of most Ministers. They cannot of course comply with every one's request; but they don't seem to think it makes against him. I have often openly said, in presence of those whom I knew to have asked, that such a request must be understood to mean one of two things: (1) Appoint me as the fittest man, for which you must take my word, as my trumpeter is dead; or (2) though I am not the fittest man, yet give me the preference, and I will show you the more gratitude.'

'October 9, 1854.

'My dear Mrs. Hill,—The paper which I sent to the Bishop contains a full report of my speech,[1] but a very slight sketch of the Bishop of New Zealand's, which was even much more interesting than the one Bishop Wilson admired so much in London. Ask him when you next meet to describe to you that, and ask him whether this does not illustrate the difference between a brilliant speech which makes you think much of the *orator*, and a quiet but impressive one which makes you think much of the *things* he is speaking of.

'When the moon shines brightly, we are taught to say, "how beautiful is this *moonlight*;" but in the day time, "how beautiful are the trees, the fields, the mountains,"

---

[1] At a meeting of the S. P. G. Society.

and in short, all the *objects* that are illuminated ; we never speak of the sun that makes them so. The really greatest orator shines like the sun, and you never think of his eloquence ; the second best shines like the moon, and is more admired as an orator.'

The following is a criticism of a Review of ' Uncle Tom ' which had just appeared :—

'Dublin: November 23, 1854.

'My dear Senior,—It is a pity your article should have been delayed, as a good part of it is likely to have lost in interest. Still there will be much that will remain interesting ; but some things perhaps may be dangerous. To set forth the dislike and jealousy of the English among a certain portion of the French, and their aversion to the war, may tend to increase those evils. I suppose you read at the time the article in the " North British Review" on " Uncle Tom." That contains most of what I have to say on the subject. A subsequent article on Slavery, in the same, contains a few more of my suggestions. The former has a good many ; and some few, important ones, from Bishop Hinds. Shall I try and procure for you the original MS. of the article? It contains one-third or one-fourth more than was printed ; some valuable parts being excluded for want of room.

'When you speak of the work being more popular than Homer, Shakespeare, &c., you leave out of account their permanence. Some very pleasant wines, for the time, will not keep like Hock.

'But the present popularity is certainly a wonderful phenomenon. No one cause will account for it. (1.) It certainly is a work of great power. The author has shown that she can't write other things as well. But I do not know that her other productions are more inferior to it than the worst of Sir W. Scott's to his best. (2.) It relates to a very interesting subject. Many of the readers in England have friends settled in the United States, and the rest can easily fancy themselves living there in the midst of slaves, and perhaps themselves slave-owners. (3.) It gives a picture which most people believe, and I conceive with good reason, to be true. The answers it called forth, the testimony of many eminent Americans, and the documents published in "the Key" all go to confirm the truth.

'Only t'other day I heard a man repeat the argument of the "Times" that self-interest is a sufficient security; as in the case of cattle, where, by-the-bye, it is so little a security that we have a law against cruelty to them. But even the most humane master of cattle treats them in a manner which one could not approve towards men, e.g. selling most of the calves that a cow bears; and knocking on the head a horse that is past work. I suggested that it would be an advantage to slaves if the masters could acquire a taste for human flesh. When a negro grows too old to be worth keeping for work, instead of being killed by inches by starvation and over-work, he would be put up to fatten like an ox. Both the above arguments are fully met in that article.

'I am in the press, as usual, though this is a bad time for publishing, except about Turks and Russians. But I must keep up the existing works by fresh editions. I have also been delivering at an Institution in Cork a lecture on the Origin of Civilisation, which the Institution in London for which I had designed it are going to print. It seems to have excited much interest.

'Poor Lord St. Germans has lost a son and a nephew in this bloody battle.

'Remember me kindly to Dr. Jeune and to your brother-in-law. What a delightful living Tenby would be if it were but of four times the value!

'Yours ever,

'RD. WHATELY.

'P.S. I have a hone now which I picked up at Tenby; and never was there a better. The rocks (up the Channel) abound in them. I wonder no one has ever thought of collecting them as a matter of trade.'

Extract from a Letter on the subject of Slavery.

'I was once in a friend's house (the Coplestons) where a lady who was visiting rebuked me for saying something against slavery, asking whether I had ever been in the West Indies. I said no; but that I was intimate with many West Indians. She said I could not be any judge. *She* had spent six weeks in Jamaica with her friend Mr. Smith or Mr. Jones, and she could testify that the slaves were well treated and very happy, and far better off than the poor of this country. Miss C. Copleston, who had much sly humour, observed to her, "Your friend Mr. Smith was a remarkably kind-hearted good man, was he not?" "Oh, yes! most singularly so." We exchanged glances, but left her contented with her supposed proof.

'It is often overlooked that there is a peculiar difficulty in giving such moral lessons to slaves as shall be consistent with slave-constitutions.

'E.g. how would you exhort a slave to abstain from pilfering or fairly running away with all the property he can lay hold of? Most would say, Teach him that theft is a sin. Granted: but he will deny that it is theft. It is enemy's property, and fair spoil. He is not a member of the community. It is a hostile one.

'Think'st thou we will not sally forth
To spoil the spoiler as we may,
And from the robber rend the prey!

'His master has stolen him, or at least is a receiver.
And he will ask whether, if you were taken prisoner by
bandits, and either kept by them or transferred by them
to others, though you might be deterred by fear in some
cases from attempting to escape, you would feel any
scruple of conscience, any doubt of the right, to seize on
anything of theirs you might need, mount their best
horses, and ride off?

'Such is the slave's case.   You cannot prove that he
has not a fair right to anything (including himself) belonging to his master, or to any other member of the community which is thus hostile to him.

'It is not coveting one's neighbour's goods to sue another
for damages for false imprisonment.

'Hence it is that most missionaries, except the Moravians,[1] have made slaves discontented and rebellious.   For
when men acquire any notion of justice, they apply it
most readily to others.'

[1] He often remarked, that the argument used commonly by the Moravian
missionaries, and also by the apostles, to keep slaves from purloining
was the only one which could be valid with them, i.e. they should abstain, in
order not to bring reproach on the Christian name.

CHAPTER XII.

1855.

Publishes the 'Lessons on Morals'—Letter to Mrs. Hill—Letter to
Mr. Senior—Publishes his edition of 'Bacon's Essays with Annota-
tions'—Letters to Mrs. Hill—His illness—Attacked by Paralysis—
Letter to Dr. Hinds—Letter to Mrs. Hill.

The year 1855 was also an uneventful one. The
Archbishop paid a short visit to London, but took little
part in what was going on. He was at this time much
engaged with the 'Lessons on Morals,' which followed
those on the British Constitution. He was always strongly
of opinion that the moral sense and perceptions of right
and wrong required as careful cultivation as any of the
intellectual powers ; and that though Christian principle
supplied the motive, the perceptions, even in those who
are truly actuated by such motives, are liable to become
blunt or to be perverted, if not carefully regulated and
directed. Conscience, if ill regulated, will not only fail
to guide us right, but positively guide us wrong, as with
those spoken of in Scripture who were 'given up to a
strong delusion.' To help his readers fully to understand
and profit by the teaching of the New Testament, and to
educate their moral perceptions, was the object of this
little book.

'Dublin : January 2, 1855.

' My dear Mrs. Hill,—I hope you inserted in my letter
to —— (though I forgot to remind you to do so) a com-

ment of your own, expressing your concurrence or dissent. If not, it must cost you another penny to write to her, as she will surely wish for your opinion. Doubtless you are right in thinking (as I collect you do) that " so that ye cannot do the things that ye would," means " so as to be an obstacle to your doing." . . . . It is a common Greek idiom to express the tendency towards a certain result as the actual result. " John forbade Jesus to be baptised " is rightly rendered—though a schoolboy would be likely to render it literally—" hindered him " (διεκώλυεν, " was in the act of hindering "). That Paul " compelled the Christians to blaspheme " (ἠνάγκαζεν) should have been " urged them," i.e. " was attempting to compel them."

' I don't know whether you ever heard my remark that the organ of Conscientiousness is the only one that never in its exercise affords any direct gratification. The organ of Love of approbation gives much pleasure when we are praised, as well as pain when we are blamed or un-noticed ; the organ of Secretiveness makes those in whom it is strong (I speak from my observation of others) feel a delight in mystifying. That of Number, as I well remember when I had it strong, about sixty years ago, affords great pleasure in the mere act of calculating ; and so of the rest. But Conscientiousness, which gives great pain to one in whom it is strong, if he at all goes against it, affords no direct pleasure when complied with. It merely says, You have paid your debt ; you are an " unprofit-able servant." And when you have triumphed nobly over some strong temptation, the pleasure—if it can be so called—is just that which you feel at having reached the shore from a strong sea, or narrowly escaped slipping down a precipice. It is the pleasure of mere safety as contrasted with a shocking disaster.

' But, indirectly, Conscientiousness affords pleasure ;

and this is what leads people to speak of delight in virtue, &c.

'It is to a conscientious man the necessary condition of all other qualifications. It is what the mosquito net (or canopy, κωνωπεῖον) is in hot climates. It affords no direct pleasure, but enables you to enjoy sweet sleep.

'But a benevolent man is gratified in doing good; and because well-directed benevolence is a virtue, he is apt to fancy this is a delight in virtue as such. But it is the organ of Benevolence that is gratified. And if he stands firm against solicitations and threats in a good cause, it is the organ of Firmness that affords the pleasure; and so of the rest. Especially to a pious Christian there is always an indirect gratification in doing his duty, through the organ of Veneration; for this, where it is strong, affords directly a high degree of gratification. Aristotle remarks this, saying that Admiration (τὸ θαυμάζειν) is in itself pleasurable. I think if he had known the Gospel he would have been a pious Christian.'

The Archbishop was anxious to have Mr. Senior's opinion on the anti-slavery article alluded to above.

'January 24, 1855.

'My dear Senior,—The MS. may be sent to "Mrs. Hill, Blackrock, Cork." But allow me to suggest that you should get Nassau or some one else to read it straight through to you first, in case, when the proof of your article comes to you for correction, you should see occasion for any insertion or modification. It would not take up three quarters of an hour, and would be well worth that. For, besides that Mrs. Hill is a very able writer, the article abounds with suggestions not only from me, but from Hinds, who had been himself a slave-owner.

'And sometimes the addition or alteration of a line, or

half line, will obviate some misapprehension, or forestall
some objection, or impart important information. (The
paper I sent yesterday was with that view.) And the
subject is not only of vast importance, but of great
difficulty ; and your opponents are active, watchful, and
some of them skilful.   If you were besieging a town, and
had erected a formidable battery, it would be a great
error to leave an unguarded opening by which a shot
might dismount your guns.

'Perhaps I may have an over-allowance of the organ of
Cautiousness ; but it is a fault, if any, on the right side.
You have sometimes in most able articles laid yourself
open to strong objections, and, in some instances, obliged
me to write against you.'

The Archbishop was this year engaged on his edition
of ' Bacon's Essays with Annotations.'   Mrs. Hill was
employed by him to assist in arranging references, &c., a
work for which her accurate habits and extensive reading
peculiarly fitted her.

'August 24, 1855.

'My dear Mrs. Hill,—I particularly wish for your opinion
of what I have said in p. 54 ; and I should like the
Bishop's[1] also, if you think he is well enough.   The man
was one in high repute : but what he said on that
occasion gave me somewhat the impression of humbug.

' You will see that I have referred to various works of
my own, and some of others, for extracts, which it should
be part of your task to make with omissions of such
passages as are not to the purpose.

' That and the arrangement and correction of the Notes
I am writing, and suggestions for more, and foot-notes

[1] The Bishop of Cork, Dr. James Wilson.

explanatory of Bacon's obsolete words and phrases, and a translation of the Antitheta, will be a considerable job for you.

'Yours very truly,

'RD. DUBLIN.

'P.S. Yours just received.

'Thanks for the valuable hints.

'Pray do not set me forth as seeking to convince any one —or as thinking myself—" that Election is not a doctrine of Scripture." I never said any such thing. But I do think many neglect to ascertain in each case " chosen to what ?"

'Calvin's reasoning, from his own data, does appear to me quite a demonstration. And I feel sure that if (according to the parallel case I have adduced) any slave-state American were to put forth such " an apparent inconsistency," he would be laughed to scorn.

'When I so freely tolerate, as I do in every one, differences of opinion, I must warn you from time to time that if I make any errors, you are in some measure responsible for confirming me in them. If you either give no reasons at all, or none that appear to me satisfactory for rejecting my views, I am disposed to consider my reasons as irrefragable.

'I mention this, because to many a one it would not occur that it is at all a compliment to be confirmed in one's own opinion by his contrary opinion.

'There is no hurry at all about Bacon. But perhaps it may be ready in the course of next season. No matter if it is not.'

'August 26, 1855.

'My dear Mrs. Hill,—Have you Bishop Hinds' " Catechist's Manual ?" If not I will send you a copy. It had been long out of print, and a new edition by Parker is lately out.   It is the substance of a portion of his lectures at St. Alban's Hall.

'In presenting a copy to one of my clergy t'other day, I took occasion (it being audience-day) to make a discourse on the subject of expounding ; and I should like your opinion thereon. (I wish you could be concealed in a closet on my audience-days, to hear and afterwards talk over with me what I say to the assembled clergy. For I generally take occasion, from business that arises, or some recent occurrence, to enter on some disquisition that may profit them ; and there are some who come almost every Wednesday to pick up matters for a sermon, or sometimes for two or three.)

'I remarked that a hortatory discourse, in a style of florid declamation, is an easier thing than a good explanation, and also more likely to be popular, and to gain a man the credit of being a fine preacher ; but that the other is more lastingly profitable.   For after all, the Apostles and Evangelists can preach the gospel better than we can.   Our first, second, and third object therefore should be to put the hearers of Scripture as nearly as we can (entirely we cannot) in the same position with the illiterate multitude whom the Apostles addressed, and who were quite familiar with many things that are made out (or not made out) by diligent study of the learned among us ; e.g. "Let him that is on the housetop," &c., is quite intelligible to one who is acquainted with the oriental mode of building, but quite a mystery to one who is not.   Paul, again, starting from Antioch (in Syria) and shortly after preaching at Antioch (in Pisidia), is quite bewildering till explained.   And the common people need to be told what is a "lawyer" and a "publican." How did Elijah so readily get the water to pour on his altar, when the land was parched with drought? easily explained, as he was close to the *sea*, but needing to be explained.

'And do not, I said, regard any matter as trifling, that tends to give men an increased interest in Scripture, or a better understanding of it.

'I used, in my own parish, to give a weekly lecture of this kind, first in a school-house and ultimately (as the number of hearers increased) in the church. Of course I did not fail to bring in practical admonitions when they sprung naturally out of the explanations; but I made the clear elucidation of Scripture the main point.

'That the hearers were interested, appeared from the large and increasing attendance; and that they understood what was said, I ascertained by examining many of them. I thought this kind of exposition more profitable than impassioned hortatory harangues.

'Of course a great deal of this kind of explanation to the uneducated, is likely to be tiresome to the educated, classes who do not need to be told what were "Pharisees and Sadducees," or what is the meaning of the name "Jesus." Nevertheless, some even of them were interested in these lectures, from picking up now and then something new to them; and in other points receiving hints how to explain to children and the vulgar.'

'September 14, 1855.

'My dear Mrs. Hill,—All the deference I claim is that my reasons should be attended to, and either admitted or refuted. And if any one chooses to do neither, the only consequence is that this is a confirmation to me of the soundness of my conclusion. But is it not possible that your dread of being unduly biassed in favour of my opinions may have sometimes led you to bend the twig a little too far in the opposite direction? There was once a

man whose extreme veneration for me led him to avoid
all personal intercourse because he " looked upon me as
a man who could prove anything." A minor degree of a
like feeling may lead a person to say, inwardly, " Probably
I am right and he wrong after all ; for though I do know
of no answer to his arguments, if I were but equal to him
as a disputant, I dare say I could refute all he has
said." '

The year 1856 was one of some trial to the Archbishop.
It began with an attack of inflammation of the tongue.
But he was now beginning to experience a warning of a
more serious character, in a symptom of 'creeping
paralysis' in the left arm and leg, which was now declaring
itself. The shaking of the left hand continued to increase,
and from this time forth never left him except in sleep ; and
the pain occasioned in the whole arm by this involuntary
muscular motion was at times very severe. The difficulty
of steadying the paper on which he wrote affected his
handwriting ; and that clear, round, bold caligraphy
now began to show somewhat of the tremulousness of
age. It was to the last more legible than that of many
persons in their best days, and exemplified the advantage
of the strenuous pains he had taken in this often-neglected
branch. He always said it was a 'mark of selfishness'
to write an illegible hand. But the alteration which
growing infirmity made in his writing was painfully felt
by him ; and from this time he made use as much as
possible of an amanuensis, latterly even in the 'Commonplace Book.' Dictation was never a painful effort to him ;
he performed it with clearness and accuracy as well as
rapidity, and would often dictate a short article or
memorandum on some interesting point while sitting at
the breakfast table.

It has been often affirmed that he refused all medical aid in his latter days. That he was a firm and decided adherent of homœopathy, all are aware; and this treatment was always adopted by him in illness, though with very little real confidence in any medicine as far as he himself was concerned. But it having been suggested that some of the foreign baths might be beneficial to this paralytic affection, he consulted the late celebrated Sir Philip Crampton, then surgeon-general, who gave it as his decided opinion, that neither mineral waters nor any other medical treatment could in any way check the progress of the disease, and that all that could be done was to keep up the strength by diet and general care.

His literary activity remained undiminished. He was constantly making additions to new editions of his works, and composing a fresh series of Easy Lessons, or superintending literary undertakings of friends or members of his own family.

'May 15, 1856.

'My dear Hinds,—I remember reading somewhere long ago, a report of a dialogue between a governor of Jamaica and a Maroon. "Top, Massa Governor, top litty bit; you say me must forsake my wife. Governor : Only *one* of them. Maroon : Which dat one ? Gar Almighty say so ? Jesus Christ say so ? No, Massa Governor ! Gar Almighty good; He no tell somebody he must forsake him *wife and children*."

'I have always thought the Maroon was in the right. But puzzle-headed people are apt to confound together the making of a contract which is (in a Christian community) not allowed, and the keeping to a contract which, when it was made, was lawful. I hold that a man who puts away a wife (even though he has another) " causeth her to commit adultery."

'You will see in the last number of the "Church Journal" some short remarks on Bacon's Essay on Marriage, having an allusion to the disputed rule of clerical monogamy. I do not see that it sets up a different rule of morality— generally for clergy and laity, supposing a man with two wives (already) was admissible into the Church, but not into the ministry, and supposing members of the Church were forbidden, when such, to take more than one wife. For, a neophyte also was not to be admitted to the ministry. Those were to be selected for it who were so circumstanced as to be the most unexceptionable.

'Mr. McNaught will, I think, make naught of his theory. He sent me his book, with a letter in which he professed to have studied mine; and then he coolly sets down among the instances of inaccuracy in the Scripture writers, the alleged discrepancy as to St. Peter's denials; utterly ignoring my solution,[1] which to me appears perfectly satisfactory, but which at least he should have noticed. He appears to be a dashing, careless sort of writer.'

'October 21, 1856.

'My dear Mrs. Hill,—Nothing tends more to deprave and corrupt the moral sense than partisanship. It turns all the virtues into its own channel. It represents as truth, and as the only truth, the Shibboleth of the party. Under its influence public spirit becomes party spirit. Candour is made to consist in putting the best possible construction on whatever is said or done by one of the party, and the worst on all that comes from the opposite, or from (what is still more hated) a neuter. Charity, and mercy, and justice are confined to those of the

---

[1] The Archbishop's view was, that the prophecy of three denials meant, that there should be *at least* three: but that probably Peter denied many more times. This view is also to be found in Thonston's 'Night of Treason.'

party, and become sins if shown towards those opposed
to it.   Everything wrong is either denied, or excused, or
applauded if it comes from one side, and exaggerated if
from the other.

'When a man is tempted by considerations of personal
interest or gratification, instead of meeting with sympathy, he is likely to be checked by the dread of disapprobation; but when he joins a party, combined for
some object which he thinks a good one, he is surrounded
by persons of whom the greater part are ready to keep
him in countenance in anything, however unreasonable,
that does but further party views.

'The Romish Church is but a picture, on a grand
scale, of what every party is in a minor degree.

'And so great a corrupter of conscience is partisanship
that it lowers the moral standard even in reference to
opponents.   They are hated as being of the opposite
party, but this is considered as their only fault.   They
are looked on as a soldier does on the soldiers of the
hostile army, whom he fights against for that reason
alone, but fully expects them to shoot at him, and thinks
none the worse of them for doing so.   It is what he
would do in their place.'

CHAPTER XIII.

1857–1858.

Appointment of Dr. Fitzgerald to the See of Cork—Letter to Mr. Senior—Letter to Mrs. Hill—Letter to Mr. Duncan—Letter to Mr. Senior on opening Places of Public Recreation on Sundays—Death of the Rev. Henry Bishop—Letter to Miss Crabtree—Letter to Mrs. Hill—Letter to Mr. Senior—Meeting of the British Association at Dublin—Interested in Dr. Livingstone's Plans—Accident to the Archbishop—His great Interest in Missions—Letter to Mr. Senior—Letter to Mrs. Hill—Dangerous Illness of his eldest Grandchild—Letter to Dr. Hinds relative to his own Paralytic Attack—Letters to Mrs. Hill—Visit of Mr. Senior—Extracts from his Journal.

In the beginning of this year the Archbishop had the pleasure of seeing his valued friend and chaplain, Dr. Fitzgerald, appointed to the see of Cork in the place of Dr. Wilson.

To Mr. Senior.

'January 1, 1857.

'Mr. (Nemo) has applied to me, and, I understand, to you also, to look over all the political economy answers, and see whether he is not, as he is sure he is, the best of the candidates.

'When I meet with any very impudent person hereafter, I shall say "Nemo impudentior."'

'January 3, 1857.

'My dear Mrs. Hill,—I hope we shall soon have a better report of your influenza.

'Mrs. W. thought Parker ought to have printed more than 1,500 copies of the Bacon. I thought he was likely to know best; but now she seems to have been right, for nearly half the number has been *subscribed*. I send you the only addition that could be struck off separate, to improve your former copy; and any of your friends who have copies may get this, gratis, from Parker. But there are other little additions pass in, to the amount of about an additional sheet.

'It is curious to observe how much more the generality relish wisdom in the form of a *hash*, than in a complete systematic work: and yet, if I am any judge, my forte is in the latter. But then, this is not what suits a lounging reader, but a *student;* and one who has something of the methodical in his own mind.

'The critic in Fraser notices (which others had done before) as something rather extraordinary, my saying that I treat of such and such a subject because erroneous views on it are prevalent; and he thence infers that I am—or at least wish to appear—at variance in most points with the generality. But surely this is a rash inference. A man may conceivably agree with all his neighbours in nine points out of ten, and yet may see reason to treat only of the one, and say nothing of the nine. There is not so much need to tell people what they already know, as to correct mistakes and clear up difficulties. Though I am fully convinced that three and two make five, and that the sun is brighter than the moon, there is no need to proclaim my conviction in a published work. One need not write a book to prove that peace is better than war, or that intemperance is noxious to health.

'As for the Essay on Gardens, my reason for saying nothing was precisely what makes the reviewer wonder; —that there was so *much* to be said. I could not say a *little* that would have been at all worth saying; and I was fearful of making the book too long.

.   .   .   .   .   .

'The "Lessons on Morals" has been brought before the S.P.C.K., but I don't think they will accept it. If they do, it will be with great mutilations. Besides the jealousy naturally felt of a successful author by men who, if not publishing authors, are at least many of them sermon-writers, there are two parties, each of which, alternately, has sometimes gained a contest in the society; and each, besides their dislike of one who openly protests against all parties, will find something to object to in that book. All disciples of Paley will be ill-disposed towards it; and I have found very few Calvinists who do not (which is very remarkable) concur with him in denying a moral faculty; indeed many of them go beyond him, representing man as having a natural preference of evil to good. Then some of the ecclesiastical party will find fault with the part about Romans vii., which the Religious Tract Society struck out in the ——.

'And most of them, together with all the "high and dry," will quarrel with what I have said of chapters and verses.   .

'By-the-bye, I wonder that you should think I represented those as inconsistent who hold one and not the other of the two interpretations I was censuring. I do not see any connexion between the two. I only said that both interpretations have danger in them, if so understood as many will be likely to understand them. But I am ready to admit the same, of some doctrines which I do hold; those being very clearly and forcibly set forth in Scripture, and attended with earnest and careful warnings against abuse.'

'Dublin: January 27, 1857.

'My dear Duncan,—I was very glad to receive from
you a letter written in as firm a hand as you wrote, when
I first became acquainted with you, forty-five years ago,
which is more than could be said of most. You have
the glory of being the first to bring Fitzgerald into notice;
he has from me a print of you to worship as his patron
saint. Most people give me the credit, or discredit, of
having obtained the bishopric for him and for Dickinson,
by making interest with Government; I never said a word
for either of them or any one else, and I will beg of
you to say so to any one who may be under this mistake.
There is a great advantage that the benevolent have over
the selfish as they grow old; the latter, seeking only their
own advantage, cannot escape the painful feeling that
any advantage they procure for themselves can last but a
short time, but one who has been always seeking the
good of others has his interest kept up to the last, because
he of courses wishes that good may befall them after he
is gone.'

The question of opening places of public recreation on
Sundays was now under discussion: and the Archbishop
wrote the following letter to Mr. Senior on the subject:—

'February 25, 1857.

'My dear Senior,—If your Sabbath question comes on
for discussion, you may as well look at what I have said
on a part of the subject, in an address to the people of
Dublin, which is appended to the last two editions of my
"Thoughts on the Sabbath." There is nothing in it
which is not, I suppose, familiar to you; but it may not
be to all. There is a distinction which should be noticed
between handicraft-work and shops. A man can cer-

tainly (if he does not overwork himself) saw more planks in seven days than in six. But there would not be more *goods sold* if shops were open seven days. *One* shopkeeper might indeed gain an advantage over his rivals, if he *alone* kept open shop on Sundays; but if *all* did it, no one would gain. I have often thought that if old clothes-men, &c., were allowed to ply only on one day in the week, all would be benefited, except indeed the sellers and buyers of stolen goods. There would not be fewer old coats or hareskins sold per week than now.

'When I lived in Suffolk, the farmers all agreed that there should be no gleaning allowed till eight o'clock, at which time a bell was tolled to give notice. This was a benefit to all, when enforced on all; for the women had time to dress their children, and give them their breakfast, &c., and there was just as much corn gleaned. But if the rule had not been enforced on *all, one* might have gone out at daybreak and forestalled all the rest.

'Do you know what ministers mean to do about transportation? A Mr. Pearson, who takes my view and that of Mr. Hill, the Recorder of Birmingham, and has exerted himself in the cause, has published a pamphlet which is worth your looking at.'

This year was saddened to the Archbishop by the death of one of his oldest and most valued friends, his brother-in-law, the Rev. Henry Bishop, with whom he had been on terms of close and affectionate intimacy for many years, and whose high qualities of heart and mind he sincerely esteemed.

The correspondence with this friend was very full and frequent; but, as in the case of Dr. Arnold, the letters have not been preserved, and no record therefore remains of many letters probably containing matter of deep interest.

'. . . . . . As for myself, I am going down hill, though not rapidly ; and I hope to be spared becoming a useless burden to the diocese, and to my family. Though sooner exhausted than I used to be, I do not find my powers fail when called forth for a short exertion. But though I am by many years the latest born of the family, I may consider myself as practically the oldest ; as one year of my life is equal in point of wear and tear to two of most people's. Not but that others have their toils and their trials ; which compared with mine, are an English thunder-shower to a West Indian hurricane.

'I sent you yesterday a copy of the first edition of the Bacon, as I can replace it with a copy of the new edition now just about to come out. There are, in this latter, a few, but trifling additions.

'I have but a limited number of copies at my disposal, as it is only the theological and educational books that I retain altogether in my own hands.

'I have no doubt I could have gained more than double what popularity I have gained, if I would have consented to point out the faults of one side only, and just kept silence as to the opposite. Many who were delighted with the " Cautions," as long as the Roman Catholics and the Tractites were exposed, " went back, and walked no more " with us, when the Low Church faults were exposed.

'I heartily sympathise with your rector about pews, but I know by experience, that even with his bishop on his side, he will have great difficulties in carrying his point. He should read the " Essay on Negotiating," with the annotations, which may furnish some useful hints to those who can apply them with discretion. But " what art ever taught its own right application ? " You should have sent earlier for the cuttings. However, you may coax them to strike under a bell-glass. I have added some of the Weigeltia, a beautiful hardy shrub, if you have it not, and also a few seeds of a beautiful and fragrant lupine, which you possibly may not have.

' I send you an order on Parker for copies of the Lessons which you may give or lend to those who are too poor to buy, and who are likely to be interested.

'With kind regards to my Halesworth friends,

' Yours very truly,

' Rd. Whately.'

'April 18, 1857.

'My dear Mrs. Hill,—It is not our identity we should lose by oblivion, but the consciousness of it; which alone makes us care about it.

' You cannot doubt that it was really *you* that suffered in your babyhood from cutting your first teeth, but you have no memory of it. And if we could as completely lose all memory of our whole life, like Virgil's ghosts, who were dipped in Lethe (*Æn.* vi.), though reason would tell us that it would be *we* who should afterwards enjoy or suffer, we could not bring our feelings to acknowledge it. . . . The sermon might be entitled " The Use of an Educated Ministry," or " Mental Culture required for Christian Ministers," or " Human Learning employed in the Cause of Religion."

' Few passages of Scripture are oftener cited than " those who *sleep in Jesus* ;" but it is an utter mistranslation, as you will at once perceive, though happily it leads to no error in doctrine. " Without God in the world " is another passage which is often cited, though in a mistaken sense.   It means that it was the ἄθεοι that were " in *the world*; " i.e. the *heathen* world.

' Ever truly yours,

' R. W.'

Miss Crabtree had sent the Archbishop a little book for children, by a friend of hers.   He was always genuinely fond of works for children and young people ; but considered they required to be written with even more care than those for adults.   The following criticism was suggested by the perusal of the book in question.

' Dublin : June 12, 1857.

' My dear Miss C.—That little book seems to me in too high-flown language for young children.

' I think it is also too uniformly tragical.   Children should be trained gradually to contemplate worldly afflictions aright ; but a very bitter dose presented to them all at once may disgust or depress them.   I don't know in what sense your friend uses " influence."   I have a very short essay on it (in my Commonplace Book), in the original and strict sense ; and if you are curious about it, I would have it transcribed for you.   My attention was early called to the subject by observing that some possess much of it, and some a little, and some—myself among them—none at all.'

' August 7, 1857.

' My dear Senior,—On receiving your letter I procured the " North British Review."   I agree with you in somewhat wondering that they received your article ; because, besides other reasons, the preface to my Bacon shows up some of their writing.   But this they probably overlooked.   I think it not unlikely your article will be

read and approved by some who, if it had appeared in
the "Edinburgh," might have never seen it, or if they
did, would have disliked it.

'Considering how many religious communities there
are in England, all of Dissenters, and that all Protestants
are Dissenters from the Roman Church, and revolted
subjects, it is no wonder that the ideas of independence,
and of disagreement, and schism should be associated in
men's minds, and that it should be taken for granted
that the only alternative is, on the one side, union under
one government, and on the other, differences of doctrine. But there is no necessary connexion between the
things thus, through custom, associated in the thoughts.
(See Lesson x. § 4, on Religious Worship.)

'The American Episcopal Church is kept distinct from
ours, not by opposition in doctrine, but simply by being
American. And the Swedish and Danish Churches, which
are subject to no common authority on earth, do not, I
believe, differ at all. The apostles, who certainly did
not seek to introduce diversity of doctrine, founded many
distinct independent churches (agreeing, I presume, with
you, that the union of vast masses of people in one community is inexpedient) even in the same province; as
Thessalonica and Philippi in Macedonia, &c. And in
early times there must have been hundreds of such
churches, distinct, but not opposed.

'But a disagreement on points purely speculative is
probably a benefit, when it so happens that the persons in
question would—but for such disagreement—have thought
themselves bound to live under one government on earth.'

In the August of this year the British Association
held its annual meeting in Dublin. The Archbishop, as
he had done in Belfast in 1852, superintended the

department of the 'Statistical Society,' of which he had so long been president. But he always regretted that the arrangements of the Association prevented his attendance on any but his own department, and often expressed a wish that the different sections could be so ordered as to occupy different days or hours, so as to permit those specially engaged in different departments to attend those of other branches, and thus avoid that exclusiveness which attention to one branch of knowledge alone is liable to produce. His own tastes were far removed from this exclusiveness; he took an interest in almost every department of science, and constantly attended the meetings of the Zoological, Natural History, Ethnological and other societies.

In the visit of Dr. Livingstone, who took a part this year in the meetings of the British Association, the Archbishop took a lively interest, and entered warmly into his plans for civilising the South African tribes.

In the early part of the year 1858, he had an accident in which he narrowly escaped being unfitted for future exertion in the way of public speaking or preaching. He had been receiving a visit from the eminent American missionary at Constantinople (since deceased), Dr. Dwight, whose account of his work had greatly interested him. He rose before Dr. D. left, to look for a copy of the Armenian translation of his 'Lessons on the Evidences of Christianity,' which he wished to present to him, when his foot caught in the carpet in crossing the room; he was tripped up and fell with much violence to the ground. At first it was apprehended that all the front teeth would have been lost; but by great care the evil was averted.

His interest in foreign missionary work was very lively and constant. His own 'Lessons on Evidences' had already, as had been observed, been translated into many different languages, and he was ever ready to help in the work of getting them printed and circulated.

His active and efficient support of the venerable Society for the Propagation of the Gospel in Foreign Parts, a branch of which he first established in Ireland, is well known; but his interest in the labours of missionaries was not confined to his own communion. In the labours of Dr. Livingstone in Africa, as before observed, and of Mr. Ellis in Madagascar, he was greatly interested; and his support and countenance were always heartily given to the missions of the Moravians. He often remarked that they, of all others, worked the most successfully among the savage heathen; and that they seemed eminently to have succeeded in the difficult task of evangelising slaves, without tempting them to revolt against their masters.

Not less constant and active was his sympathy and interest in the Waldenses, and his testimony to the prudence and Christian meekness and forbearance which they united with such resolute courage and endurance throughout their whole history, was always very strong.

The Archbishop took the chair at a meeting of the Patagonian or South American Missionary Society, and warmly advocated its claims. He pointed out that instruction in the elements of civilisation must ever accompany the introduction of Christianity—for a savage, as such, could not understand what Christianity meant. One who cannot be made to believe in to-morrow can hardly be expected to look to a future state. But by pointing out to savages advantages which they can understand and value, in the common arts of life, they may be led more willingly to attend to the teaching of those who can show them the way of salvation.

He was now engaged in preparing an edition of Paley's 'Moral Philosophy,' with annotations. He heartily appreciated Paley's excellences; but was strongly alive to the danger of following his system of morals, which he considered as, in fact, disallowing the moral faculty in man. His chief object in publishing these annotations was to put readers on their guard with respect to this danger.

He took as lively an interest in writing and arranging these annotations, as in composing an entirely original work; and bestowed indefatigable pains on the compilation of the shortest note.

'Dublin: July 8, 1858.

'My dear Senior,—As you are on an Education Commission and are going to Canada, pray make a point of seeing there Dr. Ryerson, who holds there the same office as our Irish Education Board in his own single person; and *therefore* (as he is a very able and good man) the system works, I understand, admirably.

'I hope you and your colleagues will do better than the enquiry commission we lately had here; who produced blue books in cartloads, not a word of which is at all to be depended on. For though *some* of their statements may be true, I cannot trust any; since *all* those that relate to schools which *I* am acquainted with, are grossly erroneous; though they had ample means of ascertaining the truth.

'If you go to Philadelphia you should introduce yourself to Bishop Potter, whom I have corresponded with, though not seen; and who is accounted the first man in that Church. If you see him, tell him there are now growing in the Botanical Garden some of the sweet potatoes he sent me several years ago. I am just returned from a visitation and confirmation tour. The candidates confirmed within the last half year amount to above 2,800; and since I came here, to about 30,000; though of course they are but a small proportion of the whole Protestant population of the diocese. If I were going with you, and were as young as Nassau, I would try to get two or three spirited fellows to join me, and would explore the interior of Newfoundland. It is strange that an island as large as Ireland, and the nearest spot to Europe, should never have been penetrated above thirty miles! And probably though the climate of the *coast* is foggy—as is that of Nova Scotia—the interior may be (as with Nova Scotia) clear enough. Then, for trout and salmon and deer, what sporting ground would compare with it?

'The Wales leave us next week. Their little girl has been at death's door with gastric fever, but is now gaining strength rapidly.

'Yours ever,
'R. W.'

'May 4, 1858.

'My dear Mrs. Hill,—Some people—and intelligent ones too—have in their minds an association, established by long habit, between ideas which have no natural connexion, such, that to disjoin them is like picking out the stitches (in the "Tale of a Tub") of the embroidery on the coat-tail; which Jack found so difficult, that he was fain to tear off the whole piece and fling it into the kennel.

'Even so I have known people—no fools—declare that to give up the belief that the Fourth Commandment is binding on us, and that the observance of Sunday is a compliance with it, would be to give up the whole of

Christianity. And such, allow me to say, appears to be the sort of association in your mind, as to one point or two, between things not naturally connected.

'No doubt the doctrine of perseverance does follow from the Calvinistic doctrine of election; but not *vice versâ*; as you yourself admit. Now it is the "perseverance" (as taught by me) that affords the consolation. There are two trees both bearing the same fruit. You do not eat the tree but the fruit; and no one ought to say that one of these trees is essential to his nutriment, if he might just as well have eaten from the other. That all the elect, and they only, will finally be saved, is a truth equally, if true at all, to the godly and the ungodly; why then is it not equally consolatory to both? Evidently the consolation to the godly must be, not from the doctrine generally, but from his belief that he is one of the elect.

'But supposing this latter, who was doing well, should fall into a sinful life, and so continue. Thank God the case is a rare one; and my own belief is, that of the few cases of it that do occur, a majority are of those who have imbibed the Calvinistic doctrine and fallen into careless security; you would say of such a man that he never was really one of the elect, but deceived himself in fancying it; for that else he would have persevered.

'And that all who do persevere will be saved, no one denies. "He that endureth unto the end, the same shall be saved." So that after all, it is on "patient continuance in well doing" that glory and immortality must depend; and on the expectation of that continuance that the consolation depends.'

In this year, while his son-in-law's family were again his guests, his liveliest feelings of affection were called forth by the dangerous illness of his eldest grandchild from typhus fever. In no common degree attached to all these little ones, this firstborn had been the object of special and almost passionate affection ; and his son-in-law remembered afterwards frequently finding him alone and engaged in earnest prayer for the preservation of this beloved child, with marks of the strongest emotion. His feelings were so seldom outwardly manifested that they seemed all the more intense when the veil was for a moment torn down and their depth and strength betrayed to others.

'September 1, 1858.

'My dear Hinds,—I sympathise the more with your infirmities from the increase of my own. The Confirmation of this year fatigued me much ; chiefly from the paralytic affection of the left side, which keeps one arm in constant tremor, and, latterly, pain. If I live till the time comes round again, I shall probably ask Bishop Fitzgerald to confirm for me. He is the only bishop I know of who administers the rite exactly as I do ; and I should be loth to see a change.

'If this relief prove insufficient, I shall probably look out for some ex-colonial bishop, whom I can trust, and offer him a good salary, and an apartment in the palace, to ordain and confirm, and aid me in other things, like the coadjutor of the Roman Catholics. If this also fails, I shall then offer to resign ; not stipulating for a precise sum, but asking ministers what they are willing to allow ; not on the ground of not having a subsistence, but with a view to a general rule that a retiring bishop should have this ; for want of which many a one is prevented from retiring when he ought. And this is the course I should have advised for you.

'I think I sent you the "Songs of the Night."[1]   If not, you can get it of Wertheim and Macintosh, and I should like your opinion of it.

'The lecture on Egypt,[2] I may say, who am only the compiler, is very interesting, and it was listened to with apparent interest by the crowded audiences.   I gave it to Parker, to publish for his own profit ; and it vexed me much to find that it has not yet sold enough to pay costs!   The lecture on Civilisation sold 5,000 in a few months.   Perhaps it may be that this one is not known. For, to advertise a sixpenny work would more than eat up all the profits.'

The following extracts from letters to Mrs. Hill appear to have been written at this time :—

Extract.

' There is an observation which I think your knowledge of mankind will enable you to verify.   And indeed, some part of it is in one of the " Annotations " on Bacon. A self-distrust which was in itself right, may be pushed so far, and unwisely directed, as to lead to an opposite extreme from the one originally to be guarded against. A man forgets that it is possible to warp the timber too far the contrary way.

'E.g.   Suppose A to confess with sincerity, and perhaps truly, that he is conscious of an over-saving disposition, which he is forced to be on his guard against, and that B in like manner is conscious of a tendency to profusion and carelessness.   You might be surprised to find that, practically, in almost every instance, when A did go

---

[1] By his youngest daughter, the late M's. George Wale.   Macintosh, 24 Paternoster Row.

[2] This was delivered by the Archbishop at Belfast in 1857, and on several other occasions.

wrong, it was in the way of too lavish expenditure, and B in the way of parsimony. So also if C professes with perfect sincerity, great admiration and veneration towards a certain person, it is possible that this veneration may be merely theoretical and general ; and that practically, and in almost every particular case, he will have so sedulously and excessively guarded against an over deference, as to cherish—as a point of duty—a strong prejudice against every plan, institution, decision, person, or thing, that C approves. He will have forgotten that it is possible to warp the beam too far the other way. Of this, I had had experience. And it follows that general professions, though sincere, will not furnish an unerring guide as to any one's actual conduct in particulars.'

Extract.

' Now as to another point which I have already brought before you, and on which I should like to have your answer. The candidates examined for degrees at Oxford one by one, are placed, if thought worthy, in the first, or in some lower class of honours. There is no limitation of number in each class, nor any comparison of one man with another ; but each, as soon as his own examination is over, is enrolled in his proper class. But this is " *nobis arcanum.*" Till the whole number have been examined, and the lists published, no one but the examiners know where each man is placed.

' Now when a man goes to bed the night after the close of his own examination, he knows that his place is fixed ; but it will be perhaps three or four weeks before this is published.

' Now, if any man were to say that it is a consolation and joy to him, to know that he either *is* or is *not*, in (suppose) the first class, would you, or would you not, say

that he was deceiving himself; and that the real ground
of his satisfaction must be his conviction (based on the
examination passed), that he is in the first class? And
this conviction is what he might equally have felt, as
soon as ever his examination was finished, and before the
examiners had made their decision. Nay, it sometimes
happens that a man is so well prepared, that his friends
feel confident, before his examination, that he will be in
the first class.

'But in every case, any satisfaction he may feel must
surely be, not from his knowing that he is either in the
first class, or else not, but from his belief that he is in that
class.'

Memorandum.

'There are a few points on which you have not altogether adopted my views, and on which I think you will,
on careful reconsideration.

'1. My illustration from the Oxford examinations, of
a man attributing his feelings of satisfaction to a wrong
cause, I think you will perceive on reflection to be quite
correct. All that you urge in answer, about perseverance
(just what is said on the essay thereon, which see), is
foreign to the question.

'It is curious that ordinary (and sometimes very intelligent) persons, are so apt to mistake the grounds of their
convictions, and the causes of their own feelings. This
was well pointed out by Bishop Hinds in an article in a
Review; and I have repeated it in several of my works.
Men are thus exposed to a danger of having their faith
shaken, when it is proved to them that the foundation on
which they had (erroneously) supposed it to rest, is
destroyed.

'Lord Mansfield advised a Governor of Jamaica, who

had to sit as Lord Chancellor (being no lawyer), to decide according to his common-sense view of each case, but never to state his reasons ; which, he said, will inevitably be the wrong ones, though the decision is right.

' 2. My illustration (in the last edition of the "Difficulties"), from a member of a Slave State, alleging that their law made no mention of the exclusion of slave testimony, is what, I think, you will perceive on reflection to be quite sound.

' 3. You insist on it, that you never met with any Antinomian teaching. And I dare say you have not met with any distinct avowal of it. But you could not deny that a very large majority of the Evangelical party teach an interpretation of Rom. vii. opposite to ours ; and that that is what must, practically, inculcate Antinomian views ; now, if this does not make a conclusive syllogism, I know not what can.

' 4. Any one has a right to hold one half of Calvin's theory, and reject the other half; though Calvin derides that separation. But no such person is justified in professing to be a Calvinist.

'These are points on which you have not, I think, committed yourself to a decided dissent from my views, but yet you have given no reason that I think can satisfy yourself for not adopting them.

'You have often professed a wish that you had been my pupil in your youth. So did Bishop Dickinson. And none are more greedy of mental improvement than those who are the most advanced in it. But you see I do not consider you as too old to learn.'

Extract.

' In reference to that prophecy you allude to, it should be recollected (what is not in general sufficiently dwelt

on) that the Gospel was first preached to Israelites alone,
and by them; and that for about seven years these (including Samaritans and proselytes) composed the whole
Christian Church. It was not till after the religion had
taken firm root in Israel, that the Gentiles were called
in. And it must have been, seemingly, a well-known
religion. For Cornelius and his friends are evidently
addressed as well acquainted with it, except in the one
point which had just been announced to Peter, the
admissibility of Gentiles. And they were baptised without having or needing any elementary instruction.

'It is true, the great majority of the nation rejected the
Gospel. So did the great majority of those who came
out of Egypt fall in the wilderness. But, in each case,
those were reckoned the nation who obeyed the Lord.
And probably the proportion of Jewish Christians to the
whole nation was not less than that of the Israelites
who did enter the promised land—the tribe of Levi,
and Caleb and Joshua, and the children of the rest.
Within a few days, apparently, the disciples numbered
about five thousand in Jerusalem alone, not reckoning
Galilee; and after that we hear of so rapid a spread, that
in Jerusalem alone, a few years after, there were "many
myriads" of believing Jews, besides those of the disper-
sion, and those in the rest of Judea and in Galilee. We
have indeed no statistical accounts of numbers; but there
seems every reason to think that even before the call of
the Gentiles there must have existed for several years a
very considerable Jewish-Christian Church.'

'November 5, 1858.

'My dear Mrs. Hill,—I have just lost a sister at the
age of eighty. It seems strange to me to outlive so many
of my own family. For though in years I am much the

youngest, in point of wear and tear I may be reckoned the oldest.   Hot water is not my proper element; and I have long been in it.   I am somewhat like the army in India, continually fighting, chiefly against those who ought to have been with us; continually attacked, and repulsing every attack, and losing a very few in this encounter, and a very few more in that; and so on, till by degrees it is used up, in the midst of victories.

' Yours ever,

' R. W.'

Mr. Senior again paid a visit to his old friend in the autumn of this year, and again we insert some extracts from his journal :—

Extracts from Mr. Senior's Journal.

' Nov. 13, 1858.

' My wife's maid told her this morning that my brother's coachman, a zealous Romanist, had asked her whether she believed the Apostles' Creed.

' Of course she answered, " Yes."

' " Then," he said, " you believe in the Holy Catholic Church, and you ought to obey it; and you believe in the communion of saints, and you ought to pray to them."

' " I did not know how to answer him," said she, " and in fact I am not sure what is the meaning of those words."

' I mentioned to the Archbishop her difficulty.

' " I understand," he answered, " the second branch of the sentence to be merely an explanation of the first, and read the whole thus: 'I believe in the Holy Catholic Church '—that is to say—' I believe in the communion of saints.'   In the early times in which that creed was composed, the word ' saint ' was used as opposed to ' heathen.'   It meant not a person of peculiar sanctity, but simply a professor of Christianity.   All that the creed declares is the existence of a Christian communion, or, to use a more modern word, of a Christian community—a body of which Christ is the Head; and all who believe in Him, however distinguished by varieties of belief in other respects, Protestants and Roman Catholics, Trinitarians and Arians, Latins and Greeks, whether living or dead, are the members. At the same time, I regret that the word Catholic is used in the creed, or rather I regret that we have acquiesced in its assumption by the Romanists.

'"We qualify it by adding the word 'Roman;' but that destroys its meaning.

'"It indicates, however, the confusion of the ideas which the Romanists endeavour to attach to the word 'catholic.' They claim both unity and universality. Now, if the Catholic Church is universal—that is, if it comprehends all Christians—then we and the Greeks are as Catholic as the Romanists are, and there is no unity. If the Catholic Church includes only those who assent to the conclusions of the Council of Trent, then we and the Greeks—in fact, the majority of Christians—are excluded from it, and there is no universality.

'"It is clear," he continued, "that a Catholic Church, in the Romanist sense, did not exist even in the first years of Christianity; dissensions, and even heresies, disturbed the churches addressed by St. John and by St. Paul; and the remedy suggested by St. Paul is not a recourse to any human authority—to any living depositary of infallibility, but 'watchfulness'—that is, earnest inquiry, the very conduct which Rome forbids."

'"I find," I said, "that it is not true that, in this war of conversion, the gain and loss are balanced. Your daughters tell me that the number of converts to Protestantism is large, and that to Roman Catholicism very small; but that the former belong to the lower classes, the latter to the gentry."

' " All that is true," he answered, " and it seems strange that the converts to Roman Catholicism should belong to the most educated—to the class which has been most taught to reason.

' " But, in fact, it is not by reasoning that they are converted. The Roman Catholic Church does not appeal to reason, but to authority; and she does not allow even the grounds of her authority to be examined. They are converted through their imagination or their feelings; they yield to the love of the beautiful, the ancient, the picturesque. Afterwards, indeed, they sometimes try to defend themselves by reasoning; but that is as if a jury should first deliver their verdict, and then hear the evidence."

' " One friend of mine," I said, " told me that he was converted by reasoning. He could find no medium, he said, between believing the Gospels to be mere human, uninspired records of our Saviour's doctrines, and believing that the inspiration which protected the evangelists from error is still given to the successors of St. Peter, and to the Church over which they preside."

' " That might be reasoning," said the Archbishop, " but it is bad reasoning. If it were possible that he could prove that there is no better evidence of the inspiration of St. Luke than there is of the inspiration of the Pope, he still would not have advanced a step towards proving the Pope to be inspired. Such, however, are the shifts to which those who are in search of infallibility are forced to have recourse. They cannot deny that the primitive church was infested by errors, even in the times of the apostles. They cannot deny that, if there was an infallible interpreter of Christianity, the apostles must have known of his existence, and were bound to point him out to their churches; and they cannot affirm that they did so."

'The Archbishop has been reading my journal.

' "The picture of the priests," he said, " is melancholy, but, I fear, faithful; and we, the English people, are answerable for much of their perverseness. When Lord Grenville was congratulated on the approach of Catholic Emancipation—a measure which he had always supported —he refused to rejoice in it. 'You are not going to pay the priests,' he said, 'and therefore you will do more harm than good by giving them mouthpieces in Parliament.' A priest, solely dependent on his flock, is in fact retained by them to give the sanction of religion to the conduct, whatever it be, which the majority chooses. The great merit of 'Dred' is the clearness with which this is exemplified in the Slave States. What can be more unchristian than slavery, unless indeed it be assassination? And yet a whole clergy, of different denominations, agreeing in nothing but that they are maintained on the voluntary system, combine to support slavery.

' "Notwithstanding the evils of religious controversy, I rejoice in the conversions, which, together with emigration, are altering the proportion of the numbers of the two sects.

' "The emigration," he continued, "diminishes the apparent number of the conversions; for many emigrate because they have been converted, but do not like to encounter the persecution which almost invariably awaits them here. Several circumstances have been favourable to conversion. One is the mere diffusion of education. All knowledge and all cultivation of the reasoning powers are unfavourable to error, and the religious knowledge diffused by the Education Board was of course peculiarly so. Now, indeed, the withdrawal of some books, and the power given to a single child to stop the religious instruction of all the others, have almost paralysed the Board; and the grant, which I hear is to be given to the Church Schools, will destroy it as a promoter of united education. But in its good times it did good and extensive service. The famine, too, was favourable to conversion. The priests are not alms-givers; and if they were, they were then unable to give, for they received nothing. Sometimes they refused to give even their services gratuitously, lest they should set a precedent which might be followed when the excuse was gone. All this threw the people into contact with the Protestant clergy, and created relations which have continued. The people too are learning English, and the clergy Irish. In my earlier visitations to my southern province, knowledge of Irish was the exception. The usual answer was, 'All the Protestants in my parish speak English.' 'That was to be expected,' I used to answer. *Now*, in the Irish-speaking parishes, ignorance of Irish among the Protestant clergy is the exception." '

'Nov. 14, 1858.

' "There were schools," said the Archbishop, "kept by men who rejected the national system, in which the Roman Catholic children were not required to read the entire Bible, or to listen to exclusively Protestant teaching."

'The Anglican clergy as well as the priests submitted to compromises, inconsistent with their declarations. Lord —— required all the labourers in his employ to send their children to his Protestant schools. They put their case before the priest. They could not starve, they said; what were they to do? He answered, that though the children might be forced to hear questions on the subject of their faith, they could not be forced to answer them— they might sit mute; and so they did. You may conceive what amount of Protestant knowledge or Protestant feeling they gained by the attendance which Lord —— imposed on them.

'Some Protestant schools, in order to attract the attendance of Roman Catholics, degraded the reading of the Bible into a mere form—a child read it, no explanations were given, no questions asked. It might as usefully have been read in Hebrew or in Greek. "The Protestants," the Archbishop continued, "have lost an opportunity which they never will regain. If they had accepted the national system at first, it might have been rejected by the Roman Catholics; but if at the end of the first six or seven years, when the Roman Catholics had experienced its benefits, the Protestants had thought fit, they might have established schools, under their own patrons, over a large portion of Ireland, and might have secured that the system should be honestly carried out. But a time came when the Board ceased to be unanimous, even as to the principle, on which it was originally based. One of its members actually preferred ' Sectarian education,' and said that a Roman Catholic who sent his son to a school kept by a Protestant was a fool. Another wished the Board to accept and administer grants for Sectarian schools. And then came the departure from its better practice, which forced me to resign, and is every day more impairing its utility.

' "An important subject," he added, " has not been brought under your notice—the persecution of Protestants in workhouses. It is such, that I have known of persons who have submitted to the utmost destitution rather than endure it. Insults, outrages, and violence are inflicted, and no redress can be obtained, because no legal evidence is forthcoming. A Protestant among a crowd of low, bigoted Roman Catholics, is like a slave in South Carolina. He, or more frequently she, may be subject to any indignity, and not any one of those who have witnessed it will tell the story. The only remedy would be separate wards, but the Commissioners seem to be unable or unwilling to adopt it.

'"Again," he continued, "your interlocutors have been silent as to the Lord-Lieutenancy."

'"They have not been silent," I said; "almost every one has expressed regret at its continuance. But I thought the subject too trite to be reported on."

'"Trite," he replied, "as the objections to the office are, they ought to be kept before the public, lest the concentrated interests of the few, who profit by it, and the wish, when dealing with a country in the ticklish state of Ireland, to make no change that can be avoided, should tempt government after government to defer a proposal, which will of course be opposed, and in the present state of parties might be defeated, unless it were generally called for.

'"Though your friends here," he continued, "who see and feel the evils of the Lord-Lieutenancy, may be unanimous as to its abolition, I doubt whether it is equally disapproved in England. England has no experience of the state of feeling in Ireland. There is no party there against the Queen, no party opposed to the executive as the executive. Here, in Ireland, with every change of ministry we have a change of sovereign, and the party opposed to the ministry for the time being is opposed to the Lord-Lieutenant, and does everything to make his administration unpopular and unsuccessful."

'"They are equally opposed," I said, "to the English Prime Minister and to the English Home Office."

' " Yes," he answered, " but they have not the same power to make their opposition tell. The Lord-Lieutenant lives among them ; they can worry and tease him. He is a hostage, given by the ministry to their enemies. If he likes popularity, or even dislikes censure, he tries to conciliate, or at least to avoid irritating his opponents. The Irish government therefore is generally timid. It sometimes does what it ought not to do, and still more frequently does not do what it ought to do. If Ireland were governed from the English Home Office, would the poor father and mother whose child was stolen from them from the Castle Knock National School have been treated with such bitter mockery? Would a man earning 10s. a week have been told that the remedy was to spend 50l. in suing out a Habeas Corpus?

' " People talk about the laborious duties of the office. I know what they are, for I have often been a Lord-Justice. Half-an-hour a week performs them ; and I never heard that Ireland was peculiarly ill-governed under the Lord-Justices, or in fact that the want of the Lord-Lieutenant was perceived. I have known several Lord-Lieutenants who worked hard, but they made almost all the business that they did. They were squirrels working in a cage. There is no use in sweeping a room if all the dust comes out of the broom. The only persons who would be really inconvenienced by the change would be the half-dozen tradesmen who now supply the Lodge and the Castle.

' " But I can propose an indemnity even for them. My hope is, that one day the great absentee will return— that the Queen will be an Irish resident. The short visits of Her Majesty—for less than a week at a time—only excite the people of Dublin, make them mad for two or three days, and have no results. I wish her to live among us for five or six weeks at a time, to know us, and to be known—I really believe that this would make the people loyal.

'"There *can* be no loyalty—at least no personal loyalty —to a mere idea, to a person who is never seen. Ireland now looks upon itself as a province ; it does not realise— to use an Americanism—that it is as much a part of the empire as Scotland is. It is always thinking of an Irish policy. I will not say that the Queen's annual residence in Scotland has much to do with the loyalty of the Scotch, or with their looking on Great Britain as a whole, but I cannot doubt that it has contributed to those feelings."'

'Nov. 8, 1858.

'I talked with the Archbishop about the new Roman Catholic university.

'"It is a retrograde step," he said, "on the part of the Roman Catholics. For the last seventy years they have received their lay education at Trinity College. They never whispered a complaint as to their treatment there. Now their minds are to be cramped by the narrow sec- tarianism of an exclusive education, and this too when Oxford and Cambridge have just been thrown open to them.

'"I hear that the expediency of giving them a charter has been mooted. If it is done it will be the first instance of such a charter since the Reformation. Maynooth is not an exception, for Maynooth is strictly ecclesiastical. The restrictions imposed on a Roman Catholic priest are such as a boy, educated among laymen, would hardly submit to. The Roman Catholics, therefore, were entitled to claim an ecclesiastical university, or their young men devoted to the priesthood must have been deprived of the higher portion of instruction.

' " I hear also that it has been thought that giving this charter may be an excuse for a grant to the Church Education Schools.

' " Are they prepared then," I said, " to give up the National System? for a grant to exclusively Protestant schools of course implies a grant to exclusively Roman Catholic ones."

' " Some persons," he said, " are insane enough not to see this. They must suppose that Roman Catholics are indifferent to Roman Catholic education, or that they have no one to plead their cause in Parliament, or that the present state of parties is such that fifty or sixty votes with justice on their side can be disregarded.

' " Others, not insane, but misjudging, see plainly that a grant for separate education to one body implies one to the other, and rejoice in it. They are either English or Scotchmen, unacquainted with Ireland, or Irishmen inhabiting a Protestant district, who wish to manage their own schools in their own way, and to exclude from them all Catholics as teachers or inspectors, and if they have Roman Catholic scholars, to afford them the means of conversion. They forget that throughout the Roman Catholic districts there are Protestant children who, under the separate system, would have to remain uneducated, or to be educated as Roman Catholics.

' " They may, perhaps, think that the inconvenience will be mutual—that there will be as many Roman Catholics forced into Protestant schools, as there will be Protestants driven into Roman Catholic schools. In short, that one injustice will be balanced by another. But even in this wretched calculation they are mistaken.

' " The Roman Catholics are more concentrated than the Protestants. Thousands of Protestants will be thus oppressed for hundreds of Roman Catholics."

'"Would you leave things," I said, "as they are?"

'"By no means," he answered; "that would be a much better course than the system of separate grants, but it would be a bad one.

'"The Board as now constituted, at least as now acting, allows its own rules to be habitually violated in the nunnery schools; it allows the objection of a single child to exclude a book from the use of all the rest; it excludes from religious instruction a child that offers itself, unless it brings an express formal certificate from its parents. It gives grants to rival schools, set up close to and against its own model schools—built at a great expense, with public money; it withdraws aid from schools having less than thirty scholars, though the master be competent, and there be a sufficient number of children in the neighbourhood. It is now proposing to abdicate one of its most important and most troublesome duties—the selection of inspectors—by opening the appointment to public competition. When it has done this it will have scarcely anything left to do except routine business, which any ordinary secretary and clerks could carry on. The Commissioners are merely the Lord-Lieutenant's agents, appointed and removable by him. If I were Lord-Lieutenant I would take from them what they seem ready to give up—the selection of inspectors; I would appoint clerks to perform, under my direction, the routine duties of the office, and I would inform the Commissioners that they need no longer meet periodically, but that I would summon them when I wished for their advice.

'"The system of united education unaccompanied by any compulsory religious education, would then be carried out honestly, under the superintendence of one responsible head. No child desiring Protestant instruction, or Roman Catholic instruction, would be refused it. No

child would get it whose parents especially forbade his
receiving it; no compulsion and no exclusion ought to be
the fundamental rules, as they were during the first twenty
years of the Board, and I believe that the most bigoted,
wrongheaded patrons, when they saw that there was no
remedy, that no further concession was to be hoped,
would acquiesce. This I feel convinced would be the
wisest, though perhaps the boldest course.

'"To leave the Board as it is, but require it to carry
out fully and honestly the principle on which it was
founded, would be the second best course.

'"To leave things as they are is the third best.

'"The very worst is the plan of two separate grants,
and that is the necessary result of one separate grant."

'"Do you believe," I said, "that the opposition to
united education is diminishing among the Protestants?"

'"I have no doubt of it," he answered; "it was at
the beginning rather factious than conscientious, and
more clerical than lay.

'"The Protestant people were ready to use the united
schools whenever the clergy would let them. But the
plan was a Whig plan; it was on the whole adopted by
the Roman Catholics—their taunts on it disgusted the
Orangemen. The Tories in opposition denounced it.
When they came into power they supported it feebly,
and only after a long silence, during which their partisans, after waiting in vain for a signal, had committed
themselves. But that generation has almost passed away.
The primate and I are the only relics of the Irish Bench
as I found it nearly twenty-seven years ago. The new
generation is wiser. The Church Education Society,
instead of claiming, as its predecessor the 'Kildare
Place Society' did, the whole grant, lowered its demand
to only a small portion of it.

'" It now, indeed, ceases to ask for any. I have a letter from the secretary of the committee, stating that they believe that a grant to the body which they represent would be inexpedient. I believe that if the Government hold fast to the system of united education, and take care that it is honestly carried out, the Protestant opposition to it will die out.

'" In this unhappy country, where all is see-saw, the acquiescence of the Protestants may, indeed, provoke the opposition of the Roman Catholics. The Roman Catholic Church has never been cordially friendly; it tolerated united education, only as a substitute for separate education; but the people accepted it joyfully, often even in spite of their priests; and the priests cannot tear from the people anything that they are resolved to keep.

'" Dr. S——, the patron of the Castle Knock School, dismissed the two mistresses, through whose instrumentality, or connivance, or negligence, the Protestant child was kidnapped, and appointed two others, a Roman Catholic and a Protestant, in their places. The priest told him that the Roman Catholic children should be withdrawn, unless he, the priest, was allowed to select the head mistress. Dr. S—— was firm. The children were forbidden to attend the school; they disobeyed, and the priest withdrew the prohibition.

'" Among the supporters of separate grants," he continued, " you will find some who maintain that the evil which is feared from them already exists; that in the National Schools under Roman Catholic patrons the education is now sectarian. The answer is that, where this is so, it is the fault not of the law, but of those to whom the execution is entrusted. If the Protestants are careless, if the inspectors are dishonest, if the commissioners are negligent or worse than negligent, the Roman

Catholic patrons, no doubt, have it all their own way; but such vices are not inherent in the system; they are curable, and ought to be cured.

'"One argument," he added, "is used by the friends of the Church Education Society which has some truth in one of the premises, though the conclusion is false.

'"When reproached for using coercion—for giving to the Roman Catholic children only the alternative of hearing the Bible or being excluded—they say that both the children and their parents like the coercion; that they wish for the Bible, and are glad to be able to say to the priest, as Lord ———'s tenants did, 'It is true that the children hear the Bible, but they cannot help themselves. If they were allowed to quit the schools when it is read, they would.' This is the pretence usually put forth by rebels; they say that they take up arms not against their King but against the evil counsellors, and that he in his heart approves their resistance to his authority. And sometimes what they say is true. The Stillorgan children attended our Scripture readings until the priest forbade them. It is possible that they would have been glad to say that they attended on compulsion. But though this may often be suspected, it can seldom be known: even if it were admitted, therefore, that, on the supposition that such a feeling exists in the parents and children, coercion would be justifiable, still it could seldom be right to employ it, because the truth of the supposition can seldom be ascertained."'

'Nov. 21, 1858.

'We were to have left Redesdale yesterday, but a violent gale from the SW. has raised a sea which we do not choose to encounter.

'I talked to the Archbishop of "The Society for the

Protection of the Rights of Conscience," of which he is the founder.

' "It does not attempt," he said, "to protect a man from every sort of persecution ; that is to say, from every sort of annoyance or inconvenience which he may meet with on account of his religion. It leaves the courts of law to defend his person and his property from physical injury, inflicted or threatened. It does not affect to protect him or even indemnify him against much persecution which he may have to suffer, though it may be severe, and though it may be of a kind of which the courts of law can seldom take cognisance ; such as harassing disputations, remonstrances and solicitations, derision, abuse, and denunciations of Divine wrath.

' " Such annoyances are incidental to religious schism when each party is sincere and zealous. They are to be deplored and endured. An offer of compensation for them would in many cases be a bribe, and in all cases would be an attempt to exempt men from trials to which Providence has subjected us, as tests of sincerity and as means of exhibiting patience, firmness, and faith. All that we can do in this respect is earnestly to enjoin on all within our influence to abstain from inflicting such persecutions, and to submit to them themselves, as an opportunity of showing their hearty devotion to the service of their Master.

' " But there is a third kind of persecution, for which there is no redress by law, and which inflicts physical evils for which patience and faith are no remedies.

' " This persecution is the old excommunication ; it is ' aquæ et ignis interdictio ;' it is the denial of employment, indeed of intercourse.

' " A convert, or even a few converts, surrounded by a hostile population, refused work, refused land, and refused

custom, may have to starve, or to have recourse to the
poor-house, perhaps to be refused admittance there, perhaps, if admitted, to be exposed to intolerable brutality
and indignity. This is a temptation to the weak and a
hardship on the strong, which cannot be witnessed or
heard of with indifference by any one who has any
feelings of humanity, any sense of justice, or any conscientious convictions. As the law is powerless, individuals or a combination of individuals must step in.

'"It is not as a Protestant or as a convert, or even as a
Protestant convert in distress, that any one receives aid
from us, but as an industrious and well-conducted man,
who has been excluded from employment, and left to
starvation, on merely religious grounds. And to any one
so circumstanced all who disclaim persecution are bound
to give relief, whatever be the ground of his exclusion;
whether it be his belief, whether he be excommunicated
as a Protestant, a Papist, or an atheist.

'"It is because Protestants only are so persecuted that
the society assumes in the eyes of the public a Protestant
colour. It is, in the true sense of the word, catholic. It
is open to all who are thus persecuted for conscience
sake."'

CHAPTER XIV.

1859.

Letter to Mr. Senior on ' Book grants' from the Education Board
— Letter to Lord Ebury on Liturgical Revision — Letter to a
Clergyman on the same subject—Letter to Miss Crabtree on the
Revival Movement — His family bereavements — Death of his
youngest daughter— Death of Mrs. Whately — Letters to Miss
Crabtree and Dr. Hinds—Breaking up of his family circle—Spends
the summer with Mr. Senior—Letter to Mrs. Arnold.

OF the year 1859 there is but little to record. He was
not in parliament that year; and, with the exception of a
short visit to England in the early part of it, it was spent
in his usual diocesan and literary avocations.

Lord Wicklow had suggested grants of books being
made to schools not under the Board, and on this subject
he wrote to Mr. Senior :—

'Dublin : April 14, 1859.

' My dear Senior,—As for Lord Wicklow's suggestion,
the books of the Board are to be had now, very cheap,
and so very little above prime cost, that the difference
would not afford any effectual support to any school.

' Why then should this be so eagerly sought? Evidently
for the insertion of the thin end of the wedge.   It would
be a Government recognition and sanction of denomina-
tional schools.   And soon after, a claim would be made
(no unreasonable one), and granted, for some effectual aid
to the schools set up in avowed rivalry to the National
Schools !

'If we were to send the King of Sardinia one company of soldiers to fight against Austria, he would probably be very glad. Not that this handful of men could do any valuable service, but we should have sanctioned the war, and engaged in it; and we should be expected to send, soon after, two or three regiments to support that company, and then a powerful army to support these.

'A camel, according to the Arabian fable, begged leave one cold night to put the tip of his nose inside a tent for warmth; having got his nose in, he next intruded his head and shoulders, and then his hind quarters; and then he lay down before the fire, and turned away all the rest.

'I have sent the Bishop of Cork a curious document, an Address from the Roman Catholic Bishops, claiming a separate grant. He is to have it reprinted, or not, as he may judge best. If he does not, he will send it to you to look at and show your friends.

'Yours ever,
'R. W.'

The memorandum which follows was sent to Mr. Senior a little earlier than the letter, and is the last of his notices on national education.

Lord Ebury had written to him on the question of Liturgical Revision; and the two following letters are, one an answer to the above, the other to a clergyman on the same subject.

To Lord Ebury.

'Dublin: Dec. 2, 1859.

'My dear Lord,—I am sorry to say I cannot see how to surmount the difficulties of the question your Lordship has brought before me. The pamphlet you have sent me, and one which I have since received from Mr. Proby, of the diocese of Winchester (Simpkin & Marshall), and

which probably your Lordship will have seen, do not
show me any outlet.

'The object proposed is, I presume, not to reform the
Church, but to revise the Liturgy; not to make such
fundamental changes of doctrine as might be to some
very acceptable, and would drive a great many others
out of our communion, but to make such alterations in
the formularies as might satisfy nearly all who regard
themselves as conscientious members of our Church.

'Now, if all that was wanted were the abridgment of
some services that are confessedly tedious, and the alteration of some obsolete phrases, the task of revision might
not be very difficult. But many clergymen, of various
parties, hold doctrines—I will not say at variance with
our formularies, but at variance with the most simple and
obvious sense of some passages therein; which passages
they are driven to explain away in a certain "non-natural
sense." And they earnestly desire to have these altered.
And if some revision were made which did not effect that
object, they would be much dissatisfied. They would
even be indignant, if the alterations they seek were such
as they thought ought to satisfy all parties, as containing
no express assertion of the doctrines they hold on some
point, but only excluding an assertion of the opposite, and
leaving the matter open. E.g. suppose that for "regeneration" we everywhere substituted "admission into the
visible Church." It might be said that all agree in accounting baptism an admission into the visible Church.
And the question would be left open whether the Church
is or is not a spiritually-endowed society, and whether
any or what benefit, beyond a mere empty name, is conferred on the recipient of baptism.

'Now, all this would be quite reasonable, if we were
founding a new Church and framing original formula-

ries. But, if any words are deliberately expunged from a passage where they formerly stood, this could not fail to be interpreted as a rejection of the doctrine those words were supposed to imply. which would greatly displease many. It is vain to say an omission ought not to be so understood. It will, and must be. Wherever there is an amputation there will be a wound and a scar. Suppose, e. g., we erased from the wedding service the word "obey," it would surely be understood that we meant to exempt wives from the duty of obedience; though no such inference is drawn respecting those Churches which never had that word in their marriage service. And again, some Churches never introduced the Ten Commandments into their services, and are not charged with Antinomianism thereupon; which we doubtless should be if we were to remove the commandments. And so it is in many other points. I cannot see how to get over the difficulty. It is the greater, because several of those who call out for liturgical revision do seem in reality to be seeking not merely that, but a re-cast of the Church's teaching.

'Mr. Proby. e. g., in the pamphlet above referred to, alludes to the Gorham controversy, apparently quite unconscious that he himself pronounces a decision against Mr. Gorham. For the question was not whether Mr. Gorham's doctrine was scriptural and true, but whether it was consistent with the teaching of the Church in which he sought a benefice; and Mr. Proby distinctly lays down that it was at variance with that. It is a curious circumstance, and a most unfortunate one, that the expressions which formerly, and for a very long time, satisfied those of our clergy (probably a majority, certainly a large portion) who, in the early days of the Reformation, leaned towards the Calvinistic views, are so

generally displeasing to those who lean towards those
views now.   It would seem that they have introduced a
limitation of the sense of the word "regenerate" unknown to our ancestors, both those who did and who did
not incline to Calvinism; and that now it is required to re-
model our formularies in conformity with this innovation.

'Believe me to be your

'Lordship's faithful humble servant,

'RD. DUBLIN.'

'Palace, Dublin: Dec. 10, 1859.

'Rev. Sir,—The wish that our Liturgy should be agreeable to Scripture must be common to all sincere Christians,
how much soever they may differ among themselves as to
what is agreeable to Scripture.

'But the point I was dwelling on (in the letter to Lord
Ebury) is the importance of calling each distinct thing by
its own right name, instead of confusedly blending together by means of a common title two things which are
neither identical nor inseparable.   If any one thinks that
there is need both of a doctrinal reformation of the Church
and also of a revised Liturgy, let him plainly say so.

'But evidently it is at least conceivable that some men
may wish for the one of these and not for the other—
may wish for no change in the doctrines of the Church,
and yet may wish for the abridgment of some services
that are tedious, and the alteration of some phrases that
are obsolete or ambiguous.

'This latter is what I understood Lord Ebury to have
in view.

'If I have misunderstood his Lordship, he will I presume explain to me his meaning.   To take a familiar
instance.   If I wish to make my will, I hand my lawyer
a memorandum stating in untechnical language my wishes

as to the disposal of my property, and he draws up a
will for me accordingly in legal form. If he thinks some
of my bequests unwise he may advise me, as a friend, to
alter them, but it would be very unfair in him to foist in
(as a clever lawyer might easily do) unknown to me—
under colour of merely altering an expression—words
which would defeat what he knew to be my intentions;
and the like holds good in all analogous cases.

'Suppose, for instance, the case of a Roman Catholic
priest (in our own country before the Reformation, or in
Spain or Italy in the present day) arriving at the conviction that the sacrifice of the Mass and the other distinctive tenets of the Church of Rome are fundamentally
erroneous, what would be his procedure, if he were a
sensible and fair-minded man? Surely he would not
propose merely a revision of the Liturgy, but a doctrinal
reformation of the Church. He would in the meantime
suspend his ministrations in that Church, and cease to
administer ordinances which he would consider fundamentally superstitious and erroneous; he would call on
his ecclesiastical superiors to reform the doctrines of their
Church; and if they refused to do this, he would abandon
its communion, and resign any office he might hold in it.

'But a man would not be called on to proceed thus,
who was seeking merely for such alterations in the Liturgy
as did not involve any points of doctrine.

'As for my own views upon some of the points that
are debated, it may be worth while to mention that I
very much concur with Archbishop Sumner, with the late
Bishop Ryder, and Mr. Simeon, from whose works I have
extracted some passages in the appendix to my little tract
on the Sacraments.

'Not that I have appealed to any human authority as
infallible, but I am glad to find a coincidence between

my own views and those of some who are accounted
eminent divines.'

*To Miss Crabtree, who had asked his Opinion of the Revival
Movement then going on.*

'Oct. 10, 1859.

'My dear Miss Crabtree,—The revivals are doing both
good and evil. Which will ultimately predominate is
more than I can as yet pronounce. Much will depend
on the conduct of many persons, most of whom I am unacquainted with.

'I send you the best pamphlets that have appeared.
They are by judicious and impartial men. Most of the
other publications take a part. They either condemn the
whole as an outbreak of frenzy, or proclaim hysterical
shrieks and fits as an outpouring of the Holy Spirit.

'Now to me it appears that true Christianity is a very
quiet and deliberate religion. It keeps the steam acting
on the wheels, instead of noisily whizzing out at the safety
valve.

'I cannot tell how I came to send you cuttings of the
common elder for the scarlet. But what I conjecture is
this, I have a common elder grafted with the scarlet, and
I suspect that the stock must have sent up a surreptitious
shoot which mingled with the branches of the true, and
was mistaken for one of them.

'Now this may suggest a useful parable for the present
time. When the " natural man " is grafted with true religion (by a revival, or any how) we are apt to feel carelessly confident from the certainty that the graft is of the
right sort, and has taken, and is flourishing. But without
continual vigilance shoots from the wild stock will imperceptibly grow up, and getting intermingled with the
branches of the graft will pass for one of them. A tree

that is headed down and grafted with a different kind, may be said to have undergone a "new birth," but it is not therefore safe unless it be continually and carefully watched.

'I believe that, besides other evils, the tone of some rash enthusiasts has done much to foster the kind of infidelity now prevailing, which calls itself spiritual Christianity. "You call any remarkable occurrence that favours your views miraculous; and so no doubt did the Apostles. They reckoned as inspiration any vehement excitement, any strong impression made on men's minds, just as you do," &c.'

This year was to be the last of his united family life; his home from thenceforth was to be a desolated one. Hitherto he had been singularly exempt from ordinary domestic bereavements; his elder sisters had, indeed, one by one departed, but their advanced age rendered this an event to be looked for in the course of nature, and his daily life, from his residence in Ireland, had been little affected by the removal of those out of his domestic circle. Some friends very dear and valuable to him had indeed been removed; but his own home party had been hitherto untouched. But now the time was come for the hand of affliction to be heavily laid on him, and it came in a form peculiarly affecting. His youngest daughter had been married in the November of that year to Captain George Wale, R.N., the brother of his son-in-law Charles Wale, under circumstances offering every promise of a bright future. The family festivity attending the wedding had, indeed, been shadowed with a first touch of sorrow in the sickness and death of a newborn grandchild; but this was to be the beginning of sorrows. The new-married pair were to reside in Ireland, and scarcely a month after the marriage they came to spend

Christmas under the old family roof at the palace, on their way to their new abode. Within three days the bride sickened with a fatal illness; and after ten weeks' acute suffering, the child of so many hopes was carried to her grave (in March 1860)—a bride of scarce four months. But this affliction did not come singly. Another member of the family was threatened with pulmonary symptoms and ordered to avoid the spring east winds of the Dublin coast; and the bereaved family accordingly removed to Hastings. There, in the middle of April, one short month after the daughter's death, her mother, worn out with long watching and sorrow, coming on an already over-taxed frame, was carried off by a short but sharp illness of only five days' duration.

The bereaved husband and father was, as we have said, not one to show his feelings; even those nearest to him could only guess at what passed within, and hardly they. He was now becoming very infirm, and could not, as in early days, watch by the invalid. At her own request, the day before her death, he came to read to her the service for the Visitation of the Sick. He made a strong effort to go through it, but his voice broke down at the first sentence, and he was obliged to give up the book to another.

In the midst of his own grief and increasing infirmities, he found time to write a touching letter to his grandchild in Ireland (his son's eldest daughter) on the departure of those two loved ones, exhorting her to follow in their steps.[1] From his brother-in-law and sister-in-law, who had both hastened to join him, he received the most affectionate and devoted attention; for some time he remained under the roof of the former at Tunbridge

---

[1] This much-prized letter has unhappily fallen into other hands, and cannot therefore be published.

Wells. In June he insisted, notwithstanding the entreaties of his friends, on returning to Dublin for his visitation and other duties, and went through them more easily than could have been expected. The rest of the summer was spent with his daughter and son-in-law in Cambridgeshire, and in the autumn he returned to Ireland and took up his residence in a smaller place nearer to Dublin than the former, between which and the Palace he spent the last three years of his life.

Of the letters that follow the first was written a little before the first of these bereavements; the others later.

To Miss Crabtree.

'Dublin: March 2, 1860.

.   .   .   .

'A bishop who is anxious above all things for a peaceful life will do well to imitate a bishop whom you remember by sitting still and doing nothing at all. And one who would be popular must ever swim with the stream. But one who is discreet as well as active and conscientious will consider that above half of the evils that have ever existed, have arisen from something good in itself and done well, but which has afforded a precedent and an encouragement to something evil in imitation of it. The Ass, according to the fable (which is one of most extensive application), followed the precedent of the Lapdog. Nelson gained the victory of Copenhagen by disobeying orders. If a few more such instances had occurred, and it had been thence the practice for every subaltern officer and private sailor or soldier, who might think he knew better than his commander, to collect a party of his comrades, and act as he thought best, this would before long convert the finest possible army into a rabble of undisciplined guerillas.

'If some period of great excitement had occurred when I was at Halesworth, and I had thrown myself at once into it without any precaution, I should probably have gained more reputation, and produced more striking effects, some good and some evil, than by my quiet unpretending explanatory lectures in which I laboured night after night, and week after week, in patiently laying on " line upon line, precept upon precept; here a little and there a little." '

To Bishop Hinds a few days after his Daughter's death.

'March 10, 1860.

'My dear Hinds,—We are friends of fifty years' standing; and you write like one.

'I *ought* to dwell on the *contrast* between *your* letter and that addressed to Cicero on a similar occasion, by Sulpicius, a kind-hearted friend, and a man of cultivated mind! May we find grace to think of the blessing bestowed on *us*!

'But, humanly speaking, the trial is very sharp, to have such a cup of happiness, when just tasted, dashed from the lips. And the eleven weeks of severe suffering to the dear patient, and of painful toil and anxiety to all of us, has broken down the health of the whole party.'

To Miss Crabtree he adds, two months later, 'I have faith, on Scripture warrants, in intercessory prayer; and I am sure you will be ready to pray for us, that we may be supported under these heavy strokes of affliction.'

The year 1861 was also marked by much trial; partly from alarming illness among members of his family, and partly from other causes of grief, which pressed heavily on him. His immediate circle was now a reduced one; his son-in-law was obliged to remove

with his family to the Continent in consequence of ill
health ; another daughter had been previously compelled
to reside abroad from the same cause during greater
part of the year. Only one daughter therefore remained with him ; but he bore up through all with
characteristic firmness and calm dignity ; and though
increasing infirmities might well have furnished an excuse
for withdrawing from his official duties, the visitation and
confirmations were performed as usual.   It was touching
to see the deep solemnity with which the trembling hands
were placed on the young heads ; and, though the fatigue
and exhaustion obliged him to pause and rest in the middle
of the ceremony, the usual addresses were not omitted, and
the voice which had lost much of its full clear tones, still
spoke the words of exhortation to the young candidates
with impressive earnestness.   Nor were his literary
occupations discontinued.   Writing was now become
painful and difficult : but he still corrected the proofs of
each new edition, and still dictated articles for the
'Commonplace Book,' and papers for several magazines
to which he occasionally contributed ; and frequently
sent memoranda to friends on some subject of interest
and importance.

Though unequal to much general society, he was able
to enjoy a social circle in his own home ; and many will
remember the evenings when he would discourse to a few
gathered round him, with his wonted life and power of
illustration, on a variety of topics of interest, or comment
on a passage of some favourite work he would cause to be
read aloud to him ; and at the breakfast table he was
always full of conversation and ready to enter on the
subjects of the day or to impart information on various
matters small and great.

Part of the summer of this year was passed with his

friend Mr. Senior in London, and with his relations at
Tunbridge Wells; and the change of scene and society
seemed to cheer and interest him.

His brother-in-law has preserved some recollections
of that time. 'He was always partial,' he writes, 'to
Tunbridge Wells; and in his latter visits, which continued
till within a year of his death, he had pleasure in renew-
ing intercourse with some of his old college friends.

'He had often preached for his brother-in-law in the
old chapel of ease to large and attentive congregations;
and many will remember the last time he addressed them
from that pulpit on the 4th of August 1861, when from
the effect of paralysis of one side he was hardly able to
ascend the stairs.

'A mutual esteem existed between him and Archbishop
Sumner, and the last time these met was at Tunbridge
Wells on May 29, 1860, though only to exchange
tokens of recognition on each side of the railway
platform.'

Thus far the recollections of his last visits to his
favourite old resort. The following letter to Mrs.
Arnold shows that his intellectual activity was as untiring
as ever.

To Mrs. Arnold.

'December 16, 1861.

'My dear Friend,—You must excuse my writing very
rarely and very briefly, as it is fatiguing, from the palsy
having extended to my right hand. But J—— will tell
you all about us from time to time.

'I am (as the Yankees say) most 'powerful weak.'
But I am thankful that my intellect does not yet seem
much affected; only I am soon exhausted. The last charge

was thought to be equal to any former ones.   But it took me as many weeks as it would formerly days.

'To think of such a wreck as I am having survived the poor Prince!

'He is a great loss to the public.

'Towards *me* he was always most gracious.   Two or three times I sent him little books of mine for his children, and he always acknowledged them in his own hand.'

CHAPTER XV.

1862.

Suffers from neuralgic gout.—Attends the session of the Statistical
Society, and contributes a paper on Secondary Punishments—Letter
to Rev. C. Wale—Visit of Mr. Senior—Mr. Senior's Journal—Experiments on Charring—Conversation on our Penal Code—Remarks
on the falsehood of commonly received maxims—Visit of Dr. de
Ricci, and interesting conversation on religious endowments.

IN the spring of 1862 he suffered greatly from an
affection of the leg, supposed to be neuralgic gout; the
pain was at times very severe, and the case a tedious one;
but he entirely recovered from it, and was again enabled
to pay a visit to his English friends, but being feeble,
seemed to enjoy it less. That autumn his son-in-law and
daughter paid him a visit from abroad, which greatly
cheered and refreshed him; and later his friend Mr. Senior
spent some time with him. He still continued occasionally to preach; but the weakness of his voice had increased,
and the effort was evidently a painful one.

But even in this year he came to the opening meetings
of the Statistical Society, which he had so long and steadily
supported, to receive the Lord-Lieutenant and to hear the
address of the Solicitor-General. Late in the 'session' of
the Society he contributed to their proceedings the paper
containing the notes of a conversation between himself and
Mr. Senior on Secondary Punishments, and took part in
the discussion which followed.

cc 2

388 LIFE OF ARCHBISHOP WHATELY. [1862

He continued to contribute articles to several magazines, and from time to time to add to the stores of his Commonplace Book ; but letters were more and more of an effort to him. The following letter to his son-in-law is the only one we give in this year.

'February 1, 1862.

'My dear Charles,—· . . . . To-day I enter on my seventy-sixth year. I do not think it probable I shall reach the end of it. But what I am anxious about and earnestly pray against is, continuing *alive*, after having ceased *to live*, i.e. becoming—as is a common fate of paralytic patients— a wretched burden to myself and all around me.

' I do not as yet, myself, perceive much decay of intellectual power, except that I am very *soon exhausted*. I can write nearly as well in ten days, as I formerly could in two.' . . .

We have mentioned that Mr. Senior was the Archbishop's guest in the autumn of 1862. The following extracts from his Journal will show what subjects were mostly occupying my father's mind, and illustrate the freshness and vigour of intellect which remained unabated in the midst of bodily infirmities which were gradually though slowly increasing.

Mr. Senior's Journal.

'Nov. 8, 1862.

' I left Ashton this morning to visit the Archbishop of Dublin, at the Palace in Stephen's Green.

' He is anxious that the experiment of charring instead of burning the surface turf for the purpose of reclaiming bogland should be tried. Under the present practice only a few pounds of ashes are obtained from an amount of turf which, if charred, would give hundredweights of peat-charcoal.

'"I believe," he said, "that the charcoal would form a much more useful ingredient to mix with the subsoil and manure than the ashes do.   I think it probable, indeed, that the peat charcoal would grow farming crops without any other soil.   Charcoal has the power of absorbing gases to an incredible amount, which it gives out to plants and thus furnishes to them fresh and continued supply of manure.   You may see in the Botanical Gardens of Trinity College, many plants growing in pure peat charcoal, and more luxuriantly than similar plants grow-ing in earth.

'"The charcoal is not pulverised, it is merely broken into the consistency of coarse gravel.   If by this means new land could be obtained, not only would there be a new supply of food, but new tenants; English and Scotch might be introduced without evictions."'

'Nov. 8.

'The Archbishop has been reading the earlier part of this journal.

'"There would be something," he said, "in ——'s appre-hension of evil from the dependence of a paid clergy on the State, if they were appointed, removed, and paid by the Prime Minister.   But the English, and French, and Belgian clergy, though all paid, are dependent on the State only in the sense in which every one, who is entitled by law to property or to income, is dependent on the State; that is to say, they feel that their incomes or their properties depend on the law, and on the State, as the preserver and enforcer of the law—and accordingly the clergy in all those countries are from time to time in opposition to the existing government.   The majority of

the clergy in France, in Belgium, and I am inclined to
think, in England, are now in opposition." " Though
they may have nothing to fear from the minister," I said,
" may they not have much to hope from him?"

' " From a minister," he answered, " but not necessarily
from the minister of the time being. And if the influence
of the minister be feared, it might be remedied by taking
from the Government ecclesiastical patronage. I do
not think that this would be a good change. I do not
think that a synod of bishops, or deans and chapters,
would choose so well as the prime minister does. A
synod would probably be intolerant. It would be
governed by a clique, and admit persons professing only
one set of opinions, and not the most eminent of those
men. The deans and chapters would follow the example
of the fellows of colleges, and elect only from their own
small body.

' " As the prime minister is changed every three or four
years, he has seldom time to make more than three or
four bishops, or indeed so many, and as he acts under a
strong individual responsibility, it is pretty sure that he
will endeavour to make appointments which will be
generally approved.

' "———," he continued, " when he denies that the Roman
Catholic priests are proselytisers, on the ground that he
never heard from an Irish Roman Catholic pulpit a controversial sermon, resembles a man who would say, that
a bull is an inoffensive animal because he does not bite.

' " The priests well know that controversy is not their
forte. They have no general knowledge, and a man
without general knowledge, though he may be primed
with separate texts and authorities, is soon silenced by a
disputant with extensive information.

' " On the other hand, the more enlightened of the

Roman Catholic priests probably suspect, indeed, if they are candid, *must* suspect, that when they differ from us, they are often wrong, and therefore are likely to be often defeated in argument. They are therefore forced to proselytise in a different manner.

' " They choose for their field of action large parishes where there is a Protestant population too scattered to be attended to by their own minister, and where the benefice is too poor to maintain a curate. While visiting their own flock they enter the Protestant cabins, and having the public opinion of the parish with them, they talk over the women, and then the men.

' " His opinion, that they are not anxious to make converts, is absurd. A Roman Catholic who believes that there is no salvation out of his own Church, would be a monster if he did not compass heaven and earth to make proselytes; and I *know* that they make many; but they do not boast of them, lest they should attract the notice of the Additional Curate Society.

' " I also disbelieve his statement, that the Bible readers force their way into cabins against the will of their owners.

' " They enter them often against the will of the priest and against the will of the Roman Catholic neighbours, but I do not believe that they ever enter a cabin unless the husband or the wife wishes them to do so. Under such circumstances they are often waylaid and beaten, and the converts themselves are subject to the persecution of a fanatical peasantry and a fanatical priesthood. The priests denounce and curse from the altar all who have any dealings with a convert. If it were not for the aid afforded by the Conscience Society, which endeavours to protect all who suffer for their creed, whatever that creed may be, converts would often starve.

' "———," he continued, " seems to belong to a large class of intelligent men—and a still larger class of intelligent women—who have weights without scales.

' " They notice all the arguments pro and con, but do not estimate their relative force ; any objection to a measure is to them an objection, and they *will* not or *cannot* see that it may be much overbalanced by an accompanying advantage, or by the objections to any other expedient. Such persons cannot understand the force of accumulative proof. They see that every separate bit of evidence is weak, and do not perceive that the whole body of proof built up out of those separate bits is irresistible.

' " He has summed up the objections to a clergy dependent on their flock ; he has also summed up the objections, or what he thinks the objections, to a clergy paid by the state ; but when he comes to compare those objections, his want of scales is obvious.

' " Two persons, each of them affected by this defect, cannot agree. It is as if a Stork and a Fox made a picnic, and the Fox contributed his soup in a platter, and the Stork in a bottle.

' " Such people are apt to deal in half measures. A half measure is not a medium between two extremes, but a medium between what is right and what is wrong— between what will effect its purpose and what will not.

' " A coat that fits you is not a half measure—a coat a little too tight or a little too loose, would be. Neither perfect religious impartiality, nor irresistible persecution is a half measure.

' " Each of these may effect its object. The first may enable men of different sects to live in harmony. The second may extinguish all differences, and therefore all sects.

' " But moderate persecution, such as England inflicted on Ireland, is a half measure. It produces neither peace nor unity.

' " The retention of the Lord-Lieutenancy on the Irish Union was in the nature of a half measure. It was inconsistent with the fusion of the two people, which was the object of the union.

' " When England and Ireland were two independent states, tied together as England and Hanover were, by having a common sovereign, but having no common legislative, or judicial, or administrative body, and when no one could be certain of getting from Holyhead to Dublin, in less than three weeks, such an officer may have been wanted. But when the two legislatures were fused, the Lord-Lieutenant became a phantom, the creature of the English Under-Secretary and of the English Prime Minister, forced often to look on at, and sometimes to apparently countenance a policy which he thinks mischievous, and appointments which he disapproves, with no duties but to preside at a mock Court, and make after-dinner speeches."

' " This may show," I said, " that the Lord-Lieutenancy does no good, but what harm does it do ? "

' " It does harm," he answered, " as keeping up in people's minds the notion of a separate kingdom, as affording a hot-bed of faction and intrigue, as presenting an image of majesty so faint and so feeble as to be laughed at or scorned.

' " Disaffection to the English Lord-Lieutenant is cheaply shown, and it paves the way towards disaffection to the English Crown.

' " These inconveniences would follow, *if* the Lord-Lieutenant knew his business. But he is almost always recalled before he has learnt it. Having little real power, he can

acquire influence only by cajoling people, by talking them
over, but for this purpose he ought to know his men. To
use that influence, when required, for good purposes, he
ought to know well what are the wants of Ireland. This
knowledge of men and of things he is seldom allowed
time to acquire. He is thrown into the midst of a most
corrupt, selfish, factious society, and before he has found
out the few whom he may trust, and the many who will
do all that they can do to mislead him, he leaves it. He is
placed in a country, in which many of what are considered
in more civilised nations necessary branches of administration have to be created, and many more have to be
reformed : which is governed from a distant capital by a
ministry who know little about it, and use it chiefly as a
means of party warfare, or of corruption ; and his functions cease by the time that he has acquired a half information, perhaps, not much better than ignorance." '

Nov. 16.

' " You," I said, to the Archbishop, " greatly contributed
to the abolition of transportation. With its many disadvantages—its sowing our colonies with poisoned seed—
its uncertainty, and its ill performance of the principal
purpose of punishment, the deterring men from offences
—it has one great merit. The criminal was discharged
among the antipodes. Now he is discharged at home."

' " The substitute for transportation, which I proposed,"
he answered, " was nearly what has been adopted in
Ireland—that of requiring from the convicts a certain
amount of work, compelling them to a certain moderate
quantity of daily labour, but allowing them to exceed
this as much as they pleased, and *thus* shorten the time
of their imprisonment, by accomplishing the total amount
of their task in less time than that to which they had
been sentenced.

' " I mentioned, also, that they should not again be let loose on society, till they had given some indication of amended character. And I further admitted, that the enforcement of these regulations would require much vigilance and discretion, in the superintendence of convict establishments."

' " It seems," I said, " that all these conditions are utterly neglected in England. The convict is not sentenced to the performance of any fixed amount of work. No abbreviation of imprisonment can be obtained by diligence, no indication, of amended character except quiet submission to restraints which cannot be evaded, is required ; and as to vigilance and discretion, the English prison authorities repudiate them by declaring in so many words, that ' male convicts must be treated in masses, rather than according to their individual characters.' " [1]

' " It is difficult," said the Archbishop, " to conceive the state of mind in which a man, familiar with penal jurisprudence, could come to so monstrous a conclusion as that convicts ought to be let loose on the public in masses, without reference to their individual fitness for pardon.

' " But the ill-regulated humanity which shrinks from inflicting on the convict the proper amount of punishment, may be easily explained. Those who act from feeling, not from principle, are usually led to show more tenderness towards the offending than towards the unoffending ; towards the culprit who is present, and the object of their senses, whose sufferings and apprehensions they actually witness, than towards the absent, unknown, and undefined, members of the community, whose persons or property, were endangered by him.

' " The other day," I said, " some men were tried for a

---

[1] Report of Directors of English Convict Prisons for 1857, p. 49.

crime of garotting. They had knocked a man down, broken his jaw, obliged it to be cut out of his face to prevent mortification, in fact, they had rendered him wretched for life. They were ticket-of-leave men, who, if their sentences had been carried into effect, would, at the time when the outrage was committed, have been in prison. It is computed that not one offence in twenty is detected. How many crimes did J. H. commit ; of how many people did he destroy the happiness, during each of the three periods in which, in defiance of his different sentences, he was let loose ? "

' " What were the sentences," asked the Archbishop, " passed on the garotters ? "

' " Penal servitude," I answered, " for life, or for long terms of years—which, in a very few years, will be remitted, and they will be again set to work, to maim or to murder."

' " We have nearly put an end." said the Archbishop, " to the two punishments, death and transportation, one of which was absolutely irremissible, and the other nearly so. It does seem to me, that substitutes ought to be provided. I know of but one means by which this dreadful abuse of the power of pardon can be put a stop to. It is to enact that certain sentences shall be irremissible, except by Act of Parliament.

' " Every year in which any such sentences are to be remitted, an Act should be passed, enabling the Home Secretary to grant tickets-of-leave to the persons mentioned in the schedule. The schedule should contain the names, the crimes, the sentences, and the previous convictions of the persons to be released, and the grounds on which each separate release was granted.

' " Other improvements should of course also be made, and the treatment of convicts in England should be assimilated to the Irish system, but all sentences are illusory, as long as convicts are discharged in masses, without reference to individual character.

'"If sentences for life, or for any number of years exceeding fifteen, were thus made irremissible, except by an act of the legislature, judges, the public, and the criminal population would know the real meaning and the real effect of a sentence."

'"I perfectly agree with you," I said, "as to the propriety of making long sentences irremissible, except by Act of Parliament. Nor would I allow to justices and magistrates their present discretion. Every crime should have its fixed punishment. The caprice of a magistrate or of a judge should not decide whether a murderous assault should be punished by six months imprisonment or by six weeks, or by six years. The lenity shown by our judicial authorities to acts of violence, is one of the strangest phenomena in our present penal administration. I would go further still. I would return, and return largely, to the only irremissible punishment, death. I would punish with death, three days after conviction, every person convicted a second time of robbery, accompanied by violence. Experience shows that such malefactors are never reformed. They go on from crime to crime until death. I would cut their course short, in pity to the public and in pity to themselves. The common answer, that robbery ought not to be punished by death, lest murder should be added, for the sake of concealment, does not apply. The garotter, who strikes his victim down, secures his watch and runs off, has not time to do more. He attacks him from behind, does not fear recognition, and would increase instead of diminish the chance of detection, *if* he murdered him.

'"Pity for such men is the weakest of follies. They are wild beasts, and ought to be treated as wild beasts.

What should we think of a right, claimed and exercised by a Secretary of State, to go every day to a menagerie, and let out, by mere rotation, one animal from a cage, without inquiring whether he released a monkey or a tiger? The tiger, however, would be recognised instantly, and shot down in half an hour; the ticket-of-leave *fera* may prey on society for months, or for years, in the disguise of a human being."

'We talked in the evening of the falsehood of commonly received maxims.

' " One," said the Archbishop, " which has the sanction of La Rochefoucauld is, that hypocrisy is the homage which vice pays to virtue.

' " It is not a homage to virtue but to opinion. The hypocrite affects the qualities, the reputation for which will, as he thinks, be useful to him.

' " There was a time when it was fashionable to be supposed to be a rake, to be supposed to drink, to game, to be profligate and to be extravagant. The same men who were then ' fanfarons des vices' would, under a different state of public opinion, have been ascetics."

' " It must be admitted, however," I said, " that the affectation of virtue is more common than the affectation of vice."

' " Of what Bacon calls the lowest and middle virtues," he answered. " Such as liberality, good nature, good temper, courage and fidelity to your friends or to your party. In short, of the virtues, which according to him, men praise and admire. But not of the highest virtues, of which he says that they have no sense. He does not tell us what these are, but I understand him to mean candour, perfect justice, and disregard of popularity and of party ties, when duty requires. These are qualities for which men are often blamed as eccentric, crotchety, fanciful, and absurdly scrupulous. And they are seldom affected.

' " One of the merits most pretended to, consistency— or perhaps I ought to say—one of the reproaches most dreaded is, the reproach of inconsistency. We see people trying to avoid it by persisting in what, in their own inward minds, they acknowledge to themselves to be error.

' " Now inconsistency of conduct may arise from three causes :—

' " 1. Change of circumstances.

' " 2. Change of opinion.

' " 3. The co-existence in the mind of contradictory opinions.

' " In the first of these cases, change of conduct is almost always a proof of wisdom. It is very rarely that, under altered circumstances, persistence in the same conduct is advisable.

' " Secondly, as long as man is fallible, a change of opinion must often be right. Though each separate opinion necessarily appears to the holder of it to be true, yet every one is aware, that of the mass of his opinions, some must be wholly or partially false. Just as a bad arithmetician, in adding up a long column of figures, is perfectly confident as to the truth of each separate addition, but may know from experience, that it is highly probable, that the total may be wrong.

' " Thirdly, the co-existence in the mind of irreconcilable opinions of course implies a mental defect. In a dark mind, as in a dark room, enemies may lie down in different corners, without its being known. Bring in a light, and they instantly rise and fight, until one expels the other.

' " The inconsistency of conduct, which arises from the

co-existence in the mind of opposite opinions, is not a moral, but an intellectual defect. It is to be cured only by bringing in a light.

'" On the whole, it seems to me that a man who prides himself on universal consistency ought not to be allowed to take part in public affairs. He must close his eyes before new facts and his ears against new arguments. He must be intensely obstinate, and intensely arrogant.

'" Another common error," he continued, "is to suppose the sinfulness of man was occasioned by our first parents eating the apple. The apple may have increased that sinfulness, it may have awakened passions unknown to them before; but the sin was committed as soon as they had resolved to eat the apple, and a sinful diathesis, a tendency to sin, must have existed in them, or they would not have listened to the tempter.

'" The nature of the tree of life, too, has not been well explained. I suspect that the use of its fruit completely repaired the waste of the body, and that imparted to the constitutions of our first parents a vigour which gradually wore out. The earlier generations of mankind inherited a life eleven or twelve times as long as ours. After the deluge, life gradually shortened, from 600 years, the time of Shem, to 438 years, that of his son Arphaxad; 239 years, that of Arphaxad's great grandson Peleg; 148 years, that of Peleg's great grandson Nahor; and 175 years, that of Nahor's grandson Abraham. Jacob's answer to Pharaoh, ' The days of my pilgrimage are an hundred and thirty years. Few and evil have the days of my life been, and have not attained unto the years of my forefathers,' shows, that at that time the life of man was about double of what it is now; and by the time of Moses it had receded to its present limits. Now this is what might be expected to be the effect of a food which, as long as it was habitually eaten, gave immortality, and when it was discontinued slowly lost its effect.

'"Another false maxim," I said, "is: Do not put off to to-morrow what can be done to-day. The true maxim is: Do not do to-day what can be put off till to-morrow. If you do it to-day, you will find, when to-morrow comes, that if you had delayed doing it, you *would* have done it and *ought* to have done it differently, if at all."

'"Another," he said, "is: 'Ne facias per alium quod facere potes per te.' It ought, like the former one, to be reversed and to stand, 'Ne facias per te quod facere potes per alium.'

'"The things which you ought to do, and which nobody can do for you, are so numerous and so difficult, that all your time and all your strength of body and of mind will not enable you to execute them fully. The strength and the time which you devote to things which you can do by deputy, are so much robbed from the things which you must do, if they are to be done at all, yourself.

'"A man may be great as a theorist without assistance, or with only the assistance to be derived from conversation. But he can seldom do great things in practice, unless he knows how to choose, and how to employ instruments. The Romans would have remained a petty tribe, if they had not employed every nation, as they conquered it, to aid them in conquering another."'

'November 17.

' The conversation turned this morning on *habits*.

'I said that the word "habit" was difficult of definition. That most persons, in attempting to define it, fell into tautology, calling it an habitual mode of acting or of feeling.

'"The difficulty," said the Archbishop, "is occasioned by

the confusion of two words, *custom* and *habit*, which are often used as synonymous, though really distinct; they denote respectively cause and effect. The frequent repetition of any act is a *custom*. The state of mind or of body, thereby produced, is a *habit*. The custom forms the habit, and the habit keeps up the custom. So a river is produced by a continued flow of water, which scoops for itself the bed, which afterwards confines it. And the same conduct, occasioned by different motives, will produce different habits. A man who controls his temper and who acts honestly only from prudence, acquires the habit of being gentle among his equals and of acting honestly where there is danger of detection; but he may be habitually insolent and irritable and fraudulent, when he has nothing to fear.

'"I have often said, that though 'Honesty is the best policy,' a man who acts on that motive is not really honest."

'"Aristotle's test of a habit," I said, "is that the obedience to it shall cost no effort. Defining the different virtues as habits, he therefore describes them not as duties to be performed, but as pleasures to be enjoyed. To a certain degree therefore his theory of virtue and Paley's agree. Both make virtue a matter of prudence, a means of obtaining happiness; but according to Aristotle, happiness in this life, and according to Paley, happiness in another."

'"And it *is*," he answered, "a matter of prudence. *Cæteris paribus*, a man is happy even in this life in proportion to his virtue.

'"Paley's error was, that in general (for he is not consistent) he denied a moral sense. He denied an innate instinctive feeling in man to approve of some kind of actions and to disapprove of others."

' " This seems to me," I said, " like denying an instinctive palate—denying that we instinctively perceive the difference between bitter and sweet."

' " He confounded," said the Archbishop, " an innate moral faculty with innate moral maxims, which is like denying an instinctive palate because there is no instinctive cookery; though some men, like the Germans, like the mixture of sweet and savoury, and some, like the French, detest it, all men know the difference."

' " In your lessons on morality," I said, " you do not define duty."

' " It cannot be defined," he answered; " if you attempt to do so you merely use some tautologous expression. A man's duty is to do what is *right*—to do what he *ought* to do—to do what he is *bound* to do. In short to do his duty.

' " The kind of conduct, to follow which is to do our duty, is pointed out by the scriptural rule, ' Do unto others as you would have them do unto you;' that is to say, pursue the conduct which you would wish to be universally prevalent."

' " This," I said " coincides with Bentham's principle of utility, or, as it has been sometimes called, expediency."

' " I have sometimes," said the Archbishop, " asked those who object to expediency as a motive, or as a test, whether they think that anything which is *inexpedient* ought to be done."

' I mentioned the speech of a woman, to whom the story of the Passion had been read. " Let us hope that it is not true."

' " We seldom," said the Archbishop, " think with pain on our past sufferings, unless we think that they may recur, or unless they have inflicted permanent injury.

' " If the pain has done no harm and cannot return, we

sometimes even think of it with pleasure, as enhancing
by contrast our present case.

'" But with respect to our friends, we are anxious to
believe that they have not suffered. There are no past
evils which people are so apt to grieve about, as those
which are most utterly past, the sufferings of the deceased.
One of the most usual inquiries respecting a departed
friend is, whether he died easily. Nothing is so consolatory to the survivors as to learn that he suffered little ;
and if he died in great agony, it excites their sympathy
more perhaps than the case of one who is living in
torture ; and yet this is mere imagination, the sufferings
cannot have left bad traces, and cannot recur. It is
shivering at last year's snow.

'" In our own case, present sufferings are matters of
perception, past ones of conception, and the contrast
between the two is too striking to allow us to confound
them.

'" In the cases of others, all sufferings, both present and
past, are to us matters of only conception ; we are liable,
therefore, to confound them, and to suffer real pain in
consequence of a conception of what is unreal—as we do
sometimes when reading a tragedy. It is true that the
pain of which we are speaking *once* was real, and *that*
described in the tragedy may never have been so ; but
both are equally *unreal* now—the one never was, the
other is as if it never had been.

' "Again, in our own case we resist such feeling ; every
one makes light of his own past evils.

'" But we think there is a merit in sympathising or in
imagining that we sympathise with the sufferings of our
friends, though our reason tells us, that at the very
moment at which we are bemoaning them they are perfectly free from affliction. Reason does not tell us that

a man who was burnt alive *suffered* no pain, but it does tell us that he suffers none *now*.

' " Another reason why we peculiarly lament death-bed sufferings is, that there is no hope of their being compensated by subsequent health and comfort. This, however, would be a fanciful ground of affliction in a heathen, and is utterly unchristian.

' " I believe, that by keeping these apparently obvious truths clearly and constantly before the mind, much useless sorrow may be avoided.

' " You remember," said the Archbishop, " our concocting a paper on the Trades Unions, which have destroyed the commerce, and the principal manufactures, and handicrafts of Dublin, and force us to import almost everything except poplins and porter ; which drive ships from Dublin Bay to be repaired in Liverpool, and have rendered our canals useless.

' " Well, the medical men of Dublin are almost outdoing in narrow-mindedness, selfishness, and tyranny, the ignorant weavers and carpenters.

' " They .have made an ordinance, that no fellow or licentiate of the Royal College of Surgeons, shall pretend or profess to cure diseases by the deception called ' homœopathy,' or the practice called ' Mesmerism,' or by any other form of ' quackery ' and that no fellow or licentiate of the college shall consult with, meet, advise, direct, or assist any person engaged in such deceptions or practices, or in any system of practice considered derogatory or dishonorable by the physicians or surgeons.

' " In the spirit of this ordinance, a surgeon refused to attend me unless I would promise to give up homœopathy.

' " In the midst of the disgust and shame which one must feel at such proceedings, it is some consolation to the advocates of the system denounced, that there is something of testimony borne to them by their adversaries, who dare not trust the question to the decision of reason and experience, but resort to such expedients as might be as easily employed for a bad cause as for a good one.

' " There is a notion that persecution is connected with religion, but the fact is that it belongs to human nature. In all departments of life you may meet with narrow-minded bigotry, and uncharitable party spirit. Long before the Reformation, Nominalists and Realists persecuted each other unmercifully. The majority of mankind have no real love of liberty, except that they are glad to have it themselves, and to keep it all for themselves ; but they have neither spirit enough to stand up firmly for their own rights, nor sufficient sense of justice to respect the rights of others.

' " They will submit to the domineering of a majority of their own party, and will join with them in domineering over others. I believe that several members of the Royal College of Surgeons were overawed into acquiescing in this detestable ordinance against their better judgment and their better feelings."

' " Is homœopathy," I asked, " advancing in Dublin?"

' " Rapidly," he answered. " Trades Unions among the higher orders not being able to employ personal violence, are almost powerless.

' " I do not believe that the ordinance has really done any harm, except indeed to its ordainers." '

' Dr. de Ricci, an Italian physician, settled near Dublin, and Mr. Dickson, a former fellow of Trinity College, holding a living near Omagh in Tyrone, dined with us.

' " Ireland," said Dr. de Ricci, " has utterly lost the sympathy of Italy. We thought that the Irish were like ourselves—an oppressed nation, struggling for freedom ; we

now find that they are quarrelling with England, not for
the purpose of freeing the people, but of enslaving them,
for the purpose of planting the foot of the priest still more
firmly on the necks of his flock, the foot of the bishop
still more firmly on the neck of the priest, and the foot
of the Pope still more firmly on the neck of the bishop.
We find that they would sacrifice to abject ultramontanism everything that gives dignity or strength to
human nature."

'" I deplore," I said, " the ultramontanism of the priests,
as much as you do, but both the extent of their influence
and the evil purposes for which they employ it, are
mainly our fault.　By depriving the Roman Catholic
Church in Ireland of its endowment ; by throwing the
priests on the people for support ; by forcing them to
earn a livelihood, by means of squabbling for fees, and
by means of inflaming the passions and aggravating the
prejudices of their flocks, we have excluded all gentlemen
from the priesthood ; we have given them a detestable
moral and political education ; we have enabled the Pope to
destroy all the old liberties of the Irish Roman Catholic
Church ; we have made the priests the slaves of the
Pope, and the dependants of the peasant."

'" But," said Dr. de Ricci, " they have refused an endowment."

'" It was never offered to them," said the Archbishop.

'" They were asked," said Dr. de Ricci, " if they would
take one, and they said no."

'" Of course they did," said the Archbishop.　"If I were
to go into a ball-room and say, ' Let every young lady,
who wishes for a husband, hold up her hand !' how many
hands would be held up ?　Give them endowment ; vest in
commissioners a portion of the national debt, to be appor-
tioned among the parish priests ; let each priest know the

dividend to which he is entitled, and how he is to draw for it; and protect him in its enjoyment from the arbitrary tyranny of his bishop, and you will find him no more bound by his former refusal, than any one of the young ladies would feel that not holding up her hand had bound her to celibacy. To do this," he continued, " would be not merely an act of policy, but of bare justice. It would be paying Roman Catholic priests with Roman Catholic money. The taxes are a portion of each man's income, which the State takes from him, in order to render to him certain services, which it can perform for him better than he can do for himself. Among these one of the most important is the maintenance of religion and of religious education. This service the State does not render to the Roman Catholics, and so far it defrauds them."

' " Ought it then," I said, " to pay the ministers of the Protestant Dissenters?"

' " Many of those sects," he answered, " such as the Quakers, the Baptists, and the Congregationalists, are founded on the very principle, that the State ought *not* to interfere in matters of religion—they therefore are out of the question; most of the others assent to the doctrines of the Established Church, and can take advantage of its ministrations, though they like to add the luxury of teachers peculiarly their own ; they therefore are provided for already. The Unitarians are perhaps the only sect, besides the Roman Catholics, who differ from us in doctrine, so fundamentally as to require ministers of their own. They are few, they are rich, and they ask for no aid. If they did ask for it, I do not see *how* it could be justly refused."'

CHAPTER XVI.

1863.

Gradual decline of the Archbishop—Visit of his sister-in-law—
Journal of the Rev. H. Dickinson—His last Charge—Presides at
the monthly dinner to his clergy—Increase of his bodily sufferings
—Interesting conversation with Mr. Dickinson—Apprehensions
respecting his state of health—Continued interest in literary pursuits—Tender attentions of his family in his last moments—His
patient resignation—His delight in the *Eighth* of Romans—Receives the Lord's Supper with his family—Progress of the disease
and great physical suffering—Parting interview with his favourite
grandchild—Visited by Mrs. Senior—His anxious desire to die—
His death—Lines on his death.

THE year 1863 opened tranquilly. There was some
increase of weakness, but it was very gradual. The
spring was spent much as usual. He enjoyed the society
of his friends, and especially a visit from his sister-in-law,
who spent part of the spring and early summer with him ;
and no special cause appeared for uneasiness.

The following notes, from the journal of his chaplain
and friend the Rev. Hercules Dickinson, describe the
occupations of this the last summer of his life :—

'The Archbishop gave his last charge in the cathedral
of Christ Church, Dublin, on June 18, 1863. He was
then very feeble, and felt that it was likely to be his last.
He wished to take the opportunity of letting it be understood, in contradiction of rumours diligently circulated,
that he had not changed his opinions respecting the
national system of education, but still lamented its com-

parative failure—a failure arising in great measure from the opposition of the clergy of our Church—as the greatest blow that could have been given to the cause of the Reformation in Ireland.

'Shortly after this charge was delivered, the symptoms began to show themselves of an ulcer in the right leg, similar to one from which he had endured much pain two years before. Notwithstanding the suffering this caused, he presided at his usual monthly dinner to his clergy in July, and held a special examination for a few candidates who were not ready to take orders till after the final divinity examination in Trinity College. He took his accustomed part at the examination, though the pain was so intense that he described it "as if red-hot gimlets were being put through his leg." He did not himself hold the ordination; and on the Wednesday subsequent to it he was, for the first time for many years, unable to hold his weekly reception of the clergy. He was then staying at his country residence; and, after the last day of the examination for orders, did not again enter the palace in St. Stephen's Green till he was brought there on his way to his last resting-place in the cathedral, where he had so recently delivered his farewell charge.'

Mr. Dickinson continues :—

'His sufferings increased each day, and he felt very painfully his inability to come into town for the discharge of business. His "uselessness," as he called it, was the especial trial to his active spirit. One day, early in August, when I went out to see him, on my entering his study he looked up and said, with tears in his eyes, "Have you ever preached a sermon on the text, 'Thy will be done?' How did you explain it?" When I replied. "Just so," he said; "that is the meaning;"

and added, in a voice choked with tears, " But it is hard —very hard sometimes—to say it." '

He had already consulted his usual medical advisers, and would have also seen some of the leading surgeons of Dublin, had their professional rules admitted of their meeting his own attendants; but on no other terms was he willing to consent to consultations, and indeed was little inclined to be sanguine as to the power of any remedies on himself.

But early in September it began to be manifest to all that a fatal issue must sooner or later be apprehended. His appetite, which had been always good, began to fail, and the decline of strength was more apparent. Before long, even the excursions in his garden-chair became too much for his failing powers, and he could only be wheeled from his bedroom to the adjoining sitting-room. The chess or backgammon in the evening, which had for some time been a resource, now became too fatiguing. As his powers gradually decayed, the exertion of holding a book had to be discontinued; but he listened with constant interest to reading aloud, and this was now his chief resource. One of the last things read to him in the garden had been the proof-sheets of his daughter's second volume on ' Ragged Life in Egypt.' This peculiarly pleased and interested him.

The books he preferred were chiefly of the kind that had always been his favourite reading. Works of fiction, except a few old favourites, rather wearied than entertained him; but natural history, curiosities of science, travels, histories of inventions and discoveries, &c., had a never-failing interest for him; and often, when apparently dozing, or sunk in languor and exhaustion, he would surprise the reader by remarks on the subject read, observations made in former days recurred to, or mistakes corrected.

Till within a short time of the end, he took pleasure in listening to music ; old familiar tunes played over to him by his daughters soothed and refreshed him, and he would often recognise or ask for special favourites with a clearness of memory that astonished those around him. Often such evenings of music would calm his nerves and produce sleep. It was not till very near the last, when, on music being proposed, he murmured, ' I am past that now.'

His surviving family were now almost all around him. His two unmarried daughters and his son were now joined by his brother-in-law, the Rev. W. L. Pope, who came to take a part in the attendance on his suffering friend, and to cheer and console him in this trial, as he was well fitted to do. His son-in-law and married daughter would gladly have shared these sacred offices of loving attendance, but they were detained abroad by the precarious health of the former, who was so soon to follow him. But the cares of his relatives around him were shared by the skilful and indefatigable attendance of two old and faithful servants, and of several most attached and devoted friends. To the unwearied and assiduous care and affection and personal watchfulness of these friends, and especially of his chaplains, his family cannot bear too earnest and grateful a testimony. Most especially must they remember the affectionate care of the Rev. H. H. Dickinson, who was in constant attendance on him, and whose thoughtful and judicious attentions alleviated, as far as it was possible, the intensity of the suffering which now attended every movement. His helplessness was now so great, that he who had all his life waited on himself, could not lift his hand to his mouth or turn his head ; yet never did a murmur escape his lips.

We again quote from the memoranda of Mr. Dickinson, who constantly took notes of an illness so affecting to his friends. In these notes we see the veil of reserve somewhat lifted, which hitherto had made the 'inner life' a mystery, hid even from those nearest to him. Through life he had stood forward as a resolute and powerful defender of the Christian faith, and now it was to be shown to all how the same simple trust in Christ as the only Saviour, which has smoothed so many an humble deathbed, was to be the stay and staff of the mighty thinker and writer while crossing the 'valley of the shadow of death.'

Mr. Dickinson writes:—

'*Sept.* 12.—This morning I read for the Archbishop the sixty-ninth Psalm. His appetite grows worse. When his dinner was brought he said, "Oh! how I loathe the thought of eating." Yet in these little things he shows very strongly the influence of his life-long habit of forcing all his inclinations and actions under the rule of reason. And he is so considerate for others—so fearful of giving trouble. When he could scarcely bring himself to eat he said to his attached servant, who seemed distressed, "But pray do not think I am finding fault; I know the fault is in myself." It has become extremely difficult to move him from the sofa to the bed; and it is touching to see how he tries to control the outward expression of suffering lest he should cause distress to those about him. While the perspiration streams down his face from agony, he restrains every murmur of impatience, and says to us repeatedly, "Yes, yes, I know you do all you can. The pain cannot be helped." During the night I heard him often murmur, "Lord, have mercy on me!" "Oh, my God! grant me patience!"

'Sunday, Sept. 13.—This morning he looked as if his last hour was drawing near. About one o'clock a friend standing near said, "This is death," supposing that all was over. One of his daughters stooped down and kissed his forehead. He awoke, and in the confusion of sudden waking said, with a little nervous irritation, "Oh! you should never wake an invalid!" Some time afterwards he sent for his daughter, and said, "I am afraid I spoke petulantly just now, and I am very sorry for it—I beg your pardon." If ever the fruits of the Spirit—"gentleness, patience"—were manifest in any one, they are in him. In the afternoon he was rather better. Archdeacon West, his domestic chaplain, came out and read prayers with him. He said, "Read me the eighth chapter of Romans." When Dr. West had finished the chapter, he said, "Shall I read any more?" "No; that is enough at a time. There is a great deal for the mind to dwell on in that." He dwelt especially on the thirty-second verse: "He that spared not His own Son," &c. In the very last sermon which he had preached, he had enlarged on this as the conclusive and satisfactory proof that afflictions were sent not in anger but in *love*; and he now recalled for his own comfort the train of thought by which he had so lately tried to comfort others. He has had this chapter read to him frequently during his illness.'

On the 14th of September he received the Lord's Supper with the Bishop of Killaloe, Archdeacon West, and several other friends. At his desire all the servants who wished were admitted to join, and all the members of his family united with him in the solemn service. It was a scene never to be forgotten by any who had witnessed it. A calm, earnest attention and solemn peace rested on his face; he spoke little, but evidently the soul

was communing with God. A little before this, one of
the friends in attendance on him had remarked that
his great mind was supporting him; his answer, most
emphatically and earnestly given, was, 'No; it is not
that which supports me. It is *faith in Christ*; the life
I live is by Christ alone.' I think these were his exact
words.

Meantime the disease made rapid progress. The state
of the limb was terrible. The wheeled chair could no
longer be borne; and soon even the transport from his
bed to a sofa became too painful. A distinguished
homœopathic physician had been summoned from Edinburgh to a consultation, and had agreed with the two on
the spot that nothing could avail to arrest the progress of
the disease, and that a few weeks must end it. And none
who witnessed the constant and intense suffering and
weary helplessness could dare to wish it prolonged.

His eldest grandchild, the same whose illness had so
distressed him years before, was on a visit under his roof.
He had greatly delighted in seeing her again. But the
time of her departure was now come, and the last day all
watched anxiously for a momentary revival, that she
might receive his last farewell. He had been in a doze
or stupor most of the day, but just before she left he
roused sufficiently to have her brought to the side of his
couch. He was too much overcome with emotion, in his
weak state, to speak; but as his feeble hand was guided
and placed on her head, his eye turned for the last time
to the young face before him with an expression of intense
love and deep solemnity which none who looked on could
ever forget.

His countenance had acquired an expression most
remarkable; the appearance of extreme age was gone; a
beauty of youth, or rather full manhood, seemed to rest

on it, but the brow had a smoothness and calm which
had never even in his brightest days been observed there.
That calm never left it—even through hours of intense
pain and weakness: it seemed to speak of the peace that
passeth understanding. None who saw it can forget the
majestic repose of that form, as he lay motionless on the
low couch on which the water-bed was placed, a fur
cloak thrown over him. Friends came in continually
from Dublin or from a distance, and many comparative
strangers to whom he had shown kindness, or who had long
venerated his character, would entreat for an interview.
The room door was open into the adjoining apartment,
and many would only pass in and give a last look of
affectionate reverence to one so long loved and honoured,
without speaking. Often he was sunk in slumbers of
exhaustion, and could not notice them; if able to take
notice, he would show his kindly sense of this feeling
towards him by a word or look; and often would express
warmly the comfort he felt it to be surrounded by so
many kind friends.

We again quote from Mr. Dickinson's journal :—

'*Sept.* 15.—This morning his son read to him the
fourth chapter of 2nd Corinthians. He followed the
chapter with tears and silent prayer, and at the end pronounced an emphatic AMEN. Towards evening he said,
"This has been a terrible day. Oh! this tenacity of life
is a great trial. Do pray for my release, if it be God's
will."

'*Sept.* 16.—After breakfast I read to him Hebrews ii.
He was much moved, and, when I ended, said with em-
phasis, "Every chapter in the Bible you read seems
as if it were written on purpose for me."

'*Sept.* 22.—Amongst other friends, Mrs. Henry Senior

came out to see him to-day. When she was leaving he said, " Give my love to Nassau, and give him, from me, my ' Lectures on Prayer.' Ask him, from me, to read the second Lecture."

' *Sunday, Sept.* 27.—The Archbishop's brother-in-law, Rev. Wm. Pope, read prayers to him to-day. In the evening, at eleven o'clock, there was an hæmorrhage from the leg. A messenger was immediately despatched into town for the physician. He lay quite calm and still; asking, after ten minutes, " Is the bleeding still going on? I hope so." He evidently felt thankful, as believing that his release was near. The bleeding had greatly abated before the doctor arrived. When he came in he said, " I think we can stop it, my lord." The Archbishop answered, in his old, natural manner, " I am afraid so." When the doctor left, having succeeded in stopping the hæmorrhage, the Archbishop said to me, " Is not this a very unusual hour for the doctor to come?" I answered, " Yes; but we sent for him expressly when the bleeding began." And he replied, " Oh! you had not told me of that. Did you suppose I was afraid to die?"

. . . .

' *Thursday, Oct.* 1.—This morning he listened atten- tively while several of the Psalms were read to him. He was moaning very restlessly in the night, and once, when I went to his bedside and asked, " Is there anything you wish for, my lord?" he answered, " I wish for nothing but death."

' *Oct.* 2.—When I was trying to soothe him to sleep by reading aloud an article on " Uninspired Prophecy," he unexpectedly stopped me when I came to the mention of Lord Chesterfield's well-known prediction of the French revolution, and he observed, " Oh! that is not a case in point; that was quite wide of the mark;" and he went on minutely to state the particulars of the so-called prophecy.

'*Oct.* 4.—To-day he listened while some of the Psalms were read to him. Afterwards, though hardly able to articulate—obliged, indeed, to spell the words he tried to utter—he expressed his wish that some little articles belonging to him should be given to two or three of his friends.'

It was on the night following this, I think, that another of his chaplains was watching beside him, and in making some remark expressive of sympathy for his distressing suffering and helplessness, quoted the words from Phil. iii. 21, " Who shall change our vile body." The Archbishop interrupted him with the request, "Read the words." His attendant read them from the English Bible ; but he reiterated, "Read *his own* words." The chaplain, not being able to find the Greek Testament at the moment, repeated from memory the literal translation, " This body of our humiliation." "That's right," interrupted the Archbishop, " not *vile*—nothing that He made is vile." '

The pain now began to diminish, and he lay in a calm and scarcely conscious state for the last two or three days of his life.

On the 8th of October, at eleven in the forenoon, Mr. Dickinson, who was sitting by him, perceived a change come over him. He whispered, 'The struggle is nearly over now, my lord; the rest is very near.' He then went to call the members of his family, who were all on the watch in the next room. They all came in ; and his eldest daughter knelt at his side and repeated one or two verses of Scripture-prayers from the Psalms, which we thought he heard and understood. He opened his eyes

and looked around, but was unable to speak. The pulse
became each moment weaker and his breathing more
faint. Again the verses, speaking of the Christian's hope,
were repeated in the failing ear.

Mr. Dickinson writes: 'He passed away in perfect
calm. The physician arrived at his usual hour (twelve
o'clock), ten minutes after Dr. Whately had breathed his
last. We found then that the immediate cause of death
had been the bursting of an artery in the leg.'

.   .   .   .

'Thou wilt keep him in perfect peace whose mind is
stayed upon Thee, because he trusteth in Thee.'

He was buried in the vault of St. Patrick's Cathedral.
The feeling displayed at his funeral was very deep and
universal; the Earl of Carlisle, who was so soon to follow
him, was among those who accompanied his coffin to its
last resting-place. But the whole scene, and the feelings
which it awakened in those present are best described in
the following verses by the Very Rev. William Alexander,
Dean of Emly.

THE DEATH OF ARCHBISHOP WHATELY.

Fast falls the October rain.   Skies low and leaden
    Stretch where no lustrous spot of blue is isled.
Some sorrow is abroad, the wind to deaden,
    Sad but not loud, monotonous not wild.

Faster than rain fall tear-drops—bells are tolling;
    The dark sky suits the melancholy heart;
From the church-organs awfully is rolling
    Down the draped fanes the Requiem of Mozart.

O tears beyond control of half a nation,
    O sorrowful music, what have ye to say?
Why take men up so deep a lamentation?
    What prince and great man hath there fall'n to-day?

Only an old Archbishop, growing whiter
   Year after year, his stature proud and tall
Palsied and bowed as by his heavy mitre;
   Only an old Archbishop—that is all!

Only the hands that held with feeble shiver
   The marvellous pen—by others outstretch'd o'er
The children's heads—are folded now for ever
   In an eternal quiet—nothing more!

No martyr he o'er fire and sword victorious,
   No saint in silent rapture kneeling on,
No mighty orator with voice so glorious,
   That thousands sigh when that sweet sound is gone.

Yet in Heaven's great Cathedral, peradventure,
   There are crowns rich above the rest with green,
Places of joy peculiar where *they* enter,
   Whose fires and swords no eye hath ever seen;

They who have known the truth, the truth have spoken,
   With few to understand and few to praise,
Casting their bread on waters, half heart-broken,
   For men to find it after many days.

And better far than eloquence—that golden
   And spangled juggler, dear to thoughtless youth—
The luminous style through which there is beholden
   The honest beauty of the face of Truth;

And better than his loftiness of station,
   His power of logic, or his pen of gold,
The half-unwilling homage of a nation
   Of fierce extremes to one who seem'd so cold,

The purity by private ends unblotted,
   The love that slowly came with time and tears,
The honourable age, the life unspotted,
   That is not measured merely by its years.

And better far than flowers that blow and perish
    Some sunny week, the roots deep-laid in mould
Of quickening thoughts, which long blue summers cherish,
    Long after he who planted them is cold.

Yea, there be saints, who are not like the painted
    And haloed figures fixed upon the pane,
Not outwardly and visibly ensainted,
    But hiding deep the light which they contain.

The rugged gentleness, the wit whose glory
    Flash'd like a sword because its edge was keen,
The fine antithesis, the flowing story,
    Beneath such things the sainthood is not seen,

Till in the hours when the wan hand is lifted
    To take the bread and wine, through all the mist
Of mortal weariness our eyes are gifted
    To see a quiet radiance caught from Christ;

Till from the pillow of the thinker, lying
    In weakness, comes the teaching then best taught,
That the true crown for any soul in dying
    Is Christ, not genius, and is faith, not thought.

O Death, for all thy darkness, grand unveiler
    Of lights on lights above Life's shadowy place,
Just as the night that makes our small world paler,
    Shows us the star-sown amplitudes of space!

O strange discovery, land that knows no bounding,
    Isles far off hail'd, bright seas without a breath,
What time the white sail of the soul is rounding
    The misty cape—the promontory Death!

Rest then, O martyr, pass'd through anguish mortal,
    Rest then, O saint, sublimely free from doubt,
Rest then, O patient thinker, o'er the portal,
    Where there is peace for brave hearts wearied out.

O long unrecognised, thy love too loving,
   Too wise thy wisdom, and thy truth too free!
As on the teachers after truth are moving
   They may look backward with deep thanks to thee.

By his dear Master's holiness made holy,
   All lights of hope upon that forehead broad,
Ye mourning thousands quit the minster slowly,
   And leave the good Archbishop with his God.

APPENDIX.

MISCELLANEOUS RECOLLECTIONS.

BY REV. HERCULES H. DICKINSON, M.A., VICAR OF ST. ANN'S, DUBLIN.[1]

My earliest recollections of Archbishop Whately go back to the
year 1833. And the very first thing that I remember of him left
such an impression of his kindness of heart as thirty years more
of his acquaintance and friendship served only to deepen. He
was standing on the steps of my father's house, in Baggot Street,
just as I, with my brothers and sisters, came home from our afternoon walk. I can distinctly recall his voice, and his benevolent
smile, as he cried out, three or four times, ' I see little lambs '—
' I see little lambs ; ' and coming to the edge of the steps,
gathered five or six of the younger ones into his arms, and
then walked into the house with one of us upon his shoulder.
All children naturally took to him, and seemed, with the quick
and correct intuition of childhood, to understand and trust his
love for them. In after-years I used to observe, when walking
with him in St. Stephen's Green, how the young children used
to stop and smile up at him, and how some of the little ones
who were accustomed to see him there, and whom he often
delighted by sending his dog to fetch and carry for their amusement, used even to run up to him with the familiar salutation
' Artsbissop ! ' This he was always pleased with ; often stooping
to take up some little toddler into his arms, or laying his hand
upon its head and passing on with a half-murmured word of
blessing. In the Female Orphan House, and in the National
Model Schools, which he used often to visit, he particularly
endeared himself to the children; and I think many of them

---

[1] Son of the late Bishop Dickinson.

will be not the less staunch episcopalians in after-life because their first idea of a bishop is that of one who never forgot the words of the Chief Bishop and Shepherd, 'Suffer little children to come unto me.'

The suspicion and distrust with which he was met on his arrival in Ireland, were such as he could not be wholly unprepared for. As an Englishman, and one who kept aloof from all parties, he could hardly have been generally popular; but the bitterness of opposition he encountered was such, that he must have been more or less than man had he not felt it. It was natural, therefore, that he should draw into his special confidence and friendship those few who did from the first understand the goodness and honesty which came in later years to be recognised by all; nor is he fairly to be blamed if, with his natural confidingness of disposition, he was sometimes deceived by the pretence of sympathy and a co-operation not perfectly disinterested. The very show of kindness was something refreshing in the midst of the hostility which, on all sides, encountered him.

It would give needless pain to many to refer more particularly to those years of opposition. But no one can do full justice to the character of the Archbishop who has not the records of that period before him. I well remember how the whole Irish press, day after day, month after month, year after year, continued to pour out invectives, accusations, and innuendoes, and how eagerly these were taken up and repeated from mouth to mouth. That the Archbishop was a 'Jesuit' was whispered here and there; acute physiognomists saw something suspicious in the look of his hall-porter; and when, at last, some one found out that in the words 'Ricardus Whately' might be spelt out the mystic number 666, the evidence against his Protestantism was felt to be conclusive. Things of this sort, of course, only amused him; but there was a determined opposition, and an obstinate distrust, which constantly put real difficulties in his way, and thwarted his efforts for the good of the diocese and of the Church in Ireland generally. A friend of his was one day making a journey on the top of a coach, and had for fellow-passenger a Roman Catholic gentleman. The conversation turned on the Archbishop, about whom Roman Catholic papers were then respectful or silent. 'But how is it that the members of *your* Church never abuse him?' it was asked.

'Oh, we leave that to you. You Protestants do it so well that you save us the trouble; not that we like him any better than you perhaps; but then, you see, you do our work very effectively yourselves.'

Through all this storm of obloquy, which blew with hardly diminished violence for a quarter of a century, the Archbishop held on his way unswervingly. And judging from his conduct, some might have thought he did not feel it. But that he did, and very keenly.

He was not, in his manful perseverance in duty, buoyed up by either hope or stubbornness. Many persons are kept steady to their point and purpose by a sanguine temper or an obstinate disposition. But Archbishop Whately was not at all sanguine; on the contrary, he was so hopeless as almost always to anticipate failure in everything he undertook. And, if he had given way to the bias of his natural constitution, he would have been over-yielding, indulgent and compliant.

To anything like severity of discipline it was an effort of pain to bring himself; but he held firmly to truth and duty, upon principle. He formed his convictions and purposes upon reasons which he had deliberately weighed and believed to be sound. When he had once made up his mind, he went straight on his way, as steadfastly as though he had never heard the voice of obloquy, while those who knew him well knew that he often went with a bleeding heart, feeling intensely the opposition of many whom he respected and loved, yet never flinching for that or any other consideration, from the path of duty.

It needs not to be concealed that for some of this unpopularity the Archbishop's manner was to be blamed. Nothing could have been more mild and tolerant and conciliatory than were his Charges, Pastoral Letters, and Addresses; and to all those who could appreciate his thorough truthfulness, these gave the real measure of the man, and made them comparatively indifferent to the peculiarities of manner by which those who did not know him so well or judged him hastily were apt to be offended. He gave offence to many quite unintentionally. It often happened that when he was walking through the street and much preoccupied in conversation or in thought, he either did not observe at all, or only half-noticed, in an absent way, the salutation which was offered in passing. And this was sometimes mistaken. In his manners there was at times a startling *brusquerie* by which shy people were made uncomfortable and proud people affronted. Absence of mind and shyness were very erroneously, yet not unnaturally, interpreted as rudeness. He would often enter a room, and with scant salutation or none at all begin abruptly upon the subject of which his mind was full; and then perhaps quit it as suddenly, forgetful of the usual courtesies of farewell. He had been perhaps just introduced to some one who was of consequence or else supposed himself to be so. And such a person might have been easily charmed out of his previous prejudices if the Archbishop had been an adept in those social arts by which other men are able—very harmlessly and allowably—to smooth over opposition. But he was no such adept, and had no arts of any sort. He was natural even to a fault; and in the careless familiarity of the College common-room had acquired a habit of forgetfulness as to the smaller conventionalities of life, which was, no doubt, a not unfrequent hindrance to him. And yet he could, on occasion, comport himself with a dignity and even courtly politeness, which sat gracefully enough upon him, though it was not his most characteristic and ordinary bearing. At his own dinner-table he was always courteous and particularly attentive as a host. No matter how earnestly engaged in conversation, he stood ready to receive his clergy one by one as they came in on his monthly dinner-days, and at the table never failed to take especial and friendly notice of the greatest stranger among his guests. He would occasionally, in the keenness of discussion, seem peremptory and somewhat impatient of contradiction. Seeing very clearly himself, and having reasons which he believed to be sound and logical for his opinions, he was apt sometimes to betray by his manner that he believed the persevering dissent of his opponent to be the result of obstinacy, stupidity, or prejudice, and to assume the man to be, as he would sometimes say, ' proof-proof.'

He was often merciless enough in his use of the logical weapon *reductio ad absurdum*; and as the reasoner feels generally too much sympathy with his argument to enjoy this mode of refutation, especially in public, the Archbishop's antagonists, whether convinced or not, often gave way. Yet no one, I think, ever suspected him of wishing to ride down an opponent by any official weight or force of his episcopal authority. His eagerness arose, on the contrary, from forget-

fulness of these. His clergy could hardly be expected to forget
that they were arguing with their Archbishop; and it was
not easy, even for a beneficed clergyman, under such circumstances, to hit out well, and press his points as tellingly as at
an ordinary clerical meeting. But the Archbishop on such
occasions forgot that he was anything more than Dr. Whately;
he felt and spoke as if he were back again in the common-room
debating with his equals. If he spoke *ex cathedra*, it was not
as from an episcopal throne, but rather as from the seat of the
Professor. The youngest curate was just as free to enter the list
with him as any dignitary who might be present; and, indeed,
would have been likely to receive a gentler handling than the said
dignitary; and the Archbishop was always better pleased upon
the evenings when the discussion had been open and animated.
He was so wholly free from any thought of throwing his episcopal dignity into the scale in such conversational debates, that
he would have even felt surprised and incredulous if any one
had hinted to him that his official position laid a restraint on
his antagonists in argument. He never wished people to seem
or be afraid of him in any way, and always liked most such
persons as were not. I shall ever think it a great pity that
this part of his character was not generally understood. Because,
not really knowing him, many men felt repelled and stood
aloof or drew aside, whom therefore he naturally concluded
to be either entirely opposed to him in principle or kept
away by personal dislike; and, of course, neither of these circumstances can come to any man in the light of a recommendation. It has been sometimes said of him that he liked only
those who agreed with him or who seemed to do so. I can,
however, testify that I have often heard him speak with sincere
respect and regard of many who differed from him very much,
and who spoke out their differences too. There was one clergyman who, whenever present at the monthly clerical dinner,
used with especial boldness to enter into argument with the
Archbishop, and firmly, though always with Christian and
gentlemanly mildness, would hold his ground against him.
And towards that man the Archbishop had, I know, the most
kindly feeling. He liked him all the better for his quiet
courage. But, in point of fact, there really never was an
archbishop or bishop in whose presence his clergy felt less
restraint. And though men too shy or too proud to risk

encounter with so acute a dialectician as the Archbishop, held back and were silent on these ocasions, they will remember that those who chose to take it had always full liberty of speech. There was, assuredly, no official stiffness at those gatherings of his clergy. Clergymen from other dioceses, who occasionally dined at the Palace, expressed surprise at the 'free-and-easy' friendliness of these social meetings. The Archbishop was anxious to make all feel at home. He did not even like men to stand upon the order of their going; but when the door into the other room was thrown open and dinner announced, he would sometimes call out, if he observed delay for such puncti-lios, 'Now then, bundle in, curates, rectors, archdeacons, deans, bundle in, bundle in!' He certainly 'held no man's person in admiration, because of advantage.'

Nor was he influenced by personal considerations in his ap-pointments. Whoever will take the trouble to look over the list of clergy whom he promoted may see the names of several who held opinions different from his on certain points of doctrine, or the national education question, and in politics.

His thorough dislike of party spirit made him feel sympathy with any one who made profession of the same dislike, and who disclaimed connection with any declared party in Church or State. It did not occur to him that in some cases this show of independence might be put on, from a spirit really the very opposite. Because when he, himself, took such and such steps, or refused to join in such and such measures, *he* acted from an independent love of truth, and not from the desire of pleasing any one, he forgot that some might join him in that apparently independent course of action from the less worthy motive of pleasing *him*. He gave them credit for an unworldly temper, forgetting that, in fact, the Palace was to them the world.

He saw himself morally as well as intellectually reflected in those who came near him; and often fancied congeniality of sentiment and feeling where there was little or none.

He was, besides, so wholly truthful, and free from secondary motives in what he did and said, that he was apt to take the sincerity of other people for granted. He was most unsuspicious, and was accordingly sometimes deceived.

'He drew around him a cordon of flatterers,' says an un-friendly Reviewer; and, if the truth is to be told as I desire to tell it, there is enough foundation for the sneer to claim some notice of it, particularly as the same thing has been elsewhere and frequently repeated.

There *was* a sort of flattery administered to him by some, and much too trustfully and favourably accepted by him, I will acknowledge. But it was flattery of a peculiar sort. It did not take the form of praise ; it did not appeal to the ' love of approbation,' to speak the language of the phrenologists. This principle, indeed, I have said, the Archbishop naturally had, and strongly ; but, having it, he deserves all the more credit for life-long self-denial upon this point; for conscientious perseverance, in the face of painful hostility and continued unpopularity, in saying what he thought true, and doing what he thought right. He never spoke or acted *in order to* gain praise.

There were, however, two other parts of his character quite as strong naturally, one of which a sense of duty as well as inclination helped to make constantly stronger; the other, a feeling which does not seem to ask control so obviously as does the love of approbation. Among the active principles of Archbishop Whately's mind the strongest was, doubtless, his love of teaching. He carried this to Oxford ; he fostered it there in the lecture-room, in the common-room, and in the parks, where he was always seen, at leisure hours, with some disciple. If in his personal bearing he was not always 'gentle unto all men,' yet was he eminently ' apt to teach.' His bitterest enemy could not deny to him this qualification for the episcopate.

He was above all other things διδακτικός. Nothing was more characteristic of him than the persistent energy with which he set himself to indoctrinate everybody, on all sides, right and left, with the religious, social, and ecclesiastical views which he held to be true.

Again, among passive sentiments, none was more alive in the Archbishop than his craving for sympathy, for intellectual sympathy especially. Meeting, as he continually did, with the opposition of the many, he was thrown for the satisfaction of this craving upon the few, and therefore he hailed it with unconcealed and artless delight whenever he saw or thought he saw it. It was a keener hunger with him, because so often starved ; and it was not perhaps so discriminating in its appetite as it might have been but for the painful and compulsory fasts it had so often to keep.

Some who wished to gain his favour made a habit of inquiring his opinion or asking his counsel on this question or that; he was of course delighted to get a pupil; pleased not on his own account only, but because of the opportunity of teaching others standing by. He would call such a person 'a very good anvil.' It sometimes did happen, I know, that he saw through the motive of the inquiry—obvious enough indeed to fill bystanders with disgust—but he would take advantage of the opportunity of teaching nevertheless, thereby giving the impression that he was gratified by getting it, and holding out encouragement to those who sought in this manner to please him.

Oftener than not, however, he imputed his own guileless honesty to the questioner, and gave him credit for a sincere desire to learn; and then, when he found him an apparently intelligent disciple, bringing out something which he had really learnt from one of Whately's own books, the Archbishop would hail the opinion with pleasure as a quite 'undesigned coincidence,' and think that he had found another like-minded with himself. In this way, his love of teaching and his desire for sympathy exposed him to the charge of allowing, if not accepting, what other people saw to be flattery.

It is a curious circumstance, but perhaps not so uncommon as might be at first supposed, that one who had so intense a craving for sympathy as the Archbishop had, should nevertheless have had small power of sympathy himself. And yet I think it was the want of this natural gift which deprived him of what may be properly called 'Influence.' In one of his Commonplace Books he speaks of this as a subtle sort of force, which it is difficult to account for; and he often expressed his consciousness of wanting it. 'Whatever impression I make or ever have made upon the minds of others has always been by force of arguments and never by *influence* in the correct sense of the word.' This I frequently heard him say. But it may be doubted whether any one can exercise this subtle force called 'influence' who has not either the natural power, or the art, of throwing himself into the feelings and circumstances of those he meets—in other words, the power of sympathy. And perhaps a very extraordinary strength, consistency and fixedness of character like the Archbishop's is incompatible with the possession of this in any great degree. A man who sees truths obscurely or superficially, or who has an undecided hold of his opinions, or who has an impressible imagination easily coloured by present circumstances, will not only be able to sympathise more readily with those with whom he converses, but will be unable to prevent himself from sympathising oppositely and inconsistently, just as depends upon his company. I rather think that among great men, strong leaders of speculative thought, and men who have cut their way through difficulties in action, the larger number would be classed among what may be called 'unsympathising characters.' They may be genuinely philanthropic, large-hearted, benevolent, unselfish. All this Archbishop Whately was. A man of larger or truer benevolence there never lived. And yet his habits of reflectiveness and self-concentration, his searching acuteness of judgment, his rigid consistency of principle and habit, made it difficult for him to throw himself into the thoughts and feelings of persons who widely differed from him; and his straightforward simplicity made it equally hard to assume the show of sympathy when he did not feel it.

Being unable (whether from general force of character, or from the weakness of a particular faculty, or from the natural connection of these two circumstances, need not be determined) to put himself into sympathy with other men, he required all the more that other men should be, or else should place themselves in sympathy with him. Hence he could not easily make a close friend of any one whose opinions set him at a distance. It was not, however, dogmatism or arrogance, or self-esteem, as some untruly supposed, that estranged the Archbishop from persons who diverged from him in sentiment, or led him to look coldly upon them from the first, but simply the absolute necessity for that sympathy which was, with him, an essential basis of friendship. Dr. Arnold is, I think, the only instance among his close and chosen friends of one whose opinions differed considerably from his own. But there was a thorough *moral* sympathy between the men that was quite strong enough to bridge over all differences. Arnold's intense love of truth and manly simplicity of character were thoroughly appreciated and loved by Dr. Whately.

One of the Archbishop's examining chaplains was Dr. James Wilson, afterwards Bishop of Cork. He was a man of literary tastes, and a fair share of learning, and though no writer himself, his critical acumen was valued highly by the Archbishop. He had a certain dry humour which was a constant amusement to Dr. Whately, who enjoyed greatly the recollection and repetition of some of his sayings.

Speaking one day of a newly risen sect of religionists who proscribed the use of animal food, the Archbishop said to Dr. Wilson, 'Do you know anything, Wilson, of this new sect?' 'Yes, my Lord; I have seen their confession of faith, which is a book of cookery.'

On one occasion when Dr. W. was asked to subscribe his name to a testimonial in favour of some one whom he thought not very highly of, yet did not wish to refuse, and who had had his testimonial signed already by clergymen whose names carried small weight, he got out of his difficulty by writing, 'I know the value of the above signatures. Jas. Wilson.' But the Archbishop was too straightforward himself to approve of this *ruse*, and, though amused, blamed Dr. Wilson for it at the time.

I remember hearing Dr. Wilson give, in his driest way, a very entertaining account of an interview which he had one day with a lady who called at his own house. She wanted him to bring an appeal on her behalf before the Archbishop; and stated her case with much eagerness and irrepressible volubility. Unable to stem the torrent, Dr. Wilson sat, rustic-like, waiting for the stream to spend itself, which, unlike Horace's river, it did at last. When the good lady, mistaking the Doctor's patient silence for conviction and consent, wound up her long and discursive harangue with the final appeal, 'Well now, I may depend upon you, Sir, to state all this to the Archbishop?'—the very unsatisfactory reply which she received was, 'Madam, I make it my business to intercept as many as possible of these communications.'

Archbishop Whately was, at that time, very active, and used in the afternoon to take long walks with my father (then his chaplain). The Pydgeon House[1] Wall and Sandymount Strand were their favourite places of exercise. On their way to the latter place they generally crossed over the river Dodder, by a toll-bridge (since then removed). And it very frequently happened that neither the Archbishop nor his chaplain had enough money about them to pay the penny-toll; so they had to pass over the bridge on credit. I think two of the happiest periods of the Archbishop's life were when he was engaged in concert with my father in compiling the 'Lessons on Christian Evidences,' and afterwards when in conjunction with Dr. Fitzgerald (now

---

[1] So properly spelt, being named from people of the name of 'Pydgeon,' who had a house of entertainment there in the last century.

Bishop of Killaloe) he was writing the 'Cautions for the Times.' He always enjoyed his literary occupations most when shared by one or two fellow-labourers. Some of the chapters in the Evidences were worked out in the course of walks upon Killiney shore with Dr. Dickinson, and with Archdeacon Russell, the biographer of the Rev. Charles Wolfe. When Archdeacon R. suggested to the Archbishop the chapter 'On the Character of Our Lord,' he said, 'Yes, a most important evidence indeed, but I know of only one man who could have treated that subject as it ought to be treated, and that is your friend Wolfe.' He greatly admired this writer; and showed appreciation of his poetic and imaginative eloquence by frequently reciting those passages from his sermons which he has quoted in his volume on 'Rhetoric.'

In preparing his charges or addresses, he made it his constant practice to read what he had written to several of his friends, and to ask their judgments before publication. He was remarkably candid, and ready to listen to any suggestion that might be made. He never slighted any emendation, however trifling, and never resented any criticism, however boldly offered.

He was pre-eminently a man of 'major premises'; and where his readers dissent from his conclusions, it is, in the majority of cases (I am inclined to think), in the *minor* premise that the difference will be found. In words that non-logicians will understand, his general principle is almost always true, while in his application of it to particular cases there may be, now and then, something to question. In reducing such and such a case, thing, subject, &c., to the class of which something has in the major premise been truly predicated, the soundness of the argument will often depend upon a special knowledge of facts and details. An accurate acquaintance with these, or a close and critical investigation of them, would show perhaps that there is some particular circumstance essentially distinguishing the subject of the minor premise from the class (or description of things) under which it is proposed to reduce it. Almost always sound in his general principles, invariably *logical* in his conclusion, the flaw in the Archbishop's reasonings, where there is any, arises, I think, from his not knowing or overlooking some qualifying circumstance, the knowledge of which depended on faculties of minute and patient observation, which—except

perhaps in the region of natural history—he did not very
prominently possess; or on familiarity with a certain kind of
learning which he did not much care to cultivate. He was too
wise to be far wrong in the general principle of his syllogism,
too clearly and acutely logical to blunder in his conclusion; but
he was, on some subjects, not deeply enough read to be quite
safe against objection in his *minor* premise—what some logi-
cians have called the *Argument.*

Of his examinations for Holy Orders, his daughter has spoken
in this memoir.

He never received any candidate till he had first passed the
examination of one of his chaplains. The object of this plan
was a benevolent one. It was in order that none might be
exposed to the pain of feeling and of reporting to his friends
that he was rejected by the Archbishop; for it was understood
that the chaplain's preliminary examination was quite a private
one, and that in cases where he advised the candidate not to
present himself without some further study, the recommendation
was given in confidence, and the opportunity left to him accordingly of offering himself without prejudice, when better
prepared, to the Archbishop.

When the names of the candidates were given in, and they
were reported as satisfactory, the Archbishop appointed them to
come three or four on each day. He gave them written questions to answer, and subjects on which to write short sermon-
outlines; receiving them separately into another room, where he
and his chaplains sat round a table; and always examining
them one by one. This plan he preferred, both as more agreeable
to the candidates and as testing the knowledge of each better
than he thought could be done at an examination where the
right answer may be gathered by one out of the misses of another.
As for the candidates, I think the other plan would after all
have been less formidable, if I may judge of others' feelings
from my own. For, long and intimately as I had known the
Archbishop before, I felt frightened enough at my own examination for Orders, in being the solitary object for his Grace
and five or six more divines to look at and question, and I
should have felt the presence of my companions a very
great relief. However, there was really nothing in the Archbishop's manner to alarm. He was an uncommonly patient
and indulgent examiner, always giving the candidate full time

to deliberate, and with quick kindness catching the first approach to a correct reply. In the latter years of his life, his hearing was imperfect, and his articulation less distinct than formerly. It sometimes happened, therefore, that when he put a question, and found it not heard or not answered at once, he repeated it much louder than he was himself aware. This gave the impression of impatience, and if the candidate was not prepared for it beforehand, rather increased his nervousness. But it arose from the physical causes I have referred to.

But on the whole, I think his extraordinary love of teaching made him, in the same ratio, a rather less good examiner. He often forgot the examiner altogether in the teacher, and spent so long a time in explaining and instructing, that by the end of an hour he had got much more into the candidate than he had got out of him. And I have seen him also much pleased with a candidate whose merit lay rather in being a quick and intelligent pupil than in the manifestation of any profound knowledge of his business. But the Archbishop would form his estimate of a man's general ability and intellectual fitness to teach more by the first of these tests than the second.

He never would be persuaded to prescribe any course of books for his examination. 'I shall examine,' he would say, 'in the Bible and Prayer-book. Read anything and everything, I don't care what, that will assist you to understand these two.' He used to scoff at what he was accustomed to call the *secundùm quem* style of examination which is adopted in our universities. Yet, having written on all the theological subjects which he, himself, thought most important, it was impossible for him to keep clear of these when examining, and consequently a knowledge of Whately's writings would always serve a candidate materially in the Archbishop's examination. He never, however, required any of his own books to be read; nor did he, in the least, care whether the knowledge of what he asked had been derived from him or from any one else.

He always made it a rule to examine very carefully in the Epistles. When he came over to Ireland he was asked to adopt a course of examination to which other Bishops had agreed. They had consented not to examine candidates for deacons' orders in the Epistles. The Archbishop asked, 'Are deacons then to be forbidden to *preach* from the Epistles during their diaconate?' 'Oh! no, certainly not; that is not contemplated.'

'Then,' answered his Grace, 'if they are to be allowed to preach from them, it is as well to see whether they know them or not.'

He had a sort of blunt common-sense that would march straight on to a conclusion, brushing aside all theories and plausible reasons that might be offered to the contrary. This was sometimes rather provoking to people who came to him prepared to argue out a question, and found themselves suddenly either compelled to see the matter in a strong light which had not heretofore presented itself, or to perceive that the Archbishop was not easily to be taken by surprise by any of the arguments they had provided themselves with. No matter how one might try to mystify the subject or put it another way, the Archbishop would persistently turn his lantern upon it, and would not let any sophistry divert him from the one point which he believed conclusive. He always, indeed, would give a patient hearing to arguments on the other side, but with a pitiless sort of pertinacity he would force back the arguer to the main question, till he had left him no escape. He was a very impartial chairman at committee meetings and boards, securing to every one a patient hearing. He was always very quick in seizing the salient point of a discussion, and showed the bent of his intellect in reducing a disputed question promptly, whenever it was possible to do so, under some general principle on which his mind had been made up. Whenever he could do this, he seemed to find it a relief from the consideration of details and minor points of which he soon grew weary; and there was sometimes a difficulty in making him see that the particular case did not come under the general principle so certainly as he supposed. But when the distinction was brought under his notice, no one could be more candid in reconsidering his first decision, and allowing full weight to further arguments, clearly and fairly set before him.

At public meetings he showed himself possessed of one rare and very enviable gift, which is, indeed, of much convenience to a chairman. Whenever he was obliged to listen to a speech delivered in his presence, of which he did not feel approval, and did not wish to express *dis*approval, he had the faculty of looking as if he did not hear a word. He fixed his eyes on vacancy, and banished all expression of every kind from his face, so that people who peeped forward, curious to see 'how the Archbishop was taking it', could gather as little from his countenance as if it had been carved out of stone. I remember observing this with much amusement at a certain public meeting, in the course of which one speaker made an harangue which was pre-eminently injudicious. He appealed to the Archbishop, every now and then, as cognisant of circumstances which, with singular indiscretion, he was detailing to the meeting, saying, 'Your Grace is aware of so and so; your Grace will recollect what I refer to,' and so forth. But his Grace evidently recollected nothing, and looked as if he were stone-deaf. I congratulated him, after the meeting, on his success, and asked him how he managed it. I think it was a half-unconscious art with him; however, he seemed amused, and asked me in reply, if I had ever heard a story of the late Lord Melbourne? Lord Melbourne (he told me) was in the House one evening, when —— stood up to speak on the Government side. The speech was a very indiscreet one; the speaker dashed into topics about which Ministers would rather have had nothing said, and in the course of his remarks, turned towards the bench where Lord M. was sitting, saying, 'The noble Lord at the head of the Government is fully aware of the accuracy of what I state; the noble Lord, having been present at the interview of which I speak, will bear his testimony.' The only answer from the Treasury bench was a loud *snore*.

On oratory apart from logic the Archbishop set little value. A dull speech, if sensible and to the point, would meet a much more indulgent hearing and criticism from him than one that might, perhaps, bring to the platform thunders of applause. Of clap-trap he was intolerant. His presence, therefore, as chairman was felt an uncomfortable sort of restraint by those who scarcely dared to hazard, in his unsympathetic hearing, their customary flights of Celtic fervour. In the presence of so acute a logician few could be brave enough to utter the unsubstantial nothings or use *ad captandum* arguments.

I have been asked to add a few reminiscences of my own to this Memoir, and I cannot refuse to comply, for it was my privilege to know much of that gentler side of the Archbishop's character, which was best seen by those who were admitted into the inner circle of his varied life. They can testify to his patience under heavy domestic sorrow, and to his self-control.

Ever ready to lay open the stores of his richly-filled memory, nothing pleased him more than to be asked a question by any one who really desired information: and his peculiarly happy method of impressing all that he taught upon the minds of those whom he instructed made it a great pleasure to draw him out in this way, to question him, and even to be questioned by him—a process which invariably followed his giving any reply. He would spare no pains to illustrate his meaning, nor to convey knowledge which was desired. One day he had to go some distance on very painful business; but he did not forget that about a mile out of his way was to be found a rare shrub which his visitor from London had never seen, and he drove round to procure a branch to show her.

With all his lack of 'veneration,' the Archbishop had a deep reverence for the Scriptures, and the doubts by which he lived to see them assailed were very painful to him even to hear of. 'Have you ever read any of ——'s books?' he asked me one day, mentioning one of the leaders of the 'Doubting School.' I replied that I had not. 'Then do not read them,' he added; 'if I were ——, I would deny the whole Bible at once; that would be much less trouble than picking it to pieces as he is doing.' In 1861, I was visiting the Archbishop's son-in-law and daughter at Shelford, and we visited the Geological Museum at Cambridge with him one day. On the way thither he had expressed a strong opinion against the 'Origin of Species,' which he had just been reading. When we came to the huge fossil of the Dinornis, in this Museum, turning to Mr. Wale, he exclaimed: 'I wonder how long it took for this fellow to develop from a mushroom!'

His interests in the pursuits of his daughters was great. The

music of one of those at home soothed and cheered him, while
he had the power of listening; and the sketches of the other
were a source of much amusement and delight. The Archbishop's inexhaustible flow of humour made him a constant peg
upon which to hang all sorts of bad or revived jokes. 'The Archbishop's last' was a stock title for the Irish penny-a-liners, and
he was frequently amused to see himself heralded forth as the
author of some miserable pun or antiquated witticism. A well-
known old joke thus appeared one day, and the Archbishop
showed it to me, saying in a pathetic tone, 'I ought to walk
about with my back chalked "Rubbish shot here."' Few, however,
of his sparkling utterances could be preserved, for they were
usually connected with circumstances of locality, or of individuals,
which should be reproduced in order to see their full value.
One I remember that amused us much at the time. A lady
from China who was dining with the Archbishop told him that
English flowers reared in that country lose their perfume in two
or three years. 'Indeed!' was the immediate remark, 'I had no
idea that the Chinese were such de-scent-ers.'

'What are you doing?' the Archbishop asked a visitor one
day. 'Writing for ——' was the answer. 'Very well,' he
rejoined, 'use as few words as you can, and mind your similes.'
But I must hasten on, lest I should seem to forget the first of
those two concise rules.

The morning of the day on which I arrived at Roebuck, on my
visit in 1863, was the last on which the Archbishop was wheeled
in to breakfast. I read to him during that meal, as I had so
often done before, and in spite of his painful debility, he entered
into the subject of the paper with great interest, interrupting
me with questions or remarks, as formerly. On the morning on
which the reading of his daughter's MS. of ' More about Ragged
Life in Egypt ' was finished, he took his gold pen from his pocket,
and giving it to her, said : ' I shall never use this again, M—— ;
take it, and go on.'

It was touching to see how clearly he recognised the approaching footsteps of death ; how calmly he resigned one object
of interest after another, and patiently waited for the next
indication of decay. His careful thought for others was shown
in many ways, as long as he was able to make himself understood.
'Do not read to tire yourself,' he was constantly saying. 'Is
the guard on the fire ?' he asked a few days before his death,

when speaking had already become very difficult to him, 'for I was afraid you went too near it.'

It was about that time that a clergyman from a remote part of Ireland called at the house. His name was not known to the daughters, and, Mr. Dickinson happening to be out, I was requested to see him. Apologizing for his intrusion, the gentleman said that he had come up in the hope of being permitted to see His Grace again. I hesitated, and then told him that the Archbishop could no longer receive callers, and rarely now recognised any fresh face; but our visitor urged his plea. 'The Archbishop educated my sons, and I would give anything to look at his face but once more.' I could not resist this, and I led him into the room. The Archbishop did not open his eyes, but to see him was all that the clergyman wanted; and after standing for a few minutes at his bedside, with tears running down his cheeks, he left the house, and I found that the Archbishop's munificence had not been previously known to his family.

The Sunday before his death he seemed unconscious, and I read Romans viii. (a chapter for which he had asked more than once during his illness) by his side, not being quite sure, however, that he could hear or notice it. Instinctively I read vv. 33, 34, as he had taught me to do, on a previous visit : 'Who shall lay anything to the charge of God's elect?' *Is it* God, that justifieth. Who is he that condemneth?' *Is it* Christ, that died,' &c. The eyes of the dying man opened for a moment, 'That is quite right,' he whispered.

A few days afterwards we stood round him, and saw him gently 'fall asleep,' leaving with us the lasting remembrance of the upward look, and the bright and heavenly smile which, not many moments before, had illuminated his face.

The newspapers of the day duly recorded the circumstances of the funeral, and told of every shop being shut, one only excepted; of the Cathedral being crowded as had never been before; and of such a concourse in the streets of Dublin as had not been known on any occasion of a similar kind. A little incident escaped them, which he would have noticed with great interest, in the case of any one else.

The remains of the Archbishop were removed from Roebuck to the Palace (between three and four miles off) on the evening of the day on which he died. On the morning of the funeral, a week afterwards, his little black dog 'Jet' was missing. He was found on the steps of the Palace when the porter opened the door, between six and seven o'clock, and at once went to the room in which the body lay. He watched the preparations, and when the procession set forth, Jet took up his position under the hearse. In this way he accompanied the funeral to the door of the Cathedral, and when the coffin was carried in, he left the place, and returned to Roebuck.[1]

R. A. W.

To these Notes the Writer adds a few Reminiscences of her own.

All who have read any of my father's works will be aware of his careful attention to style. He would never allow a carelessly framed sentence to escape him ; and even in ordinary familiar conversation the correctness and clearness of his manner of expressing himself was a characteristic which could not fail to strike ordinary observers. His words in general might be taken down and written in a book as they fell from his lips, without any need of alteration or omission, so free was his discourse from the colloquial slip-slop expressions and the kind of short-hand elliptical manner of speaking so common in unconstrained familiar converse.

Macaulay was his favourite modern historian, and in his Essays he took never-failing delight. He would repeat by heart whole passages from these essays, and from other favourite writers, which seemed to him to possess real eloquence, with a spirit and fervour which make these passages identified with his memory in the minds of all who knew him well. An apt and happy comparison always delighted him ; and his own peculiar excellence in this department seemed only to make his appreciation of others more lively.

He has been described as nearly destitute of poetical taste ; but this is not a fair representation of his mind. His taste in poetry was indeed somewhat limited, but what he did like he enjoyed intensely. For the modern school of poetry he had

---

[1] This dog is now in the possession of a friend near Dublin.

little taste, we might almost say little toleration. Of the poetry of his own day, he was impatient of Wordsworth, and Byron he admired without taking pleasure in him. But for the poetry of Walter Scott he had an intense admiration. He would repeat long passages of the 'Lady of the Lake' and 'Rokeby' with a spirit and enthusiasm hardly to be exceeded. He delighted in Scott's ballads, border minstrelsy, &c., in the shorter poems of Campbell and Moore, and in Burns universally. His reading of some special favourites was a thing to be long remembered; but the contemplative style of poetry had little charm for him, and of the didactic school he was positively impatient. Crabbe's 'Tales of the Hall' and 'Borough' were never-failing favourites. He did not like constantly reading aloud, but would often take a tale of Crabbe or a passage from Scott's poems, and read it with a life and expression which gave it quite a new character. 'The Parting Hour,' and the celebrated description of the Felon's last sleep in the 'Borough,' were peculiar favourites; the latter he could not read without deep emotion and a faltering voice.

Shakspeare was a never-failing favourite, and his reading of particular plays and passages was long remembered by his friends as a rich intellectual treat.

Mr. Dickinson has noticed his intense desire for sympathy. Perhaps to this strongly-marked characteristic may be referred also his dislike of others differing from him on matters of taste and feeling, as well as in opinions. This feeling may have led at times to the charge of intolerance, as it had sometimes practically the same effect; yet no one was more largely tolerant in principle. I have mentioned this peculiarity as perhaps accounting for some apparent discrepancies in his character.

His knowledge of history was more varied and extensive than critically accurate. As was the case with all his pursuits, his memory for facts was retentive, whenever those facts could be brought to illustrate principles; otherwise, as *mere* facts, he cared little for them.

Of chronology and geography, he would say, 'As they are called the *two eyes* of history, my history is stone blind.' This must be taken with some reservation. It is true he was not generally ready in remembering names and dates; but anything which threw light on the history of mankind generally, or on any important principle, moral, political, or social, was eagerly seized and carefully retained in his memory. He took great interest in military affairs; and entered even into the minute details of such changes in the art of war as might re-act on national history: even the description of warlike weapons and arms had a charm for him; and some of the female members of his family long remembered the disappointment they felt, when at a breakfast at his friend Mr. Senior's, at which he and Lord Macaulay and Sir James Stephen were to meet, instead of the 'feast of reason and flow of soul' they had looked forward to, in the meeting of four such remarkable persons, the conversation ran during the whole time on the history of improvements in the implements of war, which, to the ladies of the party, could have little interest.

The curious inventions of savages had a peculiar interest for him, and the pleasure he took in trying experiments with the Australian bomerang, the throwing-stick, &c., is remembered by all his friends.

All that concerned the history of civilisation interested and occupied him; and especially all that could throw light on his favourite axiom, that man could never have civilised himself; from which it followed necessarily that civilisation was first taught to man by his Creator.

But antiquities, as such, archæological collections, and fragments of ancient literature, interesting only as ancient, had little charm for him. To this must be ascribed the indifference to Irish antiquities with which he has been reproached. That it did not arise from want of interest in his adopted country his whole life is sufficient proof. But many who sent him 'presentation copies' of works on these and other subjects were disappointed at receiving no distinct acknowledgment; could they have taken a glance at his library table, and see the mass of volumes which were showered upon him week by week from various quarters, they would have needed no other reason for his silence. Had he acknowledged one, all must have been noticed, and the task would have been well-nigh sufficient to employ the entire time of a secretary.

In the arrangements of his own private study there was a curious mixture of order and disorder. To outward eyes the contents of his library were thrown together in the most heterogeneous manner possible—books placed side by side without the least regard to size, binding, or subject. But he always could find his way through the chaos to any book he wanted, and disliked interference with his arrangements, and, above all, an attempt to put his books to rights.

His own literary labours were usually solitary. He did not like any one, whether in or out of his immediate circle, to invade his sanctum. But after writing a memorandum for his Commonplace Book, or a note for a new edition of one of his works, he liked to bring it to his family and read it aloud to them.

Reminiscences by the late Edward Senior, Esq., P.L.C.

In the year 1836, my regiment having been sent to Dublin, I saw a good deal of the Archbishop, both at the Palace and at Redesdale. He was still misunderstood by the upper classes; they hated his politics, disliked his political economy, and were not favourably impressed by the total absence of pomp, and they dreaded his jokes.

The Archbishop was to be seen to most advantage at Redesdale, with Blanco White, Arnold and others—gardening, tree cutting, and romping with his children and dogs. His fault perhaps was 'that he too much despised popular opinion, and let people find out that he laughed at their views.'

In 1852 my duties took me to Dublin. The Archbishop had become known and trusted and honoured, especially for the perfect purity of his disposal of patronage, and the honesty of his convictions. Moreover, he had resigned his seat as a member of the Board of Education, though he continued to give it a qualified support. This withdrawal was very pleasing to a great body of his clergy.

Time, moreover, had softened the Archbishop, made him less abrupt in manner, more dignified, more tolerant of the opinions of others, less hopeful, less active in politics: age, in short, had told on him, but with a light hand.

Later, when paralysis had set in and domestic grief had bowed him down, I frequently met the Archbishop in Dublin. He was still cheerful, still clear-headed, still taking an active interest in the questions of the day, and still anxious to influence them for the best. His countenance had changed, a singularly noble and benevolent expression shone out as the earthly frame dissolved. He looked like a picture by one of the great old masters. I believe that all parties, Protestants and Roman Catholics, regretted his death, and that it was felt as a public loss. But he has left his mark on the opinions and habits of his clergy, who are themselves of the future generation, and the good that he did may, I hope, be said not to have died with him.

It was known by his friends, that the whole of the income he derived from the see (with the exception of the expenses absolutely necessary to maintain his position) was entirely devoted to charitable objects, and the promotion of the welfare of the Church in his diocese. No man was ever freer from nepotism: his only son was never raised above the dignity of rector of a modest living in Dublin, and the provision he left for his family is little more than his private means would have admitted of his making.

TABLE TALK.

I.

Remarks on Public Life as a Test of Character.

The following remarks are found in his private note-book, after some severe strictures on individual misconduct:—

'On looking back at what I have written, and observing how large a proportion of those I have mentioned I have been obliged to speak of with reprobation or contempt, it occurs to me to ask myself, how is this? Is it that the world is really so much worse than most people think? or that I look at it with a jaundiced eye? On reflection I am satisfied that it is merely this, that I have been much concerned in important *public* transactions, and that it is in these that a man can render himself so much more and more easily conspicuous by knavery or folly, or misconduct of some kind, than by good conduct. "The wheel that is weak is apt to creak." As long as matters go on smoothly and rightly they attract little or no notice, and furnish, as is proverbial, so little matter for history that fifty years of peace and prosperity will not occupy so many pages as five of wars and troubles. As soon as anything goes wrong, our attention is called to it, and there is hardly any one so contemptible in ability, or even in situation, that has it not in his power to cause something to go wrong. Ordinary men, if they do their duty well, attract no notice except among their personal intimates. It is only here and there a man, possessing very extraordinary powers, and that too combined with peculiar opportunities, that can gain any *distinction* among men by doing *good*.

> Inventas aut qui vitam excoluere per artes;
> Quique sui memores alios fecere merendo.

'But, on the other hand, almost everybody has both capacity and opportunities for doing mischief. "Dead flies cause the precious ointment to stink." A ploughman who lives a life of peaceful and honest industry is never heard of beyond his own hamlet; but arson or murder may cause him to be talked about over great part of the kingdom. And there is many a quiet and highly useful clergyman, labouring modestly in his own parish, whom one would never have occasion to mention in any record of public affairs; but two or three mischievous fanatics or demagogues, without having superior ability, or even labouring harder, may fill many a page of history.

' It is not therefore to be inferred from what I have written either that knaves and fools are so much more abundant than men of worth and sense, nor yet, again, that I think worse of mankind than others do, but that I have been engaged in a multitude of public transactions, in which none but men of very superior powers, and not always they, could distinguish themselves for *good*, while, for mischief, almost every one has capacity and opportunities.

' As for those who take what is considered as a more good-humoured view of the world, and seldom find fault with any one, as far as my observation goes, I should say that most of these think far worse of mankind than I do. At first sight this is a paradox; but if any one examine closely, he will find that it is so. He will find that the majority of those who are pretty well satisfied with men as they find them do in reality disbelieve the existence of such a thing as an honest man—I mean of what really deserves to be called so. They censure none but the most atrocious monsters, not from believing that the generality of men are upright, exempt from selfishness, baseness and mendacity, but from believing that all without exception are as base as themselves, unless perhaps it be a few half-crazy enthusiasts; and they are in a sort of good-humour with most part of the world, not from finding men good, but from having made up their minds to expect them to be bad. "*Bad*," indeed, *they* do not call them, because they feel no disgust at any but most extraordinary wickedness; but they have made up their minds that all men are what I should call utterly worthless; and "having divided (as Miss Edgeworth expresses it) all mankind into knaves and fools, when they meet with an honest man they don't know what to make of him." Now he, who from his own consciousness is certain that there is at least *one* honest man in the world, will feel all but certain that there must be more.

He will speak indeed in stronger terms of censure than the other of those who act in a way that he would be ashamed of and shocked at in himself, and which to the other seems quite natural and allowable ; but, on the other hand, if any one does act uprightly, he will give him credit for it, and not attribute his conduct (as the other will be sure to do) either to hypocrisy, or to unaccountable whim, to a secret motive, or to none at all. So that, as I said, he who at the first glance appears to think the more favourably of mankind, thinks in reality the less favourably, since he abstains from complaining of or blaming them, not from thinking them good, but from having no strong disapprobation of what is bad, and no hope of anything better.

‘ Most important is it, especially for young people, to be fully aware of this distinction. Else they naturally divide men into those who are disposed to think well of men in general, and those disposed to think ill ; and besides other sources of confusion, will usually form a judgment the very reverse of the right, from not thinking at all of the different senses in which men are said to think well or to think ill of others.

*　　*　　*　　*　　*　　*　　*　　*

‘ In short, one must make the distinction, which sounds very subtle, but is in truth great and important, between one who believes men generally to be what *he* thinks bad, and what is *in reality* bad ; between one who approves, or does not greatly disapprove, the generality, according to his *own* standard ; and one who thinks them such as *we* should approve.’

*　　*　　*　　*　　*　　*　　*　　*

II.

Public Men.

Generally speaking, I should say that most public men I have known have rather a preference for such persons as have no very high description of intellect, or high principle, but who have understanding enough to perceive readily what is wanted of them by men in power, and who can be depended on to do it faithfully and unscrupulously, and to defend it with some plausibility; avoiding all such absurdities and blunders as might get their leaders into scrapes, but wearing winkers like a gig-horse to prevent their seeing anything which they have no business with. 'None are for me, that look into me with inquiring eyes; henceforth I'll deal with ironwitted fools and unrespective boys.'

One of the errors they are apt to commit in point of policy (to say nothing of higher considerations) is to forget how incomparably more important service may be rendered them by a man of high intellectual and moral character, if he supports, suppose, only two out of three of their measures, than by all the third-rate or fourth-rate time-servers they can gather round them. A really able man, of unsuspected integrity and public spirit, carries more weight when he supports a Minister than a whole shipload of such rabble as they usually prefer to him; and when he does not support some measure, that very circumstance has at least the advantage that it proves him not to be unduly biassed, and consequently gives double importance to the support he does give in other matters.

Another mistake they are apt to make as to the same point, is to suppose too hastily that the man will be as faithful to them as a dog, while he has no more notion of fidelity to the public and to the principles of rectitude than a dog has;—that one who has no troublesome notions of honour and virtue to interfere with his being a time-server, will not leave his patrons in the lurch when he can advance himself by it. But they are apt, when any such thing occurs, to make a great outcry against treachery and ingratitude . . . . and they are apt, too, to take for granted that a person of slender ability, not likely to rival them as an eminent statesman, or to criticise very powerfully their procedure, will not have cunning enough to outwit them and play them various tricks. If they were better read in Bacon's Essays, these might have shown them (and so might daily experience) how much cunning may be possessed by men otherwise of mean abilities.

III.

On Popular Admiration.

The sort of admiration with which men such as —— are regarded in Ireland has always been a matter of perplexing difficulty to me. Not that I have not often found a similar admiration gained in England by just such qualities as his: ' versus inopes rerum, nugæque canoræ;' but then fluent bluster and fine-sounding superficial declamation are what the English generally are not gifted with.

The liking of the vulgar, whose tastes and intellect are uncultivated, for all kinds of tinsel is quite natural. But whatever *liking* savages may have for gaudy beads, they will never set a high *value* on them when very common and cheap; and the great estimation of the English vulgar for such trumpery as Prospero put in the way of Caliban and his drunken comrades might be understood to proceed from the scarcity among the English of fluent orators. But what has always puzzled me is that in Ireland, not at all less than in England, we always have from time to time certain ranting declaimers followed about and applauded by great multitudes, and yet to me, as a stranger, it seems as if three out of every four Irishmen could do nearly the same. And how a man can gain admiration for a talent so nearly universal is the puzzle. I suppose there *is* some much greater difference than I perceive; and that their appearing to me so nearly on a par with each other is just like the mistake of those who being unused to negroes fancy they are all alike. . . But some kind of talent there must always be in every one who accomplishes an object which many others *would* accomplish if they could, but *cannot*.

IV.

On the Education Committee in the House.

It was an unwise thing in me to suffer my name to be on the Lords' Committee on the Irish Education Board. I made the mistake of supposing that the Lords really regarded it—as they ought to have done—as a deliberative, not a judicial question; and that the great object of the Legislature of both Houses was to ascertain whether the system was working well for the country, and whether any better could be substituted. But they regarded it as a judicial question : the Opposition v. the Education Commissioners; with Ministry and their supporters engaged as advocates on the side of the latter, as feeling themselves bound to support the men and the measures they had brought forward. But the Ministers themselves seemed to think they were doing something of a favour to the Commissioners in giving them their support and grants of public money; and all supporters as well as opponents of Ministers spoke in a tone as if they thought that Parliament had been doing *us* the favour, in being so good as to allow us to burden ourselves with a toilsome office for the public good.

——, accordingly, when he spoke on one occasion of the unfairness of placing me on the Committee, as if to be a judge in my own cause—as if *I* had any personal interest in the matter—absurd as his remarks intrinsically were, did not depart much from the notion afloat in the House.

Unaware at the time of this kind of feeling in the House, I allowed myself to be placed on the Committee, instead of offering —as I ought to have done—to be examined as a witness.

I remember that not long after this, Lord Anglesey met me in the lobby, and was talking about the evidence that had been given, and mentioned to me, that he (who had been Lord-Lieutenant at the time of my appointment to the see of Dublin) had offered himself as a witness, but had been refused. 'I should have liked,' said he, 'to have had an opportunity of stating what I should have thought of the man who would have dared to propose conditions to your Grace.' That man knew me.

———

V.

On Lord Melbourne as a Statesman.

After all, Lord Melbourne's plan was to let everything alone, good or bad, till forced to make a change. He was the highest Conservative I ever knew. For he was not like many so-called, who have really persuaded themselves that such and such alleged abuses are really good ; he saw in many cases, and has often pointed out to me, the evils of such and such institutions; adding, however, that he was very sorry they should ever have been meddled with : 'I say, Archbishop, all this reforming gives a deuced deal of trouble, eh? eh? I wish they'd let it all alone.' Any change, in whatever department, was to him so much greater an evil than the continuance of any abuse that he would always avoid it if he could. But then he had, which most Conservatives have not, shrewdness enough to perceive when it was unavoidable, and then he always welcomed it with so much gladness that many people were alarmed with a dread of his going too far; and thus he offered the most effectual check to innovations. For John Bull becomes furious at a very obstinate opposition to some change, which he conceives called for; but if it is readily granted, the innate conservatism of the nation is called forth very strongly. He is like a restive horse, which, if you turn his head away from the ditch he is backing towards, and whip and spur him from it, will back the more violently; but if you turn him towards it, and seem rather to urge him that way, will shrink from it. Lord Melbourne took the latter mode. Yet though he thought with the Tories, and acted with the Whigs, I always vindicated him from the charge of inconsistency. A man is not a traitor for surrendering a town to the enemy when untenable, instead of waiting to have it stormed and sacked; though in so doing he is acting with those who wish the enemy to have possession of it, while his feelings and wishes are with those who are for holding out and dying in the breach. He differed from the Whigs in deprecating all changes, good or bad; he differed from the (other) Tories in conceding readily what he saw to be inevitable. Yet this man will probably go down to posterity as a zealous reformer! A monument to Sir Robert Peel and the Duke as the authors of Catholic emancipation and free trade and the Maynooth grant, and to Lord Melbourne as the friend to parliamentary reform, tithe reform, the Irish Temporalities Act, and the abolition of slavery, these should certainly stand side by side, and a most laughable pair they would be. ' I say, Archbishop, what do you think I'd have done about this slavery business, if I'd had my own way? I'd have done nothing at all! I'd have left it all alone. It's all a pack of nonsense! Always have been slaves in all the most civilised countries; the Greeks and Romans had slaves; however, they *would* have their fancy, and so we've abolished slavery; but it's great folly, &c.' And this was the general tone of his conversation, and a specimen of his political views.

VI.

On the Duke of Wellington's Administration.

Speaking of the Duke's being made Chancellor of Oxford:—
'When Fortune,' says Cicero, 'thrusts us into situations for
which nature has not adapted us, we must do our best to
perform the part as little indecorously as we can.' But when a
man thrusts himself into them, a failure, even when it would
otherwise have been very pardonable, exposes him to just
contempt.

The Duke of Wellington exposed himself to derision for not
having been able to repeat the Latin phrases put before him,
without making false quantities, on being appointed Chancellor
of the University of Oxford, though there is many an able
military and naval commander who could make no better hand
of it, and who deserves no contempt at all, because he does not
court nor accept any such office. And if I were to accept the
command of a troop of cavalry (which, in jest, I asked Lord
Wellesley to confer on me at that time), I should richly deserve
scorn for being unhorsed, as I dare say I should be, in the first
charge. But there was something more inconsistent in the zeal
with which he entered into the persecution, and refused to witness in behalf of Hampden when appealed to against the utterly
illegal proceedings that were going on. He was just equally
inflexible to the applications, during the negotiations for the
general peace of the Vaudois, for some interference to mitigate
the persecution they were exposed to; and again, to all the
claims of the Roman Catholics for civil rights; and again, of the
Jews; till he found it convenient to yield to popular opinion,
and bring forward those measures himself. It is all perfectly
consistent. He is most impartial to all religions. Those who
are the strongest in each country are, in his view, justified in
putting down and keeping down all other religionists as long as
they can; and the inferior party have nothing to do but submit,
and either profess whatever religion is established, or con-
tentedly to let themselves be trampled on till they are strong
enough; and then let them turn the tables if they can. 'Væ
victis' is his motto. And I never knew any one avow the
principle more frankly. In the debate on the Jews Relief Bill,
(when it was thrown out), in replying to me, and among other

things, to my introduction of the parallel case of the Roman
Catholic Relief Bill, he denied the parallel, 'because,' said he,
'there was "a necessity" in that case and not in this.' And,
indeed, in most of his speeches he used to take every opportunity of rather boasting than not of his readiness to grant
anything to intimidation, and nothing without; although it is
curious to observe the contrast between his military and his
political career, and also the high admiration bestowed by a
large number, at least, on *both*. What degree of ability
he showed in each is a matter of *opinion*; but his extraordinary
success in the one, and his uniform failure in the other, is
a matter of *fact*. To me it seems that the analogous course
to that which he pursued in politics would, in his campaigns,
have insured him the like defeats; in this I may be, perhaps,
mistaken; but at any rate he *did* succeed in war, and in the
field of civil government he most signally failed. I remember
that of two different persons, both men of sense (Senior was
one), to whom I made the remark, each rejoined that there was
an exception to the list of his failures; his carrying through the
difficult measure of the Emancipation. On each occasion I
expressed my astonishment at this being reckoned an instance
of success, which I had been reckoning among his most
remarkable defeats. Heaven send all my enemies such success!
He had utterly disapproved of the measure all along; he did
not at all cease to disapprove it; he granted it with a thoroughly
bad grace; and gave way because he found, to use his own expression, 'there was a necessity.' But still it is to be reckoned
among his great actions, because, forsooth, he did it himself,
and moreover showed great skill in managing the details
of the measure! I replied, that if instead of maintaining himself in the lines of Torres Vedras, he had found himself obliged to abandon them, and had accordingly destroyed
his magazines to prevent their falling into the enemy's hands,
spiked his cannon, shot his horses, and embarked his army in
safety, though he might have received credit for doing the work
well, it would hardly have been reckoned among his *triumphs*.
Now just such was the exploit of *carrying*, as it was called, the
great measure of Emancipation. If he had *carried* matters in
the same way in war, the French would soon have cleared the
Peninsula of us.

And, after all, it was done in such a way as to create no

gratitude in the parties benefited; for which, by-the-bye, they are often reproached; but who could suppose them such fools as to be grateful to those who granted what they lacked power to refuse, and who never even attempted to make a virtue of necessity, but always proclaimed that it was 'by force and against their will.' One might as well be grateful to an ox for a beef-steak. But to O'Connell, whom *they* regarded as the butcher that felled the ox, the Irish have always been even over-grateful.

The tone that the Duke always assumed was that of apologising to his own original party for a step which was as disagreeable to him as to them. And yet after all he was so far from pacifying them, that they punished themselves, to be revenged on him, by turning him out for revenge sake. It was not his own fault that he did not obtain another such triumph by passing the Reform Bill; which he offered to do, but could not find support. This, which, next to Emancipation, he had always most strenuously opposed, was carried in spite of him; and free trade, his other great aversion, is opening its buds, and will come into f'ower probably in his own time; and this measure also he has 'carried.'

He has, indeed, always proved a considerable impediment to every measure he disliked; but he has been always defeated on every point, though always making a fight; and moreover, while he always in war foresaw and made timely provision for, a retreat, when necessary, in politics he has always maintained his position to the last moment, and then surrendered at discretion.

VII.

On yielding to Popular Clamour.

To yield readily whatever is just (whenever it can be done with safety to the public and without detriment to the very persons sought to be benefited), and firmly to resist unjust claims, this, simple as it seems, is the course which, in a country like Ireland, is the most difficult to be steadily adhered to.

The difficulty arises in the case of a people who have been so very ill-governed as to have become brutalised and degraded in character. A little injustice, a short continuance of a grievance, may serve to quicken a person's perception and abhorrence of what is wrong, but a long continuance of it debases the character, and produces selfishness, ferocity, craft, and cruelty, combined. If a man loses, as Homer says, 'half his virtue the day he becomes a slave,' he is likely, if he long *continue* one, to lose most of the other half. Never was there a popular and admired remark more remote from truth than Sterne's on the negro slave : 'She had suffered persecution and had learnt mercy.' There cannot be a worse school, at least to remain long in, for the learning of mercy. It is found that slaves make the severest slave masters ; and those who have been the worst treated, as slaves, the worst masters; among others, the boys who have been the most cruelly fagged at school are observed to be generally the cruellest fag masters.

Now the result of all this is, that ninety-nine out of a hundred are completely under the dominion of one of two errors ; either from perceiving the debased, crafty, ferocious spirit, and the folly and ignorance of those who have been very long oppressed, they thereupon lose all sympathy for them, and consider them as deserving a continuance of brutal treatment, because they have been brutalised by it ; or else, sympathising with them on account of the injustice they have suffered, they are thence led to think well of them, and trust them. A man of more goodness of heart than strength of head is apt, in such a case, to put himself in the place of the sufferers, and consider what an abhorrence of injustice and cruelty he would feel, retaining those just and humane sentiments which he actually has, but which they have lost. And thence he will be for setting them quite free, and leaving them to right themselves and help themselves to what they will, and govern themselves as they please. I have always said, on the contrary, that if a persecuted or enslaved people did retain a proper sense of justice, did remain fit for complete self-government, then I should not think persecution and oppression near so great evils as I do think them. The moral and intellectual degradation they produce are among the chief of their attendant evils. But from both the one and the other of the above two errors few are found exempt. Generally speaking, the Tories fall into the former, and the Whigs into the latter, e.g. at the outbreak of the French Revolution one finds the Tory writers advocates of the old regime, and deprecating all the innovations and pointing out how unfit for liberty and self-government the French people showed themselves, and the Whigs, till fairly frightened out of their wits, exulting in the brilliant prospects opening on France from the unrestricted licence of a people so long oppressed. These latter were often converted, by the horrors of the Revolution, into the former. Sir James Mackintosh seems in a great degree to have gone through these two stages. The long-oppressed and now liberated people began by destroying their oppressors, and then the whole class they belonged to, and then all advocates of moderate measures, and lastly, one another. So it was with the negroes in Hayti. So it is, and ever will be, says Thucydides, 'as long as human nature remains the same.' And those who cannot learn from him cannot learn from experience. For with all the examples of history before us, the genuine Tories are for bringing back the penal laws or other restrictions in Ireland, and the Whigs are for either repealing the Union or letting the Irish Roman Catholics have quite their own way.

The most difficult of tasks is the cautious and gentle removal of an oppressive yoke, and the imparting of freedom and power to men, as they are able to bear it. It is more like the feeding of the famished than anything else. It is easy to say, 'This man's stomach is not in a good state for digestion, therefore give him nothing,' or, 'The man is hungry, set him down to a full table.' In the one case he dies of famine, in the other of a surfeit. In like manner, it is a very easy and coarse and clumsy procedure to go on treating as children or as brutes those who have been long oppressed, and to repress by main force all attempts on their part to free or to elevate themselves, and the result is that, at the best, you keep a certain number of your fellow-creatures degraded into brutes; at the worst, that a sudden explosion takes place, and you have a sort of servile war, or jacquerie. It is equally simple and easy to throw the reins on the neck of an unbroken horse. France, even in the memory of people now living, has furnished examples of both these plans, and their results. But a large portion of mankind are incapable of learning from experience.

VIII.

On the Protestant Church in Ireland.

The establishment of a Protestant Church in Ireland, which
by many thoughtless Liberals and designing demagogues is
spoken of as a burden to the Irish nation, and which the ultra-
Protestants speak of as nothing to be at all complained of by
the mass of the people, should be viewed, though no burden,
yet as a grievance, as being an insult. The real burden to the
Roman Catholic population is one which they are not accustomed to complain of as such : the maintenance of their own
priests. And, in like manner the Orangemen have been accustomed (as Senior has justly remarked in his Review on
Ireland, in 'The Edinburgh,' two years ago) to defend the insult
on the ground that it is no injury, and the injury on the
ground that it is no insult. They say, and truly, that the
support of the Established clergy is no burden, and again, that
it is no degradation to the people to maintain, as the Dissenters
in England do, their own clergy.

And they have an advantage in maintaining this fallacy, inasmuch as their opponents complain of that as a burden which
is not the real burden. Misled by this, the Whig ministers
thought to give satisfaction by lightening the burden—when in
fact there was no burden at all—by diminishing the revenues
of the Church. Whereas, if you were to cut off three-fourths
of the revenues, and then three-fourths of the remainder, you
would not have advanced one step towards conciliation, as long
as the Protestant Church is called the National Church. The
members of our communion here should be a branch of the
English Church, just as there is one in India, or in any other
of our foreign possessions. No one talks of the Church of
India, or of the 'United Church of England, Ireland and
India.' And there is no jealousy or displeasure excited, as
there probably would be if the Hindoos and Mussulmans, and
Parsees, and Roman Catholic Christians, &c., were told that ours
is the 'National Church' in their country. In advocating Catholic Emancipation and the payment of the priests (not, as
puzzle-headed bigots are accustomed to say, by a Protestant
government, but out of the revenues of a nation, partly Protestant and partly Romish, revenues to which both contribute,

and in which both have a right to an equitable share), and in supporting the system of schools, at which all should be *bonâ fide* admissible without doing violence to the conscience of parents, who have already, by the law of the land, had conceded to hem the right of educating their children in their own faith. In all this I and those who thought with me were considered as half Papists or Latitudinarians by one party, while by the other, the so-called Liberals, were considered as most whimsically inconsistent for our steady opposition to Roman Catholic principles.

IX.

On the Employment of Time.

—— had been speaking of the very great difference in the kind and amount of the talents with which different men are intrusted; and added that there was one which all had an equal measure of, their time. I took the liberty of remarking to him that though this at first sounds even self-evident, it is not true when one comes to reflect; for the twenty-four hours pass every day to all men alike, whether they are asleep or awake, sick or well. In this sense time is no talent at all; it is so only in respect of the quantity of vital energy, of power to act, that each person enjoys; and in this there is hardly any kind of talent more unequally distributed, the quantity of daily exertion that men are capable of being very different.

I also ventured to criticise a passage where he was saying, in speaking of the recreations of clergymen, that there must be something very bad, morally, in any man who was not made quite cheerful and happy by looking at the fields and the sunshine, &c. Knowing, as I did, that good men are not exempt from morbid depression of spirits any more than from other diseases and trials of various kinds, I deprecated the cruelty of loading them with the additional burden of harsh judgments. He took my criticism very fairly, and did not deny that there was something in what I said.

LIST OF THE WRITINGS OF DR. WHATELY.

The task of compiling a complete list of these writings is rendered extremely difficult by the fragmentary manner in which many of them appeared, and his habit of joint composition with others. The following is by no means complete; but it is believed to contain the bulk of his avowed works, and to include some to which he only contributed his name and literary assistance, and others ascribed to him on good authority: with the dates of their *first* publication, so far as these have been ascertained.

INDEX.